NORA ROBERTS

FINDING FOREVER

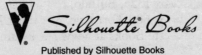

Silhouette Books

Published by Silhouette Books

America's Publisher of Contemporary Romance

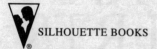 SILHOUETTE BOOKS

Finding Forever

ISBN-13: 978-1-335-54774-3

Recycling programs for this product may not exist in your area.

Copyright © 2019 by Harlequin Books S.A.

The publisher acknowledges the copyright holder of the individual works as follows:

Rules of the Game
Copyright © 1984 by Nora Roberts

Second Nature
Copyright © 1985 by Nora Roberts

This edition published by arrangement with Harlequin Books S.A.

For questions and comments about the quality of this book, please contact us at CustomerService@Harlequin.com.

® and TM are trademarks of Harlequin Books S.A., used under license. Trademarks indicated with ® are registered in the United States Patent and Trademark Office, the Canadian Intellectual Property Office and in other countries.

Visit Silhouette Books at www.Harlequin.com

Printed in U.S.A.

CONTENTS

RULES OF THE GAME

Chapter 1

"A jock. Terrific." Brooke took a long swallow of strong black coffee, tipped back in her glove-soft leather chair and scowled. "I love it."

"No need to be sarcastic," Claire returned mildly. "If de Marco wants to use an athlete for promotion, why should you object?" She gazed absently at the chunky gold ring on her right hand. "After all," Claire continued in her dry voice, "you'll be making quite a bit directing the commercials."

Brooke sent Claire a characteristic look. Direct, uncompromising gray eyes bored into the soft blue of the older woman's. One of Brooke's greatest talents, and her greatest weapons, was her ability to stare down anyone from a corporate president to a temperamental actor. She'd developed the knack early as a defense against her own insecurity and had since refined it to an art. It was an art, however, that didn't impress Claire Thorton. At forty-nine, she was the head of a multimillion-dollar company that she'd started with brains and guts. For nearly a quarter of a century, she had run things her way, and she intended to keep right on doing so.

She'd known Brooke for ten years—since Brooke had been an eighteen-year-old upstart who had wheedled her way into a job with Thorton Productions. Then she'd watched Brooke work her way up from gofer to gaffer, from gaffer to assistant cameraman and from there to director. Claire had never regretted the impulse that had led her to give Brooke her first fifteen-second commercial.

Intuition had been the basis for Claire's success with Thorton Productions, and intuitively she had sensed sharp talent in Brooke Gordon. In addition, Claire knew her, understood her, as few others did. Perhaps it was because they shared two basic traits—ambition and independence.

After a moment, Brooke gave up with a sigh. "A jock," she muttered again as she gazed around her office.

It was one small room, the pale amber walls lined with prints of stills from dozens of her commercials. There was a two-cushion sofa—reupholstered in chocolate-colored corduroy—not comfortable enough to encourage long visits. The chair with a tufted back had been picked up at a yard sale along with a coffee table that leaned slightly to the left.

Brooke sat behind an old, scarred desk that had a drawer that wouldn't quite close. On it were piles of papers, a gooseneck lamp and assorted disposable pens and broken pencils. The pens and pencils were jammed in a Sevres vase. Behind her at the window, a dieffenbachia was slowly dying in an exquisitely worked pottery bowl.

"Damn, Claire, why can't they get an actor?" Brooke tossed up her hands in her one theatrical gesture, then dropped her chin on them. "Do you know what it's like to try to coax ballplayers and rock stars to say a line without freezing or hamming it up?" With a disgusted mutter that gave no room for comment, she pushed the pile of papers into a semiordered heap. "One call to a casting agent and I could have a hundred qualified actors parading through here itching for the job."

Patiently, Claire brushed a speck of lint from the sleeve of her rose linen suit. "You know it increases sales if a production's hyped by a recognizable name or familiar face."

"Recognizable name?" Brooke tossed back. "Who's ever heard of Parks Jones? *Stupid* name," she muttered to herself.

"Every baseball fan in the country." The mild smile told Brooke it was useless to argue. Therefore, she prepared to argue further.

"We're selling clothes, not Louisville Sluggers."

"Eight Golden Gloves," Claire went on. "A lifetime batting average of three twenty-five. He's leading the league in RBIs this season. Jones has been at third base in the All-Star game for eight consecutive seasons."

Brooke narrowed her eyes. "How do you know so much? You don't follow baseball."

"I do my homework." A cool smile touched Claire's round, pampered face. She'd never had a face-lift but was religious about her visits to Elizabeth Arden. "That's why I'm a successful producer. Now you'd better do yours." She rose languidly. "Don't make any plans, I've got tickets for the game tonight. Kings against the Valiants."

"Who?"

"Do your homework," Claire advised before she closed the office door behind her.

With an exasperated oath, Brooke swiveled her chair around so that she faced her view of Los Angeles—tall buildings, glittering glass and clogged traffic. She'd had other views of L.A. during the rise in her career, but they'd been closer to street level. Now, she looked out on the city from the twentieth floor. The distance meant success, but Brooke didn't dwell on it. To do that would have encouraged thinking of the past— something Brooke meticulously avoided.

Leaning back in the oversize chair, Brooke toyed with the end of her braid. Her hair was the warm soft red shot with gold that painters attempted to immortalize. It was long and thick and unruly. Brooke was feminine enough not to want it cut to a more manageable length and practical enough to subdue it into a fat braid during working hours. It hung down the back of a thin silk blouse past the waistband of overworked blue jeans.

Her eyes as she mulled over Claire's words were thoughtful. They had misty gray irises, long lids and were surrounded by lashes in the same fragile shade as her hair. She rarely thought to darken them. Her skin was the delicate ivory-rose her hair demanded but the frailty stopped there. Her nose was small and sharp, her mouth wide, her chin aggressive. It was an unsettling face—beautiful one moment, austere the next, but always demanding. She wore a hasty dab of rose lipstick, enameled dimestore earrings and a splash of two-hundred dollar-an-ounce perfume.

She thought about the de Marco account—designer jeans, exclusive sportswear and soft Italian leather. Since they'd decided to move their advertising beyond the glossy pages of fashion magazines and into television, they had come to Thorton Productions, and so to her. It was a fat two-year contract with a budget that would give Brooke all the artistic room she could want. She told herself she deserved it. There were three Clios on the corner shelf to her right.

Not bad, she mused, for a twenty-eight-year-old woman who had walked into Thorton Productions with a high school diploma, a glib tongue and sweaty palms. And twelve dollars and fifty-three cents in her pocket, Brooke remembered; then she pushed the thought aside. If she wanted the de Marco account—and she did—she would simply have to make the ballplayer work. Grimly, she swung her chair back to face her desk. Picking up the phone, Brooke punched two buttons.

"Get me everything we have on Parks Jones," she ordered as she shuffled papers out of her way. "And ask Ms. Thorton what time I'm to pick her up tonight."

Less than six blocks away, Parks Jones stuck his hands in his pockets and scowled at his agent. "How did I ever let you talk me into this?"

Lee Dutton gave a smile that revealed slightly crooked teeth and a lot of charm. "You trust me."

"My first mistake." Parks studied Lee, a not quite homely, avuncular figure with a receding hairline, puckish face and unnerving black eyes. Yes, he trusted him, Parks thought, he even liked the shrewd little devil, but… "I'm not a damn model, Lee. I'm a third baseman."

"You're not modeling," Lee countered. As he folded

his hands, the sun glinted on the band of his thin Swiss watch. "You're endorsing. Ballplayers have been doing it since the first razor blade."

Parks snorted then walked around the tidy, Oriental-designed office. "This isn't a shaving commercial, and I'm not endorsing a mitt. It's clothes, for God's sake. I'm going to feel like an idiot."

But you won't look like one, Lee thought as he drew out a fragrant, slim cigar. Lighting it, he studied Parks over the flame. The long, lanky body was perfect for de Marco's—as was the blond, unmistakably California look. Parks's tanned lean face, navy blue eyes and tousled curling hair had already made him a favorite with the female fans, while his friendly, laid-back charm had won over the men. He was talented, easy to look at and personable. In short, Lee concluded, he was a natural. The fact that he was intelligent was at times as much a disadvantage as an advantage.

"Parks, you're hot." Lee said it with a sigh that they both knew was calculated. "You're also thirty-three. How much longer are you going to play ball?"

Parks answered with a glare. Lee knew of his vow to retire at thirty-five. "What does that have to do with it?"

"There are a lot of ballplayers, exceptional ballplayers, who slip into oblivion when they walk off the diamond for the last time. You have to think of the future."

"I *have* thought of the future," Parks reminded him. "Maui—fishing, sleeping in the sun, ogling women."

That would last about six weeks, Lee calculated, but he wisely kept silent.

"Lee." Parks flopped into a Chinese-red chair and stretched out his legs. "I don't need the money. So why am I going to be working this winter instead of lying on the beach?"

"Because it's going to be good for you," Lee began. "It's good for the game. The campaign will enhance the image of baseball. And," he added with one of his puckish smiles, "because you signed a contract."

"I'm going to get in some extra batting practice," Parks muttered as he rose. When he reached the door, he turned back with a suspiciously friendly smile. "One thing. If I make a fool of myself, I'm going to break the legs on your Tang horse."

Brooke screeched through the electronically controlled gates then swerved up the rhododendron-lined drive that led to Claire's mansion. Privately, Brooke considered it a beautiful anachronism. It was huge, white, multileveled and pillared. Brooke liked to imagine two black-helmeted guards, rifles on shoulders, flanking the carved double doors. The estate had originally belonged to a silent movie idol who had supposedly decked out the rooms in pastel silks and satins. Fifteen years before, Claire had purchased it from a perfume baron and had proceeded to redecorate it with her own passion for Oriental art.

Brooke stomped on the brake of her Datsun, screaming to a halt in front of the white marble steps. She drove at two speeds: stop and go. Stepping out of the car, she breathed in the exotic garden scents of vanilla and jasmine before striding up the stairs in the loose-limbed gait that came from a combination of long legs and preoccupation. In a crowd, her walk would cause men's heads to turn but Brooke neither noticed nor cared.

She knocked briskly on the door, then impatiently

turned the handle. Finding it unlocked, she walked into the spacious mint-green hall and shouted.

"Claire! Are you ready? I'm starving." A neat little woman in a tailored gray uniform came through a doorway to the left. "Hello, Billings." Brooke smiled at her and tossed her braid over her shoulder. "Where's Claire? I haven't the energy to search through this labyrinth for her."

"She's dressing, Ms. Gordon." The housekeeper spoke in modulated British tones, responding to Brooke's smile with a nod. "She'll be down shortly. Would you care for a drink?"

"Just some Perrier, it's muggy out." Brooke followed the housekeeper into the drawing room then slumped down on a divan. "Did she tell you where we're going?"

"To a baseball game, miss?" Billings set ice in a glass and added sparkling water. "Some lime?"

"Just a squirt. Come on, Billings." Brooke's smoky contralto became conspiratorial. "What do you think?"

Billings meticulously squeezed lime into the bubbly water. She'd been housekeeper for Lord and Lady Westbrook in Devon before being prized away by Claire Thorton. On accepting the position, she had vowed never to become Americanized. Edna Billings had her standards. But she'd never quite been able to resist responding to Brooke. A naughty young girl, she'd thought a decade before, and the opinion remained unchanged. Perhaps that was why Billings was so fond of her.

"I much prefer cricket," she said blandly. "A more civilized game." She handed Brooke the glass.

"Can you see Claire sitting in the bleachers?" Brooke demanded. "Surrounded by screaming, sweaty fans, watching a bunch of grown men swing at a little ball and run around in circles?"

"If I'm not mistaken," Billings said slowly, "there's a bit more to it than that."

"Sure, RBIs and ERAs and putouts and shutouts." Brooke heaved a long breath. "What the hell is a squeeze play?"

"I'm sure I have no idea."

"Doesn't matter." Brooke shrugged and gulped down some Perrier. "Claire has it in her head that watching this guy in action will give me some inspiration." She ran a fingertip down a shocking-orange ginger jar. "What I really need is a meal."

"You can get a hot dog and some beer in the park," Claire announced from the doorway.

Glancing up, Brooke gave a hoot of laughter. Claire was immaculately dressed in buff-colored linen slacks and tailored print blouse with low alligator pumps. "You're going to a ball game," Brooke reminded her, "not a museum. And I hate beer."

"A pity." Opening her alligator bag, Claire checked the contents before snapping it shut again. "Let's be on our way, then, we don't want to miss anything. Good night, Billings."

Gulping down the rest of her drink, Brooke bolted to her feet and raced after Claire. "Let's stop to eat on the way," she suggested. "It's not like missing the first act of the opera, and I had to skip lunch." She tried her forlorn orphan's look. "You know how cranky I get if I miss a meal."

"We're going to have to start putting you in front of the camera, Brooke. You're getting better all the time." With a slight frown at the low-slung Datsun, Claire maneuvered herself inside. She also knew Brooke's obsession with regular meals sprang from her lean adolescence. "Two hot dogs," she suggested, wisely buckling her seat belt. "It takes forty-five minutes to get to the stadium." Claire fluffed her silver-frosted brunette hair. "That means you should get us there in about twenty-five."

Brooke swore and rammed the car into first. In just over thirty minutes, she was hunting for a parking space outside of Kings Stadium. "...and the kid got it perfect on the first take," Brooke continued blithely, swerving around cars with a bullfighter's determination. "The two adult actors messed up, and the table collapsed so that it took fourteen takes, but the kid had it cold every time." She gave a loud war whoop as she spotted an empty space, swung into it, barely nosing out another car, then stopped with a jaw-snapping jerk. "I want you to take a look at the film before it's edited."

"What have you got in mind?" With some difficulty, Claire climbed out of the door, squeezing herself between the Datsun and the car parked inches beside it.

"You're casting for that TV movie, *Family in Decline.*" Brooke slammed her door then leaned over the hood. "I don't think you're going to want to look any further for the part of Buddy. The kid's good, really, really good."

"I'll take a look."

Together, they followed the crowd swarming toward the stadium. There was a scent of heated asphalt, heavy air and damp humanity—Los Angeles in August. Above them the sky was darkening so that the stadium lights sent up a white misty glow. Inside, they walked past the stands that hawked pennants and pictures and programs. Brooke could smell popcorn and grilled meat, the tang of beer. Her stomach responded accordingly.

"Do you know where you're going?" she demanded.

"I always know where I'm going," Claire replied, turning into an aisle that sloped downward.

They emerged to find the stadium bright as daylight and crammed with bodies. There was the continual buzz of thousands of voices over piped-in, soft-rock music. Walking vendors carried trays of food and drink strapped over their shoulders. Excitement. Brooke could feel the electricity of it coming in waves. Instantly, her own apathy vanished to be replaced by an avid curiosity. People were her obsession, and here they were, thousands of them, packed together in a circle around a field of green grass and brown dirt.

Something other than hunger began to stir in her.

"Look at them all, Claire," she murmured. "Is it always like this? I wonder."

"The Kings are having a winning season. They're leading their division by three games, have two potential twenty-game-winning pitchers and a third baseman who's batting three seventy-eight for the year." She sent Brooke a lifted-brow look. "I told you to do your homework."

"Mmm-hmm." But Brooke was too caught up in the people. Who were they? Where did they come from? Where did they go after the game was over?

There were two old men, perched on chairs, their hands between their knees as they argued over the game that hadn't yet started. Oh, for a cameraman, Brooke thought, spotting a five-year-old in a Kings fielder's cap gazing up at the two gnarled fans. She followed Claire down the steps slowly, letting her eyes record everything. She liked the size of it, the noise, the smell of damp, crowded bodies, the color. Navy-blue-and-white Kings pennants were waved; children crammed pink cotton candy into their mouths. A teenager was making a play for a cute little blonde in front of him who pretended she wasn't interested.

Abruptly Brooke stopped, dropping her hand on Claire's shoulder. "Isn't that Brighton Boyd?"

Claire glanced to the left to see the Oscar-winning actor munching peanuts from a white paper bag. "Yes. Let's see now, this is our box." She scooted in, then lifted a friendly hand to the actor before she sat. "This should do very well," Claire observed with a satisfied nod. "We're quite close to third base here."

Still looking at everything at once, Brooke dropped into her chair. The Colosseum in Rome, she thought, must have had the same feel before the gladiators trooped out. If she were to do a commercial on baseball, it wouldn't be of the game, but of the crowd. A pan, with the sound low—then gradually increase it as the camera closed in. Then, *bam!* Full volume, full effect. Clichéd or not, it was quintessentially American.

"Here you go, dear." Claire disrupted her thoughts by handing her a hot dog. "My treat."

"Thanks." After taking a healthy bite, Brooke continued with her mouth full. "Who does the advertising for the team, Claire?"

"Just concentrate on third base," Claire advised as she sipped at a beer.

"Yes, but—" The crowd roared as the home team took the field. Brooke watched the men move to their positions, dressed in dazzling white with navy blue caps and baseball socks. They didn't look foolish, she mused as the fans continued to cheer. They looked rather heroic. She focused on the man on third.

Parks's back was to her as he kicked up a bit of dust around the base. But Brooke didn't strain to see his face. At the moment, she didn't need it—his build was enough. Six-one, she estimated, a bit surprised by his height. No more than a hundred and sixty pounds—but not thin. She leaned her elbows on the rail, resting her chin on her hands.

He's lanky, she thought. He'll show off clothes well. Parks dipped for a grounder then returned it to short. For an instant, Brooke's thoughts scattered. Something intruded on her professional survey that she quickly brushed aside. The way he moved, she thought. Catlike? No. She shook her head. No, he was all man.

She waited, unconsciously holding her breath as he fielded another grounder. He moved loosely, apparently effortlessly, but she sensed a tight control as he stepped, bent, pivoted. It was a fluid action—feet, legs, hips, arm. A dancer had the same sort of nonchalant perfection after practicing a basic routine for years. If she could keep him moving, Brooke mused, it wouldn't matter if the man couldn't say his own name on camera.

There was an unexpected sexuality in every gesture. It was there even when he stood, idly wanting to field another practice ball. It might just work after all, Brooke reflected as her eyes roamed up his body, brushing over the blond curls that sprang around the sides and back of his cap. It might just…

Then he turned. Brooke found herself staring full into his face. It was long and lean like his body, a bit reminiscent of the gladiators she'd been thinking about earlier. Because he was concentrating, his full, passionate mouth was unsmiling; the eyes, almost the same shade as the navy hat that shaded them, were brooding. He looked fierce, almost warlike, definitely dangerous. Whatever Brooke had been expecting, it hadn't been this tough, uncompromisingly sexy face or her own reaction to it.

Someone called out to him from the stands. Abruptly, he grinned, transforming into a friendly, approachable man with an aura of easy charm. Brooke's muscles relaxed.

"What do you think of him?"

A bit dazed, Brooke leaned back in her chair and absently munched on her hot dog. "He might work," she murmured. "He moves well."

"From what I've been told," Claire said dryly, "you haven't seen anything yet."

As usual, Claire was right. In the first inning, Parks made a diving catch along the baseline at third for the final out. He batted fourth, lining a long single to left field that he stretched into a double. He played, Brooke thought, with the enthusiasm of a kid and the diabolical determination of a veteran. She didn't have to know anything about the game to know the combination was unstoppable.

In motion, he was a pleasure to watch. Relaxed now, the first staggering impression behind her, Brooke began to consider the angles. If his voice was as good as the rest of him, she mused. Well…that was yet to be seen. After polishing off another hot dog, she resumed her position leaning against the rail. The Kings were ahead 2–1 in the fifth inning. The crowd was frantic.

Brooke decided she would use some action shots of Parks in slow motion.

It was hot and still on the diamond. A fitful breeze fluttered the flag and cooled the spectators high up in the stands, but below, under the lights, the air was thick. Parks felt the sweat run down his back as he stood on the infield grass. Hernandez, the pitcher, was falling behind on the batter. Parks knew Rathers to be a power hitter who pulled to the left. He planted himself behind the bag and waited. He saw the pitch—a waist-high fast ball—heard the crack of the bat. In that one millisecond, he had two choices: catch the ball that was lined hard at him or end up with a hole in his chest. He caught it, and felt the vibration of power sing through his body before he heard the screams of the crowd.

A routine catch, most would say. Parks was surprised the ball hadn't carried him out of the stadium. "Got any leather left on your glove?" the shortstop called to him as they headed back to the dugout. Parks shot him a grin before he let his eyes drift up to the stands. His eyes locked on Brooke's, surprising them both.

In reaction, Parks slowed a bit. Now there was a face, he thought, a man wouldn't see every day. She looked a bit like a ravished eighteenth-century aristocrat with her wild mane of hair and English rose skin. He felt an immediate tightening in his stomach. The face exuded cool, forbidden sex. But the eyes… His never left them as he approached the dugout. The eyes were soft-gray and direct as an arrow. She stared back at him without a blink or a blush, not smiling as most fans would do if they were bold, or looking away if they were shy. She just stared, Parks thought, as if she were dissecting him.

With simultaneous twinges of annoyance and curiosity, he stepped into the dugout.

He thought about her as he sat on the bench. Here, the atmosphere was subdued and tense. Every game was important now if they were to maintain their lead and win the division pennant. Parks had the personal pressure of having a shot at a four hundred batting average for the year. It was something he struggled not to think about and was constantly reminded of by the press. He watched the leadoff batter ground out and thought of the redhead in the box behind third base.

Why had she looked at him like that? As if she wondered how he would look on a trophy case. With a soft oath, Parks rose and put on his batting helmet. He'd better get his mind off the little number in the stands and on the game. Hernandez was slowing down, and the Kings needed some insurance runs.

The second batter bounced one to shallow right and beat out the ball. Parks went to stand on deck. He stretched his arms over his head, one hand on the grip, the other on the barrel. He felt loose and warm and ready. Irresistibly, his eyes were drawn to his left. He couldn't see Brooke clearly from this distance, but he sensed she watched him still. Fresh annoyance broke through him. When the batter flied out, Parks approached the box.

What was her problem, anyway? he demanded as he took a testing swing. It would have been simpler if he could have characterized her as a typical Baseball Annie, but there was nothing typical about that face— or about those eyes. Planting his feet, he crouched into position and waited for the pitch. It came in high and sweet. Parks took a cut at it just before the ball dropped.

Coolly, he stepped out of the box and adjusted his helmet before he took his batting stance again. The next ball missed the corner and evened the count. Patience was the core of Parks's talent. He could wait, even when the pressure was on, for the pitch he wanted. So he waited, taking another ball and an inside strike. The crowd was screaming, begging for a hit, but he concentrated on the pitcher.

The ball came at him, at ninety miles an hour, but he had it judged. This was the one he wanted. Parks swung, getting the meat of the bat on the ball. He knew it was gone the moment he heard the crack. So did the pitcher, who watched his two-strike pitch sail out of the park.

Parks jogged around the bases while the crowd roared. He acknowledged the slap of the first base coach with a quick grin. He'd never lost his childlike pleasure in hitting the long ball. As he rounded second, he automatically looked over at Brooke. She was sitting, chin on the rail, while the crowd jumped and screamed around her. There was the same quiet intensity in her eyes—no light of congratulations, no pleasure. Irritated, Parks tried to outstare her as he rounded third. Her eyes never faltered as he turned for home. He crossed the plate, exhilarated by the homer and furious with an unknown woman.

"Isn't that marvelous?" Claire beamed over at Brooke. "That's his thirty-sixth home run this season. A very talented young man." She signaled a roving concessionaire for another drink. "He was staring at you."

"Mmm-hmm." Brooke wasn't willing to admit that her pulse rate had soared with each eye contact. She knew his type—good-looking, successful and heartless. She met them every day. "He'll look good on camera."

Claire laughed with the comfortable pleasure of a woman approaching fifty. "He'd look good anywhere."

Brooke's answer was a shrug as the game went into its seventh inning. She paid no attention to the score or to the other players as she watched Parks steadily. She remained, arms over the rail, chin on hands, booted feet crossed. There was something about him, she mused, something beyond the obvious attraction, the basic sexuality. It was that looseness of movement overlying the discipline. That's what she wanted to capture. The combination would do more than sell de Marco's clothes, it would typify them. All she had to do was guide Parks Jones through the steps.

She'd have him swinging a bat in immaculately sophisticated sports clothes—maybe riding through the surf in de Marco jeans. Athletic shots—that's what he was built for. And if she could get any humor out of him, something with women. She didn't want the usual adoring stares or knowing looks, but something fanciful and funny. If the script writers could pull it off and Jones could take any sort of direction. Refusing to look at the ifs, Brooke told herself she would make it work. Within the year, every woman would want Parks Jones and every man would envy him.

The ball was hit high and was curving foul. Parks chased after it, racing all the way to the seats before it dropped into the crowd four rows back. Brooke found herself face-to-face with him, close enough to smell the faint muskiness of his sweat and to see it run down the side of his face. Their eyes met again, but she didn't move, partly because she was interested, partly because she was paralyzed. The only thing that showed in her eyes was mild curiosity. Behind them there were shouts of triumph as someone snagged the foul as a trophy.

Enraged, Parks stared back at her. "Your name?" he demanded in undertones.

He had that fierce, dangerous look on his face again. Brooke schooled her voice to calmness. "Brooke."

"All of it, damn it," Parks muttered, pressed for time and furious with himself. He watched one thin eyebrow lift and found himself wanting to yank her out of the stands.

"Gordon," Brooke told him smoothly. "Is the game over?"

Parks narrowed his eyes before he moved away. Brooke heard him speak softly. "It's just beginning."

Chapter 2

Brooke had been expecting the call—after all, he had her name, and her name was in the book. But she hadn't been expecting it at six-fifteen on a Sunday morning.

Groggily, she groped for the phone as it shrilled, managing to grip the receiver as the cradle fell heavily to the floor. "'Lo," she mumbled without opening her eyes.

"Brooke Gordon?"

"Mmm." She snuggled back into the pillow. "Yeah."

"It's Parks Jones."

Instantly alert, Brooke opened her eyes. The light was soft and dim with dawn, early birds just beginning to chirp. She fumbled for the dented windup alarm beside her bed, then scowled at the time. Biting back a torrent of abuse, she kept her voice soft and sulky. "Who?"

Parks shifted the receiver to his other hand and scowled. "Parks Jones, third base. The Kings game the other night."

Brooke yawned, taking her time about fluffing up her pillow. "Oh," was all she said, but a smile flashed wickedly.

"Look, I want to see you. We're flying back after the game in New York this afternoon. How about a late dinner?" Why was he doing this? he asked himself as he paced the small hotel room. And why, in God's name, wasn't he doing it with a bit more style?

"Dinner," Brooke repeated languidly while her mind worked fast. Wasn't it just like his type to expect a woman to have no plans that couldn't be altered to suit him? Her first instinct was to give him a cold refusal, then her sense of the ridiculous got the better of her. "Well…" She drew out the word. "Maybe. What time?"

"I'll pick you up at nine," Parks told her, ignoring the maybe. When he couldn't get a woman out of his head for three days, he was going to find out why. "I've got the address."

"All right, Sparks, nine o'clock."

"Parks," he corrected tersely and broke the connection.

Falling back on the pillow, Brooke started to laugh.

She was still in high good humor when she dressed that evening. Still, she thought it was too bad that the file she had read on Parks hadn't contained a bit more than all those baseball statistics. A few personal details would have given her more of an edge. What would Parks Jones have to say if he knew he was taking his future director to dinner? she wondered. Somehow Brooke didn't think he'd be too pleased when he learned she'd left out that little piece of information. But the whole scenario was too good to miss. And there was the fact that he'd touched off something in her that she wanted to get out of her system before they started to work together.

Wrapped in a bath towel, Brooke pondered her wardrobe. She didn't date often—her choice. Early experience had influenced her attitude toward men. If they were good-looking and charming, Brooke steered clear of them.

She'd been only seventeen when she'd met her first good-looking charmer. He'd been twenty-two and fresh out of college. When he'd come into the diner where she had worked, Clark had been quick with a joke and generous with a tip. It had started with a late movie once or twice a week, then an afternoon picnic in the park. It hadn't bothered Brooke that he wasn't working. He'd told her he was taking the summer off before he settled down to a job.

His family was well connected, genteel and Bostonian. The genteel, Clark had explained with an acerbic humor that had fascinated her, meant there were plenty of heirlooms and little ready cash. They had plans for him that he was consistently vague about with the carelessness of the young. He'd mentioned his family now and again—grandparents, sisters—with a humor that spoke of an intimacy she envied almost painfully. Clark could make fun of them, Brooke realized, because he *was* one of them.

He'd needed a bit of freedom, he'd claimed, a few months to flow after the regimentation of college. He wanted to be in touch with the *real* world before he chose the perfect career.

Young and starved for affection, Brooke had soaked up everything he'd told her, believed every line. He had dazzled her with an education she had wished for but had never been able to have. He'd told her she was beautiful and sweet, then had kissed her as though he meant it. There had been afternoons at the beach with rented surfboards she'd hardly noticed that she'd paid for. And when she'd given him her innocence in a kind of panicked, shamed excitement, he had seemed pleased with her. He'd laughed at her naive embarrassments and had been gentle. Brooke had thought she'd never been happier.

When he'd suggested they live together, she'd agreed eagerly, wanting to cook and clean for him, longing to wake and sleep with him. The fact that her meager salary and tips now supported both of them had never crossed her mind. Clark had talked of marriage the same way he had talked of his work—vaguely. They were something for the future, something practical that people in love shouldn't dwell on. Brooke had agreed, rosily happy with what she'd thought was her first real home. One day they would have children, she had thought. Boys with Clark's handsome face, girls with his huge brown eyes. Children with grandparents in Boston who would always know who their parents were and where their home was.

For three months she'd worked like a Trojan, setting aside part of her small salary for the future Clark always talked of while he pursued what he called his studies and systematically rejected all the jobs in the want ads as unsuitable. Brooke could only agree. To her, Clark was much too smart for any manual labor, much too important for any ordinary position. When the right job came along, she knew he would simply stride into it then zoom to the top.

At times he'd seemed restless, moody. Because she

had always had to steal her own privacy, Brooke had left him to his. And when he snapped out of it, he'd always been bursting with energy and plans. Let's go here, let's go there. Now, today. Tomorrow was always years away to Clark. To Brooke, for the first time in seventeen years, today was special. She had something—*someone*—who belonged to her.

In the meantime, she'd worked long hours, cooked his meals and hoarded her tips in a small apothecary jar on a shelf in the kitchen.

One night Brooke had come home from a late shift to find that Clark had gone, taking with him her small black-and-white television set, her record collection and her apothecary jar. A note was in its place.

Brooke,
Got a call from home. My parents are putting on the pressure—I didn't know it would start so soon. I should have told you before, but I guess I kept thinking it would just go away. An old family tradition—a merger with my third cousin, as in matrimony. Hell, it sounds archaic, but it's the way my people work. Shelley's a nice girl, her dad's a connection of my dad's. I've been more or less engaged to her for a couple of years, but she was still at Smith, so it didn't seem important. Anyway, I'll slip into her family's business. Junior executive with a shot at the V.P. in five years or so. I guess I hoped I'd tell them to take a leap when the time came, but I can't. I'm sorry.

There's no fighting a wall of family and old money and stiff New England practicality, babe, especially when they keep reminding you that you're the heir apparent. I want you to know that these last couple of months I've had more breathing space than I've had in a long time, and I suppose than I'll have in an even longer time.

I'm sorry about the TV and stuff, but I didn't have the cash for the plane fare and the time wasn't right to tell my folks I'd already blown my savings. I'll pay you back as soon as I can.

I kept hoping it wouldn't have to be this way, but I'm backed into a corner. You've been great, Brooke, really great. Be happy.

Clark

Brooke had read the note twice before all the words registered. He'd gone. Her things hadn't mattered but he had. Clark was gone and she was alone—again— because she hadn't graduated from Smith or had a family in Boston or a father who could offer someone she loved a comfortable job so he'd choose her. No one had ever chosen her.

Brooke had wept until she was drained, unable to believe that her dreams, her trust and her future had been destroyed all in one instant.

Then she had grown up fast, pushing her idealism behind her. She wasn't going to be used ever again. She wasn't going to compete ever again with women who had all the advantages. And she wasn't going to slave in a steamy little diner for enough money to keep herself in a one-room apartment with dingy paint.

She had torn the note into tiny pieces, then had washed her face with icy water until all the traces of all the tears were gone.

Walking the pavement with all the money she had left in her pocket, she had found herself in front of Thorton Productions. She had gone in aggressively, belligerently, talking her way past the receptionist and into the personnel office. She'd come out with a new job, making hardly more than she had waiting tables, but with fresh ambition. She was going places. The one thing her betrayal by Clark had taught her was that she could depend on only one person: herself. No one was ever going to make her believe, or make her cry again.

Ten years later, Brooke drew a narrow black dress from her closet. It was a severely sophisticated outfit she had bought mainly for the cocktail circuit that went hand in hand with her profession. She fingered the silk, then nodded. It should do very well for her evening with Parks Jones.

As Parks drove through the hills above L.A. he considered his actions. For the first time in his career he had allowed a woman to distract him during a game— and this one hadn't even tried. For the first time, he had called a virtual stranger from three thousand miles away to make a date, and she didn't even know who the hell he was. For the first time, he was planning on taking out a woman who made him absolutely furious without having said more than a handful of words. And if it hadn't been for the road series that had followed that night game at Kings Stadium, he would have called her before this. He'd looked up her number at the airport on his way to catch a plane to New York.

He downshifted for the incline as he swung around a curve. All during the flight home, he had thought of Brooke Gordon, trying to pigeonhole her. A model or an actress, he had concluded. She had the face for it—not really beautiful, but certainly unique. Her voice was like something whispering through layers of smoke. And she hadn't sounded overly bright on the phone that morning, he reminded himself with a grimace as he stepped on the gas. There was no law that said brains had to go with intriguing looks, but something in her eyes that night… Parks shook off the feeling that he'd been studied, weighed and measured.

A rabbit darted out in front of him then stopped, hypnotized by his beams. Parks braked, swerved and swore as it raced back to the side of the road. He had a weakness for small animals that his father had never understood. Then, his father had understood little about a boy who chose to play ball rather than assume a lucrative position of power in Parkinson Chemicals.

Parks slowed to check his direction, then turned down the darkened back road that led to Brooke's tidy wooded property. He liked it instantly—the remoteness, the melodious sound of crickets. It was a small slice of country thirty-five minutes from L.A. Perhaps she wasn't so slow-witted after all. He pulled his MG behind her Datsun and looked around him.

Her grass needed trimming, but it only added to the rural charm of the house. It was a small, A-frame structure with lots of glass and a circular porch. He heard the tinkle of water from the narrow stream that ran behind the house. There was a scent of summer—hot, heavy blossoms he couldn't identify, and an inexplicable aura of peacefulness. He found himself wishing he didn't have to drive back down to a crowded restaurant and bright lights. In the distance a dog began to bark frantically, sending out echos to emphasize the openness.

Parks climbed out of the car, wondering what sort of woman would choose a house so far from city comforts.

There was an old brass knocker in the shape of a hog's head at the right of the door. It made him grin as he let it bang. When she opened the door, Parks forgot all the doubts that had plagued him on his drive through the hills. This time he thought she looked like a seductive witch—fair skin against a black dress, a heavy silver amulet between her breasts. Her hair was pulled back at the temples with two combs, then left to fall wildly down to her hips. Her eyes were as misty as hell-smoke, the lids darkened by some subtle, glittering shadow. Her mouth was naked. He caught a drift of scent that brought him a picture of East Indian harems, white silk and dusky female laughter.

"Hello." Brooke extended her hand. It took every ounce of willpower to complete the casual gesture. How was she to have known her heart would start thudding at the sight of him? It was foolish, because she had already imagined what he would look like in sophisticated clothes. She'd had to if she was to plan how to film him. But somehow his body looked rangier, even more male in a suit coat and slacks—and somehow his face was even more attractive in the shadowed half-light of her front porch. Her plans to ask him in for a drink were aborted. The sooner they were in a crowd the better. "I'm starving," she said as his fingers closed over hers. "Shall we go?" Without waiting for his answer, she shut the door at her back.

Parks led her to the car then turned. In heels, she was nearly eye level with him. "Want me to put the top up?"

"No." Brooke opened the door herself. "I like the air." She leaned back and shut her eyes as he started back down toward the city. He drove fast, but with the studied control she had sensed in him from the beginning. Since speed was one of her weaknesses, she relaxed and enjoyed.

"What were you doing at the game the other night?"

Brooke felt the smile tug at her mouth but answered smoothly, "A friend had some tickets. She thought I might find it interesting."

"Interesting?" Parks shook his head at the word. "And did you?"

"Oh, yes, though I'd expected to be bored."

"I didn't notice any particular enthusiasm in you," Parks commented, remembering her calm, direct stare. "As I recall, you didn't move through nine innings."

"I didn't need to," she returned. "You did enough of that."

Parks shot her a quick look. "Why were you staring at me?"

Brooke considered for a moment, then opted for the truth. "I was admiring your build." She turned to him with a half smile. The wind blew the hair into her face, but she didn't bother to brush it aside. "It's a very good one."

"Thanks." She saw a flash of humor in his eyes that pleased her. "Is that why you agreed to have dinner with me?"

Brooke smiled more fully. "No. I just like to eat. Why did you ask me?"

"I liked your face. And it's not every day I have a woman stare at me as if she were going to frame me and hang me on her wall."

"Really?" She gave him an innocent blink. "I'd think that pretty typical in your profession."

"Maybe." He took his eyes off the road long enough to meet hers. "But then you're not typical, are you?"

Brooke lifted a brow. Did he know he'd given her what she considered the highest compliment? "Perhaps not," she murmured. "Why don't you think so?"

"Because, Brooke Gordon, I'm not typical, either." He burst out of the woods and onto the highway. Brooke decided that she'd better tread carefully.

The restaurant was Greek, with pungent foods, spicy scents and violins. While Parks poured her a second glass of ouzo, Brooke listened to a waiter in a grease-splattered apron sing lustily as he served souvlaki. As always, atmosphere pulled at her. Caught up, she watched and absorbed while managing to put away a healthy meal.

"What are you thinking?" Parks demanded. Her eyes shifted to his, disconcerting in their directness, seducing in their softness.

"That this is a happy place," she told him. "The sort you imagine a big family running. Momma and Poppa in the kitchen fussing over sauces, a pregnant daughter chopping vegetables while her husband tends bar. Uncle Stefos waits tables."

The image made him smile. "Do you come from a large family?"

Immediately the light went out of her eyes. "No."

Sensing a boundary, Parks skirted around it. "What happens when the daughter has her baby?"

"She pops it in a cradle in the corner and chops more vegetables." Brooke broke a hunk of bread in half and nibbled.

"Very efficient."

"A successful woman has to be."

Leaning back, Parks swirled his drink. "Are you a successful woman?"

"Yes."

He tilted his head, watching the candlelight play on her skin. "At what?"

Brooke sipped, enjoying the game. "At what I do. Are you a successful man?"

"At the moment." Parks flashed a grin—the one that gave his face a young, rather affable charm. "Baseball's a fickle profession. A ball takes a bad hop—a pitcher blows a few by you. You can't predict when a slump will start or stop—or worse, why."

It seemed a bit like life to her. "And do you have many?"

"One's too many." With a shrug, he set his drink back on the table. "I've had more than one."

With her first genuine curiosity, Brooke leaned forward. "What do you do to get out of one?"

"Change bats, change batting stances." He shrugged again. "Change your diet, pray. Try celibacy."

She laughed, a warm, liquid sound. "What works best?"

"A good pitch." He, too, leaned forward. "Wanna hear one?"

When her brow rose again, he lifted a finger to trace it. Brooke felt the jolt shiver down to her toes. "I think I'll pass."

"Where do you come from?" he murmured. His fingertip drifted down her cheek, then traced her jawline. He'd known her skin would feel like that. Milkmaid soft.

"No place in particular." Brooke reached for her glass, but his hand closed over hers.

"Everyone comes from somewhere."

"No," she disagreed. His palm was harder than she had imagined, his fingers stronger. And his touch was gentler. "Not everyone."

From her tone, Parks realized she was speaking the truth as she saw it. He brushed a thumb over her wrist, finding her pulse fast but steady. "Tell me about yourself."

"What do you want to know?"

"Everything."

Brooke laughed but spoke with perfect truth. "I don't tell anyone everything."

"What do you do?"

"About what?"

He should have been exasperated, but found himself grinning. "About a job, for starters."

"Oh, I make commercials," she said lightly, knowing he would conclude she worked in front of the cameras. The game had a certain mischievous appeal for her.

"I'll be doing that myself soon," he said with a quick grimace. "Do you like it?"

"I wouldn't do it if I didn't."

He sent her a narrowed look, then nodded. "No, you wouldn't."

"You don't sound as though you're looking forward to trying it," Brooke commented, slipping her hand from his. Prolonged contact with him, she discovered, made it difficult to concentrate, and concentration was vital to her.

"Not when I have to spout some silly lines and wear somebody else's clothes." Idly, he toyed with a lock of her hair, wrapping it around his finger while his eyes remained on hers. "You've a fascinating face, more alluring than beautiful. When I saw you in the stands, I thought you looked like a woman out of the eighteenth century. The sort who had a string of anxious lovers."

With a low sound of humor, Brooke leaned closer. "Was that the first pitch, Mr. Jones?"

Her scent seemed intensified by the warmth of the candle. He wondered that every man in the room wasn't aware of it, and of her. "No." His fingers tightened briefly, almost warningly, on her hair. "When I make my first one, you won't have to ask."

Instinctively, Brooke retreated, but her eyes remained calm, her voice smooth. "Fair enough." She would definitely put him on film with women, she decided. Sultry brunettes for contrast. "Do you ride?" she asked abruptly.

"Ride?"

"Horses."

"Yeah," he answered with a curious laugh. "Why?"

"Just wondered. What about hang gliding?"

Parks's expression became more puzzled than amused. "It's against my contract, like skiing or racing." He didn't trust the light of humor in her eyes. "Should I know what game you're playing?"

"No. Can we have dessert?" She flashed him a brilliant smile he trusted less.

"Sure." Watching her, Parks signaled the waiter.

Thirty minutes later, they walked across the parking lot to his car. "Do you always eat like that?" Parks demanded.

"Whenever I get the chance." Brooke dropped into the passenger seat then stretched her arms over her head in a lazy, unconsciously sensual movement. No one who hadn't worked in a restaurant could fully appreciate eating in one. She'd enjoyed the food...and the evening. Perhaps, she mused, she'd enjoyed being with Parks because they'd spent three hours together and still didn't know each other. The mystery added a touch of spice.

In a few months, they would know each other well. A director had no choice but to get to the inside of an actor—which is what Parks would be, whether he liked it or not. For now, Brooke chose to enjoy the moment, the mystery and the brief companionship of an attractive man.

When Parks sat beside her, he reached over to cup her chin in his hand. She met his eyes serenely and with that touch of humor that was beginning to frustrate him. "Are you going to let me know who you are?"

Odd, Brooke mused, that he would have the same understanding of the evening she did. "I haven't decided," she said candidly.

"I'm going to see you again."

She gave him an enigmatic smile. "Yes."

Wary of the smile, and her easy agreement, Parks started the engine.

He didn't like knowing that she was playing him... any more than he liked knowing he'd have to come back for more. He'd known a variety of women—from icy sophisticates to bubbly groupies. There were infinite shadings in between, but Brooke Gordon seemed to fit none of them. She had both a haughty sexuality and a soft vulnerability. Though his first instinct had been to get her to bed, he now discovered he wanted more. He wanted to peel off the layers of her character and study each one until he understood the full woman. Making love to her would only be part of the discovery.

They drove in silence while an old, soft ballad

crooned on the radio. Brooke had her head thrown back, face to the stars, knowing it was the first time in months she'd fully relaxed on a date and not wanting to analyze why. Parks didn't find it necessary to break a comfortable silence with conversation, nor had he found it necessary to slip in those predictable hints about how he'd like to end the evening. She knew there wouldn't be a wrestling match on the side of the road or an embarrassing, infuriating argument when they reached the front door. He was safe, Brooke decided, and closed her eyes. It seemed things were going to work very well after all. Her thoughts began to drift toward her schedule for the next day.

The motion of the car woke her, or rather the lack of motion. Brooke opened her eyes to find the MG parked in her drive, the engine quiet. Turning her head, she saw Parks sprawled in his seat, watching her.

"You drive very well," she murmured. "I don't usually trust anyone enough to fall asleep in a car."

He'd enjoyed the moments of quiet while he'd watched her sleep. Her skin looked ethereal in the moonlight, ghostly pale with a hint of flush in her cheeks. The wind had tossed her hair so that Parks knew how it would look spread on a pillow after a wild night of loving. Sooner or later he'd see it that way, he determined. After his hands had tangled it.

"This time you're staring," Brooke pointed out.

And he smiled—not the quick grin she'd come to expect, but a slow, unsettling smile that left his eyes dark and dangerous. "I guess we'll both have to get used to it."

Leaning over, he opened her door. Brooke didn't stiffen or shift away from the brush of his body against hers; she simply watched. As if, Parks mused, she were considering his words very carefully. Good, he thought as he stepped from the car. This time she'd have something to think about.

"I like this place." He didn't touch her as they walked up the path to her house, though Brooke had expected him to take her hand or her arm. "I had a house in Malibu once."

"Not anymore?"

"Got too crowded." He shrugged as they walked up the porch steps. Their footsteps echoed into the night. "If I'm going to live out of the city, I want a place where I'm not forever stumbling over my neighbor."

"I don't have that problem here." Around them the woods were dark and quiet. There was only the bubbling sound of the stream and the music of tireless crickets. "There's a couple who live about a quarter mile that way." Brooke gestured to the east. "Newlyweds who met on a television series that folded." Leaning back against the door, she smiled. "We don't have any trouble keeping out of each other's way." She sighed, comfortably sleepy and relaxed. "Thanks for dinner." When she offered her hand, she wondered if he would take it or ignore it and kiss her. Brooke expected the latter, even wondered with a drowsy curiosity what the pressure of his lips on hers would be like.

Parks knew what she expected, and her lips, as they had from the first, tempted him. But he thought it was time this woman had something unexpected. Taking her hand, Parks leaned toward her. He saw from her eyes that she would accept his kiss with her own sultry reserve. Instead, he touched his lips to her cheek.

At the brush of his open mouth on her skin, Brooke's

fingers tightened in his. Usually she viewed a kiss or embrace distantly, as from behind a camera, wondering dispassionately how it would appear on film. Now she saw nothing, but felt. Low, turbulent waves of sensation swept through her, making her tense. Something seemed to ripple along her skin, though he never touched her—just his hand over hers, just his lips on her cheek.

Slowly, watching her stunned eyes, Parks journeyed to her other cheek, moving his lips with the same featherlightness. Brooke felt the waves rise until there was an echoing in her head. She heard a soft moan, unaware that it was her own. As hunger swept over her, Brooke turned her mouth toward his, but he glided up her skin, whispering over her eyelids so that they fluttered down. Drugged, she allowed him to roam over her face, leaving her lips trembling with anticipation, and unfulfilled. She tasted his breath on them, felt the warm flutter as they passed close, but his mouth dropped to her chin to give her a teasing touch of his tongue.

Her fingers went limp in his. Surrender was unknown to her, so she didn't recognize it. Parks did as he caught the lobe of her ear between his teeth. His body was throbbing, aching to press against hers and feel the yielding softness that came only from woman. Against his cheek, her hair was as silky as her skin, and as fragrant. It took every ounce of control to prevent his hands from diving into it, to keep himself from plundering the mouth that waited, warm and naked, for his. He traced her ear with his tongue and felt her shudder. Slowly, he brushed kisses up her temple and over her brow on his way to her other ear. He nibbled gently, letting his tongue slide over her skin until he heard her moan again.

Still he avoided her mouth, pressing his lips to the pulse in her throat, fighting the urge to move lower, to feel, to taste the subtle sweep of her breast beneath the black silk. Her pulse was jerky, like the sound of her breathing. High up in the mountains, a coyote called to the moon.

A dizzying excitement raced through him. He could have her now—feel that long, willowy body beneath his, tangle himself in that wild mane of hair. But he wouldn't have all of her. He needed more time for that.

"Parks." His name came throatily through her lips, arousing him further. "Kiss me."

Gently, he pressed his lips to her shoulder. "I am."

Her mouth felt as though it were on fire. She had thought she understood hunger, having felt it too often in the past. But she'd never known a hunger like this. "Really kiss me."

He drew away far enough to see her eyes. There was no light in them now; they were opaque with desire. Her lips were parted in invitation, her breath shuddering through them. He bent close, but kept his lips an aching whisper from hers. "Next time," he said softly.

Turning, he left her stunned and wanting.

Chapter 3

"Okay, Linda, try to look like you're enjoying this." Brooke cast a look at her lighting director and got a nod. "E.J., sweep up, starting at her toes—take your time on the legs."

E.J. gave her a blinding white grin from his smooth mahogany face. "My pleasure," he said affably and focused his camera on the actress's pink painted toenails.

"It's so hot," Linda complained, fussing with the strap of her tiny bikini. She was stretched out on a towel in the sand—long, blond and beautiful, with a rich golden tan that would hawk a popular suntan lotion. All Linda had to do was to look lush and lazy and purr that she had an *Eden* tan. The bikini would do the rest.

"Don't sweat," Brooke ordered. "You're supposed to be glowing, not wet. When we roll, count to six, then bring up your right knee—slow. At twelve, take a deep breath, pass your right hand through your hair. Say your line looking straight at the camera and think sex."

"The hell with sex, I'm roasting."

"Then let's get it in one take. All right. Speed. Roll film, and…action."

E.J. moved up from the manicured toenails, up the long, slender legs, over a rounded hip, golden midriff and barely confined bosom. He closed in on Linda's face—sulky mouth, pearly teeth and baby blues—then went back for a full shot.

"I've got an *Eden* tan," Linda claimed.

"Cut." Brooke swiped a hand over her brow. Though it was still morning, the beach was baking. She thought she could feel the sand burning through the soles of her sneakers. "Let's pump a little life into it," she suggested. "We've got to sell this stuff on one line and your body."

"Why don't you try it?" Linda demanded, falling onto her back.

"Because you're getting paid to and I'm not," Brooke snapped, then clicked her teeth together. She knew better than to lose her temper, especially with this one. The trouble was that since her evening with Parks, she'd been on a perpetual short fuse. Taking a deep breath, Brooke reminded herself that her personal life, if that's what Parks Jones was, couldn't interfere with her work. She walked over and crouched beside the pouting model. "Linda, I know it's miserable out here today, but a job's a job. You're a pro or you wouldn't be here."

"Do you know how hard I worked on this tan to get this lousy thirty-second spot?"

Brooke patted her shoulder, conveying sympathy, understanding and authority all at once. "Well then, let's make it a classic."

It was past noon before they were able to load up their equipment. E.J. reached in the back of the station wagon he used and pulled two iced drinks out of a chest cooler. "Here ya go, boss."

"Thanks." Brooke pressed the cold bottle against her forehead before she twisted off the top. "What was with her today?" she demanded. "She can be a problem, but I've never had to drag one line out of her like that before."

"Broke up with her man last week," E.J. informed Brooke before he took a greedy swallow of grape soda.

Grinning, Brooke sat on the tailgate. "Anything you don't know, E.J.?"

"Not a thing." He propped himself beside her, one of the few on the Thorton staff who wasn't leery of the Tiger-lady, as Brooke had been dubbed. "You're going to that fancy de Marco party tonight."

"Yeah." Brooke gave a slow, narrow-eyed smile that had nothing to do with the brilliance of the sun. The party would be her chance to cut Parks Jones down a few pegs. She could still remember how she had stood shaking on her porch in the moonlight after the echo of his engine had died away.

"It's going to be a kick working with Parks Jones." E.J. downed the rest of his soda in one swallow. "The man's got the best glove in the league and a bat that won't quit smoking. Knocked in two more RBIs last night."

Brooke leaned against the door frame and scowled. "Good for him."

"Don't you like baseball?" E.J. grinned, tossing his empty bottle into the back of the wagon.

"No."

"Ought to have some team spirit," he mused and gave her knee a friendly squeeze. "The better he does, the more punch the campaign'll have. And if he gets into the series—"

"If he gets into the series," Brooke interrupted, "we have to wait until the end of October before we can start shooting."

"Well." E.J. stroked his chin. "That's show biz."

Brooke tried to glare, then chuckled. "Let's get back. I've got a shoot in the studio this afternoon. Want me to drive?"

"Naw." E.J. slammed the tailgate then headed for the driver's seat. "I like living."

"You're such a wimp, E.J."

"I know," he agreed cheerfully. "I've got this thing about traveling at the speed of light." After adjusting mirror-lensed sunglasses on his face he coaxed the station wagon's engine into life. It sputtered and groaned temperamentally while he crooned to it.

"Why don't you buy a new car?" Brooke demanded. "You get paid enough."

He patted the wagon's dash when the engine caught. "Loyalty. I've been cruising in this little darling for seven years. She'll be around when that flashy machine of yours is nuts and bolts."

Brooke shrugged, then tilted back her head to drain the bottle. E.J. was the only one who worked under her who dared any intimacy, which was probably the reason she not only allowed it but liked him for it. She also considered him one of the best men with a camera on the West Coast. He came from San Francisco where his father was a high school principal and his mother owned and operated a popular beauty salon. She had met them once and wondered how two such meticulous people could have produced a freewheeling, loose-living man with a penchant for voluptuous women and B movies.

But then, Brooke mused, she'd never been able to understand families. Always she viewed them with perplexity and longing, as only one on the outside could fully understand. Settling back on the carefully patched seat, she began to plot out her strategy for her afternoon session.

"Heard you took in a Kings game the other night." E.J. caught her swift, piercing look and began to whistle tunelessly.

"So?"

"I saw Brighton Boyd at a party a couple of nights ago. Worked with him on a TV special last year. Nice guy."

Brooke remembered seeing the actor in the box next to hers and Claire's. She dropped her empty bottle on the already littered floor. "So?" she repeated coolly.

"Big Kings fan," E.J. went on, turning the radio up loud so that he had to shout over the top 40 rock. "Raved about Jones's homer—on a two-out, two-strike pitch. The man's a hell of a clutch hitter." While Brooke remained silent, E.J. tapped out the beat from the radio on the steering wheel. There was the glint of gold from a ring on his long dark fingers. "Brighton said Jones stared at you like a man who'd been hit with a blunt instrument. That Brighton, he sure does turn a phrase."

"Hmm." Brooke began to find the passing scenery fascinating.

"Said he came right over to your box chasing a foul. Had a few words to say."

Brooke turned her head and stared into E.J.'s mirrored glasses. "Are you pumping me, E.J.?"

"Hot damn! Can't pull anything over on you, Brooke. You're one sharp lady."

Despite herself she laughed. She knew a "no comment" would only cause speculation she'd like to avoid. Instead she stretched her legs out on the seat and treated it lightly. "He just wanted my name."

"And?"

"And nothing."

"Where'd you go with him?"

The faintest frown creased her brow. "I didn't say I went anywhere with him."

"He didn't ask your name because he was taking a census."

Brooke gave him a cool, haughty look that would have discouraged anyone else. "You're a gossipy old woman, E.J."

"Yep. You go to dinner with him?"

"Yes," she said on a sigh of surrender. "And that's all."

"Not as bright as he looks, then." He patted her sneakered foot. "Or maybe he felt funny about starting something up with the lady who'll be directing him."

"He didn't know," Brooke heard herself say before she could stop herself.

"Oh?"

"I didn't tell him."

"Oh." This time the syllable was drawn out and knowing.

"I didn't think it was necessary," Brooke said heatedly. "It was strictly a social meeting, and it gave me the opportunity to plan how best to film him."

"Mmm-hmm."

She turned back in her seat and folded her arms. "Shut up and drive, E.J."

"Sure thing, boss."

"As far as I'm concerned he can take his golden glove and smoking bat and sit on them."

E.J. nodded wisely, enjoying himself. "You know best."

"He's conceited and cold and inconsiderate."

"Must have been some evening," E.J. observed.

"I don't want to talk about it." Brooke kicked at the empty bottle on the floor.

"Okay," he said affably.

"He's the kind of man," she went on, "who thinks a woman's just waiting to fall all over him just because he's moderately attractive and successful and has an average mind."

"For a Rhodes scholar," E.J. mused as he slowed down for his exit.

"A what?"

"He's a Rhodes scholar."

Brooke's mouth fell open, then shut with a bang. "He is not."

E.J. shrugged agreeably. "Well, that's what it said in *Sports View.* That was supposed to be the main reason he didn't start playing professional ball until he was twenty-two."

"Probably just a publicity hype," she muttered, but she knew better. She rode the rest of the way to the studio in frowning silence.

The de Marco California villa was an eyeful. Brooke decided that it had the dubious ability of making Claire's mansion look simple and discreet. It was huge, E-shaped and dazzling white with two inner courtyards. One held a grottolike pool complete with miniature waterfall, the other a sheltered garden rich with exotic scents.

When Brooke arrived, she could hear the high liquid sounds of harps and mixed conversation. People were ranged through the house, spilling outdoors and clustered in corners. Passing through the gold-toned parlor, she caught the mingling, heady scents of expensive perfumes and spiced food. There was the glitter of diamonds, swirl of silks and flash of tanned, pampered skin.

Brooke caught snatches of conversations as she strolled through, searching for the main buffet.

"But darling, he simply can't carry a series anymore. Did you see him at Ma Maison last week?"

"She'll sign. After that fiasco in England, she's itching to come back to Hollywood."

"Can't remember a line if you feed it to him intravenously."

"Left her for the wardrobe mistress."

"My dear, have you ever seen *such* a dress!"

Hollywood, Brooke thought with halfhearted affection as she pounced on the remains of the pâté.

"I knew I'd find you here."

Brooke turned her head as she speared a chunk of smoked beef. "Hello, Claire," she managed over a mouthful of cracker. "Nice party."

"I suppose, as you always judge them by the menu." Claire gave her a long, appraising look. Brooke wore a buckskin jumpsuit, soft and smooth as cream, with a thick pewter belt cinched at her waist. She'd braided the hair at her temples and clipped it back over the flowing tousled mane, letting heavy pewter links dangle at her ears. Because she'd been distracted while applying it, she'd neglected her makeup and had only remembered to darken her eyes. As a result, they dominated her pale, sharp-featured face. "Why is it you can wear the most outlandish outfits and still look marvelous?"

Brooke grinned and swallowed. "I like yours, too," she said, noting that Claire was, as always, stylishly neat in pale blue voile. "What have they got to drink in this place?"

With a sigh, Claire motioned to a roving, red-suited waiter and chose two tulip glasses of champagne. "Try to behave yourself. The de Marcos are very old-fashioned."

"I'll be a credit to the company," Brooke promised and lifted her hand in acknowledgment of a wave from a stand-up comic she'd directed in a car commercial. "Do you think I could get a plate?"

"Gorge later. Mr. Jones's agent is here, I want you to meet him."

"I hate talking to agents on an empty stomach. Oh, damn, there's Vera. I should have known she'd be here."

Brooke answered the icy smile from the slim honey-haired model who was the current embodiment of the American look. Their paths had crossed more than once, professionally and socially, and the women had taken an instant, lasting dislike to each other. "Keep your claws sheathed," Claire warned. "De Marco's going to be using her."

"Not with me," Brooke said instantly. "I'll take the ballplayer, Claire, but someone else is going to hold the leash on that one. I don't like my poison in small doses."

"We'll discuss it," Claire muttered then beamed a smile. "Lee, we were just looking for you. Lee Dutton,

Brooke Gordon. She's going to be directing Parks." She placed a maternal hand on Brooke's arm. "My very best."

Brooke lifted an ironic brow. Claire was always lavish with praise in public and miserly with it behind closed doors. "Hello, Mr. Dutton."

Her hand was grabbed hard and pumped briskly. Discreetly, Brooke flexed her fingers while she made a swift survey. He was shorter than she was and rather round with thinning hair and startling black eyes. A creature of first impressions, she liked him on the spot.

"Here's to a long, successful relationship," he announced and banged his glass exuberantly against hers. "Parks is eager to begin."

"Is he?" Brooke smiled, remembering Parks's description of his venture into commercials. "We're just as eager to have him."

Claire sent her a brief warning look as she tucked her arm through Lee's. "And where is he? Brooke and I are both anxious to meet him."

"He has a hard time getting away from the ladies." Lee gave the proud, apologetic smile of a doting uncle. But the eyes on Brooke were shrewd.

"How awkward for him," she murmured into her glass. "But I suppose he manages to live with it."

"Brooke, you really must try the pâté." Claire sent her a teeth-clenched smile.

"I did," Brooke returned easily. "Tell me more about Parks, Mr. Dutton. I can't tell you what a fan I am."

"Oh, you follow baseball?"

Brooke tilted her glass again. "Why, we were in the park only a few weeks ago, weren't we, Claire?"

"As a matter of fact." Claire didn't bother to try to

outstare Brooke this time but turned to Lee. "Do you get to many games?"

"Not enough," he admitted, knowing a game was afoot and willing to play. "But I happen to have a few tickets for Sunday's game," he said, making a mental note to arrange for some. "I'd love to escort both you ladies."

Before Brooke could open her mouth, Claire doled out subtle punishment. "There's nothing we'd like better."

He caught Brooke's quick scowl before she smoothed her features. "Well, there's Parks now." Lee bellowed for him, causing heads to turn before conversation buzzed again.

Parks's first reaction was surprise when he saw Brooke standing beside his agent and the woman he knew was head of Thorton Productions. Then he experienced the same flare of reluctant desire he had felt on the other two occasions he'd seen her. He'd purposely let the days pass before he contacted her again, hoping the power of need would lessen. One glance at her told him it hadn't worked.

Apparently without hurry, he weaved through the crowd, stopping to exchange a few words when someone touched his arm, then gently disentangling himself. He'd learned, at an early age, how to keep from being cornered at a social occasion. In less than two minutes, Parks stood in front of Brooke.

Well done, Brooke thought. She answered Parks's smile cautiously, wondering what his reaction would be when they were introduced. She felt a jab of uneasiness then pushed it aside. After all, he'd been the one to wake her up at dawn and ask for a date.

"Parks, I want you to meet Claire Thorton, the lady who'll be producing your commercials." Lee laid his hand over Claire's in an unconsciously possessive gesture noticed only by Parks and Brooke. Parks was amused, Brooke annoyed.

"A pleasure, Ms. Thorton." He wanted to say he had expected a dragon from what he'd read of her professionally, not this soft-faced attractive woman with faded blue eyes. Instead, Parks smiled and accepted her hand.

"We're looking forward to working with you. I was just telling Mr. Dutton how much Brooke and I enjoyed your game against the Valiants a few weeks ago." Remembering his muttered demand for Brooke's name at the rail, Claire waited for the reaction.

"Oh?" So this was her friend, he thought, turning to Brooke. With her face, he concluded she must be a regular for Thorton's commercials. "Hello again."

"Hello." Brooke found her hand claimed and held. Taking a hasty sip of champagne, she waited for the bomb to drop.

"Claire tells me Ms. Gordon is her best," Lee told Parks. "Since you'll be working together closely, you'll want to get to know each other."

"Will we?" Parks ran his thumb along Brooke's palm.

"Only my best director for a project this important," Claire put in, watching them closely.

Brooke felt his thumb stop its casual caress, then his fingers tightened. There was no change in his face. To prevent a quick gasp of pain, she swallowed the rest of her champagne. "So you direct commercials," he said smoothly.

"Yes." She tugged once to free her hand, but he only increased his grip.

"Fascinating." Casually, he plucked the empty glass from her other hand. "Excuse us." Brooke found herself being dragged through the crowd of jewels and silks. Immediately, she quickened her pace so that it appeared she was walking with him rather than being led.

"Let go of me," she hissed, giving a nodding smile to another director. "You're breaking my hand."

"Consider it a preview of things to come." Parks pulled her through the open French doors, hoping to find a quiet spot. There was a three-piece band in the garden playing soft, dancing music. At least a dozen couples were taking advantage of it. Parks swore, but before he could maneuver her through the garden to a more private spot, he heard someone call her name. Immediately, he dragged her into his arms.

The hard contact with his chest stole her breath, the arm tight around her waist prevented her from finding any more. Ignoring the choking sound she made, Parks began to sway to the music. "Just wave to him," he ordered against her ear. "I'm not about to be interrupted with small talk."

Wanting to breathe again, Brooke obeyed. She was already planning revenge. When his grip lessened slightly, she drew in a sharp breath of air, letting it out on a string of abuse. "You overgrown bully, don't think you can drag me around just because you're this year's American hero. I'll only take it once, and I'll only warn you once. Don't you *ever* grab me again." Brooke stomped hard on his foot and was rewarded by having her air cut off again.

"You dance beautifully, Ms. Gordon," Parks whispered in her ear. He bit none too gently on the lobe. Between the fury and pain, Brooke felt a stir deep in her stomach. Oh, no, she thought, stiffening. Not again. The band switched to an up-tempo number but he continued to hold her close and sway.

"You're going to have a lot of explaining to do when I faint from lack of oxygen," she managed. Who would have thought that lanky body would be so hard, or the limber arms so strong?

"You won't faint," he muttered, slowly maneuvering her toward the edge of the garden. "And you're the one with the explaining to do."

She was released abruptly, but before Brooke could take a breath, he was pulling her through a clump of azalea. "Look, you jerk…" Then she was back inside, dazed by bright lights and laughter. Without pausing, Parks dragged her through the center patio and into the adjoining courtyard.

There was no music here, except the liquid sound of the water falling into the grotto, and only a few couples more intent on themselves than on a man pulling a furious woman in his wake. Parks drew her close to the pool and into the shadows behind the high wall. Brooke was effectively sandwiched between him and the smooth rocks.

"So you like to play games," he murmured.

For the first time she was able to lift her face and stare into his. Her eyes glittered in the moonlight. "I don't know what you're talking about."

"No?"

She had expected him to be annoyed, but she hadn't expected this smoldering fury. It was in his eyes, in the hard lines of his face, in the poised readiness of his body. When she felt her heart begin to thud uncomfortably, she became only more defensive. "You made all the moves," she tossed out. "You *demanded* that I give you my name. You called *me* at six o'clock in the morning for a date. All I did was let Claire drag me to a ball game."

She made an attempt to push by him and found herself pressed back against the wall by a firm hand on her chest. "You were sizing me up," he said slowly. "At the game, at dinner. Tell me, how did I come out?"

Brooke put her hand to his wrist, but was surprised when he let her push his hand away. She began a careless recital she knew would infuriate him. "You move more like a dancer than an athlete—it'll be a plus on film. Your build is good, it'll sell clothes. You can be charming at times, and your face is attractive without being handsome. That could sell anything. You have a certain sexuality that should appeal to women who'd like their men to have it, too. They're the primary target, as women still do the bulk of buying in ready-to-wear."

Her tone had been schooled to annoy. Even so, Parks couldn't prevent his temper from rising. "Do I get a rating?"

"Naturally." The bitten-off words pleased her enormously. It was a small payment for the scene on her porch, but it was payment. "Your popularity quotient is fair at the moment. It should get higher after the first commercial is aired. Claire seems to think if you could get into the World Series and do something outstanding, it would help."

"I'll see what I can do," he said dryly. "Now, why didn't you tell me who you were?"

"I did."

He leaned closer. She caught a trace of sharp cologne over the smell of wet summer leaves. "No, you didn't."

"I told you I make commercials."

"Knowing I'd conclude you were an actress."

"Your conclusions are your own problem," Brooke told him with a shrug. "I never said I was an actress." She heard a woman's laugh muffled in the distance and the rush of water into the pool beside her. The odds, she mused, were not in her favor at the moment. "I don't see what difference it makes."

"I don't like games," Parks said precisely, "unless I know the players."

"Then we won't play," Brooke countered. "Your job is to do what I tell you—no more, no less."

Parks controlled a wave of fury and nodded. "On the set." He caught the hair at her waist, then let it slide through his hands. "And off?"

"And off, nothing." She'd put more emphasis on the last word than she had intended to. It showed a weakness she could only hope he didn't notice.

"No." Parks stepped closer so that she had to tilt back her head to keep her eyes level with his. "I don't think I like those rules. Let's try mine."

Brooke was ready this time for the sneak attack on her senses. He wouldn't be permitted to seduce her, make her tremble with those featherlight teasing kisses on her skin. With a cool, hard stare, she dared him to try.

He returned the look as seconds dragged on. She caught the glint of challenge in his eyes but didn't see the slow curve of his lips. No man had ever been able to meet her stare so directly or for so long. For the first time in years, Brooke felt a weakness in her primary defense.

Then he did what he had wanted to do from the first moment he had seen her. Parks dove his hands into the lushness of her hair, letting them sink into the softness before he dragged her against him. Their eyes clashed a moment longer, even as he lowered his lips and savaged hers.

Brooke's vision blurred. She struggled to bring it back into sharp focus, to concentrate on that one sense to prevent her others from being overpowered. She fought not to taste the hot, demanding flavor of his lips, to feel the quick, almost brutal nip of his teeth that would tempt her lips to part. She didn't want to hear her own helpless moan. Then his tongue was plundering, enticing hers to answer in a seduction totally different from the teasing gentleness of his first embrace. She struggled against him, but her movements only caused more heat to flare from the friction of her body on his.

Gradually, the kiss altered. The hard pressure became sweet. He nibbled at her mouth, as if savoring the flavor, sucking gently, though his arms kept her pinned tight. She lost even her blurred vision, and her will to resist went with it.

Parks felt the change, her sudden pliancy. Her surrender excited him. She wasn't a woman to relinquish control easily, yet both times he had held her, he'd prized it from her. With gentleness, he realized, suddenly aware that the anger had fled from his body and his mouth. It was gentleness that won her, whereas force would only be met with force. Now he didn't want to think—not for a moment. He wanted only to lose himself in the soft give of her body, the white-silk scent that poured from her and the dusky flavor of her mouth. They were all the seduction of woman, only intensified by her surrender.

Brooke felt the liquid weight in her limbs, the slow insistent tug in her thighs before the muscles went lax. Her mouth clung to his, yearning for more of the magic it could bring with the gentle play of tongue and teeth. His hands began a slow exploration of her body, kneading over the soft material. When she felt him loosen the narrow zipper that ran from her throat to her waist, she roused herself to protest.

"No." The words came on a gasp of breath as his fingers slid along her skin.

Parks gathered her hair in one hand, drawing her head back so that his eyes met hers again. "I have to touch you." Watching her, he glided his fingers over her breast, pausing briefly on the taut point before he roamed down to her flat, quivering stomach. "One day I'll touch all of you," he murmured. "Inch by inch. I'm going to feel your skin heat under my hands." His fingers trailed back to her breast, leaving a path of awakened flesh in their wake. "I'm going to watch your face when I make love to you."

Bending, he touched his lips to hers again, tasting her breath as it shuddered into his mouth. Very slowly, he drew up the zipper, letting his knuckles graze along her skin. Then he ran his hands up her back until their bodies fit together again.

"Kiss me, Brooke." He rubbed his nose lightly against hers. "Really kiss me."

Tingling from his touch, aroused by the whispered words, she pressed her open mouth to his. Her tongue sought his, hungry for the moist dark tastes that had already seeped inside of her. He waited for her demands, her aggressions, feeling them build as her body strained against his. With a groan of pleasure, Brooke tangled her fingers in his hair, wanting to drag him closer. When he knew his chain of control was on its last link, Parks drew her away. He'd learned more of her, but not enough. Not yet. And he wasn't going to forget that he had a small score to settle with her.

"When the camera's rolling, it's your game and your rules." He cupped her chin in his hand, wondering how many times he'd be able to walk away from her when his body was aching to have her. "When it's not," he continued quietly, "the rules are mine."

Brooke took a shaky breath. "I don't play games."

Parks smiled, running a fingertip over her swollen mouth. "Everyone does," he corrected. "Some make a career out of it, and they aren't all on ball fields." Dropping his hand, he stepped back from her. "We both have a job to do. Maybe we're not too thrilled about it at the moment, but I have a feeling that won't make any difference in how well you work."

"No," Brooke agreed shortly. "It won't. I can detest you and still make you look fantastic on the screen."

He grinned. "Or make me look like an idiot if it suited you."

She couldn't prevent a small smile from forming. "You're very perceptive."

"But you won't, because you're a pro. Whatever happens between us personally won't make you direct any differently."

"I'll do my job," Brooke stated as she stepped around him. "And nothing's going to happen between us personally." She looked up sharply when a friendly arm was dropped over her shoulder.

"I guess we'll just wait and see about that." Parks sent her another amiable grin. "Have you eaten?"

Brooke frowned at him dubiously. "No."

He gave her shoulder a fraternal pat. "I'll get you a plate."

Chapter 4

Brooke couldn't believe she was spending a perfectly beautiful Sunday afternoon at a ball game. What was more peculiar was that she was enjoying it. She was well aware that she was being punished for the few veiled sarcastic remarks she had tossed off at the de Marco party, but after the first few innings, she found that Billings was right. There was a bit more to it than swinging a bat and running around in circles.

During her first game, Brooke had been too caught up in the atmosphere, the people, then in her initial impressions of Parks. Now she opened her mind to the game itself and enjoyed. Being a survivor, whenever she was faced with doing something she didn't want to do, Brooke simply conditioned herself to *want* to do it. She had no patience with people who allowed themselves to be miserable when it was so simple to turn a situation around to your advantage. If it wasn't always possible to enjoy, she could learn. It pleased her to be doing both.

The game had more subtlety than she had first realized, and more strategy. Brooke never ceased to be intrigued by strategy. It became obvious that there were variables to the contest, dozens of ifs, slices of chance counterbalancing skill. In a game of inches, luck couldn't be overlooked. This had an appeal for her because she had always considered luck every bit as vital as talent in winning, no matter what the game.

And there were certain aspects of the afternoon, beyond the balls and strikes, that fanned her interest.

The crowd was no less enthusiastic or vocal than it had been on her first visit to Kings Stadium. If anything, Brooke reflected, the people were more enthusiastic—even slightly wild. She wondered if their chants and screams and whistles took on a tone of delirium because the score was tied 1-1, and had been since the first inning. Lee called it an example of a superior defensive game.

Lee Dutton was another aspect of the afternoon that intrigued her. He seemed—on the surface—a genial, rather unkempt sort of man with a faint Brooklyn accent that lingered from his youth. He wore a golf shirt and checked pants, which only accented his tubbiness. Brooke might have passed him off as a cute middle-aged man had it not been for the sharp black eyes. She liked him…with a minor reservation—he seemed inordinately attentive to Claire.

It occurred to Brooke that he found a great many occasions to touch—Claire's soft manicured hands, her round shoulder, even her gabardine-clad knee. What was more intriguing to Brooke was that Claire didn't, as was her habit, freeze Lee's tentative advances with an icy smile or a stingingly polite word. As far as Brooke could tell, Claire seemed to be enjoying them—or perhaps she was overlooking them because of the importance of the de Marco account and Parks Jones. In either case, Brooke determined to keep an eye on her friend, and the agent. It wasn't unheard-of for a woman approaching fifty to be naive of men and therefore susceptible.

If she were to be truthful, Brooke would have to admit she enjoyed watching Parks. There was no doubt he was in his element in the field, eyes shaded by a cap, glove in his hand. Just as he had been in his element, she remembered, at the glossy party at the de Marco villa. He hadn't seemed out of place in the midst of ostentatious wealth, sipping vintage champagne or handling cocktail party conversation. And why should he? she mused. After their last encounter, Brooke had made it her business to find out more about him.

He'd come from money. Big money. Parkinson Chemicals was a third-generation, multimillion-dollar conglomerate that dealt in everything from aspirin to rocket fuel. He'd been born with a silver spoon in one hand and a fat portfolio in the other. His two sisters had married well, one to a restauranteur who had been her business partner before he became her husband, the other to a vice president of Parkinson attached to the Dallas branch. But the heir to Parkinson, the man who carried the old family name in front of the less unique Jones, had had a love affair with baseball.

The love affair hadn't diminished during his studies at Oxford under a Rhodes scholarship; it had simply been postponed. When Parks had graduated, he'd gone straight to the Kings' training camp—Brooke had to wonder how his family had felt about that—and there had been drafted. After less than a year on the Kings' farm team, he'd been brought up to the majors. There he had remained, for a decade.

So he didn't play for the money, Brooke mused, but because he enjoyed the game. Perhaps that was why he played with such style and steadiness.

She remembered, too, her impressions of him at the de Marcoses'—charming, then ruthless, then casually friendly. And none of it, Brooke concluded, was an act. Above all else, Parks Jones was in complete control, on or off the diamond. Brooke respected that, related to it, while she couldn't help wondering how the two of them would juggle their need to be in charge when they began to work together. If nothing else, she mused as she crunched down on a piece of ice, it would be an interesting association.

Brooke watched him now as he stood on the bag at second while the opposing team brought out a relief pitcher. Parks had started off the seventh inning with a leadoff single, then had advanced to second when the next batter walked. Brooke could feel the adrenaline of the crowd pulsing while Parks talked idly with the second baseman.

"If they take this one," Lee was saying, "the Kings lock up the division." He slipped his hand over Claire's. "We need these runs."

"Why did they change pitchers?" Brooke demanded. She thought of how furious she would be if someone pulled her off a job before it was finished.

"There's two on and nobody out." Lee gave her an easy paternal smile. "Mitchell was slowing down—he'd walked two last inning and was only saved from having runs score by that rifle shot the center fielder sent home." Reaching in his shirt pocket, he brought out a cigar in a thin protective tube. "I think you'll see the Kings going to the bullpen in the eighth."

"I wouldn't switch cameramen in the middle of a shoot," Brooke mumbled.

"You would if he couldn't focus the lens anymore," Lee countered, grinning at her.

With a laugh, Brooke dove her hand into the bag of peanuts he offered her. "Yeah, I guess I would."

The strategy proved successful, as the relief man shut down the next three batters, leaving Parks and his teammate stranded on base. The crowds groaned, swore at the umpire and berated the batters.

"Now there's sportsmanship," Brooke observed, casting a look over her shoulder when someone called the batter, who struck out to end the inning, a bum—and other less kind names.

Lee gave a snort of laughter as he draped his arm casually over Claire's shoulders. "You should hear them when we're losing, kid."

The lifted-brow look Brooke gave Claire at the gesture was returned blandly. "Enthusiasm comes in all forms," Claire observed. With a smile for Lee, she settled back against his arm to watch the top of the next inning.

Definitely an odd couple, Brooke mused; then she assumed her habitual position of elbows on rail. Parks didn't glance her way. He had only once—at the beginning of the game when he took the field. The look had been long and direct before he had turned away, and since then it was as though he wasn't even aware of her. She hated to admit it irked her, hated to admit that she would have liked to engage in that silent battle of eye to eye. He was the first man she *wanted* to spar with, though she had sparred with many since her first naive encounter ten years before. There was something exciting in the mind game, particularly since Parks had a mind she both envied and admired.

Lee was on target, as the Kings went to the bullpen when the starting pitcher walked two with one man out. Brooke shifted closer to the edge of her seat to watch Parks during the transition. What does he think about out there? she wondered.

God, what I wouldn't give for a cold shower and a gallon of beer, Parks thought as the sun beat down on the back of his neck. He'd been expecting the change of pitchers and was pleased with the choice. Ripley did well what a reliever was there to do—throw hard and fast. He gave a seemingly idle glance toward the runner at second. That could be trouble, he reflected, doing a quick mental recall of his opponent's statistics. The ability to retain and call out facts had always come naturally to Parks. And not just batting averages and stolen bases. Basically, he only forgot what he wanted to forget. The rest was stockpiled, waiting until he needed it. The trick had alternately fascinated and infuriated his family and friends, so that he generally kept it to himself. At the moment, he could remember Ripley's earned-run average, his win-loss ratio, the batting average of the man waiting to step into the batter's box and the scent of Brooke's perfume.

He hadn't forgotten that she was sitting a few yards away. The awareness of her kindled inside of him—a not quite pleasant sensation. It was more of an insistent pressure, like the heat of the sun on the back of his neck. It was another reason he longed for a cool shower. Watching Ripley throw his warm-up pitches to the catcher, Parks allowed himself to imagine what it would be like to undress her—slowly—in the daylight, just before her body went from limp surrender to throbbing excitement. Soon, he promised himself; then he forced Brooke to the back of his mind as the batter stepped up to the plate.

Ripley blew the first one by the batter—hard and straight. Parks knew that Ripley didn't throw any fancy pitches, just the fast ball and the curve. He was either going to overpower the hitters, or with the lineup of right-handers coming up, Parks was going to be very busy. He positioned himself another step back on the grass, going by instinct. He noted the base runner had a fat lead as the batter chipped the next pitch off. The runner was nearly at third before the foul was called. Ripley looked back over his shoulder at second, slid his eyes to first, then fired the next pitch.

It was hit hard, smashing into the dirt in front of third then bouncing high. There was never any opportunity to think, only to act. Parks leaped, just managing to snag the ball. The runner was coming into third in a headfirst slide. Parks didn't have the time to admire his guts before he tagged the base seconds before the runner's hand grabbed it. He heard the third base ump bellow, "Out!" as he vaulted over the runner and fired the ball at the first baseman.

While the crowd went into a frenzy, Brooke remained seated and watched. She didn't even notice that Lee had given Claire a resounding, exuberant kiss. The double play had taken only seconds—that impressed her. It also disconcerted her to discover that her pulse was racing. If she closed her eyes, she could still hear the cheers from the fans, smell the scent of sun-warmed beer and see, in slow motion, the strong, sweeping moves of Parks's body. She didn't need an instant replay to visualize the leap and stretch, the shifting of muscle. She knew a ballplayer had to be agile and quick, but how many of them had that dancerlike grace? Brooke caught herself making a mental note to bring a camera to the next game, then realized she had already decided to come back again. Was it Parks, she brooded, or baseball that was luring her back?

"He's something, isn't he?" Lee leaned over Claire to give Brooke a slap on the back.

"Something," Brooke murmured. She turned her head enough to look at him. "Was that a routine play?"

Lee snorted. "If you've got ice water for blood."

"Does he?"

As he drew on a cigar, Lee seemed to consider it. He gave Brooke a long, steady look. "On the field," he stated with a nod. "Parks is one of the most controlled, disciplined men I know. Of course—" the look broke with his quick smile "—I handle a lot of actors."

"Bless them," Claire said and crossed her short, slim legs. "I believe we all agree that we hope Parks takes to this, ah, alternate career with as much energy as he shows in his baseball."

"If he has ten percent of this skill—" Brooke gestured toward the field "—in front of the camera, I'll be able to work with him."

"I think you'll be surprised," Lee commented dryly, "at just what Parks is capable of."

With a shrug, Brooke leaned on the rail again. "We'll see if he can take direction."

Brooke waited, with the tension of the crowd seeping into her, as the game went into the bottom of the ninth inning. Still tied 1-1, neither team seemed able to break through the defensive skill of the other. It should have been boring, she mused, even tedious. But she was on the edge of her seat and her pulse was still humming. She wanted them to win. With a kind of guilty surprise, Brooke caught herself just before she shouted at the plate umpire for calling strike three on the leadoff batter. It's just the atmosphere, she told herself with a frown. She'd always been a sucker for atmosphere. But when the second batter came up, she found herself gripping the rail, willing him to get a hit.

"This might go into extra innings," Lee commented.

"There's only one out," Brooke snapped, not bothering to turn around. She didn't see the quick grin Lee cast at Claire.

On a three-and-two pitch, the batter hit a bloop single to center. Around Brooke, the fans went berserk. He might have hit a home run from the way they're reacting, she thought, trying to ignore the fast pumping of her own blood. This time Brooke said nothing as the pitcher was pulled. How do they stand the tension? she wondered, watching the apparently relaxed players as the new relief warmed up. Base runners talked idly with the opposition. She thought that if she were in competition, she wouldn't be so friendly with the enemy.

The crowd settled down to a hum that became a communal shout with every pitch thrown. The batter hit one deep, so deep Brooke was amazed at the speed with which the right fielder returned it to the infield.

The batter was content with a single, but the base runner had eaten up the distance to third with the kind of gritty speed Brooke admired.

Now the crowd didn't quiet, but kept up a continual howl that echoed and reverberated as Parks came to bat. The pressure, Brooke thought, must be almost unbearable. Yet nothing showed in his face but that dangerous kind of concentration she'd seen once or twice before. She swallowed, aware that her heart was hammering in her throat. Ridiculous, she told herself once, then surrendered.

"Come on, damn it," she muttered, "smack one out of here."

He took the first pitch, a slow curve that just missed the corner. The breath that she'd been holding trembled out. The next he cut at, fouling it back hard against the window of the press box. Brooke clamped down on her bottom lip and mentally uttered a stream of curses. Parks coolly held up a hand for time, then bent to tie his shoe. The stadium echoed with his name. As if deaf to the yells, he stepped back into the box to take up his stance.

He hit it high and deep. Brooke was certain it was a repeat of his performance in her first game, then she saw the ball begin to drop just short of the fence.

"He's going to tag up. He'll tag up!" she heard Lee shouting as the center fielder caught Parks's fly at the warning track. Before Brooke could swear, the fans were shouting, not in fury but in delight. The moment the runner crossed the plate, players from the Kings' dugout swarmed out on the field.

"But Parks is out," Brooke said indignantly.

"The sacrifice fly scored the run," Lee explained.

Brooke gave him a haughty look. "I realize that—" only because she had crammed a few basic rules into her head "—but it hardly seems fair that Parks is out."

Chuckling, Lee patted her head. "He earned another RBI and the fleeting gratitude of a stadium full of Kings fans. He was one for three today, so his average won't suffer much."

"Brooke doesn't think much of rules," Claire put in, rising.

"Because they're usually made up by people who don't have the least idea what they're doing." A little annoyed with herself for becoming so involved, she stood, swinging her canvas bag over her shoulder.

"I don't know if Parks would agree with you," Lee told her. "He's lived by the rules for most of his life. Gets to be a habit."

"To each his own," she said casually. She wondered if Lee was aware that Parks was also a man who could seduce and half undress a woman behind the fragile covering of a rock wall in the middle of a crowded, glitzy Hollywood party. It seemed to her Parks was more a man who made up his own rules.

"Why don't we go down to the locker room and congratulate him?" Genially, he hooked his arms through Claire's and Brooke's, steamrolling them through the still-cheering crowd.

Lee worked his way into the stadium's inner sanctum with a combination of panache and clout. Reporters were swarming, carrying microphones, cameras or notepads. Each one was badgering or flattering a sweaty athlete in the attempt to get a quote. In the closed-in area, Brooke considered the noise level to be every bit as high as it had been in the open stadium. Lockers slammed, shouts reverberated, laughter flowed in a kind of giddy relief. Each man knew the tension would return soon enough during the play-offs. They were going to enjoy the victory of the moment to its fullest.

"Yeah, if I hadn't saved Biggs from an error in the seventh inning," the first baseman told a reporter, deadpan, "it might have been a whole different ball game."

Biggs, the shortstop, retaliated by heaving a damp towel at his teammate. "Snyder can't catch a ball unless it drops into his mitt. The rest of us make him look good."

"I've saved Parks from fifty-three errors this season," Snyder went on blandly, drawing the sweaty towel from his face. "Guess his arm must be going. Thing is, some of the hitters are so good they just keep smacking the ball right into Parks's mitt. If you watch the replay of today's game, you'll see what fantastic aim they have." Someone dumped a bucket of water on his head, but Snyder continued without breaking rhythm. "You might notice how well I place the ball in the right fielder's mitt. That takes more practice."

Brooke spotted Parks, surrounded by reporters. His uniform was filthy, streaked with dirt, while his face fared little better. The smudges of black under his eyes gave him a slightly wicked look. Without the cap his hair curled freely, darkened with sweat. But his face and body were relaxed. A smile lingered on his lips as he spoke. That battlefield intensity was gone from his eyes, she noted, as if it had never existed. If she hadn't seen it, hadn't experienced it from him, Brooke would have sworn the man wasn't capable of any form of ruthlessness. Yet he was, she reminded herself, and it wouldn't be smart to forget it.

"With only four games left in the regular season," Parks stated, "I'll be satisfied to end up with a three eighty-seven average for the year."

"If you bat five hundred in those last games—"

Parks shot the reporter a mild grin. "We'll have to see about that."

"A little wind out there today and that game-winning sacrifice fly would've been a game-winning home run."

"That's the breaks."

"What was the pitch?"

"Inside curve," he responded easily. "A little high."

"Were you trying for a four-bagger, Parks?"

He grinned again, his expression altering only slightly when he spotted Brooke. "With one out and runners on the corners, I just wanted to keep the ball off the ground. Anything deep, and Kinjinsky scores... unless he wants the Lead Foot Award."

"Lead Foot Award?"

"Ask Snyder," Parks suggested. "He's the current holder." With another smile, Parks effectively eased himself away. "Lee." He nodded to his agent while running a casual finger down Brooke's arm. She felt the shock waves race through her, and only barely managed not to jerk away. "Ms. Thorton. Nice to see you again." His only greeting to Brooke was a slow smile as he caught the tip of her hair between his thumb and forefinger. She thought again it was wise to remember he wasn't as safe as he appeared.

"Hell of a game, Parks," Lee announced. "You gave us an entertaining afternoon."

"We aim to please," he murmured, still looking at Brooke.

"Claire and I are going out to dinner. Perhaps you and Brooke would like to join us?"

Before Brooke could register surprise at Claire having a date with Lee Dutton, or formulate an excuse against making it a foursome, Parks spoke up. "Sorry, Brooke and I have plans."

Turning her head, she shot Parks a narrowed look. "I don't recall our making any plans."

Smiling, he gave her a brief tug. "You'll have to learn to write things down. Why don't you just wait in your box? I'll be out in half an hour." Without giving her a chance to protest, Parks strolled off toward the showers.

"What incredible nerve," Brooke grumbled, only to be given a sharp but discreet elbow in the ribs by Claire.

"Sorry you can't join us, dear," she said sweetly. "But then you're not fond of Chinese food in any case. And Lee's going to show me his collection first."

"Collection?" Brooke repeated blankly as she was steered into the narrow corridor.

"We've a mutual passion." Claire gave Lee a quick and surprisingly flirtatious smile. "For Oriental art. Can you find your way back to the seats?"

"I'm not a complete dolt," Brooke muttered, while giving Lee a skeptical stare.

"Well then." Casually, Claire tucked her hand into Lee's beefy arm. "I'll see you Monday."

"Have a good time, kid," Lee called over his shoulder as Claire propelled him away.

"Thanks a lot." Stuffing her hands in her pockets, Brooke worked her way up, then out to the lower level, third base box. "Thanks a hell of a lot," she repeated and stared out at the empty diamond.

There were a few maintenance workers scooping

up the debris in the stands with humming, heavy-duty cleaners, but other than that the huge open area was deserted. Finding it strangely appealing, Brooke discovered her annoyance waning. An hour before, the air had been alive, throbbing with the pulse of thousands. Now it was serene, with only the faintest trace of the crowd—the lingering odor of humanity, a whiff of salted popcorn, a few discarded cardboard containers. She leaned back against the rail, more interested in the empty stadium than the empty field.

When had it been built? she wondered. How many generations had crammed themselves into the seats and aisles to watch the games? How many thousands of gallons of beer had traveled along the rows of seats? She laughed a little, amused by her own whimsy. When a player stopped playing, did he come here to watch and remember? She thought Parks would. The game, she concluded, would get into your blood. Even she hadn't been immune to it…or, she thought wryly, to him.

Brooke tossed her head back, letting her hair fall behind her. The shadows were lengthening, but the heat still had the sticky, sweltering capacity of high afternoon. She didn't mind—she hated being cold. Habitually, she narrowed her eyes and let herself visualize how she would approach the stadium on film. Empty, she thought, with the echo of cheers, the sound of a ball cracking off a bat, a banner left behind to flutter in the breeze. She'd use the maintenance workers, sucking up the boxes and cups and bags. She might title it *Afterthought,* and there'd be no telling if the home team had left the field vanquished or victorious. What mattered would be the perpetuity of the game, the people who played it and the people who watched.

Brooke sensed him before she heard him—only an instant, but the instant was enough to scatter her thoughts and to bring her eyes swerving toward him. Immediately, all sense of the scene she had been setting vanished from her mind. No one else had ever had the power to do that to her. The fact that Parks did baffled her nearly as much as it infuriated her. For Brooke, her work was the one stability in her life—nothing and no one was allowed to tamper with it. Defensively, she straightened, meeting his stare head-on as he walked down to her in the loose, rangy stride that masked over a decade of training.

She expected him to greet her with some smart remark. Brooke was prepared for that. She considered he might greet her casually, as if his lie in the locker room had been perfect truth. She was prepared for that, too.

She wasn't prepared for him to walk directly to her, bury his hands in her hair and crush her against him in a long, hotly possessive kiss. Searing flashes of pleasure rocketed through her. Molten waves of desire overpowered surprise before it truly had time to register. His mouth pressed against hers in an absolute command that barely hid a trace of desperation. It was that desperation, more than the authority, that Brooke found herself responding to. The need to be needed was strong in her—she had always considered it her greatest weakness. And she was weak now, with the sharp scent of his skin in her senses, the dark taste of his mouth on her tongue, the feel of his shower-damp hair on her fingers.

Slowly, Parks drew away, waiting for her heavy lids to lift. Though his eyes never left hers, Brooke felt as though he looked at all of her once, thoroughly. "I want you." He said it calmly, though the fierce look was back on his face.

"I know."

Parks ran a hand through her hair again, from the crown to the tips. "I'm going to have you."

Steadying a bit, Brooke stepped out of his arms. "That I don't know."

Smiling, Parks continued to caress her hair. "Don't you?"

"No," Brooke returned with such firmness that Parks lifted a brow.

"Well," he considered, "I suppose it could be a very pleasant experience to convince you."

Brooke tossed her head to free her hair of his seeking fingers. "Why did you lie to Lee about our having plans tonight?"

"Because I'd spent nine long, hot innings thinking about making love to you."

Again he said it calmly, with just a hint of a smile on his lips, but Brooke realized he was quite serious. "Well, that's direct and to the point."

"You prefer things that way, don't you?"

"Yes," she agreed, settling back against the rail again. "So let me do the same for you. We're going to be working together for several months on a very big project that involves a number of people. I'm very good at my job and I intend to see that you're very good at yours."

"So?"

Her eyes flashed at his amused tone, but Brooke continued. "So personal involvements interfere with professional judgment. As your director, I have no intention of becoming your lover, however briefly."

"Briefly?" Parks repeated, studying her. "Do you always anticipate the length of your relationships beforehand? I think," he continued slowly, "you're more of a romantic than that."

"I don't care what you think," she snapped, "as long as you understand."

"I understand," Parks agreed, beginning to. "You're evading the issue."

"I certainly am not!" Temper flared, reflecting in her stance and her eyes as well as her voice. "I'm telling you straight out that I'm not interested. If that bruises your ego, too bad."

Parks grabbed her arm when she would have swept by him. "You know," he began in a careful tone that warned of simmering anger, "you infuriate me. I can't remember the last time a woman affected me that way."

"I'm not surprised." Brooke jerked her arm out of his hold. "You've been too busy devastating them with your charm."

"And you're too worried about being dumped to have any kind of a relationship."

She made a quick, involuntary sound, as if she'd been struck. Cheeks pale, eyes dark, she stared at him before she shoved him aside to race up the stairs. Parks caught her before she'd made it halfway. Though he turned her back to face him firmly, his touch was gentle.

"Raw nerve?" he murmured, feeling both sympathy and guilt. It wasn't often he lost control enough to say something he'd have to apologize for. Eyes dry and hurting, Brooke glared at him. "I'm sorry."

"Just let me go."

"Brooke." He wanted to pull her into his arms and

comfort, but knew she wouldn't accept it. "I am sorry. I don't make a habit of punching women."

It wasn't charm, but sincerity. After a moment, Brooke let out a long breath. "All right. I usually take a punch better than that."

"Can we take off the gloves—at least for the rest of the day?" How deep was the hurt? Parks wondered. And how long would it take to win her trust?

"Maybe," Brooke returned cautiously.

"How about dinner?"

She responded to the smile before she realized it. "My weakness."

"We'll start there, then. How do you feel about tacos?"

She allowed him to take her hand. "Who's buying?"

They sat outdoors at a busy fast-food franchise with tiny metal tables and hard stools. Sounds of traffic and blaring car radios rolled over them. Brooke relaxed when she ate, Parks noted, wondering if she were consciously aware of the dropping of guards. He didn't think so. The relaxation was the same when she sat in an elegant restaurant with wine and exotic food as it was in a greasy little takeout with sloppy tacos and watered-down sodas in paper cups. After handing her another napkin, Parks decided to do some casual probing.

"Did you grow up in California?"

"No." Brooke drew more soda through her straw. "You did."

"More or less." Remembering how skilled she was in evading or changing the subject, Parks persisted. "Why did you move to L.A.?"

"It's warm," she said immediately. "It's crowded."

"But you live miles out of town in the middle of nowhere."

"I like my privacy. How did your family feel about you choosing baseball over Parkinson Chemicals?"

He smiled a little, enjoying the battle for control. "Stunned. Though I'd told them for years what I intended to do. My father thought, still thinks, it's a phase. What does your family think about you directing commercials?"

Brooke set down her cup. "I don't have any family."

Something in her tone warned him this was a tender area. "Where did you grow up?"

"Here and there." Quickly, she began to stuff used napkins into the empty cups. Parks caught her hand before she could rise.

"Foster homes?"

Eyes darkening with anger, Brooke stared at him. "Why are you pressing?"

"Because I want to know who you are," he said softly. "We could be friends before we're lovers."

"Let go of my hand."

Instead of obliging, Parks gave her a curious look. "Do I make you nervous?"

"You make me furious," she tossed back, evading one truth with another. "I can't be around you for more than ten minutes without getting mad."

Parks grinned. "I know the feeling. Still, it's stimulating."

"I don't want to be stimulated," Brooke said evenly. "I want to be comfortable."

With a half laugh, Parks turned her hand over, brushing his lips lightly over the palm. "I don't think so," he murmured, watching her reaction over their joined hands. "You're much too alive to settle for comfortable."

"You don't know me."

"Exactly my point." He leaned a bit closer. "Who are you?"

"What I've made myself."

Parks nodded. "I see a strong, independent woman with lots of drive and ambition. I also see a woman who chooses a quiet, isolated spot for her home, who knows how to laugh and mean it, who forgives just as quickly as she angers." As he spoke Parks watched her brows lower. She wasn't angry now, but thoughtful and wary. He felt a bit like a man trying to gain the confidence of a dove who might fly away at any time or choose to nestle in the palm of his hand. "She interests me."

After a moment, Brooke let out a long breath. Perhaps if she told him a little, she considered, he'd leave it at that. "My mother wasn't married," she began briskly. "I'm told that after six months she got tired of lugging a baby around and dumped me on her sister. I don't remember a great deal about my aunt, I was six when she turned me over to social services. What I do remember is being hungry and not very warm. I went into my first foster home." She shrugged then pushed away the debris that littered the table. "It wasn't too bad. I was there for little more than a year before I got shuffled to the next one. I was in five altogether from the age of six to seventeen. Some were better than others, but I never belonged. A lot of that may have been my fault."

Brooke sighed, not pleased to remember. "Not all foster parents take in children for the money. Some of them—most of them," she amended, "are very kind, loving people. I just never felt a part, because I always knew it would be temporary, that my sister or brother of the moment was real and I was…transient. As a result I was difficult. Maybe I challenged the people whose home I was placed in to want me—for me, not out of pity or social obligation or the extra dollars my living with them would bring in.

"My last two years in high school I lived on a farm in Ohio with a nice couple who had an angelic son who would yank my hair when his mother's back was turned." A quick grimace. "I left as soon as I graduated from high school, worked my way cross-country waiting tables. It only took me four months to get to L.A." She met Parks's quiet, steady look and suddenly flared. "Don't feel sorry for me."

The ultimate insult, he mused, taking her rigid hand in his. "I wasn't. I was wondering how many people would have had the guts to try to make their own life at seventeen, and how many would have the strength to really do it. At the same age I wanted to head for the Florida training camps. Instead I was on a plane heading for college."

"Because you had an obligation," Brooke countered.

"I didn't. If I had had the chance to go to college…" She trailed off. "In any case, we've both had a decade in our careers."

"And you can have several more if you like," Parks pointed out. "I can't. One more season."

"Why?" she demanded. "You'll only be…"

"Thirty-five," he finished with a wry smile. "I promised myself ten years ago that's when I'd stop. There aren't many of us who can play past forty like Mays."

"Yes, it's obvious you play like an old man," she returned dryly.

"I intend to stop before I do."

Taking a straw, she began to pleat it while she studied him. "Quit while you're ahead?"

"That's the idea."

That she could understand. "Does giving it up with half your life ahead of you bother you?"

"I intend to do something with the second half, but at times it does. Other times I think about all those summer evenings I'll have free. Do you like the beach?"

"I don't get there often, but yes." She thought about the long, hot commercial she'd just filmed. "With occasional exceptions," she added.

"I have a place on Maui." Unexpectedly he leaned over, caressing her cheek with fingers that were whisper soft and undeniably possessive. "I'm going to take you there one day." He shook his head as Brooke started to speak. "Don't argue, we do that too much. Let's go for a drive."

"Parks," Brooke began as they rose, "I meant what I said about not getting involved."

"Yeah, I know." Then he kissed her long and lingeringly while she stood with her hands filled with paper plates and cups.

Chapter 5

It was three days before Brooke heard from Parks. She was aware that the last four-game series in the regular season would be played out of town. She knew, too, from what she told herself was simply a casual glimpse at the sports section, that Parks had knocked in three more RBIs in the first two games. In the meantime, she was busy looking over the storyboard for his first block of commercials.

The word had come down that the first thirty-second spot would be filmed before the league play-offs, in order to capitalize on Parks's exposure in the competition. That left Brooke little time to prepare, with an already demanding schedule of studio and location shoots, editing and preproduction meetings. But challenge, like food, was vital to her.

Closed off in her office, with a half an hour's leeway before she was due at the studio, Brooke ran over the final script for the initial de Marco commercial. Casually slick, she thought, approving. It had minimal dialogue and soft sell—Parks at the plate, swinging away while dressed in de Marco's elegant sports clothes, then a slow dissolve to the next scene with him dressed in the same suit, stepping out of a Rolls with a slinky brunette on his arm.

"Clothes for anytime—anywhere," Brooke muttered. The timing had been checked and rechecked. The audio, except for Parks's one-line voice-over, was already being recorded. All she had to do was to guide Parks through the paces. The salesmanship hinged on her skill and his charm. Fair enough, she thought and reached for her half cup of cold coffee as a knock sounded at her door. "Yeah?" Brooke turned the script back to page one, running through the camera angles.

"Delivery for you, Brooke." The receptionist dropped a long white florist's box on her cluttered desk. "Jenkins said to let you know the Lardner job's been edited. You might want to check it out."

"Okay, thanks." Curiously, Brooke frowned over the top of the script at the flower box. Occasionally, she received a grateful phone call or letter from a client when they were particularly pleased with a commercial—but not flowers. Then there'd been that actor in the car spot last year, Brooke remembered. The one who was on his third wife. He'd alternately amused and annoyed Brooke by sending her batches of red roses every week. But six months had passed since she had convinced him that he was wasting her time and his money.

More likely it was one of E.J.'s practical jokes, she considered. She'd probably find a few dozen frog legs inside. Not one to spoil someone's fun, Brooke pulled off the ribbon and lifted the lid.

There were masses of hibiscus. Fragrant, dew-soft, pink-and-white petals filled the box almost to over-flowing. After the first gasp of surprise, Brooke dove her hands into them, captivated by their purely feminine scent and feel. Her office suddenly smelled like a tropical island: heady, exotic, richly romantic. With a sound of pleasure, she filled her hands with the blooms, bringing them up to her face to inhale. In contrast to the sultry scent, the petals seemed impossibly fragile. A small white card fluttered down to her littered desk.

Letting the flowers drift back into the box, Brooke reached for the envelope and tore it open.

I thought of your skin.

There was nothing else, but she knew. She shuddered, then chided herself for acting like a mooning teenager. But she read the line three times. No one had ever been able to affect her so deeply with such simplicity. Though Parks was a thousand miles away, she could all but feel those lean, strong fingers trace down her cheek. The flood of warmth, the flash of desire told her she wasn't going to escape him—had never truly wanted to. Without giving herself any time for doubts or fears, Brooke picked up the phone.

"Get me Parks Jones," she said quickly. "Try Lee Dutton, he'll have the number." Before she could change her mind, Brooke hung up, burying her hands in the flowers again.

How was it he knew just what buttons to push? she wondered, then discovered at that moment she didn't care. It was enough to be romanced—and romanced in style. Lifting a single bloom, she trailed it down her cheek. It was smooth and moist against her skin—as Parks's first kiss had been. The ringing phone caught her dreaming.

"Yes?"

"Parks Jones on line two. You've got ten minutes before they need you in the studio."

"All right. Hunt me up a vase and some water, will you?" She glanced at the box again. "Make that two vases." Still standing with the blossom in her hand, Brooke punched the button for line two. "Parks?"

"Yes. Hello, Brooke."

"Thank you."

"You're welcome."

She hesitated, then let herself speak her first thought. "I feel like a teenager who just got her first corsage."

Dropping flat on his back on the bed, he laughed. "I'd like to see you with some of them in your hair."

Experimentally she held one up over her ear. Unprofessional, she thought with a sigh, and contented herself with the scent of them. "I've a shoot in the studio in a few minutes. I don't think the lights would do them much good."

"You have your practical side, don't you, Brooke?" Parks flexed the slight ache in his shoulder and closed his eyes.

"It's necessary," she muttered but couldn't quite bring herself to drop the blossom back in the box. "How are you? I wasn't sure you'd be in."

"I got in about half an hour ago. They cut us down five to two. I went oh for three."

"Oh." She frowned, not quite sure what she was supposed to say. "I'm sorry."

"I didn't seem to have any rhythm—it'll pass." Before the play-offs, he added silently. "I thought of you, maybe too much."

Brooke felt an odd twist of pleasure that was difficult to pass off. "I wouldn't want to be responsible for a slump, particularly when I remember some of the remedies." His chuckle sounded faint and weary. "Are you tired?"

"A bit. You'd think with the division wrapped up we'd glide through this last series. Last night we went eleven innings."

"I know." She could have bitten off her tongue. "I caught the highlights on the late news," she said breezily. "I'll let you sleep, then. I just wanted to thank you."

Her inadvertent admission had his lips twitching, but he didn't bother to open his eyes. With them closed, he had no trouble bringing her face into focus. "Will I see you when I get back?"

"Of course. We'll be shooting the first segment on Friday, so—"

"Brooke," he interrupted firmly, quietly. "Will I see you when I get back?"

She hesitated, then looked down at the mass of pink-and-white hibiscus on her desk. "Yes," she heard herself saying. Pressing the flower to her cheek, she sighed. "I think I'm going to make a very big mistake."

"Good. I'll see you Friday."

The trick to being a good director, Brooke had always thought, was to be precise without being too technical, brisk without losing sympathy, then to split yourself up into several small parts so that you could be everywhere at once. It was a knack she had developed early on—on the job—without the formalized training of many of her colleagues. Perhaps because she had worked so many of the other aspects of filming, from timing a script to setting the lights to mixing sound, she was fiercely precise. Nothing escaped her eye. Because she knew actors were often overworked and insecure, she had never quite lost her sympathy for them even when she was ready to rage at a consistently flubbed line. Her early experience at waiting tables had taught her the trick of moving fast enough to all but be in two places at once.

On a set or in a studio, she had complete self-confidence. Her control was usually unquestioned because it came naturally. She never thought about being in charge or felt the need to remind others of it; she simply *was* in charge.

With a copy of the script in one hand, she supervised the final adjustments on the lights and reflectors. The ball diamond, she had noted immediately, had an entirely different feel at home plate than it had from the stands. It was like being on an island, cupped amid the high mountain of seats, with the tall green wall skirting the back. The distance from plate to fence seemed even more formidable from this perspective. Brooke wondered how men with sticks in their hands could continually hit a moving ball over that last obstacle.

She could smell the grass, freshly trimmed, the dusty scent of dirt that had dried in the sun and a whiff of E.J.'s blatantly macho cologne. "Give me a reading," she ordered the lighting director as she glanced up at the thick clouds in the sky. "I want a sunny afternoon."

Spontaneous applause broke out, along with a few whistles. "Nice pitch, Friedman," Parks commented.

The coach tossed another ball in the air. "Just making you look good, Jones. The Valiants' pitchers won't be so friendly."

Brooke swiped the back of her wrist across her damp brow. "I'd like a couple more please. What was the time on that?"

"Fourteen seconds."

"Okay. The light's shifting, check the reading. Mr. Friedman, I'd like to get a couple more."

"Anything you say, sweetheart."

"Parks, I need a full swing like last time. No matter where the ball goes, look up and out—don't forget the grin."

Laying the bat on his shoulder, he drawled, "No, ma'am."

Brooke ignored him and turned away. "Lights?"

The technician finished the adjustments, then nodded. "Set."

Although she considered the third take close to perfect, Brooke ran through another three. Edited, this segment of the commercial would run twelve and a half seconds. That it took only three hours to set up and film showed that she ran a tight schedule.

"It's a wrap. Thanks," she added as she accepted the cup of ice water from her assistant. "We'll set up in front of the restaurant in…" She glanced at her watch. "Two hours. Fred, double-check on the Rolls and the actress. E.J., I'll take the film into editing myself." Even as she spoke, Brooke walked over to the mound. "Mr. Friedman." With a smile, she held out her hand. "Thank you."

He found her grip firm and her eyes soft. "My pleasure." With a chuckle, he tossed a spare ball into his mitt. "You know, in my day ballplayers plugged razor blades or beer. We endorsed bats and gloves." He cast a glance at Parks, who was signing a baseball for a technician. "No fancy designers would have asked us to sport his clothes."

Brooke shifted her eyes to Parks. He was laughing now, shaking his head at E.J. as the cameraman ticked off some point on his fingers. The casually elegant clothes suited him, as did the dark wood bat in his hand. "I'd hate to have him know I said it, Mr. Friedman," Brooke commented as she turned back to the coach, "but Parks is a natural."

With a shout of laughter, Friedman patted her on the back. "He won't hear it from me, sweetheart. Last thing my pitchers need is a third baseman with a big head. One more thing," he added before Brooke turned away. "I watched the way you run things." He gave her an expansive grin that revealed good dentures. "You'd make a hell of a coach."

"Thanks." Pleased with the compliment, Brooke made her way toward the plate, and Parks. "You did very well."

He regarded her extended hand with amusement, but accepted it. "For a rookie?" he countered.

When she started to remove her hand, Parks held it firmly, running a light fingertip over the inside of her wrist. He had the satisfaction of feeling her pulse jump then speed up. "I didn't anticipate any problems, as you were simply playing yourself." Behind her, technicians were taking down lights and coiling cable. She heard E.J. describing the new lady he was seeing in glowing, if exaggerated, terms. Using all her willpower, Brooke concentrated on the background noises instead of the feel of Parks's finger tracing over her skin. "The next scene should be fairly easy. We'll go over it on location this afternoon. If you have any questions—"

"Just one," Parks interrupted. "Come here a minute." Without waiting for agreement, he drew her toward the dugout, stepped inside then just through the door that led to the locker rooms.

"What's the problem, Parks?" Brooke demanded. "I have to get into editing before the next shoot."

"Are we finished here for now?"

With an impatient sigh, Brooke gestured to the equipment being packed. "Obviously."

"Fine." Pressing her back against the doorway, Parks covered her mouth with his.

It was a proprietary kiss with whispers of violence. The frustrations of the past hours seeped into it as he finally let them free. There was the annoyance of wanting her—of being too far away to touch for days, then being close enough, but not being permitted to. There was the exasperation of her cool professional treatment of him while he had fought an insistent growing desire. And there was the banked fury at being put in the position of taking orders from a woman who dominated his thoughts and denied his body.

Yet it was more agitating than soothing to press his body against the softness of hers. She filled him—the exotic scent, the ripe woman-taste of her mouth, the silken skin over the sharp, strong bones of her face. Almost desperately, he pressed closer, plunged deeper. He would *not* be filled. He would find that corner, that secret place that would open her for him so that he could have her at last—body and mind. To do that he needed the edge of control, over himself, and over Brooke. Her strength made it a challenge—his desire made it a necessity.

"Hey, Brooke, want a ride to the... Whoops." E.J. poked his head into the dugout then retreated. As Parks's lips freed hers, she could hear the cameraman whistling gleefully as he strolled away. Furious that she had completely lost track of time and place, Brooke shoved against Parks's chest.

"Let go of me!"

"Why?"

Apparently her ice-pick stare more amused than wounded him. "Don't you *ever* pull something like that when I'm working," she hissed, shoving a second time as Parks blocked her exit.

"I asked if we were finished," Parks reminded her, then backed her into the wall again.

"When we're on the job," Brooke said evenly, "I'm the director, you're the product." He narrowed his eyes at her choice of words, but she continued, full steam. "You'll do *exactly* what I tell you."

"The camera's not rolling, Brooke."

"I won't have my crew speculating, circulating gossip that can undermine my authority or my credibility."

His own temper rose in direct balance with need. She only aroused him more when she challenged. "Aren't you more afraid that you enjoy being touched by me? Doesn't it infuriate you that when I kiss you, you don't really give a damn who's in charge?" He bent his head so that his lips were only a breath from hers. "I took your orders all morning, Ms. Gordon. Now it's my turn."

Her lancelike stare didn't falter as the quiet words

fluttered over her lips. With the tip of his tongue he traced them, enjoying their taste and her own suppressed passion. Merging desire stung the air—they both felt it, they both tried to rise above it in the struggle for dominance. Yet they both became aware that it was the desire that would win over each of them.

His lips rubbed over hers, without pressure or force, taunting her to demand he stop, daring her to resist her own needs. Their eyes remained open and fixed on each other. Both pairs of irises darkened as passion tempted each of them to surrender.

"We have another shoot this afternoon," Brooke managed as she fought to keep her voice steady.

"When we're filming, I'll do what you tell me." He kissed her once, hard and quick. "Tonight," he added, dealing with his own heated blood, "we'll see."

Chapter 6

Brooke chose to shoot during the late-afternoon lull using day-for-night filters, rather than compete with the evening traffic. It was a quick scene, relatively simple and very glossy. The champagne-colored Rolls would drive up in front of the posh restaurant, Parks would alight, in the same outfit, but wearing a jacket—already sponged and pressed from the morning—then offer his hand to the sleekly dressed brunette. She would step from the car, showing considerable leg, then flash Parks a look before linking her arm through his. The scene would then fade out, with Parks's voice-over dubbed in, stating the motto for the campaign.

"De Marco. For the man who's going places."

The visual would be another twelve seconds, so that combined with the stadium segment, the intro and the tag at the end, the commercial would round out at thirty seconds.

"I want a long shot of the Rolls, E.J., then come in on Parks as he steps out. We don't want to lose the impact that he's wearing the same outfit he played ball in. Don't get hung up on the lady," she added dryly as she sent him a knowing look.

"Who me?" Pulling a Kings fielder's cap out of his back pocket, he offered it to Brooke. "Want to wear it? Team spirit?"

Placing one hand on her hip, Brooke stared at him without any change of expression. With a quick chuckle, E.J. fit the cap over his own modified Afro.

"Okay, boss, I'm ready when you are."

As was her habit, Brooke rechecked the camera angle and the lighting before she signaled the first take. The Rolls cruised sedately to the curb. Brooke played the background music over in her head, trying to judge how it would fit. On cue, Parks climbed out, turning to offer his hand to the brunette still inside. Frowning, Brooke let the scene play out. It wasn't right. She saw why immediately but took the few minutes until the cut to work out how to approach Parks.

With a gesture, Brooke indicated that she would speak to Parks while the driver backed up the Rolls for the next take. Putting a hand on his arm, she led him away from the technicians. "Parks, you have to relax." Because handling fidgety actors was second nature to her, Brooke's voice and manner were markedly different from the morning session. Parks noted it and bristled anyway.

"I don't know what you mean."

She steered him well away from where a few interested pedestrians were loitering by a barricade. "Number one," she began, "you're plugging a good product. Try to believe in it."

"If I didn't think it was a good product, I wouldn't be doing this," he retorted, frowning over her shoulder at the huddle of lights.

"But you're not comfortable." When Brooke gave his shoulder a reassuring pat, Parks scowled at her. "If you insist on feeling like an idiot, it's going to show. Wait," she ordered as he started to speak. "This morning, you felt more at ease—the stadium, a bat in your hand. After the first couple of minutes, you started to play the game. That's all I want you to do now."

"Look, Brooke, I'm not an actor—"

"Who's asking you to act?" she countered. "God spare me from that." She knew she'd insulted him, so she tempered the comment with a smile. "Listen, you're a winner, out on the town in a chauffeured Rolls with a gorgeous woman. All I want you to do is have a good time and look rather pleased with yourself. You can pull it off, Parks. Loosen up."

"I wonder how you'd feel if someone asked you to field a line drive with twenty thousand people watching."

Brooke smiled again and tried not to think about the minutes ticking away. "You do that routinely," she pointed out, "because you concentrate on your job and forget those thousands of people."

"This is different," he muttered.

"Only if you let it be. Just let me see that same self-satisfied look on your face that you had when you hit that homer this morning. Pretend, Parks." Brooke straightened the collar of his shirt. "It's good for you."

"Did you know that Nina has the IQ of a soft-boiled egg?"

"Nina?"

"My date."

Brooke gave in to a sigh. "Stop being so temperamental. Nobody's asking you to marry her."

Parks opened his mouth, then shut it again. No one had ever accused him of being temperamental. He'd never *been* temperamental. If his manager told him to take a three-and-one pitch, he took it. If the third base coach told him to steal home, he ran. Not because he was malleable, but because if he was signed with a team, he followed the rules. It didn't mean he always had to like them. With a quiet oath, he ran a hand through his hair and admitted that it wasn't so much what the orders were in this case, but who was laying them out. But then, the lights and cameras would eventually shut down.

"Fine, let's do it again." He gave Brooke the slow smile she'd learned not to trust before he walked toward the Rolls. Suspicious of his easy capitulation, Brooke turned back to stand beside E.J.

Parks gave her no more cause to complain, though they were more than two hours shooting the segment. Brooke found that she had more trouble with the professional actress—and a couple of fans who recognized Parks—than she had with him. It took three takes before she convinced Nina that she wasn't looking for glowing and adoring, but for sleek and aloof. Brooke wanted the contrast and ran everyone through the twelve seconds until she was certain she had it.

Then there was the matter of two fans who sneaked through the barricade to get Parks's autograph while the camera was still rolling. Parks obliged them, and though Brooke simmered at the interruption, she noted that he dispatched the fans with the charm of a seasoned diplomat. Grudgingly, she had to admit she couldn't have done better herself.

"That's a wrap," Brooke announced, arching her back. She'd been on her feet for over eight hours, bolting down a half a sandwich between segments. She felt pleased with the day's work, satisfied with Parks's progress and ravenous. "You can break down," she told the crew. "Good job. E.J., I've scheduled the editing and dubbing for tomorrow. If you want to see what we're going to do to your film, you can come in."

"It's Saturday."

"Yeah." She pulled the bill of the fielder's cap over his face. "We'll start working at ten. Nina…" Brooke took the actress's slim, smooth hand. "You were lovely, thank you. Fred, make sure the Rolls gets back in one piece, or you'll have to face Claire. Bigelow, what's the new kid's name?" Brooke jerked her head at a young technician who was busily packing up lights.

"Silbey?"

With a nod, Brooke made a mental note of it. "He's good," she said briefly, then turned to Parks. "Well, you made it through the first one. We'll dub in the voice-over tomorrow. Any scars?"

"None that show."

"Maybe I shouldn't tell you that this one is the easiest on the schedule."

He met the humor in her eyes blandly. "Maybe you shouldn't."

"Where's your car?"

"Out at the stadium."

With a frown, Brooke checked her watch. "I'll give you a lift back there." She toyed with the idea of going by Thorton's first to take a quick look at the film, then discarded the idea. It would be better to look at it fresh in the morning. "I have to call Claire… Well." Brooke shrugged. "That can wait. Any problems?" she asked to the crew in general.

"Tomorrow's Saturday," an aggrieved E.J. stated again as he packed up his equipment. "Woman, you just don't give a man a break."

"You don't have to come in," she reminded him, knowing he would. "Good night." With Parks beside her, Brooke started down the street.

"Do you make a habit of working weekends?" he asked, noting that after a long, hectic day she still moved as though she had urgent appointments to keep.

"When it's necessary. We're rushing this through to get it aired during the play-offs or, barring that, the series." She shot him a look. "You'd better be in it." Still walking, she began to dig in the purse slung over her shoulder.

"I'll try to accommodate you. Want me to drive?"

With the keys in one hand, Brooke looked up in surprise. "Have you been talking to E.J.?"

His brows drew together. "No. Why?"

"Nothing." Dismissing the thought, Brooke paused beside her car. "Why do you want to drive?"

"It occurs to me that I may have had to stand in front of that stupid camera off and on all day, but you haven't stopped for over eight hours. It's a tough job."

"I'm a tough lady," she responded with a trace of defensiveness in her voice.

"Yeah." He grazed his knuckles over her cheek. "Iron."

"Just get in the car," Brooke muttered. After round-ing the hood, she climbed in, slamming the door only slightly. "It'll take a little while to get across town in this traffic."

"I'm not in a hurry." Parks settled comfortably beside her. "Can you cook?"

In the act of starting the car, Brooke frowned at him. "Can I what?"

"Cook. You know." Parks pantomimed the act of stirring a pan.

She laughed, shooting out of traffic with an exuberance that made Parks wince. "Of course I can cook."

"How about your place?"

Brooke zipped through a yellow light. "What about my place?" she asked cautiously.

"For dinner." Parks watched her shift into third as she scooted around a Porsche. "It seems to me I'm entitled after feeding you a couple times myself."

"You want me to cook for you?"

This time he laughed. She was going to fight him right down to the wire. "Yeah. And then I'm going to make love to you."

Brooke hit the brakes, stopping the car inches away from another bumper. "Oh, really?"

"Oh, really," he repeated, meeting her dagger-eyed stare equally. "We both just punched out on the time clock. New game." He fingered the end of her braid. "New rules."

"And if I have some objection?"

"Why don't we talk about it someplace quiet?" With his thumb, he traced her lips. "Not afraid, are you?"

The taunt was enough. When the light changed, Brooke hit the accelerator, weaving through Los Angeles traffic with grim determination.

freedom of movement, the eclectic tastes, the combination of drab colors with the garish. It occurred to him that everything she owned would have been collected during the last ten years. But how much of the past had she brought with her?

Uncomfortable with Parks's silent, thorough survey, Brooke marched to a tiny corner cabinet to pull out a bottle. "You're free to take a tour," she said abruptly. "I'm going to have a drink."

"Whatever you're having's fine," Parks said with infuriating amiability. "You can show me around later." He proceeded to make himself at home on the low, spreading sofa. Leaning back, he glanced at the fireplace, observing by the ash that Brooke made good use of it. "Fire'd be nice," he said casually. "Got any wood?"

"Out back." Ungraciously, she stuck a glass under his nose.

"Thanks." After accepting it, Parks took her hand. "Sit down," he invited with a pleasantness that put Brooke's teeth on edge. "You've been on your feet all day."

"I'm fine," she began, then let out a gasp of surprise as Parks yanked her down beside him. Realizing she should have been prepared for the move despite his outward mellowness only fanned her already strained temper. "Who do you think you are," she began, "barging in here, expecting me to whip up dinner then fall into bed with you? If you—"

"Hungry?" Parks interrupted.

She sent him a searing look. "No."

With a shrug, he draped his arm behind her, propping his feet on the hassock. "You're usually ill-tempered when you are," he commented.

"I am *not* ill-tempered," Brooke raged. "And I am *not* hungry."

"Want some music?"

Brooke drew in a deep breath. How dare he sit there acting as though she were *his* guest? "No."

"You should relax." With firm fingers, he began to knead the base of her neck.

"I'm perfectly relaxed." She pushed his hand aside, disturbed by the sensation of warmth creeping down her spine.

"Brooke." Parks set his glass on the floor, then turned to her. "When you called me a few days ago, you accepted what you knew was going to happen between us."

"I said I would see you," she corrected and started to rise. Parks hand came back to her neck and held her still.

"Knowing what *seeing* me meant," he murmured. His eyes met the fury in her gaze for a moment, then drifted down to focus on her mouth. "You might have refused to let me come here tonight...but you didn't." Slowly, he brought his eyes back to hers in a long, intense look that had her stomach muscles quivering. "Are you going to tell me that you don't want me?"

She couldn't remember the last time she had felt the need to break eye contact. It took all her strength of will to keep from faltering. "I... I don't have to tell you anything. You might remember that this is my time, my house. And—"

"What are you afraid of?"

As he watched, the confusion in her eyes turned back to fury. "I'm not afraid of anything."

"Of making love to me," he continued quietly. "Or to anyone?"

Angry color flooded her cheeks as she bolted up from the sofa. She felt a combination of rage and hurt and fear that she hadn't experienced in more than a decade. He had no right to bring the insecurity tumbling back over her, no right to make her doubt herself as a woman. Tossing her head, Brooke glared at him. "You want to make love?" she snapped. "Fine." She turned on her heel and marched to the stairs leading to the second floor. Halfway up, she threw an angry look over her shoulder. "Coming?" she demanded, then continued on without waiting for his reply.

The fury carried her across the balcony and into her bedroom, where she stood in the center of the room, seething. Her gaze landed on the bed, but she averted it quickly as she heard the sound of Parks's footsteps approaching. It was all very simple, she told herself. They would go to bed and work this attraction or animosity or whatever it was out of their systems. It would clear the air. She sent Parks another killing look as he walked into the room. Fear prodded at her again. In defense, Brooke hastily began to undress.

It was on the tip of his tongue to tell her to stop, then Parks calmly followed her example. She was trembling and didn't even know it, he observed. For the moment, they would play it her way. As with the first night he had taken her out, Parks knew what Brooke expected. Though the angry fear urged him to comfort, he was aware that it would be refused. He didn't even glance over when she dropped her T-shirt into a heap on the floor. But he noticed that she had kept a small clutch of his hibiscus on her dresser.

Naked, Brooke stomped over to the bed and pulled

off the quilt. Head high, brows arched, she turned to him. "Well?"

He looked at her. The surge of sharp desire caused him to go rigid to control it. She was long and softly rounded with fragile, china-doll skin. The proud almost challenging stance was only accented by the overall frailty—until one looked at her eyes. Stormy, they dared him to make the next move.

Parks wondered if she knew just how vulnerable she was and vowed, even as he planned to conquer, to protect. Taking his time, he walked to her until they stood face-to-face. Though her eyes never faltered, he saw the quick nervous swallow before she turned toward the bed. Parks caught her braid in his hand, forcing her to turn back. The fury in her eyes might have cooled the desire of most men. Parks smiled, comfortable with it.

"This time," he murmured as he began to unbind the braid, "I'll direct."

Brooke stood stiffly as he slowly freed her hair. Her skin tingled, as if waiting for his touch—but he never touched her. Deliberately, Parks drew out the process, working his way leisurely up the confined hair until Brooke thought she would burst. When he had finished, he spread it over her shoulders as if it were the only task he would ever perform.

"It's fabulous," Parks murmured, absorbed in its texture, at the way the slanting sunlight brought out the hidden gold within the red. Lifting a strand from her shoulder, he buried his nose in it, wanting to absorb the fragrance. Brooke felt her knees weaken, her muscles go lax. Would he ever touch her?

She kept her eyes on his face, trying to avoid a dangerous fascination with the tawny skin of his chest, the mat of dark gold hair and cords of muscles she had glimpsed in his bare shoulders. If she allowed herself to look, would she be able to prevent herself from touching? But when she noticed the thin gold chain around his neck, curiosity drove her to follow it down to the small gold circle that dangled from it. Because of this, she didn't see him shift ever so slightly to press his lips against the curve of her shoulder. The touch was a jolt, a branding shock that had her jerking back even as his hands spanned her waist.

"Relax." Fingers kneaded gently into flesh; warm lips nibbled it over his words. "I won't take you anywhere you don't want to go." Slowly, he ran the whisper-soft kisses over her shoulder, loitering at her throat. His fingertips ran down to her hips then back up in a rhythmic caress that could never soothe, but only arouse. He knew what he did to her—she knew her response was no secret. In a last attempt to hold her own, Brooke pressed her hands against his chest, arching back.

Parks still held her waist, but made no attempt to draw her back. Over the desire in his eyes, Brooke caught the light of humor. "Want me to stop?" he asked quietly. There was a trace of challenge in the question. She realized abruptly that whatever response she gave, she would still lose.

"Would you?" she countered, fighting the urge to run her suddenly sensitive fingertips over his naked chest.

It was his slow, dangerous smile. "Why don't you ask me and see?" Even as she opened her mouth to form an answer, his fastened on it. The kiss was soft and deep, the sort she knew a woman could drown in. Brooke had only the vague realization that her hands had crept up his chest to link around his neck, only the faintest knowledge that her body was melting into his. Then she was falling—or perhaps she was drowning—until the cool sheets were under her back and his weight was on her.

She didn't question how her body seemed to have become liquid, only reveled in the unaccustomed freedom of motion and space. His hands were so sure, so unhurried, as if he wished and waited for her total fluidity. With a deft caress, a strategic brush of lips, he was unlocking every restriction she had placed on herself. This pleasure was thick, fluent. Brooke luxuriated in it, no longer caring what she gave up in order to receive. Weightless, helpless, she could only sigh as he took his mouth on a lazy journey down her body.

The flick of his tongue over her nipple brought a quick tug—not quite an ache—in her stomach. This pleasure was sharp, stunning. Then it was gone, leaving her dazed as he continued to range a moist trail over her.

His hands were never still, but moved so gently, almost magically, over her, that she could never pinpoint where the source of delight came from. It seemed to radiate through the whole of her, soothing, promising, luring. He caught the point of her breast between his teeth, causing a flash of heat to spring from her center out to her fingertips. But even as she gasped from it, arching, he moved on. He brushed his fingers over her inner thigh, almost absently, so that her skin was left heated then chilled. As fire and ice coursed through her, the sound of her own moan echoed in her head.

The quivering started—a drug wearing off. And the ache—unbearable, wonderful. She was no longer soothed, but throbbing and pleasure became exquisite torment. Suddenly her fingers were in his hair as she tried to press him closer. "Make love to me," she demanded as her breath started to tremble.

He continued with the same mind-destroying caresses. "Oh, I am," he murmured.

"Now." Brooke reached for him only to have him grip her wrists. His head lifted so that their eyes met. Even through a haze of passion she could see his intense concentration—that fierce warrior look.

"It's not so simple." He could feel her pulse hammering under his fingers, but he would give her no quick moment of pleasure. When he took her, she would never forget. Parks pressed his mouth to hers, not so gently. "I've only begun."

Still holding her wrists, he began a new journey over her, with his mouth only. As he captured her breast again, taking it into the heated moistness of his mouth, she could only writhe beneath him in a frenzy that had nothing to do with a desire to escape. The breezy patience had left him to be replaced by a demand that would accept only one answer. It seemed he would feed on her skin, nipping, suckling, licking until she was half-mad from need so long suppressed. It seemed he would taste, and taste only, for hours, assuaging a steady greed she was powerless to refuse.

The heat suffused her, enervated her. Her skin trembled and grew moist from it. Down the hollow between her breasts, over the lean line of ribs to the subtle curve of hip he traced kisses until he felt her hands go limp and her pulse rage.

When his tongue plunged into the warm core of her, she shuddered convulsively, crying out with the first delirious peak. But he was relentless. Even as she struggled for breath, his hands began a new journey of possession.

With hers free, Brooke gripped his shoulders, hardly aware of the tensing of his muscles. There was no part of her body he hadn't explored, exploited, in his quest to have all of her. Now her surrender became agility and drive. Neither of them knew that her true capitulation came when she began her own demands.

Her hands sped over him, touching all she could reach while she twisted, wanting to taste—his mouth, his shoulder, the strong line of his jaw. Parks thought her scent intensified until it dominated all his senses—weakening and strengthening him at once. Her skin was moist and heated wherever his mouth nestled, bringing him another tantalizing image of white silk and forbidden passion. Husky murmurs and quick breathing broke the early-evening hush.

He was no longer thinking, nor was she. They had entered a place where thoughts were only sensations; sharp, aching, sweet and dark. Even as she fastened her mouth on his, Brooke trembled.

Then he was deep inside her, so swiftly that she dug her nails into his flesh in shock and pleasure. They merged, body to body, heart to heart, while all the sensations concentrated into one.

Chapter 7

Brooke luxuriated in the soft, warm security. As she hung between sleep and wakefulness she thought it was winter, and that she slept beneath a thick downy quilt. There was no need to get up, no need to face the cold. She could lie there for a whole lazy day and do nothing. She felt utterly peaceful, completely unburdened and pleasantly languid. Wanting to enjoy the sensations more, she struggled to shrug off sleep.

It wasn't winter, but early fall. There was no quilt, only a tangle of sheets that half covered her naked body as she curled into Parks. With sleep cleared from her mind, Brooke remembered everything—the first revelation of lovemaking, the surprise of having the secret door open without resistance, the hours of passion that had followed. There had been little talk, as the urgency to give and take had grown beyond the control of either of them. Time after time, fulfillment had led to rekindled desire, and desire to demand, until they had fallen asleep, wrapped tightly together.

Now, Brooke could remember her own insatiable thirst, the boundless energy and strength that had filled her. She remembered, too, Parks's ability to arouse her to desperation with patience…and that she had driven him beyond patience with a skill she had been unaware of possessing. But beyond the passion and pleasure, Brooke remembered one vital thing. She had needed him. This was something she had refused herself for years. To need meant dependence, dependence meant vulnerability. A woman who was vulnerable would always be hurt.

The night was behind her and dawn was breaking. In the misty gray light, Parks's face was relaxed, inches from hers, so that the warmth of his breath fluttered over her cheek. His arm was around her, his fingers curled into her hair, as if even in sleep he had to touch it. Her arm reached around to lock him close. They had slept, if only for a few hours, in a classic pose of possessing and possessed. But which one, Brooke thought hazily, was which?

With a sigh, Brooke closed her eyes. Not knowing was dangerous. The hours she had spent not caring put the independence she had taken for granted in jeopardy.

It was time to think again before it was too late, before emotions dominated her—those perilous emotions that urged her to burrow closer to Parks's warmth. If she were ever to stop the need for him from growing beyond her control, she had to do it now.

Brooke shifted in an attempt to separate her body from his. Parks tightened his hold and only brought her closer. "No," he murmured without opening his eyes. With sleepy slowness he ran his hand down the length of her naked back. "Too early to get up."

Brooke felt her breasts yield against his chest, felt the warmth in her stomach begin to smolder to heat. His lips were close—too close. The need to stay in the security of his arms was so strong it frightened her. Again Brooke tried to shift, and again Parks brought her back.

"Parks," she said, then was silenced by his lips.

Brooke told herself to struggle against the deep, musky morning kiss, but she didn't. She told herself to resist the gentle play of fingertips on her spine, but she couldn't. The gray dawn suddenly took on a rosy hue. The air seemed to grow thick. Even as he touched her, her skin quivered to be touched again. *Don't!* her brain shouted. *Don't let this happen.* But she was already sinking, and sinking quickly. She made a sound of protest that became a groan of pleasure.

Parks shifted so that his body lay across hers. Burying his face in her hair, he took his hand down the length of her; the slight swell of the side of her breast, the firm line of ribs and narrow waist, a flare of hip and long smooth thigh. He could feel the struggle going on inside her, sense her desire to separate herself from what had begun to happen between them since that first meeting of eyes. His quick flash of anger was tinged with unexpected hurt.

"Regrets already?" Lifting his head, he looked at her. Her eyes were dark, heavy with kindling passion. Her breathing was unsteady. But he knew she fought herself just as fiercely as she fought him. Her hands were on his shoulders, poised to push him away.

"This isn't smart," Brooke managed.

"No?" Controlling anger, ignoring the hurt, Parks brushed the hair from her cheek. "Why?"

Brooke met his eyes, because to look away would have admitted defeat. "It's not what I want."

"Let's be accurate." His voice was calm, his eyes steady. "It's not what you want to want."

"All right." Brooke shivered as his finger traced her ear. "It's not what I want to want. I have to be practical. We're going to be working together for quite a while. More technically, you'll be working for me. A solid professional relationship won't be possible if we're lovers."

"We are lovers," Parks pointed out, casually shifting so that the friction of his body on hers sent a shudder coursing through her.

"It won't be possible," Brooke continued, concentrating on keeping her voice steady, "if we go on being lovers."

Tilting his head, Parks smiled at her. "Why?"

"Because..." Brooke knew why. She knew dozens of logical reasons why, but no firm thought would form in her brain when he touched a light friendly kiss to her lips.

"Let me be practical a minute," Parks said after another quick kiss. "How often do you let yourself have fun?"

Brooke drew her brows together in annoyed confusion. "What do you mean?"

"You can work eight, twelve hours a day," Parks continued. "You can enjoy your job, be terrific at what you do, but you still need to throw a Frisbee now and again."

"Frisbee?" This brought on a baffled laugh that pleased him. The hands on his shoulders relaxed. "What are you talking about?"

"Fun, Brooke. A sense of the ridiculous, laziness, riding Ferris wheels. All those things that make working worthwhile."

She had the uncomfortable feeling she was being expertly led away from the subject at hand. "What does riding a Ferris wheel have to do with you and me making love?"

"Have you ever had a lover before?" Parks felt her stiffen but continued. "I don't mean someone you slept with, but someone you shared time with. I'm not asking you for any more than that." Even as he said it, Parks knew it wouldn't be true for long. He would ask for more, and she would fight him every step of the way. But then he had lived his life playing to win. "Throw a few Frisbees with me, Brooke. Ride a few waves. Let's see where it takes us."

Looking at him, she could feel her resistance melting. Before she could prevent it, her hand had lifted from his shoulder to brush at the hair that fell over his forehead. "You make it sound so simple," she murmured.

"Not simple." He took her other hand and pressed his lips to the palm. "Even fun isn't always simple. I want you…here." And his eyes came back to hers. "Naked, warm, daring me to arouse you. I want to drive with you with the top down and the wind in your hair. I want to see you caught in the rain, laughing." He ran whispering kisses over her face, then paused at her lips to drink long and deep. "I want to be with you, but I don't think it's going to be simple."

Rolling over, Parks cradled her head on his chest, allowing her to rest and think while he brushed his hands through her hair. His words had touched her in tiny vulnerable places she couldn't defend. Was she strong enough, she wondered, to try things his way without losing control? Fun, she thought. Yes, they could give each other that. He challenged her. Brooke had to admit that she had come to enjoy even the friction. What had he said once? That they could be friends before they were lovers. Odd, she mused, that both had happened almost before she realized it. Only the niggling fear that she was already afraid of losing him kept her from relaxing completely.

"I can't afford to fall in love with you," she murmured.

An odd way to put it, Parks reflected as he continued to stroke her hair. "Rule one," he drawled. "Party A will not fall in love with party B."

Making a fist, Brooke punched his shoulder. "Stop making me sound ridiculous."

"I'll try," he agreed amiably.

"Fun," she murmured, half to herself.

"A three-letter word meaning amusement, sport or recreation," Parks recited in a blandly didactic tone.

With a chuckle, Brooke lifted her head. "All right. I'll buy the Frisbee," she said before she pressed her mouth to his.

Parks cupped the back of her neck in his hand. "It's still too early to get up," he murmured.

Brooke's low laugh was muffled against his lips. "I'm not sleepy."

With a reluctant sigh, he closed his eyes. "Acting," he said thickly, "takes a lot out of you."

"Aw." Sympathetically, Brooke stroked his cheek. "I guess you'd better conserve your strength." She pressed a kiss to his jaw, then his collarbone, before continuing down his chest. Her fingers tangled with the gold chain he wore. "What's this for?"

Parks opened one eye to stare at the five-dollar gold piece that dangled from the chain Brooke held up. "Luck." He shut his eyes again. "My aunt gave it to me when I headed for the Florida training camp. She told my father he was a—" Parks reached back in his memory for the exact phrasing "—a stiff-necked old fool who thought in graphs and formulas, then gave me the gold piece and told me to go for it."

Brooke turned the shiny circle over in her palm. So he carried a little piece of the past with him, too, she mused. "Superstition?" she asked as she dropped the chain and pressed her lips to his chest.

"Luck," Parks corrected, enjoying the feel of her mouth on his skin, "has nothing to do with superstition."

"I see." She scraped her nails lightly down his side and heard his quick inhalation of breath. "Do you always wear it?"

"Mmm." She flicked her tongue over his nipple, bringing a low, involuntary groan from him. A sense of power whipped through her—light, freeing, tempting. His hands were buried in her hair again, seeking the flesh beneath. Brooke slid her body down, bringing them both a rippling slice of pleasure.

His scent was different, she discovered as she ran her lips over his skin. Different, she realized, because hers had mingled with it during the night. That was intimacy, as tangible as the act of love itself.

As the power stayed with her, she experimented. His body was strong and muscled beneath hers, tasting of man. He was taut and lean, his skin golden in the early-morning light. The palms that moved over her back were hard, calloused from his profession. Like the man, the body was disciplined, a product of that odd combination of pampering and outrageous demands any athlete subjects it to. She brushed her lips over the hard, flat stomach and felt the firm muscles quiver. Beneath her own smooth palms she could feel the sinewy strength of his thighs.

The knowledge of the pure physical strength he possessed excited her. With light touches and caresses, she could make this man breathe as though he had run to the point of collapse. With feathering kisses she could make this hardened athlete shudder with an inner weakness she alone was aware of. Though she didn't fully understand it, Brooke knew that she had given him something more than her body the night before, something more complex than surrender or passion. Without even knowing what the gift was, she wanted Parks to offer it in return.

Slowly, enjoying every movement of his body beneath hers, savoring each subtly different taste, she roamed up until her lips fastened greedily on his. How soft his mouth was. How nectarous, with a dark, secret cachet. Brooke savored it on her tongue, feeling it intensify until the draining, liquefying pleasure crept into her. Knowing she would lose that slim edge of control, she tore her mouth from his to bury it at his throat.

She felt the vibration of his groan against her lips, but she couldn't hear it. Her heartbeat raged in her head until all of her senses were confused. If it was morning, how could she feel this sultry night pleasure? If she was seducing him, how was she so thoroughly seduced? Her body pressed against his, matching itself to the slow, tortuous rhythm he set even as she raced tormenting kisses along his flesh. The heat seeping into her only seemed to add to the delirium of power, yet it wasn't

enough. She was still searching for something so neb-
ulous she wasn't certain she would recognize it when
it was found. And desire, sharp bolts of desire, were
causing everything but the quest for fulfillment to fade.

Parks gripped her hair in one hand to pull her head
up. She had only a brief glimpse of his face—the eyes
half-shut but darker and more intense than she had ever
seen them—before he brought her mouth down to his
and devoured. All will, all sense was seeping out of her.

"Brooke…" His hands were on her hips, urging her.
"Now." The demand was wrenched from him, hoarse
and urgent. She resisted, struggling to breathe, fighting to hold some part of herself separate. "I need you,"
he murmured before their lips met again. "I need you."

Then it was clear—for one breathless instant. She
needed, and knew now she was needed in return. It was
enough…perhaps everything. With a shuddering sound
of relief and joy, she gave.

At nine fifty-five, Claire swept into the editing room.
Neither the editors nor E.J. were surprised to see the
head of Thorton Productions on the job on a Saturday
morning. Anyone who had worked at Thorton more
than a week knew that Claire wasn't a figurehead but
an entity to be reckoned with. She wore one of her trim
little suits, the color of crushed raspberries, and a trace
of Parisian scent.

"Dave, Lila, E.J." Claire gave all three a quick nod
before heading toward the coffeepot. A newer member of the staff might have scurried to serve the boss,
but those lounging near the control board knew better.

"Made it myself, Ms. Thorton," E.J. told her as she

poured. "It won't taste like the battery acid these two cook up."

"I appreciate that, E.J.," she said dryly. Just the scent of it revived her. Claire inhaled it, telling herself only an old fool thought she could dance until three and still function the next day. Ah, but how nice it was to feel like a fool again, she thought with a slow smile. "I'm told that the shoot went well, with no major problems."

"Smooth as silk," E.J. stated. "Wait till you get a load of Parks knocking that sucker over the fence." He grinned reminiscently. "I won ten bucks off Brooke with that hit." His selective memory allowed him to forget that it had been his ten dollars in the first place.

Claire settled into a chair with a quiet sigh. "Is Brooke in yet?"

"Haven't seen her." E.J. began to whistle as he recalled Brooke leaving the location with Parks. Accustomed to his habits, Claire only lifted a brow.

"Are you set up, Dave?"

"Ready to run through it, Ms. Thorton. Want to see it from the top?"

"In a moment." Even as Claire checked her watch, she heard Brooke's voice in the corridor.

"As long as you understand you have absolutely no say in what gets cut and what stays in."

"I might have an intelligent comment to make."

"Parks, I'm serious."

His low chuckle rolled into the editing room just ahead of Brooke. "Morning," she said to the group at large. "Coffee hot?"

"E.J.'s special," Claire told her, watching Brooke over the rim of her mug as she sipped. She looked different, Claire thought, then slid her eyes to Parks. And there was the reason, she concluded with a small smile. "Good morning, Parks."

Her face remained bland and friendly, but he recognized her thoughts. With a slight nod, he acknowledged them. "Hello, Claire," he said, abandoning formality as smoothly as he reached for a cup for himself. "I hope you don't mind me sitting in on this." Taking the pot, he poured Brooke's coffee, then his own. "Brooke has a few reservations."

"Amateurs," Brooke said precisely as she reached for the powdered cream, "have a tendency to be pains in the—"

"Yes, well, I'm sure we're delighted to have Parks join us," Claire interrupted over E.J.'s chuckle. "Run it through, Dave. Let's see what we've got."

At her order, he flicked a series of buttons on the large control panel in front of him. Parks watched himself appear simultaneously on three monitors. He could hear Brooke's voice off camera, then the little man with the clapboard scooted in front of him announcing the scene and take.

"It's the third take that worked," Brooke announced as she settled on the arm of Claire's chair. "Casey at the bat didn't like the first pitch."

Her remark earned her a grin from Parks and a mild exclamation from Claire. "The lighting's very good." Claire studied the second take through narrowed eyes.

"The new boy, Silbey. He's got a nice touch. The clothes sell it." Brooke sipped while gesturing with her free hand. "Watch when he sets for the swing... Yes." She gave a nod of approval. "Nice moves, no apparent restriction. He looks comfortable, efficient, sexy." Intent on the screen, Brooke didn't notice the look Parks tossed at her. "This is the one I want to use." She waited, silently, watching the replay of Parks's home run. The test swings, the concentration, the connection and follow-through, the satisfied grin and the shrug.

"I want to keep in the last bit," Brooke went on. "That gee-whiz shrug. It sells the whole business. That natural cockiness is its own appeal." Parks choked over his coffee, but Brooke ignored him. "As I see it, this segment is pretty clear-cut. The next I'm not so sure about. It's going to be effective…"

Cupping his mug in both hands, Parks sat down. For the next two hours he watched himself on the screens of the monitors, listened to himself being weighed, dissected, judged. Though the latter disconcerted him initially, he found that watching himself didn't bring on the feeling of idiocy he'd been certain it would. He began to think he might find some enjoyment out of his two-year stint after all.

Though he'd heard himself picked apart and put back together countless times over the years—coaches, sports critics, other players—Parks couldn't find the same level of tolerance at hearing Brooke speak so matter-of-factly about his face and body, his gestures and expressions. All in all, he thought, it was as though he were the salable product, not the clothes he wore.

They ran the film back and forth, while Claire listened to input and made occasional comments. Yes, they would have to work in close-ups in the next shoot, his face was very good. It would be smart to fill another thirty-second spot with action to exploit the way he moved, showing the durability of the clothes as well as the versatility. They might try tennis shorts if his legs were any good.

At this Parks shot Brooke a deadly glance, half expecting her to offer her personal opinion. She caught it, then smothered a chuckle with a fit of coughing. Over Claire's head she gave him an innocent smile and an unexpectedly lewd wink. The quick response of his own body caused him to scowl at her. She was dressed like a waif, in baggy chinos and a sweater, her hair braided back and secured with a rubber band. From across the room he could smell the elusive, promising scent of her perfume.

"We taped his voice-over this morning," she told Claire. "I think you'll find his voice is good, though how he'll handle real dialogue remains to be seen. Do we have the graphics for the tag-on, Lila?"

"Right here." She flipped a series of switches. On the monitor now was the de Marco logo of a black-maned lion against a cool blue background. The signature line cartwheeled slowly onto the screen until it stopped below the cat. It held long enough for impact, then faded.

"Very classy," Brooke approved. "Then it's agreed? The third take from the first segment, the fifth from the second."

"We saved you guys from a lot of splicing," E.J. commented as he toyed with an unlit cigarette. "You should be able to put this together with your eyes closed."

"I'd appreciate it if you'd keep them open," Claire said as she rose. "Let me know when it's cut and dubbed. E.J., a splendid job, as always."

"Thanks, Ms. Thorton."

She handed him her empty mug. "On the camera-work, too," she added. The editors snickered as she turned toward the door. "Parks, I hope you didn't find all this too boring."

"On the contrary…" He thought of the objective discussions on his anatomy. "It's been an education."

She gave him a mild smile of perfect understanding. "Brooke, my office, ten minutes." As an afterthought she glanced at her watch. "Oh, dear. Perhaps you'd like to join us for lunch, Parks."

"I appreciate it, but I have a few things I have to do."

"Well then." Patting his arm, she smiled again. "Best of luck in the play-offs." She slipped away, leaving Brooke frowning after her.

"I probably won't get any lunch now," she muttered. "If you'd said yes, she'd have made reservations at Ma Maison."

"Sorry." Parks drew her out in the corridor. "Did that wink mean you approve of my legs?"

"Wink?" Brooke stared at him blankly. "I don't know what you're talking about. Winking during an editing session is very unprofessional."

He glanced at the door she had closed behind her. "The way you all talked in here, I felt that I was the product."

With a half laugh, Brooke shook her head. "Parks, you *are* the product."

His eyes came back to hers, surprising Brooke with the flare of anger. "No. I wear the product."

She opened her mouth, then closed it again on a cautious sigh. "It's really a matter of viewpoint," she said carefully. "From yours, from de Marco's, even from the consumers', the clothes are the product. From the viewpoints of your producer, your director, your cinematographer and so forth, you're as much the product as the clothes you wear because we have to see that both of you are salable. If I can't make you look good, what you're wearing might as well be flea market special."

He saw the logic but didn't care for it. "I won't be a commodity."

"Parks, you're a commodity every time you walk out on the diamond. This really isn't any different." Exasperated, she lifted her hands palms up. "You sell tickets to Kings games, baseball cards and fielder's caps. Don't be so damned sanctimonious about this."

"First it's temperamental, now it's sanctimonious," he muttered disgustedly. "I suppose what it comes down to is we look at this little…venture from two different perspectives."

Brooke felt a light flutter of fear inside her breast. "I told you," she said quietly, "that it would be difficult."

His eyes came back to her, recognizing the shield she was already prepared to bring down. Parks ran a finger down her cheek. "And I told you it would be fun." Leaning closer, he brushed his lips over hers. "We're both right. I have some things to do. Can I meet you back here later?"

Relaxing, Brooke told herself she had imagined the fear. "If you like. I'll probably be tied up until around five."

"Fine. You can cook me that dinner you promised me last night."

Brooke lifted her chin. "I never promised to cook you dinner," she corrected. "But perhaps I will."

"I'll buy the wine." Parks sent her a grin before he turned away.

"Wait." After a moment, Brooke went after him. "You don't have your car."

Parks shrugged. "I'll take a cab." He saw her hesitate then struggle with a decision.

"No," she said abruptly, digging in her bag. "You can use mine."

Parks took the keys, and her hand. He knew enough about her to realize offering the use of her car, or anything else important to her, wasn't a casual gesture. "Thank you."

Her color rose—the first truly self-conscious thing he had noticed about her. "You're welcome." Quickly, she drew her hand from his and turned away. "See you at five," she called over her shoulder without stopping.

Brooke felt a bit foolish as she rode the elevator to Claire's office. How could she have blushed over a simple thank-you for the loan of a car? She glanced up at the numbers flashing over the elevator door. Oh, he knew her too well, she realized, knew her too well when she'd hardly told him anything.

He didn't know she still had the copy of *Little Women* her second foster mother had given her. He didn't know that she had adored those temporary parents and had been devastated when a broken marriage had caused her to be placed in another foster home. He didn't know about the horrid little girl she had shared a room with during what she still considered the worst year of her life. Or the Richardsons, who had treated her more like a hired hand than a foster child. Or Clark.

With a sigh, Brooke rubbed her fingers over her forehead. She didn't like to remember—didn't like knowing that her growing feelings for Parks seemed to force her to face the past again. Oh, the hell with it, Brooke thought with a shake of her head. It *was* the past. And she was going to have enough trouble dealing with the present to dwell on it.

Steadier, she stepped out into the wide, carpeted corridor of Claire's floor. The receptionist, a pretty girl with lots of large healthy teeth, straightened in her chair at Brooke's approach. She'd worked on the top floor for over two years and was still more in awe of Brooke than of Claire.

"Good afternoon, Ms. Gordon."

"Hello, Sheila. Ms. Thorton's expecting me."

"Yes, ma'am." Sheila wouldn't have contradicted her if her life had depended on it.

Unaware of the impression she made, Brooke strode easily down the corridor and through a set of wide glass doors. Here, two secretaries, known as the twins only because of identical desks, labored away on word processors. The outer office was huge, scrupulously modern and cathedral quiet.

"Ms. Gordon." The first twin beamed a smile while a second one reached for the button on her intercom.

"She's expecting me," Brooke said simply and breezed by them into Claire's office. The door opened silently. Brooke was halfway across the pewter-colored carpet before she realized Claire was sound asleep at her desk. Totally stunned, Brooke stopped dead in her tracks and stared.

The chair Claire sat in was high-backed pale gray leather. Her desk was ebony, gleaming beneath stacks of neat papers. The glasses Claire wore for reading were held loosely in her hand. A Chinese "literary painting" in color wash and ink hung on the wall to her right, while behind her L.A. sunshine poured through a plate-glass window. Unsure what to do, Brooke considered leaving as quietly as she had come, then decided it was best to stay. Walking to the squashy leather chair facing the desk, she sat, then gently cleared her throat. Claire's eyes snapped open.

"Morning," Brooke said brightly and grinned at Claire's uncharacteristic confusion. "You'd do better on the sofa if you want a nap."

"Just resting my eyes."

"Mmm-hmm."

Ignoring the comment, Claire reached for the papers she had been reading before fatigue had won. "I wanted you to have a look at the script for the next de Marco spot."

"Okay." Brooke accepted the script automatically. "Claire, are you all right?"

"Don't I look all right?"

Deciding to take her literally, Brooke studied her. Except for the heavy eyes, she decided, Claire looked better than ever. Almost, Brooke mused, glowing. "You look marvelous."

"Well then." Claire smoothed her hair before she folded her hands.

"Didn't you sleep well last night?" Brooke persisted.

"As it happens, I was out late. Now the script."

"With Lee Dutton?" The thought went through her mind and out her lips before she could stop it. Claire gave her a tolerant smile.

"As a matter of fact, yes."

Brooke set the script back on the desk. "Claire," she began, only to be interrupted by a knock on the door.

"Your lunch, Ms. Thorton." A tray was wheeled in by twin number one.

The scent of hot roast beef had Brooke rising.

"Claire, I misjudged you." Lifting the cover from a hot plate, she inhaled. "Forgive me."

"Did you think I'd let you go hungry?" With a chuckle, Claire stood to move to the sofa. "Brooke, dear, I've known you too long. Bring me my salad and coffee like a good girl."

Nibbling on a potato wedge, Brooke obeyed. "Claire, I really want to talk with you about Lee Dutton."

"Of course." Claire speared a radish slice. "Sit down and eat, Brooke, pacing's bad for my digestion."

Plate in hand, Brooke approached the couch. She set it on the low coffee table, picked up half a roast beef sandwich and began. "Claire, are you actually dating Lee Dutton?"

"Does dating seem inappropriate to you for someone of my age, Brooke? Pass me that salt."

"No!" Flustered, Brooke looked down at Claire's out-stretched hand. She gave her the salt shaker then took a defiant bite of her sandwich. "Don't be ridiculous," she muttered over it. "I can see you dating all manner of fabulous men. I have trouble seeing you out on the town with Lee Dutton."

"Why?"

Brooke shifted her shoulders uncomfortably. This wasn't how she had intended it to go. "Well, he's nice enough, and certainly sharp, but he seems sort of... well." Brooke sighed and tried again. "Let's put it this way, I can see Lee Dutton in the neighborhood bowling alley. I can't picture you there."

"No..." Claire pursed her lips in thought. "We haven't tried that yet."

"Claire!" Exasperated, Brooke rose and began to

pace again. "I'm not getting through to you. Look, I don't want to interfere with your life—"

"No?" The mild smile had Brooke flopping back down on the couch.

"You matter to me."

Claire reached over to squeeze her hand. "I appreciate that, Brooke, I've been taking care of myself for a long time. I've even handled a few men."

A bit reassured, Brooke began to eat again. "I suppose if I thought you were really getting involved…"

"What makes you think I'm not?" At Brooke's gaping stare, Claire laughed.

"Claire, are you—are you…" She gestured, not quite certain she should put her thoughts into words.

"Sleeping with him?" Claire finished in her calm, cultured voice. "Not yet."

"Not yet," Brooke echoed numbly.

"Well, he hasn't asked me to." Claire took another bite of salad and chewed thoughtfully. "I thought he would by now, but he's quite conservative. Very sweet and old-fashioned. That's part of his appeal for me. He makes me feel very feminine. You can lose that at times in this business."

"Yes, I know." Brooke picked up her iced tea and stared into it. "Do you—are you in love with him?"

"I think I am." Claire settled back against the gray-and-rose patterned sofa. "I was only in love once before, really in love. I was your age, perhaps a bit younger." Her smile was soft for a moment, a girl's smile. "In all the years in between, I've never met anyone I was attracted to enough, comfortable enough with, trusted enough, to think of marrying."

Brooke took a long swallow of tea. She thought she

understood Claire's phrasing all too well. "You're thinking of marriage?"

"I'm thinking I'm almost fifty years old. I've built this up—" she gestured to indicate Thorton "—I have a comfortable home, a nice circle of friends and acquaintances, enough new challenges to keep me from dying of boredom, and suddenly I've found a man who makes me want to curl up in front of a fire after a long day." She smiled slowly and rather beautifully—not the girl's smile this time. "It's a good feeling." She let her eyes slide to Brooke, who was watching her closely. "I'd hate to see you have to wait twenty more years for it. Parks is a great deal more than mildly attracted to you."

For the third time, Brooke rose to pace the room. "We haven't known each other long," she began.

"You're a woman who knows her own mind, Brooke."

"Am I?" With a mordant smile, she turned back. "Perhaps I do know how I think, how I feel. I don't really know Parks, though. What if I give too much? What's to stop him from getting bored and moving on?"

Claire met her eyes steadily. "Don't compare him, Brooke. Don't make him pass tests for all those old hurts."

"Oh, Claire." Passing a hand through her hair, Brooke walked to stare out of the window. "That's the last thing I want to do."

"What's the first thing?"

"It's always been to have my own. To have my own so that nobody can come along and say, 'Whoops, you really only borrowed this, time to give it back.'" She laughed a little. "Silly, I suppose I've never really shaken that."

"And why should you?" Claire demanded. "We all

want our own. And to get it, you and I both know there are a few basic risks involved."

"I'm afraid I'm falling in love with him," Brooke said quietly. "And the closer I get, the more afraid I am that it's all going to crumble under my feet. I have a feeling I need this defense…that if I fall in love with him, I need this edge of control, this little pocket of power, to keep myself from getting demolished. Is that crazy?"

"No. You're not the kind of woman who gives herself completely without asking for something back. You did that once, but you were a child. You're a woman who needs a strong man, Brooke. One strong enough to take, strong enough not to take all." She smiled as Brooke turned to face her. "Give yourself a little time," she advised. "Things have a way of falling into place."

"Do they?"

Claire's smile widened. "Sometimes it only takes twenty years."

With a laugh, Brooke walked back to the sofa. "Thanks a lot."

Chapter 8

Brooke sat cross-legged on the softly faded Oriental rug in Claire's den. Sometime during the fourth inning she'd given up trying to sit in a chair. To her right, Lee and Claire sat on a two-cushioned brocade sofa. Billings had outdone herself by preparing her specialty, beef Wellington, then had been mutely offended when Brooke had done little more than shift the food around on her plate. Though she chided herself for being nervous, Brooke had been able to do nothing but worry about the outcome of the play-offs since Parks had taken off for the Valiants' home stadium.

She'd been able to catch part of the first afternoon game on her car radio as she had driven to a location shoot. One of the production crew had thought ahead, bringing a portable radio with an earplug, and had kept up a running commentary between takes. Brooke had felt overwhelming relief when the Kings had taken the first game, then frustration and more nerves when they had lost the second. Now, she watched the third on the television set in Claire's small, elegant den.

"That man was out at second," Brooke fumed, wriggling impotently on the faded royal-blue rug. "Anyone with two working eyes could see that."

As she launched her personal attack, the Kings' manager, a squat man with the face of a dyspeptic elf, argued with the second base umpire. If she hadn't been quite so furious herself, Brooke might have admired the manager's theatrical gestures as he spun around, rolled his eyes to heaven and pointed an accusing finger in the umpire's face. The umpire remained unmoved and the call stood. With the Kings holding on to a thin one-run lead, a runner on second with one out boded ill.

When the next batter sent one sailing over the fence and the slim lead changed hands, Brooke groaned. "I can't stand it," she decided, pounding her fists on the rug. "I just can't stand it."

"Brooke's become involved in the game," Claire murmured to Lee.

"So I've noticed." He dropped a light kiss on her cheek. "You smell wonderful!"

The sensation of blood rising to her cheeks was pleasant. She had been romanced by suave masters of the game in the more than twenty-five years of her womanhood, but she couldn't remember one who had made her feel quite the way Lee Dutton could. If they had been alone, she would have snuggled closer, but remembering Brooke, she merely squeezed his hand. "Have some wine, dear," she said to Brooke as she reached for the iced bottle beside her. "Good for the nerves."

Because she was breathing a sigh of relief as the next batter struck out, Brooke didn't acknowledge the teasing tone. "That's three out," she said as she took the cool glass from Claire.

"Two," Lee corrected.

"Only if you believe a nearsighted umpire," she countered, sipping. When he chuckled, she sent a grin over her shoulder. "At least I didn't call him a bum."

"Give yourself a little time," Lee advised, winking at Claire as she handed him a glass.

"You know, some of the players—" Brooke began, then broke off with a gasp as a smoking line drive was hit toward third. Her stomach muscles knotted instantly. Parks dove sideways, stretching his arm out toward the speeding ball. He nabbed it in the tip of his glove just before the length of his body connected with the hard Astroturf. Brooke thought she could feel the bone-rattling jolt herself.

"He got it!" Lee broke out of his casual pose with a jerk that nearly upset Claire's wine. "Look at that, look at that! He got it!" he repeated, pointing at the television image of Parks holding up the glove to show the catch while he still lay prone. "That young sonofa—" He caught himself, barely, and cleared his throat. "Parks is the best with a glove in the league," he decided. "In *both* leagues!" He leaned forward to pound Brooke companionably on the back. "Parks robbed him, kid. Stole a base hit from him as sure as God made little green apples."

Because she watched Parks stand up and brush himself off, Brooke relaxed. "I want to see it on replay," she murmured. "Slow motion."

"You'll see that play a dozen times before the night's

through," Lee predicted. "And again on the eleven-o'clock news. Hey, lookie here." Grinning, he gestured to the set. "That's what I call classy timing."

Brooke shifted her concentration to the de Marco commercial. Of course she'd seen it a dozen times in the editing room, and again on television, but each time she watched, she searched for flaws. She studied the graphics as Parks's cool clear voice spoke out to her. "It's perfect," she said with a smile. "Absolutely perfect."

"How's the next one coming?" Lee asked Claire.

"It's just waiting for Parks to be available. We hope to shoot next week."

He settled back again, one arm around Claire. "I'm going to enjoy seeing that one play during the series."

"They still have two games to win," Brooke reminded him. "They're a run behind in this one, and—"

"The opera's not over till the fat lady sings," Lee said mildly.

Brooke swiveled her head to look at him. Claire was snug beside him, a crystal glass in one hand. Lee's paunch strained against the buttons of his checked shirt. The ankle of one leg rested on the knee of the other while his foot bounced up and down to some personal tune. Abruptly, Brooke saw them as a perfect match. "I like you, Lee," she said with a wide smile. "I really like you."

He blinked twice, then his lips curved hesitantly. "Well, thanks, kid."

She's just given us her blessing, Claire thought with an inward chuckle as she took Lee's hand in hers.

Brooke made her way through the airport crowd with steady determination. In addition to the usual flow of traffic at LAX, there were fans, mobs of fans, waiting to greet the incoming Kings team. Some carried hand-made signs, others banners. There were, she noted with some amusement, a good number of truants in the Los Angeles school system that morning, not to mention a deficit in the workforce. After the twelve-inning victory, Brooke thought the players deserved a bit of adulation. She also wondered if she'd ever be able to fight her way through so that Parks would see her. The impulse to surprise him, she realized, had not been practical. A truant father hoisted a truant second-grader onto his shoulders. Brooke grinned. Maybe not practical, but it was going to be fun.

Pushing her sunglasses atop her head, Brooke narrowed her eyes against the sun and waited for the plane to touch down. As it stopped being a dot in the sky and took on form, she began to experience the first flicker of nerves. She fidgeted nervously with her bag while she stood, crushed shoulder to shoulder, with excited fans.

He'll be tired, she thought as dozens of conversations buzzed around her. *He's probably looking forward to going home and sleeping for twenty-four hours.* Brooke ran a hand through her hair. *I should have told him I was coming.* She shifted her weight to the other foot, curled her fingers around the chain link in front of her and watched the plane glide to a stop.

The moment the door opened, the cheering started, building, rising as the first men began to deplane. They waved back, looking tired and somehow vulnerable without their uniforms. Men, she thought. Simply men suffering from jet lag and perhaps a few hangovers. Then she smiled, deciding that the gladiators might have looked precisely the same the day after a bout.

As soon as she saw him, she felt warm. Beside Brooke, a teenager grabbed her companion and squealed.

"Oh, there's Parks Jones! He's bee-utiful."

Brooke swallowed a laugh as she thought of how Parks would react to the adjective.

"Every time I watch him, my knees get weak." The teenager pressed her lithe young body against the fence. "Did you see him in the commercial? When he smiled, it was like he was looking right *at* me. I nearly died."

Though she didn't take her eyes off Parks, Brooke smiled inwardly. *My plan exactly,* she thought, pleased with herself. *Why do I feel like a woman watching her man come home from the wars?*

Though her sharp director's eye had seen a group of tense and tired men, the fans saw heroes. They cheered them. Some of the players merely waved and moved on, but most came up to the fence to exchange words, jokes, a touch of hands. Brooke watched Parks walk toward the barrier with a man she recognized as Snyder, the first baseman. She wondered, by the intensity of their discussion, if they were outlining infield strategy.

"It would only take twenty-five or thirty cans of shaving cream to fill his locker," Snyder insisted.

"Takes too long and evaporates too fast," Parks commented. "You've got to be practical, George."

Snyder swore mildly and lifted his hand in acknowledgment to a shout in the crowd. "Got a better idea?"

"Carbon dioxide." Parks scanned the crowd as they neared it. "Quick and efficient."

"Hey, yeah!" Pleased, Snyder gave him a slap on the back. "Knew your brains were good for something, Einstein."

"And as long as I help you work out the mechan-

ics," Parks added, "my locker doesn't get filled with
the thinking man's shaving cream."

"There's that, too," Snyder agreed. "Would you look
at these people?" His grin widened. "Fantastic."

Parks started to agree, then spotted a mass of red hair
touched with gold in the sunlight. The fatigue drained
as though someone had pulled a cork. "Fantastic," he
murmured and walked straight toward Brooke.

The teenager beside her made a moaning, melting
sound and took a death grip on her friend's arm. "He's
coming over here," she managed in a choked whisper.
"Right over here. I know I'm going to die."

Brooke tilted her chin up so that her eyes would stay
level with his as he stopped on the other side of the
fence. "Hi." Parks's hand closed over hers on the metal
wire. The simple contact was as intimate as anything
she had ever known.

"Hi." Brooke smiled slowly, accepting the flare of
desire and the sense of closeness without question.

"Can I get a lift?"

"Anytime."

He pressed his lips to the fingers still curled around
the wire. "Meet me inside? I have to get my baggage."

Out of the corner of her eye, Brooke saw the two
teenage girls gawking. "Great catch last night."

He grinned before he stepped away. "Thanks."

Snyder caught him by the arm as Brooke melted back
into the crowd. "Hey, I like that catch better."

"Off-limits," Parks said simply, making his way
down the line of fans and outstretched hands.

"Aw, come on, Parks, we're teammates. All for one
and one for all."

"Forget it."

"The trouble with Parks," Snyder began to tell a grandfatherly type behind the fence, "is he's selfish. I make his throws look good. I bite the bullet when he lines a hospital pitch at me. And what thanks do I get?" He sent Parks a hopeful smile. "You could at least introduce me."

Parks grinned as he signed a snatch of paper a fan thrust through a hole in the fence. "Nope."

It took him nearly thirty minutes to get away from the crowd and through the terminal. Impatience was growing in him. The simple touch of fingers outside had whetted his appetite for a great deal more. He'd never been lonely on the road before. Even if there was a rainout or an off day away from home, you were surrounded by people you knew. You became as close as a family—close enough to spend endless evenings together or opt to spend one alone without bruising feelings. No, he'd never been lonely. Until this time.

Parks couldn't count the times he had thought of her over the last four days, but he knew that everything had suddenly slipped back into focus the moment he had seen her standing there. Now he saw her again.

Brooke leaned back against a pillar near the baggage belt, Parks's suitcase at her feet. She smiled but didn't straighten as she saw him. She'd hate to have him know just how crazily her pulse was racing. "You travel light," she commented.

He cupped her face in his hand and, oblivious to the people milling around them, brought her close for a long, hard kiss.

"I missed you," he murmured against her mouth, then kissed her again.

There were enough of his teammates still loitering around to start up a chorus of approval.

"Excuse me." Snyder tapped Parks on the shoulder and grinned engagingly at Brooke. "I believe you've made a mistake. *I'm* George Snyder. This is our aging batboy." He gave Parks an affectionate pat.

"How do you do." Brooke extended her hand and had it enveloped in a huge, hard palm. "Too bad about those two strikeouts last night."

There were several jeers as Snyder winced. "Actually, I'm luring the Valiants into complacency."

"Oh." Amused, Brooke gave him a big smile. "You did very well."

"Sorry, Snyder, time for your shot." Parks signaled to two teammates, who agreeably hooked their arms through Snyder's to haul him away.

"Aw, come on, Jones, give me a break!" Good-naturedly, Snyder let himself be dragged away. "I just want to discuss my strategy with her."

"Goodbye, George." Brooke waved as Parks bent to retrieve his bag.

"Let's get out of here."

With her fingers laced through his, Brooke had no choice but to follow. "Parks, you might have introduced me to your friends."

"Dangerous men," he stated. "All dangerous men."

With a chuckle, she matched her pace to his. "Yes, I could see that. Especially the one holding a toddler on each hip."

"There are a few exceptions."

"Are you one?"

Parks caught her around the waist and drew her close against him. "Uh-uh."

"Oh, good. Want to come home with me and tell me your strategy?"

"That's the best offer I've had today." After tossing his bag in the rear of her car, Parks sprawled in the passenger seat. Accustomed to her driving pattern now, he relaxed and began to unwind by rambling about the previous day's game. Brooke said little, pleased to listen, glad that she had arranged to take the day off so that they could have a few hours together, alone.

"The commercial aired during each play-off game, you know," she commented as they headed out of town.

"How'd it look?" Parks laid his head back against the seat. God, it was good to know he didn't have to go anywhere or do anything for twenty-four hours.

"Fantastic." As the road opened up, so did the Datsun's throttle. "And I have it from the source that it plays very well."

"Hmm?"

"A teenage girl in that mob today." With near perfect mimicry, Brooke related the girl's comments. She caught Parks's automatic grimace at the term *bee-utiful* but swallowed a chuckle as she continued.

"Nice to know I devastate sixteen-year-old girls," he said dryly.

"You'd be surprised at the buying power of sixteen-year-old girls." With experienced ease, Brooke negotiated the curves on the narrowing road. "Not so much directly, certainly, but indirectly through their parents. And since they'd like their teenage boyfriends to make their knees weaken, telts, *ad infinitum*." Tossing her hair back, she slid her eyes to his. "And you do have a great smile."

"Yeah." He gave a modest sigh. "I do."

Brooke stopped in her driveway with a deliberate jerk that had him swearing. Wisely slipping from the car before he could retaliate, she headed up the path.

"Just for that," Parks began as he dragged his bag out of the back, "I'm not going to give you the present I bought you."

At the door, Brooke turned, her grin changing to a look of bewilderment. "You bought me a present?"

Because she looked like a child who expected to be handed a brightly wrapped empty box, Parks treated it lightly. "I did. But I'm seriously considering keeping it myself now."

"What is it?"

"Are you going to open the door?"

Brooke shrugged, trying to pretend indifference as she turned the key. "There's a fire laid," she said as she breezed inside. "Why don't you light it while I get us some coffee?"

"Okay." Setting his bag down, Parks stretched travel-cramped muscles. With a wince, he pressed his fingers to the ribs still sore from their contact with Astroturf.

She'd brought some of her garden inside, he noted, spotting the bowl of vibrant mums and zinnias on the side table across the room. The table, he observed, was Queen Anne; the bowl, dimestore special. Grinning, he went to the hearth. The combination suited her—the exquisite and the practical.

Parks struck a match and set it to the carefully rolled paper beneath the kindling. Dry wood caught with a crackle and a *whoosh*. He inhaled the smell that brought back flickering images of the past; evenings in the cozy parlor of his family home, camping trips with his uncle and cousins, weekends in England at the home of a college friend. He wanted to add to the pictures now with the memory of Brooke lying in his arms in front of the simmering fire while they made slow, endless love.

When he heard her returning, Parks stood, turning to face her as she entered with a tray holding a bottle and two glasses. "I thought you might want wine instead."

Smiling, Parks took the tray from her. "Yes." After setting the tray on the hassock, Parks lifted the bottle, examining the label with a lifted brow. "Is this a celebration?"

"A precelebration," Brooke countered. "I expect you to win tomorrow." She picked up both glasses, holding them out. "And if you don't, we'll have had the wine in any case."

"Seems fair." Parks poured pale gold liquid into the stemmed glasses. Taking one from her, he clinked the rims together. "To the game?" he asked with a slow smile.

Brooke felt the quick nervous flutter in her stomach and nodded. "To the game," she agreed and drank. Her eyes widened but remained steady when he reached out to take a handful of her hair.

"I saw this in the sunlight," he murmured. "Even in that mob of people at the airport, I'm not sure what I would have done if that fence hadn't been in the way." He let it sift through his fingers. "It was a long four days, Brooke."

She nodded, taking his hand to draw him onto the sofa beside her. The curves of her body seemed to fit naturally against the lines of his. "You're tense," she said quietly.

"Postseason games." He drew her closer, knowing the nerves would gradually drain before they built again the next day. "Maybe the lucky ones are the players raking leaves in their backyards in October."

"But you don't really think so."

Parks laughed. "No, I don't really think so. The playoffs pump you up until you're ready to explode, but the series…" He trailed off with a shake of his head. He didn't want to let his mind run that far ahead. The rules were three out of five—they weren't there yet. For now he didn't want to think of it, but of the woman beside him, the quiet afternoon and the long evening ahead. He thought that he'd remember her this way, a little pensive, with the smell of woodsmoke and fall flowers mixing with her own perfume. His mind drifted lazily, comfortably, as he sipped the iced wine and watched the flames dance.

"Have you been busy?"

Brooke tilted her head in absent agreement. She didn't want to think of work any more than Parks did. "The usual," she said vaguely. "E.J. talked me into seeing a perfectly dreadful movie where the cast pranced around in mythological costumes and shot lightning bolts."

"Olympian Revenge?"

"It had a talking three-head dragon."

"That's the one. I caught it in Philadelphia last month when we had a rainout."

"I saw the mike in the frame three times."

Parks chuckled at her professional disdain. "Nobody else did," he assured her. "They were all asleep."

"Gross ineptitude keeps me awake." She leaned her head against his shoulder. It occurred to her how empty her home had been for the last few days, and how cozy it felt again. Brooke had never felt the need to share it before. In fact, she had always had a strong proprietary feeling about what was hers. Now, sitting quietly on the sofa, she realized she had already begun to give up her privacy, willingly and with total unawareness. Turning her head, she studied Parks's profile. "I missed you," she said at length.

He turned his head as well so that their lips were close, not quite touching. "I'd hoped you would." Then he shifted so that his mouth grazed her cheek. She trembled. Not yet, he told himself as the heat flared inside him. Not quite yet. "Maybe I'll give you that present after all."

Brooke's lips curved against his throat. "I don't believe you bought me anything at all."

Recognizing the ploy but willing to play, Parks rose. "You'll have to apologize for that," he said soberly as he walked to his suitcase. He flipped open the case then rummaged inside. When he stood again, Parks had a white box in his hands. Brooke regarded it curiously but with some of the wariness he had noted outside.

"What is it?"

"Open it and find out," he suggested, dropping it into her lap.

Brooke turned it over, examining the plain white box, testing it for weight. She wasn't a woman accustomed to spontaneous gifts and in the short time he had known her, Parks had already given her two. "You didn't have to—"

"You *have* to give your sister a Christmas present," he said mildly, sitting beside her again. "You're not my sister and it isn't Christmas."

Brooke frowned. "I'm not sure I understand the logic in that," she murmured then opened the lid. Packed in wads of tissue paper was a fat pink ceramic hippo with heavily lashed eyes, a flirtatious grin and varicolored polka dots. With a laugh, Brooke drew it out. "She's gorgeous!"

"She reminded me of you," Parks commented, pleased with the laugh and the look of humor in her eyes when she turned them to him.

"Is that so?" She held the hippo up again. "Well, she does have rather fetching eyes." Touched, she stroked the wide ceramic flank. "She really is sweet, Parks. What made you think of it?"

"I thought she'd fit into your menagerie." Seeing the puzzled look on her face, he gestured toward the shelf that held her monkey and bear. "Then there's that pig on the front door, the little carving of a jackrabbit in your bedroom, the china owl on the windowsill in the kitchen."

Comprehension came slowly. There were animals of varying types and materials scattered all through the house. She'd been collecting them for years without having the slightest idea what she was doing. But Parks had seen. Without an instant of warning to either of them, Brooke burst into tears.

Stunned, then alarmed, Parks reached for her, not having a clue what he would offer comfort for. Still, he'd seen enough tears from his sisters to know that logic often had nothing to do with tears. Ashamed, and unable to stem the flow, Brooke evaded his arms and rose. "No, no, please. Give me a minute. I *hate* to do this."

Even as he told himself to respect her wishes, Parks was going to her. Despite her resistance, he pulled her against him. "I can't stand to *see* you do it," he muttered; then, with a hint of exasperation, "Why are you doing it?"

"You'll think I'm stupid. I hate being stupid."

"Brooke." Firmly, he cupped a hand under her chin and lifted it. Tears rolled freely down her cheeks. Knowing no other remedy, he kissed her—the soft lips, the wet cheeks, the damp eyelids. What began as a blind effort to comfort grew to smoldering passion.

He could feel it build in him as his mouth sought hers again. His hands moved through her hair like those of a man making his tentative way through bolts of silk. She trembled against him—sobs or desire Parks was no longer sure as the kiss went deeper and deeper. She opened for him, more giving than he could remember. Her defenses were down, he reminded himself, fighting the impatience to fill his own needs quickly. His murmurs were quiet-pitched to soothe, his hands gently stroking to arouse.

Even recognizing her own vulnerability, Brooke didn't resist. She wanted to drift into that smoky, weightless world where every movement seemed to be in slow motion. She wanted to feel that fire and flash that left you breathless. She wanted the down-soft contentment that would lull you to sleep and linger in the morning.

As he lowered her to the floor, the scent of woodsmoke grew stronger. Brooke could hear the pop and hiss of the logs as flames ate at them. His long patient kisses held her suspended—half in the reality of the wool rug beneath her back, the red flickers of firelight and sun on her closed lids, half in the world of dreams lovers understand. While her mind floated, flirting with each separate sensation, he undressed her.

Parks took infinite care with the tiny round buttons of her blouse, as if he could wait until the seasons changed outside the tall windows. There was no time here, no winter, no spring, only one everlasting moment. Brooke slipped her hands under his shirt, fingertips gliding over the warmth and the strength. As patient as he, she drew the material up, over his shoulders, then discarded it.

Flesh against flesh, they lay before the fire while the sun streamed through the massive windows and pooled over them. Kisses grew longer, interrupted only for sighs, for murmurs. She tasted the mellow warmth of wine on his tongue and was intoxicated.

Slowly, his mouth never leaving hers, Parks began to explore her body. Tiny, needlelike chills ran over her flesh, chasing the path of his hands. Feeling the light graze of his knuckles against the side of her breast, Brooke moaned, a liquid sound of pleasure. He took his tongue deeper into her mouth, gently exploiting this small weakness until the drug took full effect. She was limp, languid, utterly his. Then and only then did he give his lips the freedom to taste her skin again. It was as pungent as her scent, and somehow more erotic.

With moist, openmouthed kisses he savored her, entranced her. Then the quick pressure of his teeth on some sensitive spot would bring her sharply aware, gasping with the change. His lips would soothe again, lulling her back into pliancy. Again and again he yanked her toward the flame, then guided her back to the clouds, until Brooke was no longer certain which she most desired.

She felt him draw her slacks down over her hips while he pressed those soul-wrenching kisses along her stomach. A mindless excitement filled her, rendering her helpless to do any more than move as he requested. His breath was warm on her intimate flesh so that the long muscles in her thighs trembled then went lax.

Still his mouth moved slowly. The hands that had already discovered every secret point of pleasure continued to caress and linger, keeping her trapped beneath a thin sheet of silken passion. The power she had experienced before moved through her, but her mind was too dazed to recognize it. She felt herself balanced on a slender edge—desire's tightrope—and wanted to continue to walk it as much as she longed to fall headlong into the wild, churning sea below. Then he was above her again, his eyes looking down into hers for a long, long, moment before his lips descended. He was waiting, and she understood. Their mouths still clinging, Brooke guided him inside her.

Her moan melted into his mouth, hot and passionate. Though she was clinging to him now with a sudden, fierce strength, Parks moved slowly. Brooke felt herself fill, fill to the desperate point of explosion. Then the shudders, racking, convulsive, until she seemed to slide back down some smooth cool path to the torrent again. Like a swimmer trapped in rushing white water, she was swept from peak to peak while he moved with tortuous slowness. She could feel the tight, tense control in him, hear it in the quick labored breaths that merged with hers as he prolonged the pleasure, and the agony. Then he murmured something—a prayer, a plea, an oath—and took them both tumbling off the tightrope.

He must have slept. Parks thought he had closed his eyes for only an instant, but when he opened them again, the slant of the sun was different. Brooke was beside him, her hair wrapping them to each other. Her eyes were wide and aware as she stared into his. She'd been watching him for nearly an hour. Parks smiled and pressed his mouth to her shoulder.

"Sorry. Did I fall asleep?"

"For a little while." She hid her face against his neck a moment. It was as though he had stripped off her flesh, exposing all her thoughts. She wasn't quite certain what she should do about it. "You must have been exhausted."

"Not anymore," he said truthfully. He felt alert, pumped with energy and…clean. The last made him give a quick shake of his head. He stroked a hand down her arm. "There was something I wanted to ask you before I got…distracted." Propping himself on his elbow, Parks looked down at her. "Why were you crying?"

Brooke moved her shoulders in a shrug and started to shift away. With a firm hand, Parks stopped her. He could feel the effort she was making to draw back from him, but he realized he could no longer permit it. Whether she knew it or not, she had given herself to him completely. He was going to hold her to it.

"Brooke, don't try to block me out," he said quietly. "It won't work anymore."

She started to protest, but the quiet, steady look in his eyes told her he spoke nothing less than the truth. That alone should have been a warning of where her heart was taking her. "It was a sweet thing to do," she said at length. "I'm not used to sweetness."

Parks lifted a brow. "That's part of it, perhaps. What's the rest?"

With a sigh, Brooke sat up. This time he let her. "I

hadn't realized I'd been collecting." With both hands, she pushed her hair back, then wrapped her arms around her knees. "I overreacted when you pointed it out. I always wanted a dog, a cat, a bird, anything when I was growing up. It wasn't feasible the way I shifted around." She moved her shoulders again, causing her tumbled hair to shiver over her naked back. "It was kind of shattering to realize I was still compensating."

Parks felt a chord of sympathy and suppressed it. There was no quicker way to alienate her. "You've got your own home, your own life now. You could have anything you wanted." Reaching around her, he poured more wine for both of them. "You don't have to compensate." He sipped, studying her profile.

"No," she agreed in a murmur. "No, I don't."

"What kind of dog do you want?"

Brooke twirled the glass in her hand, then suddenly laughed. "Something homely," she said, turning to grin at him. "Something down-to-the-ground homely." She reached out, laying a hand on his cheek. "I didn't even thank you."

Parks considered, nodding solemnly as he took the glass from her hand. "No, you didn't." In a quick move, he had her rolling on top of him. "Why don't you thank me now?"

Chapter 9

Claire came down to give the set her final approval. At the far end of the studio, serenely indifferent to the piles of equipment, lights and shades, was a cozy living room scene. A deep, cushy sofa in shades of masculine brown was spotlighted as technicians made adjustments. On a table beside it was a Tiffany lamp which would appear to give the soft, sexy lighting the crew was working to achieve. Claire worked her way around cable and cases to a new angle.

Tasteful, she decided. And effective. De Marco was pleased with the first spot. So pleased, Claire thought with a mild grimace, that he had insisted his current inamorata appear in this one. Well, that was show business, she decided as she checked her watch. Brooke had moaned and groaned at the casting, then had given in with the mutter that at least he hadn't insisted they write her any dialogue.

The studio segment was being filmed first, though it would appear at the end of the ad when aired. Judging Parks's temperament, Brooke had decided to go with what would probably be the most difficult portion for him first, then ease him into the rest. And, Claire mused as she checked her watch, their luck was holding. The Kings would compete in the World Series the following week, giving the commercials just that much more impact.

Outside the studio, a long buffet had been set up in the hall. E.J., the production coordinator and the assistant cameraman were already making the most of it. Brooke was in the studio, nibbling on a hunk of cheese as she supervised the finer details.

"Damn it, Bigelow, that light's flickering again. Change the bulb or get a new fixture in here. Silbey, let me see what kind of effect we get with that new gel."

Obediently, he hit a switch so that the light filtered through the colored sheet and came out warm and sultry. "Okay, not bad. Sound?"

The sound technician walked under the boom mike. With her face innocently bland, she began to recite a nursery rhyme with a few interesting variations. At the polite volley of applause, she curtsied.

"Any problems?" Claire asked as she moved to stand beside Brooke.

"We've smoothed them out. Your end?"

"Everyone's accounted for. The talent's changing." Absently, she straightened the hem of her sleeve. "I got a glimpse of de Marco's lady. She's gorgeous."

"Thank God," Brooke said with feeling. "Are we expecting him?"

"No." Claire smiled at the resigned tone of Brooke's

voice. She heartily disliked relatives, friends or lovers hanging around a shoot. "He tells me Gina claims he would make her nervous, but he left no doubt she's to be given the royal, kid-glove treatment."

"I won't bite her," Brooke promised. "I ran through Parks's lines with him. He has it cold...if he doesn't fumble it on camera."

"He doesn't appear to be a fumbler."

Brooke smiled. "No. And I think he's starting to enjoy this whole business despite himself."

"Good. I have a script I want him to read." Above their heads on a ladder, someone cursed pungently. Claire's smooth features never registered she had even heard. "There's a part, a small one, I think he's perfect for."

Brooke turned to give Claire her full attention. "A feature?"

She nodded. "For cable. We won't be casting for another month or two, so he's got plenty of time to think about it. I'd like you to read it, too," she added casually.

"Sure." Mulling over the idea of Parks as an actor, Brooke turned to call out another instruction.

"You might like to direct it."

The order froze in her throat. "What?"

"I know you're happy directing commercials," Claire went on as if Brooke weren't gaping at her. "You've always said you enjoy creating the quick and intense, but this script might change your mind."

"Claire—" Brooke might have laughed if she hadn't been stunned "—I've never directed anything more complex than a sixty-second spot."

"Like the promo for the new fall shows you filmed last summer? Three major network stars told me you were one of the best they'd ever worked with." It was said dryly, hardly like a compliment. "I've wanted to ease you into something like this for a long time, but I didn't want to push." Claire patted her hand. "I'm still not pushing, just read the script."

After a moment, Brooke nodded. "All right, I'll read it."

"Good girl. Ah, there's Parks now." Her eyes ran over him with professional discrimination. "My, my," she murmured, "he does wear clothes well."

He looked as though he had chosen the pale blue cashmere sweater and slate-gray jeans at random, shrugging into them without a thought. That they fit with tailored precision wasn't nearly as important as the sense of rightness—that careless style that comes not from money but from basic class.

That he had, Brooke thought. Beneath the attractive face and athletic body was a sense of class that one was born with or one was not. It could never be taught. He held a glass of ginger ale in his hand, looking over the rim as he studied the room.

He found it crowded and cluttered and apparently disorganized but for the small island of order that was a sofa, table and lamp. He wondered fleetingly how anyone could work sanely around the coiled snakes of cable, huge black cases and poles of light. Then he saw Brooke. She could, he thought with a smile. She would simply steamroll over the chaos until she got exactly what she wanted. She might have wept like a child in his arms only a few nights before, but when she was on the job she was as tough as they came.

Perhaps, he mused, that was why he'd fallen in love with her—and perhaps that was why he was going to keep that little bit of information to himself for a while. If he'd nearly panicked when he'd realized it, Brooke would undoubtedly do so. She wasn't quite ready to sit trustingly in the palm of his hand.

Brooke moved toward him, eyes narrowed. Parks thought uncomfortably that she could always make him feel like a department store dummy when she looked at him that way. It was her director's look, appraising, searching for flaws, mulling over the angles.

"Well?" he said at length.

"You look marvelous." If she had noticed the faint irritation in his voice, she ignored it. Reaching up, she disheveled his hair a bit, then studied the effect. "Yes, very good. Nervous?"

"No."

Her face softened with a smile. "Don't frown, Parks, it won't help you get into the mood. Now…" Linking her arm in his, she began to lead him toward the set. "You know your lines, but we'll have cue cards in case you draw a blank, so there's nothing to worry about. The main thing we want is that sort of laid-back, understated machismo. Remember this is the end of the segment; the first scene you're on the field in uniform, then there's the business in the locker room while you're changing, then this. Soft lights, a little brandy, a beautiful woman."

"And I owe it all to de Marco," he said dryly.

"The woman in any case," she returned equably. "It's simply a statement that clothes suit a man's image. Hopefully, men will be convinced that de Marco's right for theirs. You'll sit here." Brooke gestured toward the end of the couch. "Give me that relaxed slouch of yours when you're unwinding. It's casual but not sloppy."

He frowned again, helplessly annoyed that she could dissect his every gesture and put a label on it. "Now?"

"Yes, please." Brooke stood back while Parks settled himself on the couch. "Yes, good… Bring your elbow back just a bit on the arm. Okay." She smiled again. "That's what I want. You're getting very good at this, Parks."

"Thanks."

"You'll talk right into the camera this time," she told him, gesturing behind her to where the machine sat on a dolly. "Easy, relaxed. The girl will come up behind you, leaning over as she hands you the brandy snifter. Don't look at her, just touch her hand and keep talking. And smile," she added, looking at her watch. "Where is the girl?"

On cue, Gina entered, tall and voluptuous, followed by a stern-looking blonde and two men in business suits. Better than the photo de Marco sent over, Brooke noted, and that had been impressive. The woman was young, but not too young, a ripe twenty-five, Brooke estimated, with large sloe eyes and raven hair. Her body was curvy, shown to advantage in a clingy low-cut gown that stopped just short of censorship. She wouldn't get aloof from this one, Brooke mused, watching Gina make her way across the studio. Heat vibrated in every movement. This time she would go for pure sex—for the five and a half seconds Gina was on screen. For a thirty-second television ad, it would be more than enough.

Ignoring the appreciative mutters and elbowing of her crew, Brooke walked to meet de Marco's lady. "Hello." She extended her hand with a smile. "I'm Brooke Gordon, I'll be directing you."

"Gina Minianti," she purred in a voice that instantly made Brooke regret she'd have no lines.

"We're very pleased to have you, Ms. Minianti. Do you have any questions before we begin?"

Gina gave her a slight smile. *"Come?"*

"If there's anything you don't understand," Brooke began, only to have the blonde interrupt her.

"Signorina Minianti doesn't speak English, Ms. Gordon," she said briskly. "Weren't you informed?"

"Doesn't—" Breaking off, Brooke rolled her eyes to the ceiling. "Lovely."

"I'm Mr. de Marco's personal secretary. I'll be glad to translate."

Brooke gave the blonde a long hard look, then turned around. "Places," she called. "It's going to be a long day."

"A little stumbling block?" Parks murmured as she passed him.

"Shut up and sit down, Parks."

Controlling a grin, he stepped forward to take Gina's hand. "Signorina," he began, then caught Brooke's full attention when he continued in fluid Italian. Beaming, Gina answered in a rapid spate, gesturing freely with her other hand.

"She's excited," Parks commented, knowing Brooke had stopped in her tracks behind him.

"So I gathered."

"She's always wanted to do an American movie." He spoke to Gina again, something that made her throw back her magnificent head and laugh throatily. Turning, she dismissed the blonde with a flick of the wrist and tucked her arm through Parks's. When they faced her, the tawny Californian, the raven Italian, Brooke was struck with the perfection of the contrast. That five and a half seconds of film, she thought, was going to crackle like a forest fire—and sell one hell of a lot of de Marco merchandise.

"You seem to speak Italian well enough to suit her," Brooke commented.

"Apparently." He grinned again, noting that Brooke wasn't the least jealous but appraising, as if he and Gina were already in a view screen. "She'd like me to interpret for her."

"All right, tell her we'll run through it once to show her what she needs to do. Let's have the lights!" Striding to the set, Brooke waited impatiently while Gina and Parks strolled behind her, heads close as he relayed Brooke's instructions. "Sit down, Parks, and tell her to watch closely. I'll run through it with you." Parks settled on the couch as she had instructed him. "Take it from the top, just as if the camera were rolling."

He began, talking easily, as if to a few friends on a visit. Perfect, Brooke thought as she picked up the prop brandy snifter and walked into camera range behind the couch. She leaned over, letting her cheek come close to his as she offered it. Without glancing from the camera, Parks accepted it, raising the fingers of his other hand to run down the back of Brooke's as it rested on his shoulder. She straightened slowly, moving out of camera range as he finished the dialogue.

"Now ask her if she understands what she's to do," Brooke ordered.

Gina lifted an elegant hand at Parks's question, silently communicating "of course."

"Let's try one." Brooke backed behind E.J. and the assistants who would dolly the camera platform forward for the close-ups. "Quiet on the set," she called, effectively cutting off a few discreet murmurs. "Roll film…" The clapper struck—Parks Jones for de Marco, scene three, take one. She narrowed her eyes at Parks. "Action."

He ran through it well enough for a first take, but Brooke decided he hadn't warmed to it yet. Gina followed instructions, bringing the snifter, leaning over him suggestively. Then she glanced up, startled, as the camera rolled in.

"Cut. Parks, explain to Gina not to look at the camera, please." She smiled at the woman, hoping she communicated patience and understanding. She needed a great deal of both by the fifth take. Instead of becoming more used to the camera, Gina seemed to be growing more unnerved. "Five minutes," Brooke announced. The hot lights switched off, and the crew began a pilgrimage toward the buffet. With another smile, Brooke gestured for Gina to join her and Parks on the sofa. "Parks, will you tell her she need only be natural. She's gorgeous, the few seconds she's going to be on film will make a tremendous impact."

Gina listened with brows knit, then tossed Brooke a smile. *"Grázie."* Taking Parks's hand, she launched into a long, emotional torrent that turned out to be an apology for her clumsiness and a request for something cold to calm her nerves.

"Bring Signorina Minianti some orange juice," Brooke demanded. "Tell her she's not clumsy at all," Brooke continued diplomatically. "Ah, tell her to try to imagine you're lovers, and when the camera turns off—"

"I get the idea," Parks said with a grin. When he

spoke to Gina again, she gave her throaty laugh then shook her head before she answered. "She says she'll try to imagine it," Parks relayed to Brooke, "but if she imagines it too well, Carlo will step on my face...or words to that effect."

"We have to sacrifice for our art," Brooke told him dryly. "Parks, it would help if you could put a little more steam into it."

"Steam?" he repeated, lifting a brow.

"A man who doesn't steam a bit with a woman like that hanging over his shoulder needs a transfusion." Rising, Brooke patted his shoulder. "See what you can do?"

"Anything for art," he returned, sending her a wolfish grin.

As E.J. sat behind his camera again, Brooke walked to stand at his shoulder. "Let's see if we can make one this time," she muttered.

"Boss, I can do this all day long." He focused his lens on Gina and sighed. "I think I've died and gone to heaven."

"De Marco might arrange it if you don't watch your step. Places!"

Better, she mused. Yes, definitely better as they completed the sixth take. But not perfect. She told Parks to ask Gina to give the camera a languid look before she slid Parks an under-the-lashes smile. The direction lost something in the interpretation. "Cut. Here, tell her to stand next to the camera and watch again." Brooke took Gina's place, moving behind him as he spoke, cupping the snifter of lukewarm tea. This time when Parks took it from her, he brought her other hand to his lips, pressing a soft kiss against it without breaking the rhythm of the dialogue. Brooke felt a jolt shoot up her arm and forgot to move away.

"Just seemed natural," Parks told her, linking his fingers through hers.

Brooke cleared her throat, aware that her crew was watching with avid interest. "Give it a try that way, then," she said matter-of-factly. She walked back to E.J., but when she turned, Parks's eyes were still on her. Brooke gave a quick, frustrated shake of her head. She knew that look. Slowly, the meaning crystal clear, Parks smiled.

"Places!" Brooke called in her own defense.

It took three more takes before she got just what she wanted. A hot but self-satisfied Gina gave Parks two exuberant kisses, one on each cheek, then came over and chattered something at Brooke. Glancing up at Parks, Brooke saw that amused and all too innocent look on his face.

"Just say thank you," he advised.

"Thank you," Brooke said obediently as Gina took her hand and squeezed it. She swept off with her entourage. "What was I thanking her for?" Brooke used the sleeve of her shirt to dry the sweat on her forehead.

"She was complimenting your taste."

"Oh?"

"She said your lover was magnificent."

Dropping her arm, Brooke stared at him. "Really?" she said coolly.

Parks grinned, gave a deprecatory shrug then strolled off to see if anything was left at the buffet.

Hands on her hips, Brooke stared after him. She wouldn't give him the satisfaction of letting her own smile escape. "Location, one hour," she called out.

* * *

Brooke had been right in thinking that the third brief scene of the commercial would be the most difficult to film. She shot the second scene next, crowding lights, equipment and crew into the Kings locker room. Claire had arranged, with a little negotiating, to have a few of the better-known of Parks's teammates available for background or cameos. Once Brooke got them settled down so that they stopped waving at the camera or making fictitious announcements into the mike, it began to work. And work well.

Because of the relative ease with which the segment was progressing, Brooke found the headache growing at the base of her skull unexplainable. True, the locker room was noisy between takes, and after the first hour of many bodies under hot lights, it *smelled* like a locker room, but this headache was pure tension.

At first she simply ignored it; then, when that became impossible, she grew annoyed with herself. There was nothing to be tense about. Parks did what he was told, pulling the cashmere sweater over his naked chest for each take. And every time he smiled at her, Brooke felt the headache pulse.

By the time the crew was setting up for the scene on the diamond, Brooke had convinced herself she had it under control. It was just a nagging ache, something she would take care of with a couple of aspirin when she got home. As she watched the sound technician work on a mike, she felt a beefy arm slip over her shoulders.

"Hi." Snyder grinned down at her, drawing an automatic smile of response from Brooke. He was, she thought, about as dangerous as a cocker spaniel.

"Ready for the next scene, George? You did very well before. Of course, you won't be on camera this time."

"Yeah, I wanted to mention that you're making a big mistake using Parks. Too skinny." He flexed a well-muscled arm.

Brooke gave his biceps a nod of approval. "I'm afraid I don't have anything to do with the casting."

"Too bad. Hey, now that I'm a star, are you going to pick me up at the airport?"

"Forget it, Snyder." Before Brooke could answer, Kinjinsky strolled over, a bat in one hand, a ball in the other. "She's out of your league." He grinned at Brooke, jerking his head at his teammate. "He specializes in belly dancers."

"Lies." Snyder looked amazingly like an overgrown choirboy. "All lies."

"When my daughter grows up," Kinjinsky said mildly, "I'm going to warn her about men like him." Walking to the plate, he tossed the ball up in the air then drilled it out to center field.

"Kinjinsky's the best fungo hitter on the team," Snyder told Brooke. "Too bad he has such trouble with a pitched ball."

"At least I can make it from first to second in under two and a half minutes," Kinjinsky tossed back.

Snyder, well used to ribbing about his base running, feigned an offended look. "I have this genetic anatomical problem," he explained to Brooke.

"Oh." Playing along, she looked sympathetic. "That's too bad."

"It's called a lead foot," Parks commented as he came up behind them.

Hearing his voice had the headache she'd nearly forgotten drumming again. She turned to find him watching her and his teammates with a lazily amused smile. Parks wore full uniform, the blazing white that brought out the gold of his skin. The navy cap shaded his eyes, giving him a cocky, assured look. Quietly possessive, his eyes skimmed over her. This time Brooke felt a flutter in her stomach in addition to the throb at the base of her neck.

"Just keeping your woman entertained," Snyder said genially.

"Brooke's her own woman." But there was something unmistakably proprietary in the disclaimer.

Hearing it, Snyder realized there was something deeper here than he had imagined. So the lightning's finally hit the Iceman, he thought. Snyder had the wit to rib unmercifully and the nature of a man who mends the broken wings of small birds. "When she sees how good I come across on camera, you're going to be out of a job."

"De Marco doesn't have a line for sumo wrestlers," Parks countered.

"Gentlemen," Brooke spoke, cutting them off. "The crew's ready. George, if you'd take your place at first to give Parks his target."

"Ouch." He winced. "Try not to take that literally, Jones. I don't want to be on the disabled list next week."

"Mike." Brooke stepped over to Kinjinsky. "If you'll just hit them to Parks—don't make it too easy for him, I want to see a little effort."

With a grin, Kinjinsky tossed up another ball. "I'll see what I can do."

Nodding, Brooke walked toward the crew. "Places. Parks, any questions?"

"I think I can handle this one." He stepped up to third, automatically kicking up a bit of dust with his spikes.

She looked through the lens, feeling another flutter in her stomach as she focused on Parks. Shifting his weight to one hip, he grinned at her, Brooke stepped back, gesturing to E.J.

"Hey, boss, you okay?"

"Yes, I'm fine. Roll film."

It went perfectly. Brooke knew she could have used the first take without a hitch, but opted for two more. They were equally smooth. Kinjinsky blasted the ball at Parks, enough to make him dive or leap before Parks in turn fired the ball at Snyder on first.

"Third take's the winner," E.J. announced when Brooke called the session a wrap.

"Yes." Unconsciously, she rubbed the back of her neck.

"He shouldn't have even caught it," E.J. went on, watching Brooke as he began to load his equipment.

"He seems to excel at doing the impossible," she murmured.

"Headache?"

"What?" Glancing down, she found E.J. watching her steadily. "It's nothing." Annoyed, she dropped her hand. Parks was already in a conference on the mound with his two teammates. He had his glove hand on his hip, grinning at Snyder's newest concept for a practical joke. "It's nothing," Brooke repeated in a mutter, reaching for one of the sodas in the ice chest.

It had to be nothing, she told herself as she tipped the bottle and drank deeply. Whatever was rolling around inside her was just a product of fatigue after a long day's work. She needed aspirin, a decent meal and eight hours' sleep. She needed to stay away from Parks.

The minute the thought entered her head, Brooke was infuriated. *He has nothing to do with it*, she told herself fiercely. *I'm tired, I've been working too hard, I've—* She caught E.J.'s speculative stare and bristled.

"Would you get out of here?"

His face cleared with a wide grin. "On my way. I'll drop off the film at editing."

With a curt nod, Brooke strode out to the mound to thank Snyder and Kinjinsky. She heard the tail of Snyder's brainstorm, something about frogs in the bullpen, before Parks turned to her.

"How'd it go?"

"Very well." Heat was running along her skin now, too physical, too tangible. She gave her attention to his teammates. "I want to thank both of you. Without your help, it never would have gone so smoothly."

Snyder leaned his elbow on Kinjinsky's shoulder. "Just keep me in mind when you want something more than a pretty face in one of these commercials."

"I'll do that, George."

Parks waited through the rest of the small talk, adding comments easily though his concentration was all for Brooke. He waited until the ballplayers had wandered off toward the locker room before he took Brooke's chin in his hand. Closely, patiently, he examined her. "What's wrong?"

Brooke stepped away so that they were no longer touching. "Why should anything be wrong?" she countered. Her nerves had gone off like bells in her head at his touch. "It went very well. I think you'll be pleased with it when it's edited. With the two spots running throughout the series, we won't shoot another until November." Turning, she noted that most of the crew had gone. She found she wanted to be away before she and Parks were completely alone. "I have a few things to clear up back at the office, so—"

"Brooke." Parks cut her off cleanly. "Why are you upset?"

"I'm *not* upset!" Biting back fury, she whirled back to him. "It's been a long day, I'm tired. That's all."

Slowly, Parks shook his head. "Try again."

"Leave me alone," she said in a trembling undertone that told her, and him, just how close she was to the edge. "Just leave me alone."

Dropping his mitt to the ground, he took both her arms. "Not a chance. We can talk here, or we can go back to your place and hash it out. Your choice."

She shoved away from him. "There's nothing to hash out."

"Fine. Then let's go have dinner and see a movie."

"I told you I had work to do."

"Yeah." He nodded slowly. "You lied."

Sharp, bubbling anger filled her eyes. "I don't have to lie, all I have to do is tell you no."

"True enough," he agreed, holding on to his own temper. "Why are you angry with me?" His voice was calm, patient. His eyes weren't. The sun fell against his face, accenting that fierce sexuality.

"I'm not angry with you!" she nearly shouted.

"People usually shout when they're angry."

"I'm *not* shouting," she claimed as her voice rose.

Curiously, he tilted his head. "No? Then what are you doing?"

"I'm afraid I'm falling in love with you." Her expression became almost comically surprised after the words had tumbled out. She stared in simple disbelief, then covered her mouth with her hand as if to shove the words back inside.

"Oh, yeah?" He didn't smile as he took another step toward her. Something was scrambling inside his stomach like a squirrel in a cage. "Is that so?"

"No, I..." In defense, she looked around, only to find that she was alone with him now. Alone in his territory. The stands rose up like walls to trap them inside the field of grass and dirt. Brooke backed off the mound. "I don't want to stay here."

Parks merely matched his steps to hers. "Why afraid, Brooke?" He lifted his hand to her cheek, causing her to stop her retreat. "Why should a woman like you be afraid of being in love?"

"I know what happens!" she said suddenly with eyes that were dark and stormy in contrast to the trembling tone.

"Okay, why don't you tell me?"

"I'll stop thinking. I'll stop being careful." She ran an agitated hand through her hair. "I'll give until I lose the edge, then when it's over I won't have anything left. Every time," she whispered, thinking of all the transient parents, thinking of Clark. "I won't let it happen to me again. I can't be involved with you for the fun of it, Parks. It just isn't working." Without being aware of the direction, Brooke had turned to pace to the third base bag. Parks felt the warmth of the gold piece against his chest and decided it was fate. Taking his time, he followed her. His percentage of errors at the corner was very small.

"You are involved with me, whether you're having fun at it or not."

She sent him a sharp glance. This wasn't the easygoing man but the warrior. Brooke straightened her shoulders. "That can be remedied."

"Try it," he challenged, calmly gripping her shirt in his hand and pulling her toward him.

Brooke threw her head back, infuriated, and perhaps more frightened than she had ever been in her life. "I won't see you again. If you can't work with me, take it up with Claire."

"Oh, I can work with you," he said softly. "I can even manage to take your orders without too much of a problem because you're damn good at what you do. I told you once before I'd follow your rules while the camera was on." He glanced around, silently relaying that there was no camera this time. "It's tough to beat a man on his own ground, Brooke, especially a man who's used to winning."

"I'm not a pennant, Parks," she said with amazing steadiness.

"No." With one hand still gripping her shirt, he traced the other gently down her cheek. "Pennants are won through teamwork. A woman's a one-on-one proposition. Seventh-inning stretch, Brooke. Time to take a quick breath before the game starts again." The hand on her cheek moved up to cup her neck. She wondered that he couldn't feel the sledgehammers pounding there. Then he smiled, that slow dangerous smile that always drew her. "I'm in love with you."

He said it so calmly, so simply, that it took her a moment to understand. Every muscle in her body went rigid. "Don't."

He lifted a brow. "Don't love you or don't tell you?"

"Stop." She put both hands on his chest in an attempt to push him away. "It's not a joke."

"No, it's not. What are you more afraid of?" he asked, studying her pale face. "Loving or being loved?"

Brooke shook her head. She'd been so careful to keep from crossing that thin line—been just as careful to keep others from crossing from the other side. Claire had done it, and E.J., she realized. There was love there. But *in* love... How could a tiny, two-letter word petrify her?

"You could ask me when," Parks murmured, kneading the tense muscles in her neck, "and I couldn't tell you. There wasn't a bolt of lightning, no bells, no violins. I can't even say it snuck up on me because I saw it coming. I didn't try to step out of the way." He shook his head before he lowered his mouth to hers. "You can't wish it away, Brooke."

The kiss rocked her back on her heels. It was hard and strong and demanding without the slightest hint of urgency. It was as if he knew she could go nowhere. She could fight him, Brooke thought. She could still fight him. But the tension was seeping out of her, filling her with a sense of freedom she had thought she would never fully achieve. She was loved.

Feeling the change in her, Parks pulled back. He wouldn't win her with passion. His needs ran too deep to settle for that. Then her arms were around him, her cheek pressed against his chest in a gesture not of desire, but of trust. Perhaps the beginning of trust.

"Tell me again," she murmured. "Just tell me once more."

He held her close, stroking her hair while the breeze whispered through the empty stadium. "I love you."

With a sigh, Brooke stepped over the line. Lifting her head, she took his face in her hands. "I love you, Parks," she murmured before she urged his lips to take hers.

Chapter 10

Clubhouses have their own smell. Sweat, foot powder, the tang of liniments, the faint chemical aroma of whirlpools and the overlying fragrance of coffee. The mixture of odors was so much a part of his life, Parks never noticed it as he pulled on his sweatshirt. What he did notice was tension. That was inescapable. Even Snyder's determined foray of practical jokes couldn't break the curtain of nerves in the locker room that afternoon. When a team had spent months together—working, sweating, winning and losing—aiming toward one common goal, nothing could ease the nerves of facing the seventh game of the World Series.

If the momentum had been with them, the atmosphere would have been different. All the minor aches that plague the end of a season would barely have been noticed—the tired legs, the minor pulls. But the Kings had dropped the last two games to the Herons. A professional athlete knows that skill is not the only determining factor in winning. Momentum, luck, timing are all added for balance.

Even if the Kings could have claimed they'd fallen into a slump there might have been a little more cheer in the clubhouse. The simple fact was that they'd been outplayed. The number of hits between the opponents was almost even—but the Herons had made theirs count while the Kings had left their much needed runs stranded on base. Now it came down to the last chance for both teams. Then when it was over, they'd pick up their off-season lives.

Parks glanced at Snyder, who'd be on his charter boat in Florida the following week. Catching fish and swapping lies, he called it, Parks mused. Kinjinsky, getting heat applied to his ribs, would be playing winter ball in Puerto Rico. Maizor, the starting pitcher, would be getting ready to play daddy for the first time when his wife delivered in November. Some would go on the banquet circuit and the talk show circuit—depending on the outcome of today's game. Others would go back to quiet jobs until February and spring training.

And Parks Jones makes commercials, he reflected with a small grimace. But the idea didn't bring on the sense of foolishness it had only a few months before. It gave him a certain pleasure to act—though Brooke wouldn't call it that—in front of the camera. But he wasn't too thrilled with the poster deal Lee had cooked up.

He smiled a little as he drew on his spikes. Hype, Brooke had called it, saying simply it was part of the game. She was right, of course; she usually was about that aspect of things. But Parks didn't think he'd ever be completely comfortable with the way she could look him over with those calm eyes and sum him up with a few choice words. Wouldn't it disconcert any man to have fallen in love with a woman who could so accurately interpret his every expression, body move or careless word? *Face it, Jones,* he told himself, *you could have picked an easier woman.* Could have, he reflected, but didn't. And since Brooke Gordon was who and what he wanted, she was worth the effort it took to have her, and to keep her. He wasn't so complacent that he believed he had truly done either yet.

Yes, she loved him, but her trust was a very tenuous thing. He sensed that she waited for him to make a move so that she could make a countermove. And so the match continued. Fair enough, he decided; they were both programmed to compete. He didn't want to master her...did he? With a frown, Parks pulled a bat out of his locker and examined it carefully. If he had to answer the question honestly, he'd say he wasn't sure. She still challenged him—as she had from the very first moment. Now, mixed with the challenge were so many emotions it was difficult to separate them.

He'd been angry when Brooke wouldn't change her schedule and fly East during the games at the Herons' home stadium. And when he'd become angry, she'd become very cool. Her work, she had told him, couldn't be set aside to suit him or even herself...any more than his could. Even though he'd understood, Parks had been angry. He had simply wanted her there, wanted to know she was in the stands so that he could look up and see her. He had wanted to know she was there when the long game was over. Pure selfishness, he admitted. They both had an ample share of that.

With a grim smile Parks ran a hand down the smooth barrel of the bat. She'd told him it wouldn't be easy. Brooke had been her own person long before he had pushed his way into her life. Circumstances had made her the person she was—though they were circumstances she had still not made completely clear to him. Still it was that person—the strong, the vulnerable, the practical and the private, whom he had fallen for. Yet he couldn't quite get over the urge he had at times to shake her and tell her they were going to do it his way.

He supposed what epitomized their situation at this point was their living arrangement. He had all but moved in with her, though neither one of them had discussed it. But he knew Brooke considered the house hers. Therefore, Parks was living with her, but they weren't living together. He wasn't certain his patience would last long enough to break through that final thin wall—without leaving the entrance hole a bit jagged.

With a quiet oath he reached into the locker and grabbed a batting glove, sticking it in his back pocket. If he had to use a bit of dynamite, he decided, he would.

"Hey, Jones, infield practice."

"Yeah." He grabbed his mitt, sliding his hand into its familiar smoothness. He was going to handle Brooke, he told himself. But first there was a pennant to win.

Alternately cursing and drumming her fingers against the steering wheel, Brooke cruised the parking lot in search of a space. "I knew we should've left earlier," she muttered. "We'll be lucky to get anything within a mile of the stadium."

Leaning back against the seat, E.J. interrupted his humming long enough to comment. "Still fifteen minutes before game time."

"When somebody gets you a free ticket," Brooke said precisely, "the least you can do is be ready when they pick you up. There's one!" Brooke gunned the motor and slipped between two parked cars with inches to spare. Hitting the brake, she glanced at her companion. "You can open your eyes now, E.J.," she said dryly.

Cautiously, one at a time, he did so. "Okay…" He looked at the car beside him. "Now how do we get out?"

"Open the door and inhale," she advised, wiggling out her side. "And hurry up, will you? I don't want to miss them taking the field."

"I've noticed your interest in baseball's increased over the summer, boss." Thankful for his thin frame, E.J. squeezed out of the Datsun.

"It's an interesting game."

"Yeah?" Joining her, he grinned.

"Careful, E.J., I still have your ticket. I could scalp it twenty times before we reach the door."

"Aw, come on, Brooke, you can tell your friend what's already in the papers."

She scowled at that, stuffing her hands in her pockets. There'd been pictures of her and Parks, tantalizing little articles and hints in every paper she'd looked at for more than a week. In L.A., gossip carried quickly—a hot ballplayer and his attractive director were definitely food for gossip.

"I even caught a bit in one of the trades," E.J. went on, blithely ignoring the storm clouds in Brooke's eyes. "Speculation is that Parks might take up, ah…show business," he said, giving her another grin, "seriously."

"Claire has a part for him if he wants it," Brooke returned, evading his obvious meaning. "It's small but meaty. I didn't want to go into it in depth with Parks until after the series. He has enough on his mind."

"Yeah, I'd say the man's had a few things on his mind for some time now."

"E.J.," Brooke began warningly as she passed over her tickets.

"You know," he continued when they fought their way through the inside crowd, "I've always wondered when somebody'd come along who'd shake that cool of yours a little."

"Is that so?" She didn't want to be amused, so she slipped her sunglasses down to conceal the humor in her eyes. "And you apparently think someone has?"

"Honey, you can't get within ten feet of the two of you and not feel the steam. I've been thinking..." He fussed with the front of his T-shirt as if straightening a tie. "As your close friend and associate, maybe I should ask Mr. Jones his intentions."

"Just try it, E.J., and I'll break all of your lenses." Caught between amusement and irritation, Brooke plopped down in her seat. "Sit down and buy me a hot dog."

He signaled. "What do you want on it?"

"All I can get."

"Come on, Brooke." He fished in his pocket for a couple of bills, exchanging them for hot dogs and cold drinks. "Buddy to buddy, how serious is it?"

"Not going to let up, are you?"

"I care."

Brooke glanced over at him. He was smiling, not the wisecracking grin she so often saw on his face, but a simple smile of friendship. It was, perhaps, the only weapon she had no defense against. "I'm in love with him," she said quietly. "I guess that's pretty damn serious."

"Grade-A serious," he agreed. "Congratulations."

"Am I supposed to feel like I'm walking on a cliff?" she demanded, only half joking.

"Don't know." E.J. took a considering bite of his hot dog. "Never had the experience."

"Never been in love, E.J.?" Leaning back in her seat, Brooke grinned. "You?"

"Nope. That's why I spend so much time looking." He gave a heavy sigh. "It's a tough business, Brooke."

"Yeah." She took off his fielder's cap and swatted him with it. "I bet it is. Now shut up, they're going to announce the starting lineup."

A tough business, she thought again. Well, he wasn't far wrong, even if he had been joking. Looking for love was a lonely occupation, one she'd given up—or thought she'd given up—years before. Finding it—or having it tackle you from behind—was even tougher. Once it found you it clung, no matter how much you tried to shake it off. But she wasn't trying to shake it off, Brooke mused. She was just trying to understand how it fit and make a few adjustments. The fabric kept changing.

"Playing third and batting fourth, number twenty-nine, Parks Jones."

The already boisterous crowd went frantic as Parks jogged out on the field to take his place in the lineup. When he stood beside Snyder, he let his eyes drift over. They locked on Brooke's. With a smile, he gave the customary tip of his cap. It was a gesture for the crowd, but she knew it had been aimed at her personally. It was all the acknowledgment he would give her until it was over. It was all she expected.

"I'm going to outhit you today, Iceman," Snyder warned, grinning at the crowd. "Then Brooke's going to realize her mistake."

Parks never took his eyes off her. "She's going to marry me."

Snyder's jaw dropped. "No kidding! Well, hey..."

"She just doesn't know it yet," Parks added in a murmur. He slapped hands with the right fielder, batting fifth. "But she will."

Brooke detected a change in Parks's smile, something subtle, but to her unmistakable. Narrowing her eyes, she tried to decipher it. "He's up to something," she muttered.

E.J. perfected a shot with a small still camera. "What?"

"Nothing." She swirled her drink so that ice chunks banged together. "Nothing."

A well-known blues singer stepped up to the mike to sing the national anthem. Two lines of athletes removed their caps. The crowd rose, silent for what would be the last time in more than two hours. The excitement was so tangible Brooke thought she could reach out into the warm October air and grab a handful of nerves. It built and built until it exploded with cheers and shouts and whistles as the last note of the song trembled. The Kings took the field.

Sportscasters are fond of saying that the seventh game of the World Series is the ultimate in sports events—the pinnacle test of teamwork and individual effort. This was no exception. In the first inning, Brooke saw the Kings' center fielder charge a ball, stretching forward to catch it on the run then holding on to it as the momentum carried him into a forward roll. She saw the Herons shortstop seem to throw heart and body after a ball to prevent it from going through the hole for a base hit. At the end of the fourth, the teams had one run apiece, each on solo home runs.

Brooke had seen Parks guard his position at third, stealing, as Lee would have put it, two certain base hits and starting the execution of a clutch double play. Watching him, Brooke realized he played this game just as he played every other—with total concentration, with steady determination. If he had nerves, if somewhere in his mind was the thought that this was *the* game, it didn't show. As he stepped up to bat, she leaned out on the rail.

Before he stepped into the box, Parks ran a hand up and down his bat as though checking for splinters. He was waiting for calm, not the calm of the shouting fans but inner calm. In his mind's eye he could see Brooke leaning on the rail, her hair tumbling over her shoulders, her eyes cool and direct. The knot of tension in his stomach eased.

When he stepped up to the plate his predominant thought was to advance the runner. With Snyder on first, he'd have to put it well out of the infield. And they'd be pitching him carefully. Both times he had come to bat, Parks had clipped a single through the hole between third and short.

Parks took his stance and looked directly into the pitcher's eyes. He watched the windup, saw the ball hurtling toward him, shifted his weight, then checked his swing. The slider missed the corner. Ball one.

Stepping out of the box, Parks knocked the bat against his spikes to clear them of dirt. Yeah, they were going to be careful what they gave him. But he could get Snyder to second just as easily on a walk as on a hit. The trouble was, second wasn't a sure scoring position for Snyder.

The second pitch missed, low and outside. Parks checked the signal from the third base coach. He didn't allow his eyes to drift over to where Brooke sat. Parks knew even that brief contact would destroy his concentration.

The next pitch came in on him, nearly catching him on the knuckles then bouncing foul. The crowd demanded a hit. Parks checked Snyder, who was keeping very cozy with the bag, before he stepped into the box again.

Hoping to even the count, the pitcher tried another fast curve. In that fraction of a second, Parks shifted his weight. Wrists square and unbroken, he connected, letting his hips bring the bat around. He had the satisfaction of hearing the ball crack off the bat before the crowd was on its feet, screaming.

The ball sailed over center field, and though three men gave chase, no one reached it before it smashed into the dirt of the warning track and bounced high over the wall. With the fans roaring on all sides, Parks settled for the ground-rule double. There was sweat trickling down his back, but he barely felt it. He thought once that if he'd pulled the ball a bit to the right, it would have gone over clean, scoring two. Then he forgot it.

With Snyder on third, he couldn't take a sizable lead, so he contented himself with putting only a couple of feet between himself and the bag. The odds that Farlo would sacrifice to score Snyder were slim. The out-fielder could spray a ball to all fields, but he wasn't a power hitter. Parks crouched, shaking his arms to keep the muscles loose.

Farlo fell behind quickly, fouling off two pitches and frustrating the crowd. Parks simply refused to think of the possibility of being stranded on base again. The in-field was playing them tight, looking for that ground ball that could be turned into a double play.

Parks saw the pitch, judged it to be a low curve and tensed. Farlo showed his teeth and smacked it to right field. Parks was running on instinct before he con-sciously told his feet to move. The third base coach was waving him on. Years of training had Parks round-ing third at top speed and heading home without hesita-tion or question. He saw the catcher crouched, ready to receive the ball, shielding the plate like a human wall. It flashed through Parks's mind that the Herons' right fielder was known for his arm and his precision before he threw himself at the plate in a feet-first slide that had dirt billowing in the clouds. He felt the red flash of pain as his body connected with the catcher, heard his opponent's *whoosh* of air at the hit and saw the small white ball swallowed by the mitt.

They were a tangle of bodies and mutual pain as the umpire spread his arms. "Safe!"

The crowd went wild, stranger pounded on stranger, beer sloshed over cups. Brooke found that E.J. had grabbed her for a quick dance. His camera cut into her chest but it was several moments before she felt it.

"My man!" E.J. shouted, whirling her into the man on her right, who tossed his box of popcorn into the air.

No, she thought breathlessly. *My man.*

At the plate, Parks didn't concentrate on the adulation of the crowd, but on drawing enough breath into his lungs so he could stand again. The catcher's knee had slammed solidly into his ribs. Rising, he gave his uniform a perfunctory brush then headed to the dugout, where his teammates waited for him. This time, he allowed his eyes to find her. She was standing, her arms still around E.J. But her face softened with a smile that was only for him.

Touching his cap, he disappeared into the dugout. The trainer had the cold spray ready for his ribs.

Parks had forgotten his aches long before he had taken his defensive position in the top of the ninth. The Herons had whittled their lead down to one run with some blood and guts baserunning in the seventh. Since then, both teams had held like rocks. But now, Maizor was in trouble.

With only one out, he had a runner on second and a power hitter coming to the plate. *We could walk him and put him on,* Parks considered as the catcher tipped back his mask on his way to the mound for a conference. But the Herons had more big bats in the lineup and a few pinch hitters who couldn't be underestimated. Parks sauntered over to the mound, noting as he did that Maizor was strung tight.

"Gonna go for him?" Parks asked as the catcher chewed on a wad of gum the size of a golf ball.

"Yeah, Maizor's gonna take care of him, aren't you, Slick?"

"Sure." He turned the ball over and over in his hand. "We all want a ride in Jones's new sports car."

Parks took the mention of the Most Valuable Player Award with a shrug. They were still two outs away, and all three men knew it. "One thing." He adjusted his cap. "Don't let him hit it toward me."

Maizor swore and grinned and visibly relaxed. "Let's play ball."

Over his shoulder, Maizor checked the runner on second. Satisfied that his lead wasn't too greedy, he fired the ball at the plate. Parks could almost hear the rush of the wind as the bat cut, just over the ball. Kinjinsky called out, telling him to bear down and do it again. He did, but this time the batter got a solid piece of it.

As if a button had been pushed, Parks went for it, lunging from his side as Kinjinsky dashed to cover him. He had only seconds to judge the speed and the height. Even as he let his body fall in the direction of the ball, he felt the runner pass him on his way to third. Landing on his knees, Parks caught in on the short bounce. Without taking the time to rise, he fired the ball toward third. Kinjinsky nabbed it and held his ground as the runner slid into him.

"Still trying to make the easy plays look hard," the shortstop commented as they passed each other. They were both coated with dirt and sweat. "One more, baby, just one more."

Parks let the long, mixed roar of the crowd wash over him as he crouched at third. His face was utterly impassive. The tying run was on first. By the time the count reached three and two, being on the diamond was like being in the eye of a hurricane. Noise and turbulence whirled around them from the stands. On the field, the tension was dead silent.

Maizor went inside, handcuffing the batter. The ball was hit, drifting foul. Parks gave chase as it drifted toward the seats, running at full speed as though the wall weren't looming up in front of him. He could get it, he knew he could get it—if an excited fan didn't reach over and make a grab.

With his free hand, he caught the rail and lifted his glove. He felt the impact of the ball as he closed his leather over it. While the crowd started to scream, he found he was looking directly into Brooke's eyes. The foul had all but fallen into her lap.

"Nice catch." Leaning over, she kissed him full on the mouth.

Then one of his teammates had him around the waist, and the rest was madness.

Parks had more champagne dumped on him than he could possibly have drunk. It mixed with sweat and washed some of the grime away. Snyder had positioned himself on top of a locker and from there emptied two bottles on anyone in sight—reporters and league brass included. Accused of showboating, Parks was tossed, fully dressed, into the whirlpool. Grateful, he stripped and remained where he was with half a bottle of champagne. From there he gave interviews while the water beat the aches from his body and bedlam raged around him.

The pitch on his double had been an outside fast ball. Yeah, his slide into home had been risky, considering the arm of the right fielder, but he'd had a good lead. He continued to answer questions as Snyder, in a champagne-drenched uniform, was not so gently assisted into the whirlpool with him. Parks slid down farther in the soothing water and drained the cold wine straight from the bottle. Yes, the redhead in the stands was Brooke Gordon, his director on the de Marco commercials. Parks smiled as Snyder wisecracked the reporters' attention to himself. Teammates might poke and prod into each other's business, but they protected their own.

Parks closed his eyes a moment, just a moment. He wanted to recapture that instant when she had leaned over and touched her lips to his. Everything had been heightened in that split second of victory. He had thought he could hear each individual shout from the crowd. He'd seen the sunlight glint on the chipped paint of the railing, felt the baking heat as his hand had wrapped around it. Then he'd seen her eyes, close, soft, beautiful. Her voice had been quiet, conveying excitement, humor and love all in two words. When they had touched his, her lips had been warm and smooth, and for an instant that had been all he had felt. Just the silky texture of her lips. He hadn't even heard the last out called. When he'd been dragged back on the field by his teammates, she had simply lowered her chin to the rail and smiled at him. *Later.* He had heard her thought as clearly as if she had spoken it.

It took two hours to urge the last reporter out of the clubhouse. The players were quieting. The first rush of victory was over, replaced by a mellowness that would very quickly become nostalgia. The year was over. There'd be no more infield practice, batting practice, night rides on planes with card games and snoring. They were in a business where today was over quickly and tomorrow took all their efforts. Now there wasn't a tomorrow, but next year.

Some were sitting, talking quietly on the benches in the midst of the locker room litter, as Parks dressed. He glanced at the second-string catcher, a boy of barely nineteen, completing his first year in the majors. He held his shin guards in his hands as if he couldn't bear to part with them. Parks put his mitt into his duffel bag and felt suddenly old.

"How're the ribs?" Kinjinsky asked as he slung his own bag over his shoulder.

"Fine." Parks gestured to the boy on the bench. "The kid's barely old enough to vote."

"Yeah." Kinjinsky, a ripe thirty-two, grinned. "It's hell, isn't it?" They both laughed as Parks closed his locker for the last time that year. "See you in the spring, Jones. My woman's waiting for me."

Parks zipped up his bag while the thought warmed in him. He, too, had a woman, and it would take him thirty minutes to drive to the mountains.

"Hey, Parks." Snyder caught him before he'd reached the door. "You really going to marry her?"

"As soon as I can talk her into it."

Snyder nodded, not questioning the phrasing of the answer. "Give me a call when you set it up. I'm the best man."

With a smile, Parks held out a hand and shook the beefy one. "Damned if you're not, George." He walked into the corridor, closing the door on the clubhouse and the season.

When he emerged outside, it was dusk. Only a few fans lingered, but he signed autographs for them and gave them the time they wanted. Parks thought idly about picking up another bottle of champagne for himself and Brooke as he signed his name to the bill of a twelve-year-old's battered hat. Champagne, a fire burning low, candles. It seemed like a good setting to propose marriage. It was going to be tonight, because tonight he didn't think he could lose.

The parking lot was all but deserted. The overhead lights were just flickering on as twilight deepened. Then he saw her. Brooke was sitting on the hood of his car, spotlighted in the flood of a security light, her hair like tongues of flame around her strong-boned, delicate-skinned face. Love welled up in him, a fierce possessive love that took his breath away. Except for the lips that curved, she didn't move. He realized then she had been watching him for some time. He struggled to regain some control over his muscles before he continued toward her.

"If I'd known you were waiting here, I'd have come out sooner." He felt the ache in his ribs again, but not from the bruise this time. This was from a need he was still not quite used to.

"I told E.J. to take my car. I didn't mind waiting." Reaching up, she put both hands on his shoulders. "Congratulations."

Very deliberately, Parks set his bag down on the asphalt then dove his hands into her hair. Their eyes held briefly, endlessly, before he lowered his mouth and took what he needed.

His emotions were more finely tuned than he had realized. All the pleasure of victory, the weariness that came from winning it, the dregs of excitement and tension surfaced, to be doubled then swept away by one all-encompassing need. Brooke. How was he to have known that she would grow to be everything—and all things? A bit unnerved by the intensity, Parks drew away. A man couldn't win when his knees were buckling. He ran his knuckles down her cheek, wanting to see that very faint, very arousing clouding of her eyes.

"I love you."

At his words, Brooke rested her head against his chest and breathed deeply. She could smell his shower on him, some subtle soap fragrance that spoke of gymnasiums and locker rooms that were inhabited only by men. For some reason, it made her feel acutely a woman. The light grew dimmer as they remained, held close and silent.

"Too tired to celebrate?" she murmured.

"Uh-uh." He kissed her hair.

"Good." Drawing away, she slid from the hood. "I'll buy you dinner to start it off." Brooke opened the passenger door and smiled. "Hungry?"

Until that moment, Parks hadn't realized that he was starving. What little he'd eaten before the game had been devoured by nerves. "Yeah. Do I get to pick the place?"

"Sky's the limit."

Fifteen minutes later, Brooke gazed around the garishly colored Hamburger Heaven. "You know," she mused, studying the overhead lights that were shaped like sesame seed rolls. "I'd forgotten your penchant for junk food."

"A hundred percent pure beef," Parks claimed, picking up an enormous double-decker sandwich.

"If you believe that, you believe anything."

Grinning, he offered her a french fry. "Cynic."

"If you call me names, I won't read you the sports page." She put her hand over the folded paper she'd just bought. "Then you won't hear the accolades the press have heaped on you." When he shrugged, unconcerned, she opened the paper. "Well, I want to hear them." With one hand on her milk shake, Brooke began to thumb her way through. "Here… Oh." She stopped dead and scowled.

"What is it?" Parks leaned over. On the front page were two pictures, side by side. The first was of his over-the-seats catch of the final out. The second was of Brooke's impulsive kiss. The caption read:

JONES SCORES… TWICE

"Cute," he decided, "considering I didn't score but snagged a pop fly." He twisted his head, skimming down the article which ran through the highlights of the game—critiques and praise. "Hmm… 'And Jones ended it with a race to the rail, snagging Hennesey's long foul out of the seats in one of the finest plays of the afternoon. As usual, the MVP makes the impossible look routine. He got his reward from the luscious redhead—'" here he shot Brooke a brief glance "'—Brooke Gordon, a successful commercial director who's been seen with the third baseman on and off the set.'"

"I really hate that," Brooke said with such vehemence that Parks looked up in surprise.

"Hate what?"

"Having my picture splashed around that way. And this—this half-baked speculation. This, and that silly business in the *Times* a couple days ago."

"The one that called you a willowy, titian-haired gypsy with smoky eyes?"

"It's not funny, Parks." Brooke shoved the paper aside.

"It's not tragic, either," he pointed out.

"They should mind their own business."

Leaning back, Parks nibbled on a fry. "You'd probably be the first to tell me that being in the public eye makes you public property."

Brooke scowled at that, knowing they were precisely her words when they'd discussed the poster deal. "*You're* in the public eye," she countered. "It's the way you make your living. *I* don't. I work behind the camera, and I have a right to my privacy."

"Ever heard of guilty by association?" He smiled before she could retort. Instead of a curt remark, she let out a long sigh. "At least they're accurate," he added. "I've often thought of you as a gypsy myself."

Brooke picked up her cheeseburger, frowned, then bit into it. "I still don't like it," she muttered. "I think…" She shrugged, not certain how foolish she was going to sound. "I've always been a little overly sensitive about my privacy, and now…what's happening between us is too important for me to want to share with anyone who has fifty cents for a paper."

Parks leaned forward again and took her hand. "That's nice," he said softly. "That's very nice."

The tone of his voice had fresh emotion rising in her. "I don't want to hole up like a couple of hermits, Parks, but I don't want every move we make to be on the evening news, either."

With a bit more nonchalance than he was feeling at the moment, he shrugged and began to eat again. "Romance is news… So's divorce, when it involves public people."

"It's not going to ease up with the de Marco campaign, either, or if you decide to take that part in the film." She took another french fry out of its paper scoop and glared at it. "The hotter you are, the more the press will buzz around. It's maddening."

"I could break my contract," he suggested.

"Don't be ridiculous."

"There's another solution," he considered, watching Brooke swallow the french fry and reach for another.

"What?"

"We could get married. Want some salt for those?"

Brooke stared at him, then found she had to search for her voice. "What did you say?"

"I asked if you wanted some salt." Parks offered her a tiny paper packet. "No?" he said when she neither answered nor moved. "I also said we could get married."

"Married?" Brooke echoed stupidly. "You and me?"

"The press would ease off after a while. Quietly married couples don't make news the same way lovers do. Human nature." He pushed his sandwich aside and leaned toward her. "What do you think?"

"I think you're crazy," Brooke managed in a whisper. "And I don't think this is funny."

Parks gripped her arm when she started to scoot out of the booth. "I'm not joking."

"You—you want to get married so we won't get our picture in the paper?"

"I don't give a damn if we get our picture in the paper or not, you do."

"So you want to get married to—to placate me." She stopped struggling against his hold on her arm, but her eyes filled with fury.

"I've never had any intention of placating you," he countered. "I couldn't placate you if I dedicated my life to it. I want to get married because I'm in love with you. I'm *going* to marry you," he corrected, suddenly angry, "if I have to drag you, kicking and screaming."

"Is that so?"

"Yes, that's exactly so. You might as well get used to it."

"Maybe I don't want to get married." Brooke shoved the food in front of them aside. "What about that?"

"Too bad." He leaned back, eyeing her with the same simmering temper with which she eyed him. "*I* want to get married."

"And that's supposed to be enough, huh?"

"It's enough for me."

Brooke crossed her arms over her chest and glared at him. "Kicking and screaming?"

"If that's the way you want it."

"I can bite, too."

"So can I."

Her heart was thudding against her ribs, but Brooke realized it wasn't from anger. No, it had nothing to do with anger. He was sitting there, across a laminated table littered with food from a twelve-year-old's fantasy, telling her he was going to marry her whether she liked it or not. Brooke discovered, somewhat to her own amazement, that she liked it just fine. But she wasn't going to make it easy for him.

"Maybe winning the series went to your head, Parks. It's going to take more than a temper tantrum to get me to marry you."

"What do you want?" he demanded. "Candlelight and soft music?" Annoyed that he had scuttled his own plans, he leaned over again and grabbed her hands. "You're not the kind of woman who needs scenery,

Brooke. You know just how easy it is to come by and how little it means. What the hell do you want?"

"Take two," she said very calmly. "You know your motivation," she began in her cool director's voice, "but this time tone down the force and try for a little finesse. Ask," she suggested, looking into his eyes, "don't tell."

He felt the anger, or perhaps it had been fear, slide out of him. The hands that held hers gentled. "Brooke—" he lifted a hand and pressed her fingers to his lips "—will you marry me?" Parks smiled over their joined hands. "How was that?"

Brooke laced the fingers with hers. "Perfect."

Chapter 11

What was she doing? In a sudden panic, Brooke stared at herself in the freestanding long-length mirror. How could things be happening so fast and be so much out of her control? A year ago—no, even six months ago—she hadn't known Parks Jones existed. In something under an hour, she would be married to him. Committed. For life. Forever.

From somewhere deep inside her brain came a panicked call to run and run fast. Brooke hadn't realized she'd made a move until she was summarily jerked back into place.

"Be still, Ms. Gordon," Billings ordered firmly. "There are two dozen of these little buttons if there's one." She used a complaining tone, though privately she thought Brooke's choice of an ivory satin gown with its snug bodice and flowing skirt was inspired. A good, traditional wedding dress, she decided, not one of those flighty trouser suits or miniskirted affairs in scarlet or fuchsia. Billings continued to fasten the range of tiny pearl buttons in back.

"Stand still now," she ordered again as Brooke fidgeted.

"Billings," Brooke said weakly, "I really think I'm going to be sick."

The housekeeper looked up at Brooke's reflection. Her face was pale, her eyes huge, made darker by the merest touch of slate-gray shadow. In Billings's staunch opinion, a bride was supposed to look ready to faint. "Nonsense," she said briskly. "Just a case of the flutters."

"Flutters," Brooke repeated, creasing her brow. "I never flutter. That's ridiculous."

The Englishwoman smiled fleetingly as Brooke straightened her shoulders. "Flutters, jitters, nerves—every woman born has them on her wedding day."

"Well, I don't," she claimed as her stomach muscles quivered.

Billings only sniffed as she finished her fastening. "There now, that's the last one."

"Thank God," Brooke muttered, heading for a chair before Billings caught her.

"No, you don't. You're not putting creases in that skirt."

"Billings, for heaven's sake—"

"A woman has to suffer now and again."

Brooke's opinion was a short four-letter word. Lifting a brow, Billings picked up a hairbrush from the vanity. "A fine way for a blushing bride to talk."

"I'm not a blushing bride." Brooke swept away before Billings could apply the brush. "I'm twenty-eight years old," she continued, pacing. "I must be crazy, I must be absolutely crazy. No sane woman agrees to marry a man in a fast-food restaurant."

"You're getting married in Ms. Thorton's garden," Billings corrected. "And it's quite a lovely day for it."

The practical tone caused Brooke to scowl. "And I should never have let her talk me into that, either."

"Hah!" The exclamation had Brooke's brows lifting. Billings gestured threateningly with the hairbrush. "Hah!" she said again, effectively closing Brooke's mouth. "No one talks you into anything. You're a hard-headed, stubborn, single-minded young woman, and you're shaking in your shoes because there's a hard-headed, stubborn, single-minded young man downstairs who's going to give you a run for your money."

"I certainly am not shaking in my shoes," Brooke corrected, insulted. Billings saw the faint pink flush rise to the pale cheeks.

"Scared to death."

Brooke stuck both fists on her hips. "I am most certainly not afraid of Parks Jones."

"Hah!" Billings repeated as she pulled over a footstool. Climbing on it, she began to draw the brush through Brooke's hair. "You'll probably stammer and quake when you take your vows, just like some silly girl who doesn't know her own mind."

"I've never stammered in my life." Enunciating each word precisely, Brooke glared at their twin reflections in the mirror. "And nothing makes me quake."

"We'll just see about that, won't we?" Rather pleased with herself, Billings arranged Brooke's mane of hair into a cunningly tumbled mass. In this, she secured a delicate clip of pale pink-and-white hibiscus. She had fussed that lily of the valley or rosebuds would have been more suitable, but secretly thought the exotic flowers were stunning.

"Now, where are those lovely pearl drops Ms. Thorton gave you?"

"Over there." Still fuming, Brooke pointed to the tiny jeweler's box that held Claire's gift.

They should have eloped as Parks had suggested, Brooke thought. What had made her think she wanted all this fuss and bother? What had made her think she wanted to get married in the first place? As her nerves started jumping again, she caught Billings's ironic stare. Brooke lifted her chin.

"Well, put them on," the housekeeper ordered, holding the pink-blushed pearls in her palm. "It was very clever of Mr. Jones to send you flowers to match them."

"If you like him so much, why don't you marry him?" Brooke muttered, fastening the earrings with fingers that refused to stop trembling.

"I suppose you'll do," Billings said briskly, swallowing a lump in her throat. "Even without a proper veil and train." She wanted badly to press a kiss to Brooke's cheek, but knew it would weaken both of them. "Come along, then," she said instead. "It's time."

I could still call it off, Brooke thought as she let Billings draw her down the hall. There's still time. No one can make me go through with this. The little skips of nerves in her stomach had increased to thumps. There's absolutely nothing that can make me walk out into that garden. What was the phrase? she wondered. Marry in haste, repent at leisure? This was certainly haste.

It had only been four days since Parks had asked her. Four days. Maybe the big mistake had been in telling Claire. Good God, she'd never seen anyone move so fast once they'd gotten the bit between their teeth. Brooke decided she must have been in a state of shock to have let Claire sweep her along with plans and arrangements. An intimate ceremony in her terraced garden, a champagne reception. *Elope?* Claire had brushed that aside with a wave of her hand. Elopements were for silly teenagers. And wouldn't a three-piece ensemble be lovely? Brooke had found herself caught up. And now she was just caught.

But no, Brooke corrected as she and Billings reached the foot of the stairs. All she had to do was turn around and head for the door. She could get into her car and just drive away. That was the coward's way. Straightening her shoulders, Brooke rejected it. She wouldn't run, she would simply walk outside and explain very calmly she had changed her mind. Yes, that's all it would take. *I'm very sorry,* she practiced mentally, *but I've decided not to get married after all.* She'd be very calm and very firm.

"Oh, Brooke, you look lovely." And there was Claire, dressed in powder-blue silk with the sheen of tears in her eyes.

"Claire, I—"

"Absolutely lovely. I wish you'd let me have them play the wedding march."

"No, I—"

"It doesn't matter, as long as you're happy." Claire pressed her cheek to Brooke's. "Isn't it silly, I feel just like a mother. Imagine having your first pangs of motherhood at my age."

"Oh, Claire."

"No, no, I'm not going to get sloppy and sentimental

and ruin my face." Sniffling, she drew away. "It's not every day I'm maid of honor."

"Claire, I want to—"

"They're waiting, Ms. Thorton."

"Yes, yes, of course." Giving Brooke's hand a quick squeeze, she went out on the terrace.

"Now you, Ms. Gordon." Brooke stood where she was, wondering if the coward's way wasn't basically sound. Billings put a firm hand on her back and pushed. Brooke found herself out on the terrace facing Parks.

He took her hand. He was firm as he brought hers to his lips. She noticed his eyes, smiling, sure. He was in a pearl-gray suit, more formal than anything she had seen him wear. But his eyes held that complete intensity she knew they had when he waited for a pitch. She found herself walking with him to the center of the terrace that was surrounded by flowers and the ornamental trees Claire loved.

Still time, Brooke thought as the minister began to speak in a calm, clear voice. But she couldn't open her mouth to stop what was already happening.

She'd remember the scent always. Jasmine and vanilla, and the sweet drift of baby roses. But she didn't see the flowers because her eyes were locked on Parks's. He was repeating the words the minister spoke, the traditional words spoken countless times by countless couples. But she heard them as if they were uttered for the first time.

Love, honor, cherish.

She felt the ring slip onto her finger. Felt, but again didn't see because she couldn't take her eyes from his. From the branches of a weeping cherry, a bird began to trill.

She heard her own voice, strong and assured, repeat the same promises. And her hand, with no trembling, placed the symbol of the promise on Parks's finger.

A pledge, a promise, a gift. Then their lips moved together, sealing it.

I was going to run, she remembered.

"I'd have caught you," Parks murmured against her mouth.

Astonished and annoyed, Brooke drew back. He was grinning at her, his hands still caught in her hair. To the confusion of the others in the quiet, fragrant garden, Brooke cursed then threw her arms around his neck and laughed.

"Hey." Snyder gave Parks a firm shove. "Give somebody else a chance."

Claire's idea of a small gathering was the epitome of a producer's understatement. Though Brooke didn't bother to count heads, she knew there were well over a hundred "absolutely essential guests." She found she didn't mind—the glitter was her gift to Claire. There was a bubbly fountain of champagne, a five-tiered pink-and-white cake and silver platters of food that for once Brooke had no interest in. Which turned out for the best, as she was swept from one person's arms to another, kissed, hugged and congratulated until it all became a blur of color and sound.

She met Parks's mother, a tiny, exquisite woman who kissed her cheek then burst into tears. His father crushed Brooke in a hug and murmured that now that Parks was married, he would stop the nonsense and come into the company. She found herself inheriting a family in a lump—a large, confusing family that didn't quite fit any of the imaginings of her youth. And through it all, she had barely more than glimpses of Parks as she was passed from cousin to cousin to be weighed, measured and discussed like a fascinating new acquisition.

"Leave the girl be a minute." A sturdy, pewter-haired woman swept the others aside with an imperious wave of her hand. "These Joneses are a silly bunch." She sighed, then summed Brooke up with one long look. "I'm your Aunt Lorraine," she said and extended her hand.

Brooke accepted the handshake, knowing instinctively the gesture was somehow more sincere and more intimate than all the kisses she had received. Then with a flash of insight, she knew. "The gold piece."

Lorraine smiled, pleased. "Told you about that, did he? Well, he's a good boy…more or less." A straight, no-nonsense brow lifted. "And he won't bully you, will he?"

With a grin, Brooke shook her head. "No, ma'am, he won't."

Lorraine nodded, giving Brooke's hand a quick pat. "Good. I'll expect a visit in six months. It takes a couple that long to work out the first kinks. Now, if I were you, I'd get my husband and sneak out of this rabble." With this advice, she strode away. Brooke had her first twinge of genuine kinship.

Even so, it seemed like hours before they could slip away. Brooke had intended to steal back upstairs and change, but Parks had seen his opportunity and had pulled her outside, bundled her into his car and driven off. Now he stopped the car in the driveway of the A-frame and sighed.

"We made it."

"It was rude," Brooke mused.

"Yeah."

"And very smart." Leaning over, she kissed him. "Especially since you managed to cop a bottle of champagne on the way."

"Quick hands," he explained as he stepped from the car.

Brooke chuckled, but felt a fresh ripple of unease as they walked up the path. Parks's hand was closed over hers. She could feel the slight, unfamiliar pressure of her wedding ring against her skin. "One problem," she began, pushing the feeling aside. "You dragged me out of there without my purse." She glanced at the door, then back at Parks. "No keys."

Parks reached in his pocket and drew out his own. A faint frown creased her brow as she remembered he had a key to the door now. A key to her life. Though he noticed her reaction, Parks said nothing, only slipping the key into the lock. It opened silently. He swept her up into his arms, and with her laughter, the subtle disharmony was forgotten.

"I hadn't realized you were such a traditionalist," Brooke murmured, nuzzling at his neck, "but…" She trailed off at the sound of high, sharp yapping. Astonished, she looked down to see a small brown dog with a black muzzle racing around Parks's feet, making occasional dives for his ankles. "What's that?" she managed.

"Your wedding present." With his toe, he nudged the puppy, sending him rolling over on his back. "Homely enough?"

Brooke stared down at the pushed-in mongrel face. "Oh, Parks," she whispered, close to tears. "You fool."

"E.J. should've dropped him off about an hour ago,

if he was on schedule. Guy at the pound thought I was crazy when I told him I wanted something down-to-the-ground homely."

"Oh, I love you!" Brooke squeezed his neck fiercely then wriggled out of his arms. In her satin wedding dress, she knelt on the floor to play with the puppy.

She looked young, Parks thought, too young, as she buried her face in the little dog's fur. Why would he constantly expose her vulnerabilities then be uncertain how to handle them? There was so much sweetness in her, and yet, was he somehow more comfortable with the vinegar she could serve him? It was the mix, Parks thought as he knelt to join her, the fascinating mix he couldn't resist.

"Our first child." Brooke chuckled when the puppy lay in exhausted slumber on the rug.

"He has your nose."

"And your feet," she retorted. "He's going to be enormous from the size of them."

"Maybe you can cast him in a few dog food commercials," he commented as he drew Brooke to her feet. Gently he kissed her cheek, then trailed his lips over her chin to the other one. He felt the sudden tremble of her breath on his skin. "Champagne's getting warm," he murmured.

"I'm not thirsty."

He was leading her slowly toward the stairs, still planting those soft, whispering kisses over her face on the journey, leaving her lips—her heating, seeking lips—subtly tormented. And they started to climb the stairs, without rush or hurry, while Parks began unfastening that long range of tiny buttons.

"How many are there?" he murmured against her mouth.

"Dozens," Brooke answered, loosening his tie as they reached the halfway point.

His fingers were nimble. Before they reached the door of the bedroom, he had the gown loosened to her waist. Brooke pushed the jacket from his shoulder, and with her teeth nipping at his neck, tugged his shirt from the waistband of his pants.

"Are you ever going to kiss me?" she demanded breathlessly.

"Mmm-hmm." But he only drove her mad by running his lips over her shoulder as he nudged the satin aside. Then he drew it from her, running his hands slowly down her body until the material was only a pool of white at her feet. He toyed with the bits of lace she wore, tiny, filmy wisps designed to torment men. And even as they tormented him, Parks fought for control. There was always that last struggle for control before he found he was lost in her.

Her fingers slid down his naked ribs to brush over his stomach before she found the hook to his trousers. She heard his quick, indrawn breath before his hands became more demanding. Needing, wanting, she pulled him with her onto the bed.

Why should there be such desperation when they were now so securely bound to each other? Though neither of them understood it, they both felt it. The urgency to touch, taste. To possess. Gentleness was abandoned while hungry, primitive passion took its place. The teasing kisses stopped with a hard, burning pressure of mouth on mouth. Her hands sought, as skillfully as his, to find weaknesses. Every moan brought a fresh thrill of arousal, each sigh an increase of tortuous desire until neither knew if the sounds were from pleasure or desperation. And both refused to succumb to the fire.

He found her breast taut and firm. Greedily, his mouth sought it, sending a tearing thread of delight into the core of her. Even as she moaned in surrender, her hands pressed him closer, her body moving sinuously under his until he was lost in the taste of her.

Flesh heated against flesh. The pace quickened. Faster, faster, until they were breathless and clinging but still not ready to yield. She ran her hands over his damp back, over the roping of muscles that accented his superior strength. But physical strength meant nothing in the inescapable quicksand of passion. They were both trapped in it, both equally incapable of freeing themselves.

With sudden strength, she shifted, so that they were tangled together, side by side. Her mouth fastened on his, devouring as eagerly as she was devoured, taking as mindlessly as she was taken. Her hair fell over them, curtaining their faces so that Parks couldn't breathe without breathing her. If he had been capable of thought, he might have imagined himself absorbed by her. But there was no thought for either of them, and the need had grown too great to be resisted.

She went willingly when he shifted her, drawing his mouth down to hers even as he entered her with something close to violence. Then there was only speed and heat, driving them beyond everything but each other.

"Should I need you more each time?" Brooke wondered aloud.

"Mmm." Parks didn't want to move from the warm

comfort of her body. It yielded under his, pressed deep into the mattress. "Just don't stop."

It was dusk. The light filtering through the windows was soft—and soon it would be night. Her wedding night. Yet she still felt only like a lover. How would it be to feel like a wife? Lifting her hand, she stared at the band on her finger. It was encrusted with diamonds and sapphires that glowed softly in the room's twilight. "I don't want it to be different tomorrow," she thought aloud. "I don't want it to change."

Parks raised his head. "Everything changes. You'll get mad if I use all the hot water for my shower. I'll get mad if you've drunk the last of the coffee."

Brooke laughed. "You have a way of simplifying things."

"Those are the nuts and bolts of a relationship, Mrs. Jones," he claimed and kissed her.

The eyes that had begun to close for the kiss opened wide. "Jones," she repeated. "I'd forgotten about that part of it." She considered for a minute. "It makes me think of your mother...though of course she was very nice."

Parks gave a muffled chuckle. "Don't worry. Just remember she lives three hundred miles away."

Brooke rolled over until she lay on top of him. "You have a very nice family."

"Yeah, and we don't want to get tangled up with them any more than we have to."

"Well..." Brooke laid her head on his chest. "No. At least not too soon," she added, thinking of his aunt. She relaxed again as he began to lazily stroke her hair. "Parks?"

"Hmm?"

"I'm glad we decided to come here instead of flying off somewhere."

"We'll go to Maui for a couple of weeks around Christmas. I want you to see my place there."

Brooke thought of her schedule if she decided to take Claire up on the feature for cable. Somehow or other, she'd managed to get the two weeks. "I love you."

His hand stopped a moment, then pressed her closer. They were three words she didn't say often. "Did I tell you how beautiful you looked when Billings shoved you out on the terrace?"

Brooke's head shot up. "You saw that?"

Grinning he traced her ear with his fingertip. "Funny, I didn't expect you to be as terrified as I was."

Brooke regarded him a moment, then a smile curved on her lips. "Were you really?"

"A half hour before the wedding, I'd run up a list of all the reasons why we should call it off."

She lifted a brow. "Were there many?"

"I lost count," he told her, ignoring the narrowing of her eyes. "I could only think of one good reason to go through with it."

"Oh, really?" Her chin came up as she tossed her head. "And what was that?"

"I love you."

Brooke dropped her forehead onto his. "That's it, huh?"

"The only one I could think of." He slid a hand down to her hip. "Though one or two others are beginning to occur to me."

"Mmm. Like it being good for the campaign." She began to nuzzle, just behind his ear.

"Oh, sure. That's top on my list." He groaned when

the first shudder rippled through him. "Right next to having somebody to sort my socks."

"You can forget that one," Brooke murmured, moving down to his shoulder. "But there's always having an in with the director when you do that part for cable."

"Haven't decided to do it." His legs tangled with hers as they altered positions. "Have you?"

"Not yet." Her thoughts began to drift as he cupped her breast. "But you should."

"Why?"

Lazily, her eyes opened to look into his. "I shouldn't tell you."

Intrigued, he propped himself on his elbow and toyed with her hair. "Why not?"

She sighed a little, while managing to convey a shrug. "The last thing you need is someone feeding your ego."

"Go ahead." He kissed her nose. "I can take it."

"Damn it, Parks, you're good."

He stopped in the action of twining her hair around his finger and stared at her. "What did you say?"

Brooke shifted again. "Well, I don't mean you can *act*," she began. "Don't start getting delusions."

He grinned, enjoying her ironic lift of brow. "That's more like it."

"You have good camera presence," she went on. "Do you have any idea how many big stars stay big simply by playing themselves?" Parks grunted, more interested in the curve of her shoulder. "You know how to play yourself, Parks," Brooke persisted, drawing him back for a moment. "And if you were to stick to parts, at least for a while, that suited you…well, when you really are ready to retire from baseball you could walk right into a movie career."

He started to laugh, then stopped when he saw the look in her eyes. "You're not joking."

Brooke stared at him, then let out a long breath. "I'm really going to hate myself when I've got to deal with you as a director in a couple of weeks, but you're very, very good, and you should think about it. And if you get a star complex when I tell you to run through some business on camera a half a dozen times, I'll…"

"What?" he challenged.

"Something," Brooke said ominously. "Something despicable."

He gave her a wicked grin. "Promise?"

Since she couldn't stop the laugh, she rolled him over forcibly so that she was lying across him again. "Yeah. And now I'm going to make love to you until your bones dissolve."

"Is this in my contract?" he demanded.

"You better believe it."

Chapter 12

Though it was November, Los Angeles was suffering from a heat wave that fried tempers and melted patience. Brooke's was no exception. She and Parks had had ten long, isolated days before she had begun work again—but they hadn't been trouble-free. Nothing's trouble-free, Brooke reminded herself as she knotted her blouse beneath her breasts. What fool thought a honeymoon would be? She had, she admitted ruefully as the camera crane was unloaded. But then how much thought had she really given to adjustments, to changes and, as Parks had termed it, the nuts-and-bolts business that made up a marriage?

She had accepted his name, and though she would keep her own professionally, it was Brooke Jones that she would sign to all legal documents. He had given up his apartment and moved into her house. She had his name, he had her key. Why did she feel she was tallying a balance sheet? Frustrated, Brooke wiped her forearm over her brow.

Was that what marriage was, she wondered, a series of checks and balances? With her marriage barely three weeks old, she should be blissfully happy, glowing. Instead, Brooke felt frustrated, annoyed and unsettled—perhaps more unsettled because she knew Parks was no more blissfully happy than she.

With a shake of her head, she told herself to put it aside. Bringing her personal problems to work wouldn't solve them—and more than likely it would make them worse, since she was directing Parks.

"Let's go up, E.J., I want to see the angle." Sitting in the basket beside him, she gave the crane operator a nod to take them up.

Below them, the beach spread gold. The surf kicked up, white and frothy, catching the glint of the sun and rainbowing through the lens. She thought she could feel the heat steam from the metal casing of the camera. "All right, I'll want a wide shot when he starts, then zoom in, but not too tight. At this angle, we'll get a good profile of the horse. The palomino's a nice contrast with the jeans. Set the speed. I want it slow enough so they see every muscle ripple."

"On Parks or the horse?" E.J. asked with a grin.

"On both," Brooke answered curtly, nodding to be brought down. Wiping her palms on the seat of her pants, she strode over to where Parks waited. He wore nothing but snug, low-slung de Marco jeans. "We're ready for you."

"All right." Parks gave her a long, steady look as he hooked his thumbs in his front pockets. He wasn't sure why he was dissatisfied, or why he felt the need to annoy her. The friction had been growing between them for the past few days, building and shifting like some electric storm. But there'd been no boom of thunder, no slash of lightning to release the pressure. "What do you want?"

"You've seen the script," she reminded him.

"Aren't you going to give me my motivation?"

"Don't be a smart aleck, Parks," she snapped. "It's too damn hot."

"Just want to make sure I've got the right mood so you won't make me do it a half dozen times."

Temper flared in her eyes and was forcefully suppressed. She wouldn't let him taunt her into a public sniping. "You'll do it two dozen times if I feel it's necessary," she said as calmly as possible. "Now get on the horse, gallop straight down the beach in the shallows. And enjoy it."

"Is that an order?" he murmured, deceptively mild.

"It's a direction," she returned evenly. "I'm the director, you're the talent. Got it?"

"Yeah, I got it." Catching her close, he crushed her mouth with his. He felt the dampness of her blouse under his palm, the angry rigidity of her body and the yielding softness of her breasts. Why was he angry? he wondered even as his temper inched higher. Why did he feel he was dragging her close and shoving her away at the same time? "Got that?" he demanded as he turned and swung onto the horse.

She glared at him, a half-naked man astride a golden horse, as he smiled down at her with the cocky assurance she both loved and detested. Making him pay for that small victory would be a pleasure. Turning on her heel, Brooke strode back to her crew. "Take one," she ordered, then waited, turning ideas for vengeance over in her mind. She took the bullhorn her assistant handed her. "Places!" Parks led the palomino into the surf. Brooke stared at him, forcing herself to put her personal feelings on hold while she thought and felt and saw only as a director. "Roll film, and…action!"

He's magnificent, Brooke thought with a twin surge of pride and irritation. He took the horse into an easy, rolling gallop, kicking up the surf so that the streams of water rose high. Beads glistened on his skin, darkly tanned so that he and the palomino merged into one golden form. Parks's hair and the horse's mane lifted in the wind the motion caused. Strength, an elegance of movement and the simplicity of two beautiful animals. Brooke didn't need special effects to show her how it would look in slow motion.

"Cut. E.J.?"

"Fantastic," he called down. "Sales of de Marco jeans just went up ten percent."

"Let's make sure." Pulling her damp shirt away from her back, Brooke walked to where Parks waited, astride the horse. It had been fantastic, she mused, but not perfect. Spotting her, Parks broke off his conversation with the palomino's trainer.

"Well?"

"It looked pretty good. Let's do it again."

"Why?"

Ignoring the question, she absently patted the gelding's smooth throat. "I want you to look down the beach as you ride…all the way down." She didn't want that comfortable, freewheeling sexuality this time, but a dash of aloofness, the solitary-man appeal flavored with the sensuality any female over twelve would recognize.

He shifted in the saddle, his eyes never leaving hers. "Why?"

"Ride the horse, Parks," she countered. "Let me sell the jeans."

Very slowly, he dismounted. The trainer quickly remembered something he had to do somewhere else. Behind them, the crew became very busy. Parks held the reins in one hand while he and Brooke measured each other. "Ever considered asking?" he said quietly.

"Ever considered following directions?" she tossed back.

He felt the salt spray drying on his skin. "Too bad you've never been a team player, Brooke."

"This isn't a ball game," she retorted, firing up. "We all have our jobs to do. Yours is whatever I tell you it is."

The flash of anger in his eyes suited her mood. She wanted a fight, a rip-roaring screamer that would tear through the tension of their last few days together. Planting her feet, Brooke prepared to attack and defend.

"No," he said with a sudden deadly calm that put her at a disadvantage, "it's not. My job is to endorse de Marco."

"And that's what I'm telling you to do." She forced herself to match his tone, though she badly wanted to shout. "If you want to be a prima donna, wait until after we wrap. Take your complaints and talk to your agent."

His hand snaked out to grab her arm before she could stalk away. "I'm talking to my wife."

Heart hammering in her throat, she looked down at the hand that held her. "Your director," Brooke icily corrected, meeting his eyes. "My crew's hot, Parks. I'd like to finish this before someone faints from heat exhaustion."

His grip tightened. But he saw that her face was flushed from the heat and damp with sweat. "We're not finished with this," he told her as he released her arm. "This time, you're going to take a good hard look at the rules." Swinging onto the horse, Parks rode away before she could think of an appropriate comment.

Brooke frowned after him as she stalked back to the crane. "Take two."

He could have given no logical, succinct explanation for his anger. Parks only knew he was furious. He had only one motivation as he stalked down the corridors to Brooke's office—to have it out with her. He wasn't certain what *it* was, but he would have had it out with her on location if she hadn't been gone before he'd realized it. Though he wasn't thrilled about coming to terms with her in her office, he'd had plenty of experience in meeting a challenge on the opposition's home field. All it meant was that he would take the offensive first.

Brushing by her secretary without a word, Parks pushed open the door to Brooke's office. Empty.

"I'm sorry, Mr. Jones." The secretary hurried up to him, warned by the dangerous light in his eye. "Ms. Gordon... Mrs. Jones isn't in."

"Where?" Parks demanded curtly.

"I— Perhaps Ms. Thorton's office. If you'll wait, I'll check for you..." But he was already heading out with a long, determined stride that had her chewing on the nail of her forefinger. It looked like Brooke was in trouble. And some people have all the luck, the secretary mused before she went back to her desk.

In less than five minutes, Parks walked by the twins in Claire's outer office and opened her door without knocking. "Where's Brooke?" he demanded, not bothering to greet Claire or his agent.

"Good afternoon, Parks," Claire said easily. "Tea?" She continued to pour Lee's cup as if a furious man weren't at that moment glaring at her.

Parks gave the classic little tea service a brief glance. "I'm looking for Brooke."

"You've missed her, I'm afraid." Claire sipped her tea, then offered Lee a plate of macaroons. "She was in and out a half an hour ago. Would you like a cookie, Parks?"

"No…" He managed to get a tenuous hold on his manners. "Thanks. Where did she go?"

Claire nibbled on a macaroon, then dusted her fingers on a pink linen napkin. "Didn't she say she was going home, Lee?"

"Yep. And she wasn't in any better mood than Parks is." He sent his client a bland smile before he wolfed down a cookie.

"No, she wasn't, was she?" Claire folded her hands on her lap. "Tell me, dear, are you two having a tiff?"

"No, we're not having a tiff," Parks muttered, not certain what they were having. It occurred to him suddenly how cozy his agent and his producer were on the small two-cushioned sofa. "What are you two having?" he countered.

"Tea." Claire smiled her dry smile.

"Why don't you have a seat and cool off?" Lee invited. "You look like you've just played nine full innings."

"We were shooting on the beach," Parks murmured. Did Lee Dutton have his arm around Claire Thorton, or was he seeing things?

"It went well?" Claire asked, noting his expression, amused by the reason for it.

"Apparently Brooke was satisfied."

"Apparently," Claire murmured, then shot him a level stare. "When are you and Brooke going to relax and enjoy yourselves?"

Parks's speculative look changed to a frown. "What do you mean?"

"I mean I've never in my life seen two people spend so much time poking at each other."

"Is that what you call it?" Parks muttered, stuffing his hands in his pockets.

"For want of a better term." Claire set her teacup carefully in its saucer. "I realize, of course, that the power game is a founding part of your relationship, and provides its own stimulation, but don't you think it's time you became a family as well as opponents?" Keeping her eyes level, Claire settled into the crook of Lee's arm.

Parks stared at her for nearly a full minute. Power game, he repeated silently. Well, yes, it was an intricate part of what they were to each other. They had both looked for strength, challenge, and would have walked the other way if they hadn't found the combination. But as for the rest—a family... Was that what was niggling at the back of his mind?

Wasn't it true that he couldn't resolve himself to the fact that they were living in *her* house, surrounded by *her* things? He still felt uncomfortably like a guest. Even as fresh annoyance grew, he remembered their discussing a trip to Maui. He had told Brooke he wanted her to see *his* place. But... Even as he searched for an excuse, he knew he wouldn't find one.

Turning, Parks paced to the window and scowled out. "I don't think Brooke's ready for a family relationship." The brief, undignified answer Claire gave him had Parks turning back, half-amused. Lee merely reached forward and snatched another cookie.

"She's looked for one all of her life. If you know anything about her, you know that." Suddenly angry, Claire rose. "Is it possible for two people to live together and not understand the other's needs, the other's hurts? How much has she told you about how she grew up?"

"Barely anything," Parks began. "She—"

"How much did you ask?" Claire demanded. "Don't tell me you didn't want to pry," she said quickly, cutting him off. "You're her husband, it's your business to pry. You can be civilized enough to respect her privacy and never touch on what she really needs from you."

"I know that she needs to know she can make her own place," he tossed back. "I know that it doesn't matter if it's a chipped cup or a Hepplewhite table, as long as it's hers."

"Things!" Claire raged. "Yes, she needs things. God knows she never had them as a child, and the child in her still hurts because of it. But they're only a symbol of what she really wants. Brooke walked in here, an eighteen-year-old adult with nothing more than a few dollars in her pocket and a lot of guts. Someone she thought she loved had taken everything from her, and she wasn't ever going to let that happen again." Her mouth tightened, her eyes frosting over at the memory. "It's your job to show her that it won't."

"I don't want to *take* anything from her," Parks retorted heatedly.

"But you want her to give," Claire shot back.

"Of course I do, damn it. I love her."

"Then listen to me. Brooke's struggled all her life to have something of her own, to have some*one* of her own. She has the things. She's earned them. If you want to share them with her, share her life, you'd better have something pretty special to offer in return. Love isn't enough."

"What is?" Parks tossed back, furious at being lectured by someone half his size.

"You'd better figure it out."

Parks measured her another moment. "All right," he said coolly and left without another word.

Lee rose from the sofa to stand beside Claire. Her pampered skin was flushed with temper, her faded blue eyes icy. "You know," he mused as he studied her, "I've never seen you in full gear before."

"I don't often lose my temper." Claire fluffed at her hair. "Young people," she stated, as if the two words explained everything.

"Yeah." Taking her shoulders, he turned her to face him. "They don't know a good thing when they've got it." His puckish round face creased with a grin. "How'd you like to spend the rest of your life with an overweight theatrical agent?"

The ice melted from Claire's eyes, but the flush remained. "Lee, I thought you'd never ask."

Parks was fighting his way through L.A. traffic when he heard the first report of the fire. His anger at Claire, his frustration that she had spoken no more than the truth, was switched off instantly as he caught the tail end of a news broadcast reporting brush fires in Liberty Canyon—less than an hour away from Brooke's isolated

A-frame. No, there wasn't anger now, but a sick sense of fear that had his palms slipping damply on the wheel.

Had she gone home? he wondered frantically as he sped around a cruising Ferrari. Would she have the television set on, the radio, or would she be in one of her solitary moods? After a hot, enervating day on location, she would often simply shower and sleep for an hour. Recharging, he had called it jokingly. Now the idea terrified him.

As he drove higher, he began to scent the fragrance of dry leaves burning. A faint haze of smoke rose into the sky to the east. Thirty minutes, Parks estimated as he pressed his foot on the accelerator. Forty, if they were lucky. It would take him nearly half that to get there.

There was no wind to hurry the fire along, he reminded himself, fighting to keep calm. They weren't calling it a firestorm...not yet. Brooke was probably already packing up her most important things—he might even meet her on the road on her way down. Any minute she could come zipping around one of the curves in the road leading back down the mountain. They'd get a hotel, talk this business out. Claire was right, he hadn't dug deep enough. Once he had promised himself he would learn the whole woman. It was long past time to make good on the promise.

Parks could almost taste the smoke now, the thick black smoke that led the way for the fire. He saw a pack of small animals—rabbits, raccoons, a fox—race down the road on the other side in their migration to lower elevation. It was close, then, he thought, too close. Why in God's name wasn't she speeding down the road toward safety? He drove the last fifteen miles in a blur of speed and fear.

Parks only took the time to register that Brooke's car was in the driveway before he was out of his own and racing toward the house. She had to be asleep, he decided, not to know the fire was closing in. Even without the radio on, the haze of smoke and smell of burning brought the news. He burst through the front door, calling her name.

The house was silent. There was no sound of hurried movement, of drawers slamming, nothing to indicate frantic packing. Parks was racing up the stairs two at a time when he heard the dog barking. He swore, but kept going. He'd forgotten the dog completely in his fear for Brooke. And the fear grew again when he saw the bed was empty. He was racing through the second floor, still calling, when a movement outside the window caught his eye.

Rain? he thought, pausing long enough to stare. No, water—but not rain. Going to the window, he saw her. Relief was immediately overlapped by irritation, and irritation by fury. What the hell was she doing standing in the backyard watering the lawn when the smoke was thick enough to block out the trees to the east?

With a quick jerk, he pulled up the window and shouted through the screen. "Brooke, what the hell are you doing?"

She jolted, then looked up. "Oh, Parks, thank God! Come down and help, there isn't much time. Close the window!" she shouted. "The sparks could get inside. *Hurry!*"

He moved, and moved quickly, intending on shaking her until she rattled then dragging her to the car. Halfway down the stairs, he leaped over the banister and headed to the back door. "What the hell are you doing?" he demanded again. Then, instead of shaking her, he found he was holding her tight enough to make her bones crack. If he hadn't heard the radio, if she'd been sleeping… *If.* A thousand ifs ran through his mind as his mouth came down frantically on hers.

It was the sudden howl of wind that brought him back. A sudden ripple of terror ran down his spine. The wind would speed the fire and feed the flames. Brush fire became firestorm. "We've got to get out of here."

He had dragged her nearly two feet before he realized she was fighting him. "No!" With a show of pure strength, Brooke broke away from him then picked up the hose she had dropped.

"Damn it, Brooke, we can't have more than fifteen minutes."

He took her arm again and again she broke away. "I know how much time there is." She aimed the spray of water toward the house again, soaking the wood. The sound drummed in the air over the growing fierceness of the wind.

For the first time, Parks noticed that she was wet and filthy and wearing only a bathrobe. She'd just been stepping from the shower when the special report on the radio had warned her of the approaching fire. He looked at the dirt and grass stains on the silk of her robe and realized what she'd been doing. The land around the house had been cleared. She'd done it with her hands. He saw the scratches and dried blood on them and on her legs and ankles. Now, with the puppy barking frantically around her, she was wetting down the house.

"Are you crazy!" he demanded as the first flash of admiration was drowned in fresh fury. Parks grabbed her arm again, ripping the shoulder seam of her robe. "Do you know what a firestorm is?"

"I know what it is." Her elbow connected with his ribs as she struggled away. "If you won't help, stay out of my way. Half the house hasn't been wetted down yet."

"You're getting out of here." Parks pulled the hose out of her hand and started dragging her. "If I have to knock you unconscious."

Brooke shocked them both by planting her fist solidly on his jaw. The blow was enough to free her so that she stumbled back, losing her balance and landing on all fours.

"I said stay out of my way," she hissed, then choked as the smoke clogged her lungs.

Parks dragged her to her feet. His eyes were as wild with fear and fury as hers. "You idiot, are you going to fight a firestorm with a garden hose? It's wood and glass!" he shouted as he shook her. "Wood and glass," he repeated, coughing as he threw a hand toward the house. "Is it worth dying for?"

"It's worth fighting for!" she shouted back against smoke and wind as the tears started to flow. "I won't give in to the fire, I *won't!*" She began fighting him again, more desperately than before.

"Damn it, Brooke, stop!" He took her shoulders until his fingers bit into her flesh. "There isn't time."

"The fire won't have it. Not our home, don't you understand?" Her voice rose, not in hysteria but in fierce determination. "Not *our* home."

Parks stopped shaking her, again finding that his arms had wrapped around to hold her close. Understanding flooded through him, and in its wake came every emotion he'd ever experienced. Is that what Claire had meant, he wondered, when she'd said love wasn't enough? Love was enough for beginning, but sustaining took every feeling a human being was capable of. *Our home,* she had said. And with the two words Brooke had cemented everything.

He drew her away. The tears were streaming, her breath was labored. Her eyes were rimmed with red but steady. He knew he had never felt more for another, and never would. And suddenly he knew that questions and answers weren't necessary for him to know the whole woman. Without speaking, he let her go and picked up the hose himself. Brooke stayed where she was while he turned the water onto the house. With the back of her wrist, she wiped the stinging tears from her face.

"Parks..."

He turned, smiling the grim gladiator smile. "It's worth fighting for." Brooke let out a shuddering sigh as she closed her hand over his. "We'll need towels to breathe through, a couple of blankets. Get them while I hose down the rest of the house."

It seemed like hours passed while they worked together, soaking the wood and each other, the dog, again and again while the smoke grew thicker. The wind screamed, threatening to rip the blanket Parks had tossed over her out of her hands. The heat, Brooke thought. She wouldn't be able to bear the heat. But the flames still held off. There were moments she almost believed the fire would veer away, then she would be choking on the smoke and taking her turn with the hose until she couldn't think at all. There was only one goal—to save the house she'd shared with Parks— the symbol of everything she had ever needed. Home, family, love.

With the towels pressed to their faces, they worked their way around and around the house, soaking the roof, the sides, all the surfaces the heat seemed to dry again so quickly. They no longer spoke, but worked systematically. Two pairs of arms, two sets of legs, working with one mind—to protect what was theirs.

Parks saw the flames first, and was almost too awed to move. It wasn't a furnace, he thought, or an oven. It was hell. And it was racing toward them. Great, greedy towers of fire belched out of the main body like spears. And in the midst of unbearable heat, he felt the icy sweat of human fear.

"No more." In a quick move, he grabbed Brooke's arm and scooped up the puppy.

"What are you doing? We can't leave now." Stumbling and choking, Brooke fought to free herself.

"If we don't leave now, we could be dead." He pushed Brooke into his car and shoved the puppy into her arms. "Damn it, Brooke, we've done all we can." His hands were slick with sweat as he turned the key. "Nothing you can buy is worth dying for."

"You don't understand!" With the back of her hand she smeared grime and tears together on her face. "Everything—everything I have is back there. I can't let the fire take it all—everything that means anything to me."

"Everything," he repeated in a murmur. Parks stopped the car to stare at her with red-rimmed, stinging eyes. "All right, if that's how you feel, I'll go back and do what I can." His voice was curiously flat and emotionless. "But, by God, you stay here. I won't risk you."

Before she could take in what he'd said or what he was doing, he was gone. For a moment, the hysteria had complete control. She trembled with it, unable to move or think. The fire was going to take her home, all her possessions. She'd be left with nothing, just as she had been so many times before. How could she face it again after all the years of struggling, of work, of wanting?

The puppy squirmed in her arms and whimpered. Blankly, Brooke stared down at him. What was she doing sitting there when her house was in danger? She had to go back, go back and save... Parks.

Fear froze her, then had her springing from the car and racing through the smoke. She'd sent him back—he'd gone back for her. For what? she thought desperately. What was she trying to save? Wood and glass—that's what he'd called it. It was nothing more. He was her home, the real home she'd searched for all her life. She shouted for him, sobbing as the smoke blocked everything from view.

She could hear the fire—or the wind. Brooke was no longer certain one was separate from the other. All that was clear now was that if she lost him now, she truly lost everything. So she shouted his name again and again, fighting her way through the smoke to get to him.

For an instant she could no longer breathe, no longer be certain where she was or where to run. An image flashed through her mind, one of herself as a young girl approaching a small two-story house where she would spend a year of her life. She couldn't remember the names of the people who would be her parents for those twelve months, only that sense of disorientation and loneliness. She'd always felt as lonely going in as she had coming out. She'd always been separate, always an outsider, until she'd met Parks.

She saw him racing back to her, misted through the

curtain of smoke. Before she could separate one image from another, she was in his arms.

"What happened?" he demanded. "I heard you shouting, I thought—" He buried his face against her neck a moment as the fear ebbed. "Damn it, Brooke, I told you to stay in the car."

"Not without you. Please, let's go." She was dragging on his arm, pulling him back down the road toward the car.

"The house—"

"Means nothing," she said fiercely. "Nothing does without you." Before he could react, Brooke was climbing into the driver's seat herself. The moment Parks was beside her, she started down the twisting road.

After nearly a mile, the smoke thinned. It was then Brooke felt the reaction set in with shudders and fresh tears. Pulling off the road, she laid her head on the steering wheel and wept.

"Brooke." Gently, he brushed a hand over her wet, tangled hair. "I'm sorry. I know the house was important to you. We don't know yet that it's gone or beyond repair. We can—"

"Damn the house!" Lifting her head, she looked at him with eyes that were both angry and desolate. "I must've been crazy to act that way. To send you back there when…" Trailing off, she swore and slammed out of the car. Slowly, Parks got out and followed her.

"Brooke."

"You're the most important thing in my life." She turned to him then, taking deep breaths to keep the tears back. "I don't expect you to believe that after the way I behaved, but it's true. I couldn't let go of the house, the things, because I'd waited so long to have them. I needed the identity they gave me." Because the words were painful, she swallowed. "For so long everything I had was only mine on loan. All I could think of was that if I didn't keep that house, those things, I'd be lost again. I don't expect you to understand—"

"I will understand." He took her face in his hands. "If you'll let me."

She let out a long, shuddering breath. "I never belonged anywhere, to anyone. Ever. It makes you afraid to trust. I always told myself that there'd be a day when I'd have my own things, my own place—I wouldn't have to share them, I wouldn't have to ask. It was something I promised myself because I couldn't have survived without that one hope. I forgot to let go of that when I didn't need it anymore."

"Maybe." He stroked a thumb over her cheek. "Or maybe you had without realizing it. Back there, you called it *our* home."

"Parks." She reached up to place her hands on him. "I don't care if the house is gone, if everything in it's gone. I have everything I need, everything I love, right here in my hands."

They were wet, filthy, exhausted. Alive. Parks looked at her blackened face and matted hair, the red-rimmed eyes. She'd never looked more beautiful to him. Throats raw from smoke, eyes stinging, he reached for her. Together, they fell to the grass.

Brooke was laughing and weeping as he kissed her. Her face was streaked with soot and tears, but his lips raced wildly over it. Passion met passion. Bruises were unfelt as they touched each other while a need, as volatile as the fire they had challenged, raged through them. When the tatters of her robe were gone, his sodden clothes joined it, they lay tangled, naked on the grass. Again and again, their mouths clung, drawing the strength and victory of the moment from each other, climbing beyond the smoke and stench of the fire left behind to a clean, bright world.

She knew she had never been so aware, so stunningly alive. Her body seemed to hum from a thousand pulses that grew more erratic as he touched her. With her arms tight around him, his body pressed against hers, she felt the sensation of absolute trust. He would protect, she would defend, against any outside forces that threatened. During the fire, they had ceased to be a man and a woman. They had become a unit. Somewhere beneath the swirling passion, Brooke felt peace. She had found her own.

They made love while the smoke broke into mists above their heads. And when they were spent, they clung still, unwilling to break the unity so newly discovered.

"You've hurt yourself," Parks murmured, touching a bruise on her shoulder.

"I don't feel hurt." She buried her lips at his throat and knew she would never forget the smell of smoke and ash and loving. "I hit you."

"Yeah, I noticed."

Hearing the grin in his voice, she closed her eyes. "You were only thinking of me. I'm sorry."

"Now you're thinking of us." He pressed his lips to her temple. "I'm glad."

"We won," she whispered.

Parks lifted his head to look down at her. Taking his thumb, he rubbed a streak of soot from her skin. It was the color of her eyes, he thought, seeing it on his own flesh. "We won, Brooke."

"Everything."

His lips curved before he brought them down to hers. "Everything."

She cradled his head on her shoulder, gently stroking his hair. Tiny pieces of ash continued to float above her like memories. "I said once I didn't want anything to change... I was afraid to let it change. I was wrong." Closing her eyes, she let herself absorb his closeness. "It's not quite the same now."

"Better," he murmured. "It makes a difference. It'll always make a difference."

She sighed, knowing the contentment she had always searched for was irrevocably bound up in one man, one love. "But we'll still play the game, won't we?"

This time when he lifted his head, he grinned. Brooke's lips curved in response. "By our own rules."

* * * * *

SECOND NATURE

To Deb Horm, for the mutual memories

Prologue

...with the moon full and white and cold. He saw the shadows shift and shiver like living things over the ice-crusted snow. Black on white. Black sky, white moon, black shadows, white snow. As far as he could see there was nothing else. There was such emptiness, an absence of color, the only sound the whistling moan of wind through naked trees. But he knew he wasn't alone, that there was no safety in the black or the white. Through his frozen heart moved a trickle of hot fear. His breath, labored, almost spent, puffed out in small white clouds. Over the frosted ground fell a black shadow. There was no place left to run.

Hunter drew on his cigarette, then stared at the words on the terminal through a haze of smoke. Michael Trent was dead. Hunter had created him, molded him exclusively for that cold, pitiful death under a full moon. He felt a sense of accomplishment rather than remorse for destroying the man he knew more intimately than he knew himself.

He'd end the chapter there, however, leaving the details of Michael's murder to the reader's imagination. The mood was set, secrets hinted at, doom tangible but unexplained. He knew his habit of doing just that both frustrated and fascinated his following. Since that was precisely his purpose, he was pleased. He often wasn't.

He created the terrifying, the breathtaking, the unspeakable. Hunter explored the darkest nightmares of the human mind and, with cool precision, made them tangible. He made the impossible plausible and the uncanny commonplace. The commonplace he would often turn into something chilling. He used words the way an artist used a palette and he fabricated stories of such color and simplicity a reader was drawn in from the first page.

His business was horror, and he was phenomenally successful.

For five years he'd been considered the master of his particular game. He'd had six runaway bestsellers, four of which he'd transposed into screenplays for feature films. The critics raved, sales soared, letters poured in from fans all over the world. Hunter couldn't have cared less. He wrote for himself first, because the telling of a story was what he did best. If he entertained with his writing, he was satisfied. But whatever reaction the critics and the readers had, he'd still have written. He had his work; he had his privacy. These were the two vital things in his life.

He didn't consider himself a recluse; he didn't consider himself unsociable. He simply lived his life exactly as he chose. He'd done the same thing six years before…before the fame, success and large advances.

If someone had asked him if having a string of best-sellers had changed his life, he'd have answered, why should it? He'd been a writer before *The Devil's Due* had shot to number one on the *New York Times* list. He was a writer now. If he'd wanted his life to change, he'd have become a plumber.

Some said his lifestyle was calculated—that he created the image of an eccentric for effect. Good promotion. Some said he raised wolves. Some said he didn't exist at all but was a clever product of a publisher's imagination. But Hunter Brown had a fine disregard for what anyone said. Invariably, he listened only to what he wanted to hear, saw only what he chose to see and remembered everything.

After pressing a series of buttons on his word processor, he set up for the next chapter. The next chapter, the next word, the next book, was of much more importance to him than any speculative article he might read.

He'd worked for six hours that day, and he thought he was good for at least two more. The story was flowing out of him like ice water: cold and clear.

The hands that played the keys of the machine were beautiful—tanned, lean, long-fingered and wide-palmed. One might have looked at them and thought they would compose concertos or epic poems. What they composed were dark dreams and monsters—not the dripping-fanged, scaly-skinned variety, but monsters real enough to make the flesh crawl. He always included enough realism, enough of the everyday, in his stories to make the horror commonplace and all too plausible. There was a creature lurking in the dark closet of his work, and that creature was the private fear of every man. He found it, always. Then, inch by inch, he opened the closet door.

Half-forgotten, the cigarette smoldered in the overflowing ashtray at his elbow. He smoked too much. It was perhaps the only outward sign of the pressure he put on himself, a pressure he'd have tolerated from no one else. He wanted this book finished by the end of the month, his self-imposed deadline. In one of his rare impulses, he'd agreed to speak at a writers' conference in Flagstaff the first week of June.

It wasn't often he agreed to public appearances, and when he did it was never at a large, publicized event. This particular conference would boast no more than two hundred published and aspiring writers. He'd give his workshop, answer questions, then go home. There would be no speaker's fee.

That year alone, Hunter had summarily turned down offers from some of the most prestigious organizations in the publishing business. Prestige didn't interest him, but he considered, in his odd way, the contribution to the Central Arizona Writers' Guild a matter of paying his dues. Hunter had always understood that nothing was free.

It was late afternoon when the dog lying at his feet lifted his head. The dog was lean, with a shining gray coat and the narrow, intelligent look of a wolf.

"Is it time, Santanas?" With a gentleness the hand appeared made for, Hunter reached down to stroke the dog's head. Satisfied, but already deciding that he'd work late that evening, he turned off his word processor.

Hunter stepped out of the chaos of his office into the tidy living room with its tall, many-paned windows and lofted ceiling. It smelled of vanilla and daisies. Large and sleek, the dog padded alongside him.

After pushing open the doors that led to a terra-cotta patio, he looked into the thick surrounding woods. They shut him in, shut others out. Hunter had never considered which, only knew that he needed them. He needed the peace, the mystery and the beauty, just as he needed the rich red walls of the canyon that rose up around him. Through the quiet he could hear the trickle of water from the creek and smell the heady freshness of the air. These he never took for granted; he hadn't had them forever.

Then he saw her, walking leisurely down the winding path toward the house. The dog's tail began to swish back and forth.

Sometimes, when he watched her like this, Hunter would think it impossible that anything so lovely belonged to him. She was dark and delicately formed, moving with a careless confidence that made him grin even as it made him ache. She was Sarah. His work and his privacy were the two vital things in his life. Sarah was his life. She'd been worth the struggles, the frustration, the fears and the pain. She was worth everything.

Looking over, she broke into a smile that flashed with braces. *"Hi, Dad!"*

Chapter 1

The week a magazine like *Celebrity* went to bed was utter chaos. Every department head was in a frenzy. Desks were littered, phones were tied up and lunches were skipped. The air was tinged with a sense of panic that built with every hour. Tempers grew short, demands outrageous. In most offices the lights burned late into the night. The rich scent of coffee and the sting of tobacco smoke were never absent. Rolls of antacids were consumed and bottles of eye drops constantly changed hands. After five years on staff, Lee took the monthly panic as a matter of course.

Celebrity was a slick, respected publication whose sales generated millions of dollars a year. In addition to stories on the rich and famous, it ran articles by eminent psychologists and journalists, interviews with both statesmen and rock stars. Its photography was first-class, just as its text was thoroughly researched and concisely written. Some of its detractors might have termed it quality gossip, but the word *quality* wasn't forgotten.

An ad in *Celebrity* was a sure bet for generating sales and interest and was priced accordingly. *Celebrity* was, in a tough, competitive business, one of the leading monthly publications in the country. Lee Radcliffe wouldn't have settled for less.

"How'd the piece on the sculptures turn out?"

Lee glanced up at Bryan Mitchell, one of the top photographers on the West Coast. Grateful, she accepted the cup of coffee Bryan passed her. In the past four days, she'd had a total of twenty hours' sleep. "Good," she said simply.

"I've seen better art scrawled in alleys."

Though she privately agreed, Lee only shrugged. "Some people like the clunky and obscure."

With a laugh, Bryan shook her head. "When they told me to photograph that red-and-black tangle of wire to its best advantage, I nearly asked them to shut off the lights."

"You made it look almost mystical."

"I can make a junkyard look mystical with the right lighting." She shot Lee a grin. "The same way you can make it sound fascinating."

A smile touched Lee's mouth but her mind was veering off in a dozen other directions. "All in a day's work, right?"

"Speaking of which—" Bryan rested one slim jean-clad hip on Lee's organized desk, drinking her own coffee black. "Still trying to dig something up on Hunter Brown?"

A frown drew Lee's elegant brows together. Hunter

Brown was becoming her personal quest and almost an obsession. Perhaps because he was so completely inaccessible, she'd become determined to be the first to break through the cloud of mystery. It had taken her nearly five years to earn her title as staff reporter, and she had a reputation for being tenacious, thorough and cool. Lee knew she'd earned those adjectives. Three months of hitting blank walls in researching Hunter Brown didn't deter her. One way or the other, she was going to get the story.

"So far I haven't gotten beyond his agent's name and his editor's phone number." There might've been a hint of frustration in her tone, but her expression was determined. "I've never known people so closemouthed."

"His latest book hit the stands last week." Absently, Bryan picked up the top sheet from one of the tidy piles of papers Lee was systematically dealing with. "Have you read it?"

"I picked it up, but I haven't had a chance to start it yet."

Bryan tossed back the long honey-colored braid that fell over her shoulder. "Don't start it on a dark night." She sipped at her coffee, then gave a laugh. "God, I ended up sleeping with every light in the apartment burning. I don't know how he does it."

Lee glanced up again, her eyes calm and confident. "That's one of the things I'm going to find out."

Bryan nodded. She'd known Lee for three years, and she didn't doubt Lee would. "Why?" Her frank, almond-shaped eyes rested on Lee's.

"Because—" Lee finished off her coffee and tossed the empty cup into her overflowing wastebasket "—no one else has."

"The Mount Everest syndrome," Bryan commented, and earned a rare, spontaneous grin.

A quick glance would have shown two attractive women in casual conversation in a modern, attractively decorated office. A closer look would have uncovered the contrasts. Bryan, in jeans and a snug T-shirt, was completely relaxed. Everything about her was casual and not quite tidy, from her smudged sneakers to the loose braid. Her sharp-featured, arresting face was touched only with a hasty dab of mascara. She'd probably meant to add lipstick or blusher and then forgotten.

Lee, on the other hand, wore a very elegant ice-blue suit, and the nerves that gave her her drive were evident in the hands that were never quite still. Her hair was expertly cut in a short swinging style that took very little care—which was every bit as important to her as having it look good. Its shade fell somewhere between copper and gold. Her skin was the delicate, milky white some redheads bless and others curse. Her makeup had been meticulously applied that morning, down to the dusky blue shadow that matched her eyes. She had delicate, elegant features offset by a full and obviously stubborn mouth.

The two women had entirely different styles and entirely different tastes but oddly enough, their friendship had begun the moment they'd met. Though Bryan didn't always like Lee's aggressive tactics and Lee didn't always approve of Bryan's laid-back approach, their closeness hadn't wavered in three years.

"So." Bryan found the candy bar she'd stuck in her jeans pocket and proceeded to unwrap it. "What's your master plan?"

"To keep digging," Lee returned almost grimly. "I do

have a couple of connections at Horizon, his publishing house. Maybe one of them'll come through with something." Without being fully aware of it, she drummed her fingers on the desk. "Damn it, Bryan, he's like the man who wasn't there. I can't even find out what state he lives in."

"I'm half-inclined to believe some of the rumors," Bryan said thoughtfully. Outside Lee's office someone was having hysterics over the final editing of an article. "I'd say the guy lives in a cave somewhere, full of bats with a couple of stray wolves thrown in. He probably writes the original manuscript in sheep's blood."

"And sacrifices virgins every new moon."

"I wouldn't be surprised." Bryan swung her feet lazily while she munched on her chocolate bar. "I tell you the man's weird."

"*Silent Scream*'s already on the bestseller list."

"I didn't say he wasn't brilliant," Bryan countered, "I said he was weird. What kind of a mind does he have?" She shook her head with a half-sheepish smile. "I can tell you I wished I'd never heard of Hunter Brown last night while I was trying to sleep with my eyes open."

"That's just it." Impatient, Lee rose and paced to the tiny window on the east wall. She wasn't looking out; the view of Los Angeles didn't interest her. She just had to move around. "What kind of mind *does* he have? What kind of life does he live? Is he married? Is he sixty-five or twenty-five? Why does he write novels about the supernatural?" She turned, her impatience and her annoyance showing beneath the surface of the sophisticated grooming. "Why did you read his book?"

"Because it was fascinating," Bryan answered immediately. "Because by the time I was on page three, I was so into it you couldn't have gotten the book away from me with a crowbar."

"And you're an intelligent woman."

"Damn right," Bryan agreed and grinned. "So?"

"Why do intelligent people buy and read something that's going to terrify them?" Lee demanded. "When you pick up a Hunter Brown, you know what it's going to do to you, yet his books consistently spring to the top of the bestseller list and stay there. Why does an obviously intelligent man write books like that?" She began, in a habit Bryan recognized, to fiddle with whatever was at hand—the leaves of a philodendron, the stub of a pencil, the left earring she'd removed during a phone conversation.

"Do I hear a hint of disapproval?"

"Yeah, maybe." Frowning, Lee looked up again. "The man is probably the best colorist in the country. If he's describing a room in an old house, you can smell the dust. His characterizations are so real you'd swear you'd met the people in his books. And he uses that talent to write about things that go bump in the night. I want to find out why."

Bryan crumpled her candy wrapper into a ball. "I know a woman who has one of the sharpest, most analytical minds I've ever come across. She has a talent for digging up obscure facts, some of them impossibly dry, and turning them into intriguing stories. She's ambitious, has a remarkable talent for words, but works on a magazine and lets a half-finished novel sit abandoned in a drawer. She's lovely, but she rarely dates for any purpose other than business. And she has a habit of twisting paper clips into ungodly shapes while she's talking."

Lee glanced down at the small mangled piece of

metal in her hands, then met Bryan's eyes coolly. "Do you know why?"

There was a hint of humor in Bryan's eyes, but her tone was serious enough. "I've tried to figure it out for three years, but I can't precisely put my finger on it."

With a smile, Lee tossed the bent paper clip into the trash. "But then, you're not a reporter."

Because she wasn't very good at taking advice, Lee switched on her bedside lamp, stretched out and opened Hunter Brown's latest novel. She would read a chapter or two, she decided, then make it an early night. An early night was an almost sinful luxury after the week she'd put in at *Celebrity*.

Her bedroom was done in creamy ivories and shades of blue from the palest aqua to indigo. She'd indulged herself here, with dozens of plump throw pillows, a huge Turkish rug and a Queen Anne stand that held an urn filled with peacock feathers and eucalyptus. Her latest acquisition, a large ficus tree, sat by the window and thrived.

She considered this room the only truly private spot in her life. As a reporter, Lee accepted that she was public property as much as the people she sought out. Privacy wasn't something she could cling to when she constantly dug into other people's lives. But in this little corner of the world, she could relax completely, forget there was work to do, ladders to climb. She could pretend L.A. wasn't bustling outside, as long as she had this oasis of peace. Without it, without the hours she spent sleeping and unwinding there, she knew she'd overload.

Knowing herself well, Lee understood that she had a tendency to push too hard, run too fast. In the quiet of her bedroom she could recharge herself each night so that she'd be ready for the race again the following day.

Relaxed, she opened Hunter Brown's latest effort.

Within a half hour, Lee was disturbed, uncomfortable and completely engrossed. She'd have been angry with the author for drawing her in if she hadn't been so busy turning pages. He'd put an ordinary man in an extraordinary situation and done it with such skill that Lee was already relating to the teacher who'd found himself caught up in a small town with a dark secret.

The prose flowed and the dialogue was so natural she could hear the voices. He filled the town with so many recognizable things, she could have sworn she'd been there herself. She knew the story was going to give her more than one bad moment in the dark, but she had to go on. That was the magic of a major storyteller. Cursing him, she read on, so tense that when the phone rang beside her, the book flew out of her hands. Lee swore again, at herself, and lifted the receiver.

Her annoyance at being disturbed didn't last. Grabbing a pencil, she began to scrawl on the pad beside the phone. With her tongue caught between her teeth, she set down the pencil and smiled. She owed the contact in New York an enormous favor, but she'd pay off when the time came, as she always did. For now, Lee thought, running her hand over Hunter's book, she had to make arrangements to attend a small writers' conference in Flagstaff, Arizona.

She had to admit the country was impressive. As was her habit, Lee had spent the time during the flight from L.A. to Phoenix working, but once she'd changed to the small commuter plane for the trip to Flagstaff, her work had been forgotten. She'd flown through thin clouds over a vastness almost impossible to conceive after the skyscrapers and traffic of Los Angeles. She'd looked down on the peaks and dips and castlelike rocks of Oak Creek Canyon, feeling a drumming excitement that was rare in a woman who wasn't easily impressed. If she'd had more time…

Lee sighed as she stepped off the plane. There was never time enough.

The tiny airport boasted a one-room lobby with a choice of concession stand or soda and candy machines. No loudspeaker announced incoming and outgoing flights. No skycap bustled up to her to relieve her of her bags. There wasn't a line of cabs waiting outside to compete for the handful of people who'd disembarked. With her garment bag slung over her shoulder, she frowned at the inconvenience. Patience wasn't one of her virtues.

Tired, hungry and inwardly a little frazzled by the shaky commuter flight, she stepped up to one of the counters. "I need to arrange for a car to take me to town."

The man in shirtsleeves and loosened tie stopped pushing buttons on his computer. His first polite glance sharpened when he saw her face. She reminded him of a cameo his grandmother had worn at her neck on special occasions. Automatically he straightened his shoulders. "Did you want to rent a car?"

Lee considered that a moment, then rejected it. She hadn't come to do any sightseeing, so a car would hardly be worthwhile. "No, just transportation into Flagstaff." Shifting her bag, she gave him the name of her hotel. "Do they have a courtesy car?"

"Sure do. You go on over to that phone by the wall there. Number's listed. Just give 'em a call and they'll send someone out."

"Thank you."

He watched her walk to the phone and thought he was the one who should have said thank-you.

Lee caught the scent of grilling hot dogs as she crossed the room. Since she'd turned down the dubious tray offered on the flight, the scent had her stomach juices swimming. Quickly and efficiently, she dialed the hotel, gave her name and was assured a car would be there within twenty minutes. Satisfied, she bought a hot dog and settled in one of the black plastic chairs to wait.

She was going to get what she'd come for, Lee told herself almost fiercely as she looked out at the distant mountains. The time wasn't going to be wasted. After three months of frustration, she was finally going to get a firsthand look at Hunter Brown.

It had taken skill and determination to persuade her editor-in-chief to spring for the trip, but it would pay off. It had to. Leaning back, she reviewed the questions she'd ask Hunter Brown once she'd cornered him.

All she needed, Lee decided, was an hour with him. Sixty minutes. In that time, she could pull out enough information for a concise, and very exclusive, article. She'd done precisely that with this year's Oscar winner, though he'd been reluctant, and a presidential candidate, though he'd been hostile. Hunter Brown would probably be both, she decided with a half smile. It would only add spice. If she'd wanted a bland, simple life, she'd have bent under the pressure and married Jonathan. Right now she'd be planning her next garden party rather than calculating how to ambush an award-winning writer.

Lee nearly laughed aloud. Garden parties, bridge parties and the yacht club. That might have been perfect for her family, but she'd wanted more. More what? her mother had demanded, and Lee could only reply, Just more.

Checking her watch, she left her luggage neatly stacked by the chair and went into the ladies' room. The door had hardly closed behind her when the object of all her planning strolled into the lobby.

He didn't often do good deeds, and then only for people he had a genuine affection for. Because he'd gotten into town with time to spare, Hunter had driven to the airport with the intention of picking up his editor. With barely a glance around, he walked over to the same counter Lee had approached ten minutes before.

"Flight 471 on time?"

"Yes, sir, got in ten minutes ago."

"Did a woman get off?" Hunter glanced at the nearly empty lobby again. "Attractive, midtwenties—"

"Yes, sir," the clerk interrupted. "She just stepped into the restroom. That's her luggage over there."

"Thanks." Satisfied, Hunter walked over to Lee's neat stack of luggage. Doesn't believe in traveling light, he noticed, scanning the garment bag, small Pullman and briefcase. Then, what woman did? Hadn't his Sarah taken two suitcases for the brief three-day stay with his sister in Phoenix? Strange that his little girl should be two parts woman already. Perhaps not so strange, Hunter reflected. Females were born two parts woman, while males took years to grow out of boyhood—if they ever did. Perhaps that's why he trusted men a great deal more.

Lee saw him when she came back into the lobby. His

back was to her, so that she had only the impression of a tall, leanly built man with black hair curling carelessly down to the neck of his T-shirt. Right on time, she thought with satisfaction, and approached him.

"I'm Lee Radcliffe."

When he turned, she went stone-still, the impersonal smile freezing on her face. In the first instant, she couldn't have said why. He was attractive—perhaps too attractive. His face was narrow but not scholarly, raw-boned but not rugged. It was too much a combination of both to be either. His nose was straight and aristocratic, while his mouth was sculpted like a poet's. His hair was dark and full and unruly, as though he'd been driving fast for hours with the wind blowing free. But it wasn't these things that caused her to lose her voice. It was his eyes.

She'd never seen eyes darker than his, more direct, more…disturbing. It was as though they looked through her. No, not through, Lee corrected numbly. Into. In ten seconds, they had looked into her and seen everything.

He saw a stunning, milk-pale face with dusky eyes gone wide in astonishment. He saw a soft, feminine mouth, lightly tinted. He saw nerves. He saw a stubborn chin and molten copper hair that would feel like silk between the fingers. What he saw was an outwardly poised, inwardly tense woman who smelled like spring evenings and looked like a *Vogue* cover. If it hadn't been for that inner tension, he might have dismissed her, but what lay beneath people's surfaces always intrigued him.

He skimmed her neat traveling suit so quickly his eyes might never have left hers. "Yes?"

"Well, I…" Forced to swallow, she trailed off. That

alone infuriated her. She wasn't about to be set off into stammers by a driver for the hotel. "If you've come to pick me up," Lee said curtly, "you'll need to get my bags."

Lifting a brow, he said nothing. Her mistake was simple and obvious. It would have taken only a sentence from him to correct it. Then again, it was her mistake, not his. Hunter had always believed more in impulses than explanations. Bending down, he picked up the Pullman, then slung the strap of the garment bag over his shoulder. "The car's out here."

She felt a great deal more secure with the briefcase in her hand and his back to her. The oddness, Lee told herself, had come from excitement and a long flight. Men never surprised her; they certainly never made her stare and stammer. What she needed was a bath and something a bit more substantial to eat than that hot dog.

The car he'd referred to wasn't a car, she noted, but a Jeep. Supposing this made sense, with the steep roads and hard winters, Lee climbed in.

Moves well, he thought, and dresses flawlessly. He noted, too, that she bit her nails. "Are you from the area?" Hunter asked conversationally when he'd stowed her bags in the back.

"No. I'm here for the writers' conference."

Hunter climbed in beside her and shut the door. Now he knew where to take her. "You're a writer?"

She thought of the two chapters of her manuscript she'd brought along in case she needed a cover. "Yes."

Hunter swung through the parking lot, taking the back road that led to the highway. "What do you write?"

Settling back, Lee decided she might as well try her routine out on him before she was in the middle of two hundred published and aspiring writers. "I've done articles and some short stories," she told him truthfully enough. Then she added what she'd rarely told anyone. "I've started a novel."

With a speed that surprised but didn't unsettle her, he burst onto the highway. "Are you going to finish it?" he asked, showing an insight that disturbed her.

"I suppose that depends on a lot of things."

He took another careful look at her profile. "Such as?"

She wanted to shift in her seat but forced herself to be still. This was just the sort of question she might have to answer over the weekend. "Such as if what I've done so far is any good."

He found both her answer and her discomfort reasonable. "Do you go to many of these conferences?"

"No, this is my first."

Which might account for the nerves, Hunter mused, but he didn't think he'd found the entire answer.

"I'm hoping to learn something," Lee said with a small smile. "I registered at the last minute, but when I learned Hunter Brown would be here, I couldn't resist."

The frown in his eyes came and went too quickly to be noticed. He'd agreed to do the workshop only because it wouldn't be publicized. Even the registrants wouldn't know he'd be there, until the following morning. Just how, he wondered, had the little redhead with the Italian shoes and midnight eyes found out? He passed a truck. "Who?"

"Hunter Brown," Lee repeated. "The novelist."

Impulse took over again. "Is he any good?"

Surprised, Lee turned to study his profile. It was infinitely easier to look at him, she discovered, when those eyes weren't focused on her. "You've never read any of his work?"

"Should I have?"

"I suppose that depends on whether you like to read with all the lights on and the doors locked. He writes horror fiction."

If she'd looked more closely, she wouldn't have missed the quick humor in his eyes. "Ghouls and fangs?"

"Not exactly," she said after a moment. "Not that simple. If there's something you're afraid of, he'll put it into words and make you wish him to the devil."

Hunter laughed, greatly pleased. "So, you like to be scared?"

"No," Lee said definitely.

"Then why do you read him?"

"I've asked myself that when I'm up at 3:00 a.m. finishing one of his books." Lee shrugged as the Jeep slowed for the turn-off. "It's irresistible. I think he must be a very odd man," she murmured, half to herself. "Not quite, well, not quite like the rest of us."

"Do you?" After a quick, sharp turn, he pulled up in front of the hotel, more interested in her than he'd planned to be. "But isn't writing just words and imagination?"

"And sweat and blood," she added, moving her shoulders again. "I just don't see how it could be very comfortable to live with an imagination like Brown's. I'd like to know how he feels about it."

Amused, Hunter jumped out of the Jeep to retrieve her bags. "You're going to ask him."

"Yes." Lee stepped down. "I am."

For a moment, they stood on the sidewalk, silently.

He looked at her with what might have been mild interest, but she sensed something more—something she shouldn't have felt from a hotel driver after a ten-minute acquaintance. For the second time she wanted to shift and made herself stand still. Wasting no more words, Hunter turned toward the hotel, her bags in hand.

It didn't occur to Lee until she was following him inside that she'd had a nonstop conversation with a hotel driver, a conversation that hadn't dwelt on the usual pleasantries or tourist plugs. As she watched him walk to the desk, she felt an aura of cool confidence from him and traces, very subtle traces, of arrogance. Why was a man like this driving back and forth and getting nowhere? she wondered. Stepping up to the desk, she told herself it wasn't her concern. She had bigger fish to fry.

"Lenore Radcliffe," she told the clerk.

"Yes, Ms. Radcliffe." He handed her a form and imprinted her credit card before he passed her a key. Before she could take it, Hunter slipped it into his own hand. It was then she noticed the odd ring on his pinky, four thin bands of gold and silver twisted into one.

"I'll take you around," he said simply, then crossed through the lobby with her again in his wake. He wound through a corridor, turned left, then stopped. Lee waited while he unlocked the door and gestured her inside.

The room was on the garden level with its own patio, she was pleased to note. As she scanned the room, Hunter carelessly switched on the TV and flipped through the channels before he checked the air conditioner. "Just call the desk if you need anything else," he advised, stowing her garment bag in the closet.

"Yes, I will." Lee hunted through her purse and came up with a five. "Thank you," she said, holding it out.

His eyes met hers again, giving her that same frozen jolt they had in the airport. She felt something stir deep within but wasn't sure if it was trying to reach out to him or struggling to hide. The fingers holding the bill nearly trembled. Then he smiled, so quickly, so charmingly, she was speechless.

"Thank you, Ms. Radcliffe." Without a blink, Hunter pocketed the five dollars and strolled out.

Chapter 2

If writers were often considered odd, writers' conferences, Lee was to discover, were oddities in themselves. They certainly couldn't be considered quiet or organized or stuffy.

Like nearly every other of the two hundred or so participants, she stood in one of the dozen lines at 8:00 a.m. for registration. From the laughing and calling and embracing, it was obvious that many of the writers and would-be writers knew one another. There was an air of congeniality, shared knowledge and camaraderie. Overlaying it all was excitement.

Still, more than one member stood in the noisy lobby like a child lost in a shipwreck, clinging to a folder or briefcase as though it were a life preserver and staring about with awe or simple confusion. Lee could appreciate the feeling, though she looked calm and poised as she accepted her packet and pinned her badge to the mint-green lapel of her blazer.

Concentrating on the business at hand, she found a chair in a corner and skimmed the schedule for Hunter Brown's workshop. With a dawning smile, she took out a pen and underlined.

CREATING HORROR THROUGH ATMOSPHERE AND EMOTION
Speaker to be announced.

Bingo, Lee thought, capping her pen. She'd make certain she had a front-row seat. A glance at her watch showed her that she had three hours before Brown began to speak. Never one to take chances, she took out her notebook to skim over the questions she'd listed, while people filed by her or merely loitered, chatting.

"If I get rejected again, I'm going to put my head in the oven."

"Your oven's electric, Judy."

"It's the thought that counts."

Amused, Lee began to listen to the passing comments with half an ear while she added a few more questions.

"And when they brought in my breakfast this morning, there was a five-hundred-page manuscript under my plate. I completely lost my appetite."

"That's nothing. I got one in my office last week written in calligraphy. One hundred and fifty thousand words of flowing script."

Editors, she mused. She could tell them a few stories about some of the submissions that found their way to *Celebrity*.

"He said his editor hacked his first chapter to pieces so he's going into mourning before the rewrites."

"I always go into mourning before rewrites. It's after a rejection that I seriously consider taking up basket weaving as a profession."

"Did you hear Jeffries is here again trying to peddle that manuscript about the virgin with acrophobia and telekinesis? I can't believe he won't let it die a quiet death. When's your next murder coming out?"

"In August. It's poison."

"Darling, that's no way to talk about your work."

As they passed by her, Lee caught the variety of tones, some muted, some sophisticated, some flamboyant. Gestures and conversations followed the same wide range. Amazed, she watched one man swoop by in a long, dramatic black cape.

Definitely an odd group, Lee thought, but she warmed to them. It was true she confined her skill to articles and profiles, but at heart she was a storyteller. Her position on the magazine had been hard-earned, and she'd built her world around it. For all her ambition, she had a firm fear of rejection that kept her own manuscript unfinished, buried in a drawer for weeks and sometimes months at a time. At the magazine, she had prestige, security and room for advancement. The weekly paycheck put the roof over her head, the clothes on her back and the food on her table.

If it hadn't been so important that she prove she could do all this for herself, she might have taken the chance of sending those first hundred pages to a publishing house. But then... Shaking her head, Lee watched the people mill through the registration area, all types, all sizes, all ages. Clothes varied from trim professional suits to jeans to flamboyant caftans and smocks. Apparently style was a matter of taste and taste a matter of individuality. She wondered if she'd see quite the same variety anywhere else. Absently, she glanced at the partial manuscript she'd tucked into her briefcase. Just for cover, she reminded herself. That was all.

No, she didn't believe she had it in her to be a great writer, but she knew she had the skill for great reporting. She'd never, never settle for being second-rate at anything.

Still, while she was here, it wouldn't hurt to sit in on one or two of the seminars. She might pick up some pointers. More important, she told herself as she rose, she might be able to stretch this trip into another story on the ins and outs of a writers' conference. Who attended, why, what they did, what they hoped for. Yes, it could make quite an interesting little piece. The job, after all, came first.

An hour later, a bit more enthusiastic than she wanted to be after her first workshop, she wandered into the coffee shop. She'd take a short break, assimilate the notes she'd written, then go back and make certain she had the best seat in the house for Hunter Brown's lecture.

Hunter glanced up from his paper and watched her enter the coffee shop. Lee Radcliffe, he mused, finding her of more interest than the local news he'd been scanning. He'd enjoyed his conversation with her the day before, and as often as not, he found conversations tedious. She had a quality about her—an innate frankness glossed with sophistication—that he found intriguing enough to hold his interest. An obsessive writer who believed that the characters themselves were the plot of any book, Hunter always looked for the unique and the individual. Instinct told him Lee Radcliffe was quite an individual.

Unobserved, he watched her. From the way she looked absently around the room it was obvious she was preoccupied. The suit she wore was very simple but showed both style and taste in the color and cut. She was a woman who could wear the simple, he decided, because she was a woman who'd been born with style. If he wasn't very much mistaken, she'd been born into wealth as well. There was always a subtle difference between those who were accustomed to money and those who'd spent years earning it.

So where did the nerves come from? he wondered. Curious, he decided it would be worth an hour of his time to try to find out.

Setting his paper aside, Hunter lit a cigarette and continued to stare at her, knowing there was no quicker way to catch someone's eye.

Lee, thinking more about the story she was going to write than the coffee she'd come for, felt an odd tingle run up her spine. It was real enough to give her an urge to turn around and walk out again when she glanced over and found herself staring back at the man she'd met at the airport.

It was his eyes, she decided, at first not thinking of him as a man or the hotel driver from the previous day. It was his eyes. Dark, almost the color of jet, they'd draw you in and draw you in until you were caught, and every secret you'd ever had would be secret no longer. It was frightening. It was…irresistible.

Amazed that such a fanciful thought had crept into her own practical, organized mind, Lee approached him. He was just a man, she told herself, a man who worked for his living like any other man. There was certainly nothing to be frightened of.

"Ms. Radcliffe." With the same unsmiling stare, he gestured to the chair across from him. "Buy you a cup of coffee?"

Normally she would've refused, politely enough. But now, for some intangible reason, Lee felt as though she had a point to prove. For the same intangible reason, she felt she had to prove it to him as much as to herself. "Thank you." The moment she sat down, a waitress was there, pouring coffee.

"Enjoying the conference?"

"Yes." Lee poured cream into the cup, stirring it around and around until a tiny whirlpool formed in the center. "As disorganized as everything seems to be, there was an amazing amount of information generated at the workshop I went to this morning."

A smile touched his lips, so lightly that it was barely there at all. "You prefer organization?"

"It's more productive." Though he was dressed more formally than he'd been the day before, the pleated slacks and open-necked shirt were still casual. She wondered why he wasn't required to wear a uniform. But then, she thought, you could put him in one of those nifty white jackets and neat ties and his eyes would simply defy them.

"A lot of fascinating things can come out of chaos, don't you think?"

"Perhaps." She frowned down at the whirlpool in her cup. Why did she feel as though she was being sucked in, in just that way? And why, she thought with a sudden flash of impatience, was she sitting here having a philosophical discussion with a stranger when she should be outlining the two stories she planned to write?

"Did you find Hunter Brown?" he asked her as he studied her over the rim of his cup. Annoyed with herself, he guessed accurately, and anxious to be off doing.

"What?" Distracted, Lee looked back up to find those strange eyes still on her.

"I asked if you'd run into Hunter Brown." The whisper of a smile was on his lips again, and this time it touched his eyes as well. It didn't make them any less intense.

"No." Defensive without knowing why, Lee sipped at her cooling coffee. "Why?"

"After the things you said yesterday, I was curious what you'd think of him once you met him." He took a drag from his cigarette and blew smoke out in a haze. "People usually have a preconceived image of someone but it rarely holds up in the flesh."

"It's difficult to have any kind of an image of someone who hides away from the world."

His brow went up, but his voice remained mild. "Hides?"

"It's the word that comes to my mind," Lee returned, again finding that she was speaking her thoughts aloud to him. "There's no picture of him on the back of any of his books, no bio. He never grants interviews, never denies or substantiates anything written about him. Any awards he's received have been accepted by his agent or his editor." She ran her fingers up and down the handle of her spoon. "I've heard he occasionally attends affairs like this, but only if it's a very small conference and there's no publicity about his appearance."

All during her speech, Hunter kept his eyes on her,

watching every nuance of expression. There were traces of frustration, he was certain, and of eagerness. The lovely cameo face was calm while her fingers moved restlessly. She'd be in his next book, he decided on the spot. He'd never met anyone with more potential for being a central character.

Because his direct, unblinking stare made her want to stammer, Lee gave him back the hard, uncompromising look. "Why do you stare at me like that?"

He continued to do so without any show of discomfort. "Because you're an interesting woman."

Another man might have said beautiful, still another might have said fascinating. Lee could have tossed off either one with light scorn. She picked up her spoon again, then set it down. "Why?"

"You have a tidy mind, innate style, and you're a bundle of nerves." He liked the way the faint line appeared between her brows when she frowned. It meant stubbornness to him, and tenacity. He respected both. "I've always been intrigued by pockets," Hunter went on. "The deeper the better. I find myself wondering just what's in your pockets, Ms. Radcliffe."

She felt the tremor again, up her spine, then down. It wasn't comfortable to sit near a man who could do that. She had a moment's sympathy for every person she'd ever interviewed. "You have an odd way of putting things," she muttered.

"So I've been told."

She instructed herself to get up and leave. It didn't make sense to sit there being disturbed by a man she could dismiss with a five-dollar tip. "What are you doing in Flagstaff?" she demanded. "You don't strike me as someone who'd be content to drive back and forth to an airport day after day, shuttling passengers and hauling luggage."

"Impressions make fascinating little paintings, don't they?" He smiled at her fully, as he had the day before when she'd tipped him. Lee wasn't sure why she'd felt he'd been laughing at her then, any more than why she felt he was laughing at her now. Despite herself, her lips curved in response. He found the smile a pleasant and very alluring surprise.

"You're a very odd man."

"I've been told that, too." His smile faded and his eyes became intense again. "Have dinner with me tonight?"

The question didn't surprise her as much as the fact that she wanted to accept, and nearly had. "No," she said, cautiously retreating. "I don't think so."

"Let me know if you change your mind."

She was surprised again. Most men would've pressed a bit. It was, well, expected, Lee reflected, wishing she could figure him out. "I have to get back." She reached for her briefcase. "Do you know where the Canyon Room is?"

With an inward chuckle, he dropped bills on the table. "Yes, I'll show you."

"That's not necessary," Lee began, rising.

"I've got time." He walked with her out of the coffee shop and into the wide, carpeted lobby. "Do you plan to do any sightseeing while you're here?"

"There won't be time." She glanced out one of the wide windows at the towering peak of Humphrey Peak. "As soon as the conference is over I have to get back."

"To where?"

"Los Angeles."

"Too many people," Hunter said automatically. "Don't you ever feel as though they're using up your air?"

She wouldn't have put it that way, would never have thought of it, but there were times she felt a twinge of what might be called claustrophobia. Still, her home was there, and more important, her work. "No. There's enough air, such as it is, for everyone."

"You've never stood at the south rim of the canyon and looked out, and breathed in."

Again, Lee shot him a look. He had a way of saying things that gave you an immediate picture. For the second time, she regretted that she wouldn't be able to take a day or two to explore some of the vastness of Arizona. "Maybe some other time." Shrugging, she turned with him as he headed down a corridor to the right.

"Time's fickle," he commented. "When you need it, there's too little of it. Then you wake up at three o'clock in the morning, and there's too much of it. It's usually better to take it than to anticipate it. You might try that," he said, looking down at her again. "It might help your nerves."

Her brows drew together. "There's nothing wrong with my nerves."

"Some people can thrive on nervous energy for weeks at a time, then they have to find that little valve that lets the steam escape." For the first time, he touched her, just fingertips to the ends of her hair. But she felt it, experienced it, as hard and strong as if his hand had closed firmly over hers. "What do you do to let the steam escape, Lenore?"

She didn't stiffen, or casually nudge his hand away as she would have done at any other time. Instead, she stood still, toying with a sensation she couldn't remember ever experiencing before. Thunder and lightning, she thought. There was thunder and lightning in this man, deep under the strangely aloof, oddly open exterior. She wasn't about to be caught in the storm.

"I work," she said easily, but her fingers had tightened on the handle of her briefcase. "I don't need any other escape valve." She didn't step back, but let the haughtiness that had always protected her enter her tone. "No one calls me Lenore."

"No?" He nearly smiled. It was this look, she realized, the secret amusement the onlooker could only guess at rather than see, that most intrigued. She thought he probably knew that. "But it suits you. Feminine, elegant, a little distant. *And the only word there spoken was the whispered word, 'Lenore!'* Yes." He let his fingertips linger a moment longer on her hair. "I think Poe would've found you very apt."

Before she could prevent it, before she could anticipate it, her knees were weak. She'd felt the sound of her own name feather over her skin. "Who are you?" Lee found herself demanding. Was it possible to be so deeply affected by someone without even knowing his name? She stepped forward in what seemed to be a challenge. "Just who are you?"

He smiled again, with the oddly gentle charm that shouldn't have suited his eyes yet somehow did. "Strange, you never asked before. You'd better go in," he told her as people began to gravitate toward the open doors of the Canyon Room. "You'll want a good seat."

"Yes." She drew back, a bit shaken by the ferocity of the desire she felt to learn more about him. With a last look over her shoulder, Lee walked in and settled in the front row. It was time to get her mind back on the business she'd come for, and the business was Hunter Brown. Distractions like incomprehensible men who drove Jeeps for a living would have to be put aside.

From her briefcase, Lee took a fresh notebook and two pencils, slipping one behind her ear. Within a few moments, she'd be able to see and study the mysterious Hunter Brown. She'd be able to listen and take notes with perfect freedom. After his lecture, she'd be able to question him, and if she had her way, she'd arrange some kind of one-on-one for later.

Lee had given the ethics of the situation careful thought. She didn't feel it would be necessary to tell Brown she was a reporter. She was there as an aspiring writer and had the fledgling manuscript to prove it. Anyone there was free to try to write and sell an article on the conference and its participants. Only if Brown used the words *off the record* would she be bound to silence. Without that, anything he said was public property.

This story could be her next step up the ladder. Would be, Lee corrected. The first documented, authentically researched story on Hunter Brown could push her beyond *Celebrity*'s scope. It would be controversial, colorful and, most important, exclusive. With this under her belt, even her quietly critical family would be impressed. With this under her belt, Lee thought, she'd be that much closer to the top rung, where her sights were always set.

Once she was there, all the hard work, the long hours, the obsessive dedication would be worth it. Because once she was there, she was there to stay. At the top, Lee thought almost fiercely. As high as she could reach.

On the other side of the doors, on the other side of

the corridor, Hunter stood with his editor, half listening to her comments on an interview she'd had with an aspiring writer. He caught the gist, that she was excited about the writer's potential. It was a talent of his to be able to conduct a perfectly lucid conversation when his mind was on something entirely different. It was something he roused himself to do only when the mood was on him. So he spoke to his editor and thought of Lee Radcliffe.

Yes, he was definitely going to use her in his next book. True, the plot was only a vague notion in his head, but he already knew she'd be the core of it. He needed to dig a bit deeper before he'd be satisfied, but he didn't foresee any problem there. If he'd gauged her correctly, she'd be confused when he walked to the podium, then stunned, then furious. If she wanted to talk to him as badly as she'd indicated, she'd swallow her temper.

A strong woman, Hunter decided. A will of iron and skin like cream. Vulnerable eyes and a damn-the-devil chin. A character was nothing without contrasts, strengths and weaknesses. And secrets, he thought, already certain he'd discover hers. He had another day and a half to explore Lenore Radcliffe. Hunter figured that was enough.

The corridor was full of laughter and complaints and enthusiasm as people loitered or filed through into the adjoining room. He knew what it was to feel enthusiastic about being a writer. If the pleasure went out of it, he'd still write. He was compelled to. But it would show in his work. Emotions always showed. He never *allowed* his feelings and thoughts to pour into his work—they would have done so regardless of his permission.

Hunter considered it a fair trade-off. His emotions,

his thoughts, were there for anyone who cared to read them. His life was completely and without exception his own.

The woman beside him had his affection and his respect. He'd argued with her over motivation and sentence structure, losing as often as winning. He'd shouted at her, laughed with her and given her emotional support through her recent divorce. He knew her age, her favorite drink and her weakness for cashews. She'd been his editor for three years, which was as close to a marriage as many people come. Yet she had no idea he had a ten-year-old daughter named Sarah who liked to bake cookies and play soccer.

Hunter took a last drag on his cigarette as the president of the small writers' group approached. The man was a slick, imaginative science fiction writer whom Hunter had read and enjoyed. Otherwise, he wouldn't be there, about to make one of his rare appearances in the writing community.

"Mr. Brown, I don't need to tell you again how honored we are to have you here."

"No—" Hunter gave him the easy half smile "—you don't."

"There's liable to be quite a commotion when I announce you. After your lecture, I'll do everything I can to keep the thundering horde back."

"Don't worry about it. I'll manage."

The man nodded, never doubting it. "I'm having a small reception in my suite this evening, if you'd like to join us."

"I appreciate it, but I have a dinner engagement."

Though he didn't know quite what to make of the smile, the organization's president was too intelligent to press his luck when he was about to pull off a coup. "If you're ready, then, I'll announce you."

"Any time."

Hunter followed him into the Canyon Room, then loitered just inside the doors. The room was already buzzing with anticipation and curiosity. The podium was set on a small stage in front of two hundred chairs that were nearly all filled. Talk died down when the president approached the stage, but continued in pockets of murmurs even after he'd begun to speak. Hunter heard one of the men nearest him whisper to a companion that he had three publishing houses competing for his manuscript. Hunter skimmed over the crowd, barely listening to the beginning of his introduction. Then his gaze rested again on Lee.

She was watching the speaker with a small, polite smile on her lips, but her eyes gave her away. They were dark and eager. Hunter let his gaze roam down until it rested on her lap. There, her hand opened and closed on the pencil. A bundle of nerves and energy wrapped in a very thin layer of confidence, he thought.

For the second time Lee felt his eyes on her, and for the second time she turned so that their gazes locked. The faint line marred her brow again as she wondered what he was doing inside the conference room. Unperturbed, leaning easily against the wall, Hunter stared back at her.

"His career's risen steadily since the publication of his first book, only five years ago. Since the first, *The Devil's Due,* he's given us the pleasure of being scared out of our socks every time we pick up his work." At the mention of the title, the murmurs increased and heads began to swivel. Hunter continued to stare at Lee, and she back at him, frowning. "His latest, *Silent Scream,* is already solid in the number-one spot on the bestseller list. We're honored and privileged to welcome to Flagstaff—Hunter Brown."

The effusive applause competed with the growing murmurs of two hundred people in a closed room. Casually, Hunter straightened from the wall and walked to the stage. He saw the pencil fall out of Lee's hand and roll to the floor. Without breaking rhythm, he stooped and picked it up.

"Better hold on to this," he advised, looking into her astonished eyes. As he handed it back, he watched astonishment flare into fury.

"You're a—"

"Yes, but you'd better tell me later." Walking the rest of the way to the stage, Hunter stepped behind the podium and waited for the applause to fade. Again he skimmed the crowd, but this time with such a quiet intensity that all sound died. For ten seconds there wasn't even the sound of breathing. "Terror," Hunter said into the microphone.

From the first word he had them spellbound, and held them captive for forty minutes. No one moved, no one yawned, no one slipped out for a cigarette. With her teeth clenched tight, Lee knew she despised him.

Simmering, struggling against the urge to spring up and stalk out, Lee sat stiffly and took meticulous notes. In the margin of the book she drew a perfectly recognizable caricature of Hunter with a dagger through his heart. It gave her enormous satisfaction.

When he agreed to field questions for ten minutes, Lee's was the first hand up. Hunter looked directly at her, smiled and called on someone three rows back.

He answered professional questions professionally

and evaded any personal references. She had to admire his skill, particularly since she was well aware he so seldom spoke in public. He showed no nerves, no hesitation and absolutely no inclination to call on her, though her hand was up and her eyes shot fiery little darts at him. But she was a reporter, Lee reminded herself. Reporters got nowhere if they stood on ceremony.

"Mr. Brown," Lee began, and rose.

"Sorry." With his slow smile, he held up a hand. "I'm afraid we're already overtime. Best of luck to all of you." He left the podium and the room, under a hail of applause. By the time Lee could work her way to the doors, she'd heard enough praise of Hunter Brown to turn her simmering temper to boil.

The nerve, she thought as she finally made it into the corridor. The unspeakable nerve. She didn't mind being bested in a game of chess; she could handle having her work criticized and her opinion questioned. All in all, Lee considered herself a reasonable, low-key person with no more than her fair share of conceit. The one thing she couldn't, wouldn't, tolerate was being made a fool of.

Revenge sprang into her mind, nasty, petty revenge. Oh, yes, she thought as she tried to work her way through the thick crowd of Hunter Brown fans, she'd have her revenge, somehow, some way. And when she did, it would be perfect.

She turned off at the elevators, knowing she was too full of fury to deal successfully with Hunter at that moment. She needed an hour to cool off and to plan. The pencil she still held snapped between her fingers. If it was the last thing she did, she was going to make Hunter Brown squirm.

Just as she started to push the button for her floor,

Hunter slipped inside the elevator. "Going up?" he asked easily, and pushed the number himself.

Lee felt the fury rise to her throat and burn. With an effort, she clamped her lips tight on the venom and stared straight ahead.

"Broke your pencil," Hunter observed, finding himself more amused than he'd been in days. He glanced at her open notebook, spotting the meticulously drawn caricature. An appreciative grin appeared. "Well done," he told her. "How'd you enjoy the workshop?"

Lee gave him one scathing look as the elevator doors opened. "You're a font of trivial information, Mr. Brown."

"You've got murder in your eyes, Lenore." He stepped into the hall with her. "It suits your hair. Your drawing makes it clear enough what you'd like to do. Why don't you stab me while you have the chance?"

As she continued to walk, Lee told herself she wouldn't give him the satisfaction of speaking to him. She wouldn't speak to him at all. Her head jerked up. "You've had a good laugh at my expense," she grated, and dug in her briefcase for her room key.

"A quiet chuckle or two," he corrected while she continued to simmer and search. "Lose your key?"

"No, I haven't lost my key." Frustrated, Lee looked up until fury met amusement. "Why don't you go away and sit on your laurels?"

"I've always found that uncomfortable. Why don't you vent your spleen, Lenore. You'd feel better."

"Don't call me Lenore!" she exploded as her control slipped. "You had no right to use me as the brunt of a joke. You had no right to pretend you worked for the hotel."

"You assumed," he corrected. "As I recall, I never pretended anything. You asked for a ride yesterday. I simply gave you one."

"You knew I thought you were the hotel driver. You were standing there beside my luggage—"

"A classic case of mistaken identity." He noted that her skin tinted with pale rose when she was angry. An attractive side effect, Hunter decided. "I'd come to pick up my editor, who'd missed her Phoenix connection, as it turned out. I thought the luggage was hers."

"All you had to do was say that at the time."

"You never asked," he pointed out. "And you did tell me to get the luggage."

"Oh, you're infuriating." Clamping her teeth shut, she began to fumble in her briefcase again.

"But brilliant. You mentioned that yourself."

"Being able to string words together is an admirable talent, Mr. Brown." Hauteur was one of her most practiced skills. Lee used it to the fullest. "It doesn't make you an admirable person."

"No, I wouldn't say I was, particularly." While he waited for her to find her key, Hunter leaned comfortably against the wall.

"You carried my luggage to my room," she continued, infuriated. "I gave you a five-dollar tip."

"Very generous."

She let out a huff of breath, grateful that her hands were busy. She didn't know how else she could have prevented herself from slapping his calm, self-satisfied face. "You've had your joke," she said, finding her key at last. "Now I'd like you to do me the courtesy of never speaking to me again."

"I don't know where you got the impression I was

courteous." Before she could unlock the door, he'd put his hand over hers on the key. She felt the little tingle of power and cursed him for it even as she met his calmly amused look. "You did mention, however, that you'd like to speak to me. We can talk over dinner tonight."

She stared at him. Why should she have thought he wouldn't be able to surprise her again? "You have the most incredible nerve."

"You mentioned that already. Seven o'clock?"

She wanted to tell him she wouldn't have dinner with him even if he groveled. She wanted to tell him that and all manner of other unpleasant things. Temper fought with practicality. There was a job she'd come to do, one she'd been working on unsuccessfully for three months. Success was more important than pride. He was offering her the perfect way to do what she'd come to do, and to do it more extensively than she could've hoped for. And perhaps, just perhaps, he was opening the door himself for her revenge. It would make it all the sweeter.

Though it was a large lump, Lee swallowed her pride.

"That's fine," she agreed, but he noticed she didn't look too pleased. "Where should I meet you?"

He never trusted easy agreement. But then Hunter trusted very little. She was going to be a challenge, he felt. "I'll pick you up here." His fingers ran casually up to her wrist before he released her. "You might bring your manuscript along. I'm curious to see your work."

She smiled and thought of the article she was going to write. "I very much want you to see my work." Lee stepped into her room and gave herself the small satisfaction of slamming the door in his face.

Chapter 3

Midnight-blue silk. Lee took a great deal of time and gave a great deal of thought to choosing the right dress for her evening with Hunter. It was business.

The deep blue silk shot through with thin silver threads appealed to her because of its clean, elegant lines and lack of ornamentation. Lee would, on the occasions when she shopped, spend as much time choosing the right scarf as she would researching a subject. It was all business.

Now, after a thorough debate, she slipped into the silk. It coolly skimmed her skin; it draped subtly over curves. Her own reflection satisfied her. The unsmiling woman who looked back at her presented precisely the sort of image she wanted to project—elegant, sophisticated and a bit remote. If nothing else, this soothed her bruised ego.

As Lee looked back over her life, concentrating on

her career, she could remember no incident where she'd found herself bested. Her mouth became grim as she ran a brush through her hair. It wasn't going to happen now.

Hunter Brown was going to get back some of his own, if for no other reason than that half-amused smile of his. No one laughed at her and got away with it, Lee told herself as she slapped the brush back on the dresser smartly enough to make the bottles jump. Whatever game she had to play to get what she wanted, she'd play. When the article on Hunter Brown hit the stands, she'd have won. She'd have the satisfaction of knowing he'd helped her. In the final analysis, Lee mused, there was no substitute for winning.

When the knock sounded at her door, she glanced at her watch. Prompt. She'd have to make a note of it. Her mood was smug as, after picking up her slim evening bag, she went to answer.

Inherently casual in dress, but not sloppy, she noted, filing the information away as she glanced at the open-collared shirt under his dark jacket. Some men could wear black tie and not look as elegant as Hunter Brown looked in jeans. That was something that might interest her readers. By the end of the evening, Lee reminded herself, she'd know all she possibly could about him.

"Good evening." She started to step across the threshold, but he took her hand, holding her motionless as he studied her.

"Very lovely," Hunter declared. Her hand was very soft and very cool, though her eyes were still hot with annoyance. He liked the contrast. "You wear silk and a very alluring scent but manage to maintain that aura of untouchability. It's quite a talent."

"I'm not interested in being analyzed."

"The curse or blessing of the writer," he countered. "Depending on your viewpoint. Being one yourself, you should understand. Where's your manuscript?"

She'd thought he'd forget—she'd hoped he would. Now, she was back to the disadvantage of stammering. "It, ah, it isn't…"

"Bring it along," Hunter ordered. "I want to take a look at it."

"I don't see why."

"Every writer wants his words read."

She didn't. It wasn't polished. It wasn't perfect. Without a doubt, the last person she wanted to allow a glimpse of her inner thoughts was Hunter. But he was standing, watching, with those dark eyes already seeing beyond the outer layers. Trapped, Lee turned back into the room and slipped the folder from her briefcase. If she could keep him busy enough, she thought, there wouldn't be time for him to look at it anyway.

"It'll be difficult for you to read anything in a restaurant," she pointed out as she closed the door behind her.

"That's why we're having dinner in my suite."

When she stopped, he simply took her hand and continued on to the elevators as if he hadn't noticed. "Perhaps I've given you the wrong impression," she began coldly.

"I don't think so." He turned, still holding her hand. His palm wasn't as smooth as she'd expected a writer's to be. The palm was as wide as a concert pianist's, but it was ridged with calluses. It made, Lee discovered, a very intriguing and uncomfortable combination. "My imagination hasn't gone very deeply into the prospect of seducing you, Lenore." Though he felt her stiffen in outrage, he drew her into the elevator. "The point is, I don't care for restaurants and I care less for crowds and interruptions." The elevator hummed quietly on the short ascent. "Have you found the conference worthwhile?"

"I'm going to get what I came for." She stepped through the doors as they slid open.

"And what's that?"

"What did you come for?" she countered. "You don't exactly make it a habit to attend conferences, and this one is certainly small and off the beaten path."

"Occasionally I enjoy the contact with other writers." Unlocking the door, he gestured her inside.

"This conference certainly isn't bulging with authors who've attained your degree of success."

"Success has nothing to do with writing."

She set her purse and folder aside and faced him straight on. "Easy to say when you have it."

"Is it?" As if amused, he shrugged, then gestured toward the window. "You should drink in as much of the view as you can. You won't see anything like this through any window in Los Angeles."

"You don't care for L.A." If she was careful and clever, she should be able to pin him down on where he lived and why he lived there.

"L.A. has its points. Would you like some wine?"

"Yes." She wandered over to the window. The vastness still had the power to stun her and almost…almost frighten. Once you were beyond the city limits, you might wander for miles without seeing another face, hearing another voice. The isolation, she thought, or perhaps just the space itself, would overwhelm. "Have you been there often?" she asked, deliberately turning her back to the window.

"Hmm?"

"To Los Angeles?"

"No." He crossed to her and offered a glass of pale gold wine.

"You prefer the East to the West?"

He smiled and lifted his glass. "I make it a point to prefer where I am."

He was very adept at evasions, she thought, and turned away to wander the room. It seemed he was also very adept at making her uneasy. Unless she missed her guess, he did both on purpose. "Do you travel often?"

"Only when it's necessary."

Tipping back her glass, Lee decided to try a more direct approach. "Why are you so secretive about yourself? Most people in your position would make the most of the promotion and publicity that's available."

"I don't consider myself secretive, nor do I consider myself most people."

"You don't even have a bio or a photo on your book covers."

"My face and my background have nothing to do with the stories I tell. Does the wine suit you?"

"It's very good." Though she'd barely tasted it. "Don't you feel it's part of your profession to satisfy the readers' curiosity when it comes to the person who creates a story that interests them?"

"No. My profession is words—putting words together so that someone who reads them is entertained, intrigued and satisfied with a tale. And tales spring from imagination rather than hard fact." He sipped wine himself and approved it. "The teller of the tale is nothing compared to the tale itself."

"Modesty?" Lee asked with a trace of scorn she couldn't prevent.

The scorn seemed to amuse him. "Not at all. It's a matter of priorities, not humility. If you knew me better, you'd understand I have very few virtues." He smiled, but Lee told herself she'd imagined that brief predatory flash in his eyes. Imagined, she told herself again and shuddered. Annoyed at her own reaction, she held out her wineglass for a refill.

"Have you any virtues?"

He liked the fact that she struck back even when her nerves were racing. "Some say vices are more interesting and certainly more entertaining than virtues." He filled her glass to just under the rim. "Would you agree?"

"More interesting, perhaps more entertaining." She refused to let her eyes falter from his as she drank. "Certainly more demanding."

He mulled this over, enjoying her quick response and her clean, direct thought patterns. "You have an interesting mind, Lenore. You keep it exercised."

"A woman who doesn't finds herself watching other people climb to the top while she fills water glasses and makes the coffee." She could have cursed in frustration the moment she'd spoken. It wasn't her habit to speak that freely. The point was, she was here to interview him, Lee reminded herself, not the other way around.

"An interesting analogy," Hunter murmured. Ambition. Yes, he'd sensed that about her from the beginning. But what was it she wanted to achieve? Whatever it was, he mused, she wouldn't be above stepping over a few people to get it. He found he could respect that, could almost admire it. "Tell me, do you ever relax?"

"I beg your pardon?"

"Your hands are rarely still, though you appear to

have a great deal of control otherwise." He noted that at his words her fingers stopped toying with the stem of her glass. "Since you've come into this room, you haven't stayed in one spot more than a few seconds. Do I make you nervous?"

Sending him a cool look, she sat on the plush sofa and crossed her legs. "No." But her pulse thudded a bit when he sat down beside her.

"What does?"

"Small, loud dogs."

He laughed, pleased with the moment and with her. "You're a very entertaining woman." He took her hand lightly in his. "I should tell you that's my highest compliment."

"You set a great store by entertainment."

"The world's a grim place—worse, often tedious." Her hand was delicate, and delicacy drew him. Her eyes held secrets, and there was little that intrigued him more. "If we can't be entertained, there're only two places to go. Back to the cave, or on to oblivion."

"So you entertain with terror." She wanted to shift farther away from him, but his fingers had tightened almost imperceptibly on her hand. And his eyes were searching for her thoughts.

"If you're worried about the unspeakable terror lurking outside your bedroom window, would you worry about your next dentist appointment or the fact that your washer overflowed?"

"Escape?"

He reached up to touch her hair. It seemed a very casual, very natural gesture to him. Lee's eyes flew open as if she'd been pinched. "I don't care for the word *escape*."

She was a difficult combination to resist, Hunter

thought, as he let his fingertips skim down the side of her throat. The fiery hair, the vulnerable eyes, the cool gloss of breeding, the bubbling nerves. She'd make a fascinating character and, he realized, a fascinating lover. He'd already decided to have her for the first; now, as he toyed with the ends of her hair, he decided to have her for the second.

She sensed something when his gaze locked on hers again. Decision, determination, desire. Her mouth went dry. It wasn't often that she felt she could be outmatched by another. It was rarer still when anyone or anything truly frightened her. Though he said nothing, though he moved no closer, she found herself fighting back fear—and the knowledge that whatever game she challenged him to, she would lose because he would look into her eyes and know each move before she made it.

A knock sounded at the door, but he continued to look at her for long silent seconds before he rose. "I took the liberty of ordering dinner," he said, so calmly that Lee wondered if she'd imagined the flare of passion she'd seen in his eyes. While he went to the door, she sat where she was, struggling to sort her own thoughts. She was imagining things, Lee told herself. He couldn't see into her and read her thoughts. He was just a man. Since the game was hers, and only she knew the rules, she wouldn't lose. Settled again, she rose to walk to the table.

The salmon was tender and pink. Pleased with the choice, Lee sat down at the table as the waiter closed the door behind him. So far, Lee reflected, she'd answered more questions than Hunter. It was time to change that.

"The advice you gave earlier to struggling writers about blocking out time to write every day no matter how discouraged they get—did that come from personal experience?"

Hunter sampled the salmon. "All writers face discouragement from time to time. Just as they face criticism and rejection."

"Did you face many rejections before the sale of *The Devil's Due?*"

"I suspect anything that comes too easily." He lifted the wine bottle to fill her glass again. She had a face made for candlelight, he mused as he watched the shadow and light flicker over the cream-soft skin and delicate features. He was determined to find out what lay beneath, before the evening ended.

He never considered he was using her, though he fully intended to pick her brain for everything he could learn about her. It was a writer's privilege.

"What made you become a writer?"

He lifted a brow as he continued to eat. "I was born a writer."

Lee ate slowly, planning her next line of questions. She had to move carefully, avoid putting him on the defensive, maneuver around any suspicions. She never considered she was using him, though she fully intended to pick his brain for everything she could learn about him. It was a reporter's privilege.

"Born a writer," she repeated, flaking off another bite of salmon. "Do you think it's that simple? Weren't there elements in your background, circumstances, early experiences, that led you toward your career?"

"I didn't say it was simple," Hunter corrected. "We're all born with a certain set of choices to make. The matter of making the right ones is anything but simple.

Every novel written has to do with choices. Writing novels is what I was meant to do."

He interested her enough that she forgot the unofficial interview and asked for herself, "So you always wanted to be a writer?"

"You're very literal-minded," Hunter observed. Comfortable, he leaned back and swirled the wine in his glass. "No, I didn't. I wanted to play professional soccer."

"Soccer?"

Her astonished disbelief made him smile. "Soccer," he repeated. "I wanted to make a career of it and might have been successful at it, but I had to write."

Lee was silent a moment, then decided he was telling her precisely the truth. "So you became a writer without really wanting to."

"I made a choice," Hunter corrected, intrigued by the orderly logic of her mind. "I believe a great many people are born writer or artist, and die without ever realizing it. Books go unwritten, paintings unpainted. The fortunate ones are those who discover what they were meant to do. I might have been an excellent soccer player. I might have been an excellent writer. If I'd tried to do both, I'd have been no more than mediocre. I chose not to be mediocre."

"There're several million readers who'd agree you made the right choice." Forgetting the cool facade, she propped her elbows on the table and leaned forward. "Why horror fiction, Hunter? Someone with your skill and your imagination could write anything. Why did you turn your talents toward that particular genre?"

He lit a cigarette so that the scent of tobacco stung the air. "Why do you read it?"

She frowned; he hadn't turned one of her questions

back on her for some time. "I don't as a rule, except yours."

"I'm flattered. Why mine?"

"Your first was recommended to me, and then…" She hesitated, not wanting to say she'd been hooked from the first page. Instead, she ran her fingertip around the rim of her glass and sorted through her answer. "You have a way of creating atmosphere and drawing characters that make the impossibility of your stories perfectly believable."

He blew out a stream of smoke. "Do you think they're impossible?"

She gave a quick laugh, a laugh he recognized as genuine from the humor that lit her eyes. It did something very special to her beauty. It made it accessible. "I hardly believe in people being possessed by demons or a house being inherently evil."

"No?" He smiled. "No superstitions, Lenore?"

She met his gaze levelly. "None."

"Strange, most of us have a few."

"Do you?"

"Of course, and even the ones I don't have fascinate me." He took her hand, linking fingers firmly. "It's said some people are able to sense another's aura, or personality if the word suits you better, by a simple clasp of hands." His palm was warm and hard as he kept his eyes fixed on hers. She could feel, cool against her hand, the twisted metal of his ring.

"I don't believe that." But she wasn't so sure, not with him.

"You believe only in what you see or feel. Only in what can be touched with one of the five senses that you understand." He rose, drawing her to her feet. "Everything that is can't be understood. Everything that's understood can't be explained."

"Everything has an explanation." But she found the words, like her pulse, a bit unsteady.

She might have drawn her hand away, and he might have let her, but her statement seemed to be a direct challenge. "Can you explain why your heart beats faster when I step closer?" His face looked mysterious, his eyes like jet in the candlelight. "You said you weren't afraid of me."

"I'm not."

"But your pulse throbs." His fingertip lightly touched the hollow of her throat. "Can you explain why when we've yet to spend even one full day together, I want to touch you, like this?" Gently, incredibly gently, he ran the back of his hand up the side of her face.

"Don't." It was only a whisper.

"Can you explain this kind of attraction between two strangers?" He traced a finger over her lips, felt them tremble, wondered about their taste.

Something soft, something flowing, moved through her. "Physical attraction's no more than chemistry."

"Science?" He brought her hand up, pressing his lips to the center of her palm. She felt the muscles in her thighs turn to liquid. "Is there an equation for this?" Still watching her, he brushed his lips over her wrist. Her skin chilled, then heated. Her pulse jolted and scrambled. He smiled. "Does this—" he whispered a kiss at the corner of her mouth "—have to do with logic?"

"I don't want you to touch me like this."

"You want me to touch you," Hunter corrected. "But you can't explain it." In an expected move, he thrust his hands into her hair. "Try the unexplainable," he challenged before his lips closed over hers.

Power. It sped through her. Desire was a rush of heat. She could feel need sing through her as she stood motionless in his arms. She should have refused him. Lee was experienced in the art of refusals. There was suddenly no wit to evade, no strength to refuse.

For all his intensity, for all the force of his personality, the kiss was meltingly soft. Though his fingers were strong and firm in her hair, so firm if she'd tried to move away she'd have found herself trapped, his lips were as gentle and warm as the light that flickered on the table beside them. She didn't know when she reached for him, but her arms were around him, bodies merging, silk rustling. The quiet, intoxicating taste of wine was on his tongue. Lee drank it in. She could smell the candle wax and her own perfume. Her ordered, disciplined mind swam first with confusion, then with sensation after alluring sensation.

Her lips were cool but warmed quickly. Her body was tense but slowly relaxed. He enjoyed both changes. She wasn't a woman who gave herself freely or easily. He knew that just as he knew she wasn't a woman often taken by surprise.

She seemed very small against him, very fragile. He'd always treated fragility with great care. Even as the kiss grew deeper, even as his own need grew surprisingly greater, his mouth remained gentle on hers, teasing, requesting. He believed that lovemaking, from first touch to fulfillment, was an art. He believed that art could never be rushed. So, slowly, patiently, he showed her what might be, while his hands stayed only in her hair and his mouth stayed softly on her.

He was draining her. Lee could feel her will, her strength, her thoughts, seeping out of her. And as they drained away, a flood of sensation replenished what she lost. There was no dealing with it, no…explaining. It could only be experienced.

Pleasure this fluid couldn't be contained. Desire this strong couldn't be guided. It was the lack of control more than the flood of feeling that frightened her most. If she lost her control, she'd lose her purpose. Then she would flounder. With a murmured protest, she pulled away but found that while he freed her lips, he still held her.

Later, he thought, at some lonely, dark hour, he'd explore his own reaction. Now he was much more interested in hers. She looked at him as though she'd been struck—face pale, eyes dark. Though her lips parted, she said nothing. Under his fingers he could feel the light tremor that coursed through her—once, then twice.

"Some things can't be explained, even when they're understood." He said it softly, so softly she might have thought it a threat.

"I don't understand you at all." She put her hands on his forearms as if to draw him away. "I don't think I want to anymore."

He didn't smile as he let his hands slide down to her shoulders. "Perhaps not. You'll have a choice to make."

"No." Shaken, she stepped away and snatched up her purse. "The conference ends tomorrow and I go back to L.A." Suddenly angry, she turned to face him. "You'll go back to whatever hole it is you hide in."

He inclined his head. "Perhaps." It was best she'd put some distance between them. Very abruptly, he realized that if he'd held her a moment longer, he wouldn't have let her go. "We'll talk tomorrow."

She didn't question her own illogic, but shook her head. "No, we won't talk anymore."

He didn't correct her when she walked to the door, and he stood where he was when the door closed behind her. There was no need to contradict her; he knew they'd talk again. Lifting his glass of wine, Hunter gathered up the manuscript she'd forgotten and settled himself in a chair.

Chapter 4

Anger. Perhaps what Lee felt was simple anger, without other eddies and currents of emotion, but she wasn't certain whom she felt angry with.

What had happened the evening before could have been avoided—should have been, she corrected as she stepped out of the shower. Because she'd allowed Hunter to set the pace and the tone, she'd put herself in a vulnerable position *and* she'd wasted a valuable opportunity. If Lee had learned anything in her years as a reporter, it was that a wasted opportunity was the most destructive mistake in the business.

How much did she know of Hunter Brown that could be used in a concise, informative article? Enough for a paragraph, Lee thought in disgust. A very short paragraph.

She might have only one chance to make up for lost time. Time lost because she'd let herself feel like a woman instead of thinking like a reporter. He'd led her along on a leash, she admitted bitterly, rubbing a towel over her dripping hair while the heat lamp in the ceiling warmed her skin. Instead of balking, she'd gone obediently where he'd taken her. And had missed the most important interview of her career. Lee tossed down the towel and stalked out of the steamy bathroom.

Telling herself she felt nothing but annoyance for him and for herself, Lee pulled on a robe before she sat down at the small writing desk. She still had some time before room service would deliver her first cup of coffee, but there wasn't any more time to waste. Business first...and last. She pulled out a pad and pencil.

HUNTER BROWN. Lee headed the top of the pad in bold letters and underlined the name. The problem had been, she admitted, that she hadn't approached Hunter—the assignment—logically, systematically. She could correct that now with a basic outline. She had, after all, seen him, spoken to him, asked him a few elementary questions. As far as she knew, no other reporter could make such a claim. It was time to stop berating herself for not tying everything up neatly in a matter of hours and make the slim advantage she still had work for her. She began to write in a decisive hand.

APPEARANCE. Not typical. Now there was a positive statement, she thought with a frown. In three bold strokes, she crossed out the words. Dark; lean, rangy build, she wrote. Like a long-distance runner, a cross-country skier. Her eyes narrowed as she brought his face to the foreground of her memory. Rugged face, offset by an air of intelligence. Most outstanding feature—eyes. Very dark, very direct, very...unnerving.

Was that editorializing? she asked herself. Would

those long, quiet stares disturb everyone? Shrugging the question away, Lee continued to write. Tall, perhaps six-one, approximately a hundred sixty pounds. Very confident. Musician's hands, poet's mouth.

A bit surprised by her own description, Lee went on to her next category.

PERSONALITY. Enigmatic. Not enough, she decided, huffing slightly. Arrogant, self-absorbed, rude. Definitely editorializing. She set down her pen and took a deep breath, then picked it up again. A skilled, mesmerizing speaker, she admitted in print. Perceptive, cool, taciturn and open by turns, physical.

The last word had been a mistake, Lee discovered, as it brought back the memory of that long, soft, draining kiss, the gentleness of the mouth, the firmness of his hands. No, that wasn't for publication, nor would she need notes to bring back all the details, all the sensations. She would, however, be wise to remember that he was a man who moved quickly when he chose, a man who apparently took precisely what he wanted.

Humor? Yes, under the intensity there was humor in him. She didn't like recalling how he'd laughed at her, but when she had such a dearth of material, she needed every detail, uncomfortable or not.

She remembered every word he'd said on his philosophy of writing. But how could she translate something so intangible into a few clean, pragmatic sentences? She could say he thought of his work as an obligation. A vocation. It just wasn't enough, she thought in frustration. She needed his own words here, not a translation of his meaning. The simple truth was, she had to speak to him again.

Dragging a hand through her hair, she read over her

orderly notes. She should have held the reins of the conversation from the very beginning. If she was an ex-
pert on anything, it was on channeling and steering talk
along the lines she wanted. She'd interviewed subjects
more closemouthed than Hunter, more hostile, but she
couldn't remember any more frustrating.

Absently, she began to tap the end of her pencil
against the table. It wasn't her job to be frustrated, but
to be productive. It wasn't her job, she added, to allow
herself to be so utterly seduced by an assignment.

She could have prevented the kiss. It still wasn't clear
to Lee why she hadn't. She could have controlled her
response to it. She didn't want to dwell on why she
hadn't. It was much too easy to remember that long,
strangely intense moment and in remembering, to feel
it all again. If she was going to prevent herself from
doing that, and remember instead all the reasons she'd
come to Flagstaff, she had to put Hunter Brown firmly
in the category of assignment and keep him there. For
now, her biggest problem was how she was going to
manage to see him again.

Professionally, she warned herself. But she couldn't
sit still thinking of it, or him. Pacing, she tried to block
out the incredibly gentle feel of his mouth on hers. And
failed.

A flood of feeling; she'd never experienced anything
like it. The weakness, the power—it was beyond her to
understand it. The longing, the need—how could she
know the way to control it?

If she understood him better perhaps… No. Lee
lifted her hairbrush, then set it down again. No, understanding Hunter would have nothing to do with fighting her desire for him. She'd wanted to be touched by

him, and though she had no logical reason for it, she'd
wanted to be touched more than she'd wanted to do her
job. It was unprecedented, Lee admitted as she absently
pushed bottles and jars around on her dresser. When
something was unprecedented, you had to make up your
own guidelines.

Uneasy, she glanced up and saw a pale woman with
sleepy eyes and unruly hair reflected in the glass. She
looked too young, too…fragile. No one ever saw her
without the defensive shield of grooming, but she knew
what was beneath the fastidiousness and gloss. Fear.
Fear of failure.

She'd built her confidence stone by meticulous stone,
until most of the time she believed in it herself. But at
moments like this, when she was alone, a little weary,
a little discouraged, the woman inside crept out, and
with her, all the tiny doubts and fears behind that labo-
riously built wall.

She'd been trained from birth to be little more than
an intelligent, attractive ornament. Well-spoken, well-
groomed, well-disciplined. It was all her family expected of her. No, Lee corrected. It was *what* had been
expected of her. In that respect, she'd already failed.

What trick of fate had made it so impossible for her
to fit the mold she'd been fashioned for? Since childhood she'd known she needed more, yet it had taken her
until after college to store up enough courage to break
away from the road that would have led her from proper
debutante to proper matron.

When she'd told her parents she wasn't going to be
Mrs. Jonathan T. Willoby, but was leaving Palm Springs
to live and work in Los Angeles, she'd been quaking
inside. Not until later did she realize it had been their

training that had seen her through the very difficult meeting. She'd been taught to remain cool and composed, never to raise her voice, never to show any vulgar signs of temper. When she'd spoken to them, she'd seemed perfectly sure of her own mind, while in truth she'd been terrified of leaving that comfortable gilt cage they'd been fashioning for her since before she was born.

Five years later, the fear had dulled, but it remained. Part of her drive to reach the top in her profession came from the very basic need to prove herself to her parents.

Foolish, she told herself, turning away from the vulnerability of the woman in the glass. She had nothing to prove to anyone, unless it was to herself. She'd come for a story, and that was her first, her only priority. The story was going to gel for her if she had to dog Hunter Brown's footsteps like a bloodhound.

Lee looked down at her notebook again, and at the notes that filled less than a page. She'd have more before the day was over, she promised herself. Much more. He wouldn't get the upper hand again, nor would he distract her from her purpose. As soon as she'd dressed and had her morning coffee, she'd look for Hunter. This time, she'd stay firmly behind the wheel.

When she heard the knock, Lee glanced at the clock beside her bed and gave a little sigh of frustration. She was running behind schedule, something she never permitted herself to do. She'd deliberately requested coffee and rolls for nine o'clock so that she could be dressed and ready to go when they were delivered. Now she'd have to rush to make certain she had a couple of solid hours with Hunter before check-out time. She wasn't going to miss an opportunity twice.

Impatient with herself, she went to the door, drew off the chain and pulled it open.

"You might as well eat nothing if you think you can subsist on a couple of pieces of bread and some jam." Before she could recover, Hunter swooped by her, carrying her breakfast tray. "And an intelligent woman never answers the door without asking who's on the other side." Setting the tray on the table, he turned to pin her with one of his long, intrusive stares.

She looked younger without the gloss of makeup and careful style. The traces of fragility he'd already sensed had no patina of sophistication over them now, though her robe was silk and the sapphire color flattering. He felt a flare of desire and a simultaneous protective twinge. Neither could completely deaden his anger.

She wasn't about to let him know how stunned she was to see him, or how disturbed she was that he was here alone with her when she was all but naked. "First a chauffeur, now a waiter," she said coolly, unsmiling. "You're a man of many talents, Hunter."

"I could return the compliment." Because he knew just how volatile his temper could be, he poured a cup of coffee. "Since one of the first requirements of a fiction writer is that he be a good liar, you're well on your way." He gestured to a chair, putting Lee uncomfortably in the position of visitor. As though she weren't the least concerned, she crossed the room and seated herself at the table.

"I'd ask you to join me, but there's only one cup." She broke a croissant in two and nibbled on it, unbuttered. "You're welcome to a roll." With a steady hand, she added cream to the coffee. "Perhaps you'd like to explain what you mean about my being a good liar."

"I suppose it's a requirement of a reporter as well." Hunter saw her fingers tense on the flaky bit of bread then relax, one by one.

"No." Lee took another bite of her roll as if her stomach hadn't just sunk to her knees. "Reporters deal in fact, not fiction." He said nothing, but the silent look demanded more of her than a dozen words would have. Taking her time, determined not to fumble again, she sipped at her coffee. "I don't remember mentioning that I was a reporter."

"No, you didn't mention it." He caught her wrist as she set down the cup. The grip of his fingers told her immediately just how angry he was. "You quite deliberately didn't mention it."

With a jerk of her head, she tossed the hair out of her eyes. If she'd lost, she wouldn't go down groveling. "It wasn't required that I tell you." Ignoring the fact that he held one of her hands prisoner, Lee picked up her croissant with the other and took a bite. "I paid my registration fee."

"And pretended to be something you're not."

She met his gaze without flinching. "Apparently, we both pretended to be something we weren't, right from the start."

He tilted his head at her reference to their initial meeting. "I didn't want anything from you. You, on the other hand, went beyond the harmless in your deception."

She didn't like the way it sounded when he said it— so petty, so dirty. And so true. If his fingers hadn't been biting into her wrist, she might have found herself apologizing. Instead, Lee held her ground. "I have a perfect right to be here and a perfect right to try to sell an article on any facet of this conference."

"And I," he said, so mildly her flesh chilled, "have a perfect right to my privacy, to the choice of speaking to a reporter or refusing to speak to one."

"If I'd told you that I was on staff at *Celebrity*," she threw back, making her first attempt to free her arm, "would you have spoken to me at all?"

He still held her wrist; he still held her eyes. For several long seconds, he said nothing. "That's something neither of us will ever know now." He released her wrist so abruptly, her arm dropped to the table, clattering the cup. Lee found that she'd squeezed the flaky pastry into an unpalatable ball.

He frightened her. There was no use denying it even to herself. The force of his anger, so finely restrained, had tiny shocks of cold moving up and down her back. She didn't know him or understand him, nor did she have any way of being certain of what he might do. There was violence in his books; therefore, there was violence in his mind. Clinging to her composure, she lifted her coffee again, drank and tasted absolutely nothing.

"I'm curious to know how you found out." Good, her voice was calm, unhurried. She took the cup in both hands to cover the one quick tremor she couldn't control.

She looked like a kitten backed into a corner, Hunter observed. Ready to spit and scratch, even though her heart was pounding hard enough to be almost audible. He didn't want to respect her for it when he'd rather strangle her. He didn't want to feel a strong urge to touch the pale skin of her cheek. Being deceived by a woman was perhaps the only thing that still had the power to bring him to this degree of rage.

"Oddly enough, I took an interest in you, Lenore. Last night—" He saw her stiffen and felt a certain satisfaction. No, he wasn't going to let her forget that, any more than he could forget it himself. "Last night," he repeated slowly, waiting until her gaze lifted to his again, "I wanted to make love with you. I wanted to get beneath the careful layer of polish and discover you. When I had, you'd have looked as you do now. Soft, fragile, with your mouth naked and your eyes clouded."

Her bones were already melting, her skin already heating, and it was only words. He didn't touch her, didn't attempt to, but the sound of his voice flowed over her skin like the gentlest of caresses. "I don't— I had no intention of letting you make love to me."

"I don't believe in making love to a woman, only with." His eyes never left hers. She could feel her head begin to swim with passion, her breath tremble with it. "Only with," Hunter repeated. "When you left, I turned to the next best way of discovering you."

Lee gripped her hands together in her lap, knowing she had to control the shudders. How could a man have such power? And how could she fight it? Why did she feel as though they were already lovers? Was it just the sense of inevitability that they would be, no matter what her choice? "I don't know what you mean." Her voice was no longer calm.

"Your manuscript."

Uncomprehending, she stared. She'd completely forgotten it the night before in her fear of him, and of herself. Anger and frustration had prevented her from remembering it that morning. Now, on top of a dazed desire, she felt the helplessness of a novice confronted by the master. "I never intended for you to read it," she began. Without thinking, she was shredding her napkin in her lap. "I don't have any aspirations toward being a novelist."

"Then you're a fool as well as a liar."

All sense of helplessness fled. No one, no one in all of her memory, had ever spoken to her like that. "I'm neither a fool nor a liar, Hunter. What I am is an excellent reporter. I want to write an exclusive, in-depth and accurate article on you for our readers."

"Why do you waste your time writing gossip when you've got a novel to finish?"

She went rigid. The eyes that had been clouded with confused desire became frosty. "I don't write gossip."

"You can gloss over it, you can write it with style and intelligence, but it's still gossip." Before Lee could retort, he rose up so quickly, so furiously, her own words were swallowed. "You've no right working forty hours a week on anything but the novel you have inside you. Talent's a two-headed coin, Lenore, and the other side's obligation."

"I don't know what you're talking about." She rose, too, and found she could shout just as effectively as he. "I know my obligations, and one of them's to write a story on you for my magazine."

"And what about the novel?"

Flinging up her hands, she whirled away from him. "What about it?"

"When do you intend to finish it?"

Finish it? She should never have started it. Hadn't she told herself that a dozen times? "Damn it, Hunter, it's a pipe dream."

"It's good."

She turned back, her brows still drawn together with anger but the eyes beneath them suddenly wary. "What?"

"If it hadn't been, your camouflage would have worked very well." He drew out a cigarette while she stared at him. How could he be so patient, move so slowly, when she was ready to jump at every word? "I nearly called you last night to see if you had any more with you, but decided it would keep. I called my editor instead." Still calm, he blew out smoke. "When I gave the chapters to her to read, she recognized your name. Apparently she's quite a fan of *Celebrity*."

"You gave her…" Astonished, Lee dropped into the chair again. "You had no right to show anyone."

"At the time, I fully believed you were precisely what you'd led me to believe you were."

She stood again, then gripped the back of her chair. "I'm a reporter, not a novelist. I'd like you to get the manuscript from her and return it to me."

He tapped his cigarette in an ashtray, only then noticing her neatly written notes. As he skimmed them, Hunter felt twin surges of amusement and annoyance. So, she was trying to put him into a few tidy little slots. She'd find it more difficult than she'd imagined. "Why should I do that?"

"Because it belongs to me. You had no right to give it to anyone else."

"What are you afraid of?" he demanded.

Of failure. The words were almost out before Lee managed to bite them back. "I'm not afraid of anything. I do what I'm best at, and I intend to continue doing it. What are you afraid of?" she retorted. "What are you hiding from?"

She didn't like the look in his eyes when he turned his head toward her again. It wasn't anger she saw there, nor was it arrogance, but something beyond both. "I do what I do best, Lenore." When he'd come into the room, he hadn't planned to do any more than rake her to the bone for her deception and berate her for wasting her talent. Now, as he watched her, Hunter began to think there was a better way to do that and at the same time learn more about her for his own purposes. He was a long way from finished with Lenore Radcliffe. "Just how important is doing a story on me to you?"

Alerted by the change in tone, Lee studied him cautiously. She'd tried everything else, she decided abruptly, perhaps she could appeal to his ego. "It's very important. I've been trying to learn something about you for over three months. You're one of the most popular and critically acclaimed writers of the decade. If you—"

He cut her off by merely lifting a hand. "If I decided to give you an interview, we'd have to spend a great deal of time together, and under my terms."

Lee heard the little warning bell, but ignored it. She could almost taste success. "We can hash out the terms beforehand. I keep my word, Hunter."

"I don't doubt that, once it's given." Crushing out his cigarette, Hunter considered the angles. Perhaps he was asking for trouble. Then again, he hadn't asked for any in quite some time. He was due. "How much more of the manuscript do you have completed?"

"That has nothing to do with this." When he merely lifted a brow and stared, she clenched her teeth. *Humor him,* Lee told herself. *You're too close now.* "About two hundred pages."

"Send the rest to my editor." He gave her a mild look. "I'm sure you have her name by now."

"What does that have to do with the interview?"

"It's one of the terms," Hunter told her easily. "I've

plans for the week after next," he continued. "You can join me—with another copy of your manuscript."

"Join you? Where?"

"For two weeks I'll be camping in Oak Creek Canyon. You'd better buy some sturdy shoes."

"Camping?" She had visions of tents and mosquitoes. "If you're not leaving for your vacation right away, why can't we set up the interview a day or two before?"

"Terms," he reminded her. "My terms."

"You're trying to make this difficult."

"Yes." He smiled then, just a hint of amusement around his sculpted mouth. "You'll work for your exclusive, Lenore."

"All right." Her chin came up. "Where should I meet you and when?"

Now he smiled fully, appreciating determination when he saw it. "In Sedona. I'll contact you when I'm certain of the date—and when my editor's let me know she's received the rest of your manuscript."

"I hardly see why you're using that to blackmail me."

He crossed to her then, unexpectedly combing his fingers through her hair. It was casual, friendly and uncannily intimate. "Perhaps one of the first things you should know about me is I'm eccentric. If people accept their own eccentricities, they can justify anything they do. Anything at all." He ended the words by closing his mouth over hers.

He heard her suck in her breath, felt her stiffen. But she didn't struggle away. Perhaps she was testing herself, though he didn't think she could know she tested him, too. He wanted to carry her to the rumpled bed, slip off that thin swirl of silk and fit his body to hers. It would fit; somehow he already knew. She'd move with him, for him, as if they'd always been lovers. He knew, though he couldn't explain.

He could feel her melting into him, her lips growing warm and moist from his. They were alone and the need was like iron. Yet he knew, without understanding, that if they made love now, sated that need, he'd never see her again. They both had fears to face before they became lovers, and after.

Hunter gave himself the pleasure of one long, last kiss, drawing her taste into him, allowing himself to be overwhelmed, just for a moment, by the feel of her against him. Then he forced himself to level, forced himself to remember that they each wanted something from the other—secrets and an intimacy both would put into words in their own ways.

Drawing back, he let his hands linger only a moment on the curve of her cheek, the softness of her hair, while she said nothing. "If you can get through two weeks in the canyon, you'll have your story."

Leaving her with that, he turned and strolled out the door.

"If I can make it through two weeks," Lee muttered, pulling a heavy sweater out of her drawer. "I tell you, Bryan, I've never met anyone who says as little who can irritate me as much." Ten days back in L.A. hadn't dulled her fury.

Bryan fingered the soft wool of the sweater. "Lee, don't you have *any* grub-around clothes?"

"I bought some sweatshirts," she said under her breath. "I haven't spent a great deal of my time in a tent."

"Advice." Before another pair of the trim slacks could

be packed into the knapsack Lee had borrowed from her, Bryan took her hand.

Lee lifted one thin coppery brow. "You know I detest advice."

Grinning, Bryan dropped down on the bed. "I know. That's why I can never resist dishing it out. Lee, really, I know you have a pair of jeans. I've *seen* you wear them." She brushed at the hair that escaped her braid. "Designer or not, take jeans, not seventy-five-dollar slacks. Invest in another pair or two," she went on while Lee frowned down at the clothes still in her free hand. "Put that gorgeous wool sweater back in your drawer and pick up a couple of flannel shirts. That'll take care of the nights if it turns cool. Now…"

Because Lee was listening with a frown of concentration, she continued. "Put in some T-shirts—blouses are for the office, not for hiking. Take at least one pair of shorts and invest in some good thick socks. If you had more time, I'd tell you to break in those new hiking boots, because they're going to make you suffer."

"The salesman said—"

"There's nothing wrong with them, Lee, except they've never been out of the box. Face it." She stretched back among Lee's collection of pillows. "You've been too concerned about packing enough paper and pencils to worry about gear. If you don't want to make an ass of yourself, listen to momma."

With a quick hiss of breath, Lee replaced the sweater. "I've already made an ass of myself, several times." She slammed one of her dresser drawers. "He's not going to get the best of me during these next two weeks, Bryan. If I have to sleep out in a tent and climb rocks to get this story, then I'll do it."

"If you tried real hard, you could have fun at the same time."

"I'm not looking for fun. I'm looking for an exclusive."

"We're friends."

Though it was a statement, not a question, Lee glanced over. "Yes." For the first time since she'd begun packing, she smiled. "We're friends."

"Then tell me what it is that bothers you about this guy. You've been ready to chew your nails for over a week." Though she spoke lightly, the concern leaked through. "You wanted to interview Hunter Brown, and you're going to interview Hunter Brown. How come you look like you're preparing for war?"

"Because that's how I feel." With anyone else, Lee would have evaded the question or turned cold. Because it was Bryan, she sat on the edge of the bed, twisting a newly purchased sweatshirt in her hands. "He makes me want what I don't want to want, feel what I don't want to feel. Bryan, I don't have room in my life for complications."

"Who does?"

"I know exactly where I'm going," Lee insisted, a bit too vehemently. "I know exactly how to get there. Somehow I have a feeling that Hunter's a detour."

"Sometimes a detour is more interesting than a planned route, and you get to the same place eventually."

"He looks at me as though he knows what I'm thinking. More, as if he knows what I thought yesterday, or last year. It's not comfortable."

"You've never looked for the comfortable," Bryan stated, pillowing her head on her folded arms. "You've always looked for a challenge. You've just never found one in a man before."

"I don't want one in a man." Violently, Lee stuffed the sweatshirt into the knapsack. "I want them in my work."

"You don't have to go."

Lee lifted her head. "I'm going."

"Then don't go with your teeth gritted." Crossing her legs under her, Bryan sat up. She was as rumpled as Lee was tidy but seemed oddly suited to the luxurious pile of pillows around her. "This is a tremendous opportunity for you, professionally and personally. Oak Creek's one of the most beautiful canyons in the country. You'll have two weeks to be part of it. There's a man who doesn't bore or cater to you." She grinned at Lee's arch look. "You know damn well they do one or the other and you can't abide it. Enjoy the change of scene."

"I'm going to work," Lee reminded her. "Not to pick wildflowers."

"Pick a few anyway. You'll still get your story."

"And make Hunter Brown squirm."

Bryan gave her throaty laugh, tossing a pillow into the air. "If that's what you're set on doing, you'll do it. I'd feel sorry for the guy if he hadn't given me nightmares." After a quick grimace, her look softened into one of affection. "And, Lee…" She laid her hand over her friend's. "If he makes you want something, take it. Life isn't crowded with offers. Give yourself a present."

Lee sat silently for a moment, then sighed. "I'm not sure if I'd be giving myself a present or a curse." Rising, she went to her dresser. "How many pairs of socks?"

"But is she pretty?" Sarah sat in the middle of the rug, one leg bent toward her while she tried valiantly to hook the other behind her neck. "*Really* pretty?"

Hunter dug into the basket of laundry. Sarah had

scrupulously reminded him it was his turn to sort and fold. "I wouldn't use the word *pretty*. A carefully arranged basket of fruit's pretty."

Sarah giggled, then rolled and arched into a back bend. She liked nothing better than talking with her father, because no one else talked like him. "What word would you use, then?"

Hunter folded a T-shirt with the name of a popular rock band glittered across it. "She has a rare, classic beauty that a lot of women wouldn't know precisely what to do with."

"But she does?"

He remembered. He wanted. "She does."

Sarah lay down on her back to snuggle with the dog that stretched out beside her. She liked the soft, warm feel of Santanas's fur, in much the same way she liked to close her eyes and listen to her father's voice. "She tried to fool you," Sarah reminded him. "You don't like it when people try to fool you."

"To her way of thinking, she was doing her job."

With one hand on the dog's neck, Sarah looked up at her father with big, dark eyes so much like his own. "You never talk to reporters."

"They don't interest me." Hunter came upon a pair of jeans with a widening hole in the knee. "Aren't these new?"

"Sort of. So why are you taking her camping with you?"

"Sort of new shouldn't have holes already, and I'm not taking her, she's coming with me."

Digging in her pocket, she came up with a stick of gum. She wasn't supposed to chew any because of her braces, so she fondled the wrapped piece instead. In six months, Sarah thought, she was going to chew a dozen pieces, all at once. "Because she's a reporter or because she has a rare, classic beauty?"

Hunter glanced down to see his daughter's eyes laughing at him. She was entirely too clever, he decided, and threw a pair of rolled socks at her. "Both, but mostly because I find her interesting and talented. I want to see how much I can find out about her, while she's trying to find out about me."

"You'll find out more," Sarah declared, idly tossing the socks up in the air. "You always do. I think it's a good idea," she added after a moment. "Aunt Bonnie says you don't see enough women, especially women who challenge your mind."

"Aunt Bonnie thinks in couples."

"Maybe she'll incite your simmering passion."

Hunter's hand paused on its way to the basket. "What?"

"I read it in a book." Expertly, she rolled so that her feet touched the floor behind her head. "This man met this woman, and they didn't like each other at first, but there was this strong physical attraction and this growing desire, and—"

"I get the picture." Hunter looked down at the slim, dark-haired girl on the floor. She was his daughter, he thought. She was ten. How in God's name had they gotten involved in the subject of passion? "You of all people should know that things don't often happen in real life the way they do in books."

"Fiction's based on reality." Sarah grinned, pleased to throw one of his own quotes back at him. "But before you do fall in love with her, or have too much simmering passion, I want to meet her."

"I'll keep that in mind." Still watching her, Hunter held up three unmatched socks. "Just how does this happen every week?"

Sarah considered the socks a moment, then sat up. "I think there's a parallel universe in the dryer. On the other side of the door, at this very minute, someone else is holding up three unmatched socks."

"An interesting theory." Reaching down, Hunter grabbed her. As Sarah's laughter bounced off the lofted ceiling, he dropped her, bottom first, into the basket.

Chapter 5

It was like every Western she'd ever seen. With the sun bright in her eyes, Lee could almost see outlaws outrunning posses and Indians hiding in wait behind rocks and buttes. If she let her imagination go, she could almost hear the hoofbeats ring against the rock-hard ground. Because she was alone in the car, she could let her imagination go.

The rich red mountains rose up into a painfully blue sky. There was a vastness that was almost outrageous in scope, with no lushness, with no need for any, with no patience for any. It made her throat dry and her heart thud.

There was green—the silvery-green of sage clinging to the red, rocky soil and the deeper hue of junipers, which would give way to a sudden, seemingly planned sparseness. Yet the sparseness was rich in itself. The space, the overwhelming space, left her stunned and humble and oddly hungry for more. Everywhere there were more rocky ridges, more color, more... Lee shook her head. Just more.

Even when she came closer to town, the houses and buildings couldn't compete with the openness. Stop signs, streetlights, flower gardens were inconsequential. Her car joined more cars, but five times the number would still have been insignificant. It was a view you drank in, she thought, but its taste was hot and packed a punch.

She liked Sedona immediately. Its tidy Western flavor suited the fabulous backdrop instead of marring it. She hadn't been sure anything could.

The main street was lined with shops with neat signs and clean plate glass. She noticed lots of wood, lots of bargains and absolutely no sense of urgency. Sedona clung to the aura of town rather than city. It seemed comfortable with itself and with the spectacular spread of sky. Perhaps, Lee mused as she followed the directions to the rental-car drop-off, just perhaps, she'd enjoy the next two weeks after all.

Since she was early for her arranged meeting time with Hunter even after dealing with the paperwork on her rental car, Lee decided she could afford to indulge herself playing tourist. She had nearly an hour to vacation before work began again.

The liquid silver necklaces and turquoise earrings in the shop windows tempted her, but she moved past them. There'd be plenty of opportunities after this little adventure for something frivolous—as a reward for success. For now, she was only passing time.

But the scent of fudge drew her. Slipping inside the little shop that claimed to sell the world's best, Lee bought a half pound. For energy, she told herself as the sample melted in her mouth. There was no telling what kind of food she'd get over the next two weeks. Hunter had very specifically told her when he contacted her by phone that he'd handle the supplies. The fudge, Lee told herself, would be emergency rations.

Besides, some of Bryan's advice had been valid enough. There was no use going into this thing thinking she'd be miserable and uncomfortable. There wasn't any harm getting into the spirit a bit, Lee decided as she strolled into a Western-wear shop. If she viewed the next two weeks as a working vacation, she'd be much better off.

Though she toyed with conch belts for a few minutes, Lee rejected them. They wouldn't suit her, any more than the fringed or sequined shirts would. Perhaps she'd pick one up for Bryan before heading back to L.A. Anything Bryan put on suited her, Lee mused with something closer to a sigh than to envy. Bryan never had to feel restricted to the tailored, the simple or the proper.

Was it a matter of suitability, Lee wondered, or a matter of image? With a shrug, she ran a fingertip down the shoulder of a short suede jacket. Image or not, she'd locked herself into it for too long to change now. She didn't want to change, in any case, Lee reminded herself as she wandered through rows and rows of hats. She understood Lee Radcliffe just as she was.

Telling herself she'd stay only another minute, she set her knapsack at her feet. She wasn't particularly athletic. Lee tried on a dung-colored Stetson with a curved brim. She wasn't flighty. She exchanged the first hat for a smaller one with a spray of feathers in the band. What she was, was businesslike and down-to-earth.

She dropped a black flat-brimmed hat on her head and studied the result. Sedate, she decided, smiling a little. Practical. Yes, if she were in the market for—

"You're wearing it all wrong."

Before Lee could react, two strong hands were tilting the hat farther down on her head. Critically, Hunter angled it slightly, then stepped away. "Yes, it's the perfect choice for you. The contrast with your hair and skin, that practical sort of dash." Taking her shoulders, he turned her toward the mirror, where both his image and hers looked back at her.

She saw the way his fingers held her shoulders, long and confident. She could see how small she looked pressing against him. In no more than an instant, Lee could feel the pleasure she wanted to ignore and the annoyance she had to concentrate on.

"I've no intention of buying it." Embarrassed, she drew the hat off and returned it to the shelf.

"Why not?"

"I've no need for it."

"A woman who buys only what she needs?" Amusement crossed his face even as anger crossed hers. "A sexist remark if I've ever heard one," Hunter continued before she could speak. "Still, it's a pity you won't buy it. It gives you a breezy air of confidence."

Ignoring that, Lee bent down and picked up her knapsack again. "I hope I haven't kept you waiting long. I got into town early and decided to kill some time."

"I saw you wander in here when I drove in. Even in jeans you walk as though you were wearing a three-piece suit." While she tried to work out if that had been a compliment, he smiled. "What kind did you buy?"

"What?" She was still frowning over his comment.

"Fudge." He glanced down at the bag. "What kind did you buy?"

Caught again, Lee thought, nearly resigned to it. "Some milk chocolate and some rocky road."

"Good choice." Taking her arm, he led her through the shop. "If you're determined to resist the hat, we may as well get started."

She noted the Jeep parked at the curb and narrowed her eyes. This was certainly the same one he'd had in Flagstaff. "Have you been staying in Arizona?"

He circled the hood, leaving her to climb in on her own. "I've had some business to take care of."

Her reporter's sense sharpened. "Research?"

He gave her that odd ghost of a smile. "A writer's always researching." He wouldn't tell her—yet—that his research on Lenore Radcliffe led him to some intriguing conclusions. "You brought a copy of the rest of your manuscript?"

Unable to prevent herself, Lee shot him a look of intense dislike. "That was one of the conditions."

"So it was." Easily he backed up, then pulled into the thin stream of traffic. "What's your impression of Sedona?"

"I can see that the weather and the atmosphere would draw the tourist trade." She found it necessary to sit very erect and to look straight ahead.

"The same might be said of Maui or the South of France."

She couldn't stop her lips from curving, but turned to look out the side window. "It has the air of having been here forever, with very little change. The sense of space is fierce, not at all soothing, but it pulls you in. I suppose it makes me think of the people who first saw it from horseback or the seat of a wagon. I imagine some of them would have been compelled to build right away, to set up a community so that the vastness didn't overwhelm them."

"And others would have been drawn to the desert or the mountains so that the buildings wouldn't close them in."

As she nodded, it occurred to her that she might fit into the first group, and he into the second.

The road he took narrowed and twisted down. He didn't drive sedately, but with the air of a man who knew he could negotiate whatever curve was thrown at him. Lee gripped the door handle, determined not to comment on his speed. It was like taking the downhill rush of a roller coaster without having had the preparatory uphill climb. They whooshed down, a rock wall on one side, a spiraling drop on the other.

"Do you camp often?" Her knuckles were whitening on the handle, but though she had to shout to be heard she was satisfied that her voice was calm enough.

"Now and again."

"I'm curious..." She stopped and cleared her throat as Hunter whipped around a snaking turn. "Why camping?" Did the rocks in the sheer wall beside them ever loosen and tumble onto the road? She decided it was best not to think about it. "A man in your position could go anywhere and do anything he chose."

"This is what I chose," he pointed out.

"All right. Why?"

"There are times when everyone needs simplicity."

Her foot pressed down on the floorboard as if it were a brake pedal. "Isn't this just one more way you have of avoiding people?"

"Yes." His easy agreement had her turning her head to stare at him. He was amused to note that her hand loosened on the handle and that her concentration was on him now rather than the road. "It's also a way of getting away from my work. You never get away from writing, but there are times you need to get away from the trappings of writing."

Her gaze sharpened. Though her fingers itched for her notebook, Lee had faith in her own powers of retention. "You don't like trappings."

"We don't always like what's necessary."

Oblivious to the speed and the curves now, Lee tucked one leg under her and turned toward him. That attracted him, Hunter reflected. The way she'd unconsciously drop that careful shield whenever something challenged her mind. That attracted him every bit as much as her cool, nineteenth-century beauty.

"What do you consider trappings as regards your profession?"

"The confinement of an office, the hum of a machine, the paperwork that's unavoidable but interferes with the story flow."

Odd, but that was precisely what she needed in order to maintain discipline. "If you could change it, what would you do?"

He smiled again. Hunter had never known anyone who thought in more basic terms or straighter lines. "I'd go back a few centuries to when I could simply travel and tell the story."

She believed him. Though he had wealth and fame and critical acclaim, Lee believed him. "None of the rest means anything to you, does it? The glory, the admiration?"

"Whose admiration?"

"Your readers and the critics."

He pulled off the road next to a small wooden building that served as a trading post. "I'm not indifferent to my readership, Lenore."

"But to the critics."

"I admire the orderliness of your mind," he said and stepped from the Jeep.

It was a good beginning, Lee thought, pleased, as she climbed out the passenger side. He'd already told her more than anyone else knew, and the two weeks had barely begun. If she could just keep him talking, learn enough generalities, then she could pin him down on specifics. But she'd have to pace herself. When you were dealing with a master of evasion, you had to tread carefully. She couldn't afford to relax.

"Do we have to check in?"

From behind her back Hunter grinned, while Lee struggled to pull out her knapsack. "I've already taken care of the paperwork."

"I see." Her pack was heavy, but she told herself she'd refuse any offer of assistance and carry it herself. A moment later, she saw it wouldn't be an issue. Hunter merely stood aside, watching as she wriggled into the shoulder straps. So much for chivalry, she thought, annoyed that he hadn't given her the opportunity to assert her independence. She caught the gleam in his eye. He read her mind much too easily.

"Want me to carry the fudge?"

She closed her fingers firmly over the bag. "I'll manage."

With his own gear on his back, Hunter started down a path, leaving her no choice but to follow. He moved as though he'd been walking dirt paths all his life—as if perhaps he'd cut a few of his own. Though she felt out of place in her hiking boots, Lee was determined to keep up and to make it look easy.

"You've camped here before?"

"Mmm-hmm."

"Why?"

He stopped, turning to fix her with that dark, intense stare that always took her breath away. "You only have to look."

She did and saw that the walls and peaks of the canyon rose up as if they'd never stop. They were a color and texture unique to themselves, enhanced by the snatches of green from rough, hardy trees and shrubs that seemed to grow out of the rock. As she had from the air, Lee thought of castles and fortresses, but without the distance the plane had given her, she couldn't be sure whether she was storming the walls or being enveloped by them.

She was warm. The sun was strong, even with the shade of trees that grew thickly at this elevation. Though she saw other people—children, adults, babies carried papoose-style—she felt no sense of crowding.

It's like a painting, she realized all at once. *It's as though we're walking into a canvas.* The feeling it gave her was both eerie and irresistible. She shifted the pack on her back as she kept pace with Hunter.

"I noticed some houses," she began. "I didn't realize people actually lived in the canyon."

"Apparently."

Sensing his mind was elsewhere, Lee lapsed into silence. She'd done too well to start pushing. For now, she'd follow Hunter, since he obviously knew where he was going.

It surprised her that she found the walk pleasant. For years her life had been directed by deadlines, rush and self-imposed demands. If someone had asked her where she'd choose to spend two weeks relaxing, her mind would have gone blank. But when ideas had begun to come, roughing it in a canyon in Arizona wouldn't have made the top ten. She'd never have considered that the purity of air and the unimpeded arch of sky would be so appealing to her.

She heard a quiet, musical tinkle that took her several moments to identify. The creek, Lee realized. She could smell the water. The new sensation gave her a quick thrill. Her guide, and her project, continued to move at a steady pace in front of her. Lee banked down the urge to share her discovery with him. He'd only think her foolish.

Did she realize how totally out of her element she looked? Hunter wondered. It had taken him only one glance to see that the jeans and the boots she wore were straight out of the box. Even the T-shirt that fit softly over her torso was obviously boutiqueware rather than a department-store purchase. She looked like a model posing as a camper. She smelled expensive, exclusive. Wonderful. What kind of woman carried a worn knapsack and wore sapphire studs in her ears?

As her scent wafted toward him again, carried on the breeze, Hunter reminded himself that he had two weeks to find out. Whatever notes she would make on him, he'd be making an equal number on her. Perhaps both of them would have what they wanted before the time was up. Perhaps both of them would have cause to regret it.

He wanted her. It had been a long time since he'd wanted anything, anyone, that he didn't already have. Over the past days he'd thought often of her response to that long, lingering kiss. He'd thought of his own response. They'd learn about each other over the next two weeks, though they each had their own purposes. But nothing was free. They'd both pay for it.

The quiet soothed him. The towering walls of the canyon soothed him. Lee saw their ferocity, he their tranquillity. Perhaps they both saw what they needed to see.

"For a woman, and a reporter, you have an amazing capacity for silence."

The weight of her pack was beginning to take precedence over the novelty of the scenery. Not once had he asked if she wanted to stop and rest, not once had he even bothered to look back to see if she was still behind him. She wondered why he didn't feel the hole her eyes were boring into his back.

"You have an amazing capacity for the insulting compliment."

Hunter turned to look at her for the first time since they'd started out. There was a thin sheen of perspiration on her brow and her breath came quickly. It didn't detract an iota from her cool, innate beauty. "Sorry," he said, but didn't appear to be. "Have I been walking too fast? You don't look out of shape."

Despite the ache that ran down the length of her back, Lee straightened. "I'm *not* out of shape." Her feet were killing her.

"The site's not much farther." Reaching down to his

hip, he lifted the canteen and unscrewed the top. "It's perfect weather for hiking," he said mildly. "Mid-seventies, and there's a breeze."

Lee managed to suppress a scowl as she eyed the canteen. "Don't you have a cup?"

It took Hunter a moment to realize she was perfectly serious. Wisely, he decided to swallow the chuckle. "Packed away with the china," he told her soberly enough.

"I'll wait." She hooked her hands in the front straps of her knapsack to ease some of the weight.

"Suit yourself." While Lee looked on, Hunter drank deeply. If he sensed her resentment, he gave no sign as he capped the canteen again and resumed the walk.

Her throat was all the drier at the thought of water. He'd done it on purpose, she thought while she gritted her teeth. Did he think she'd missed that quick flash of humor in his eyes? It was just one more thing to pay him back for when the time came. Oh, she couldn't wait to write the article and expose Hunter Brown for the arrogant, coldhearted demigod he'd set himself up to be.

She wouldn't be surprised if he was walking her in circles, just to make her suffer. Bryan had been all too right about the boots. Lee had lost count of the number of campsites they'd passed, some occupied and some empty. If this was his way of punishing her for not revealing from the start that she worked for *Celebrity,* he was certainly doing an elaborate job.

Disgusted, exhausted, with her legs feeling less like flesh and more like rubber, she reached out and grabbed his arm. "Just why, when you obviously have a dislike for women and for reporters, did you agree to spend two weeks with me?"

"Dislike women?" His brows arched. "My likes and dislikes aren't as generalized as that, Lenore." Her skin was warm and slightly damp when he curled his fingers around the back of her neck. "Have I given you the impression I dislike you?"

She had to fight the urge to stretch like a cat under his hand. "I don't care what your personal feelings are toward me. This is business."

"For you." His fingers squeezed gently, bringing her an inch closer. "I'm on vacation. Do you know, your mouth's every bit as appealing now as it was the first time I saw it."

"I don't want to appeal to you." But her voice was breathy. "I want you to think of me only as a reporter."

The smile hovered at the edges of his mouth, around the corners of his eyes. "All right," he agreed. "In a minute."

Then he touched his lips to hers, as gently as he had the first time, and as devastatingly. She stood still, amazed to feel as intense a swirl of sensation as she had before. When he touched her, hardly touching her, it was as if she'd never been kissed before. A new discovery, a fresh beginning—how could it be?

The weight on her back seemed to vanish. The ache in her muscles turned into a deeper, richer ache that penetrated to the bone. Her lips parted, though she knew what she invited. Then his tongue joined with hers, slipping into the moistness, drinking up her flavor.

Lee felt the urgency scream through her body, but he was patient. So patient, she couldn't know what the patience cost him. He hadn't expected pain. No woman had ever brought him pain with desire. He hadn't expected the need to flame through him like brushfire, fast and out of control. Hunter had a vision, with perfect clarity, of what it would be like to take her there, on the ground, under the blazing sun with the canyon circling like castle walls around them and the sky like a cathedral dome.

But there was too much fear in her. He could sense it. Perhaps there was too much fear in him. When they came together, it might have the power to topple both their worlds.

"Your lips melt against mine, Lenore," he whispered. "It's all but impossible to resist."

She drew back, aroused, alarmed and all too aware of how helpless she'd been. "I don't want to repeat myself, Hunter," she managed. "And I don't want to amuse you with clichés, but this is business. I'm a reporter on assignment. If we're to make it through the next two weeks peacefully, it'd be wise to remember that."

"I don't know about the peace," he countered, "but we'll try your rules first."

Suspicious, but finding no room to argue, Lee followed him again. They walked out of the sunlight into the dim coolness of a stand of trees. The creek was distant but still audible. From somewhere to the left came the tinny sound of music from a portable radio. Closer at hand was the rustling of small animals. With a nervous look around, Lee convinced herself they were nothing more than squirrels and rabbits.

With the trees closing around them, they might have been anywhere. The sun filtered through, but softly, on the rough, uneven ground. There was a clearing, small and snug, with a circle of stones surrounding a long-dead campfire. Lee glanced around, fighting off the uneasiness. Somehow, she hadn't thought it would be this remote, this quiet, this…alone.

"There're shower and bathroom facilities a few hundred yards east," Hunter began as he slipped off his pack. "Primitive but adequate. The metal can's for trash. Be sure the lid's tightly closed or it'll attract animals. How's your sense of direction?"

Gratefully, she slipped out of her own pack and let it drop. "It's fine." Now, if she could just take off the boots and rest her feet.

"Good. Then you can gather some firewood while I set up the tent."

Annoyed with the order, she opened her mouth, then firmly shut it again with only a slight hiss. He wouldn't have any cause to complain about her. But as she started to stalk off, the rest of his sentence hit home.

"What do you mean *the* tent?"

He was already unfastening the straps of his pack. "I prefer sleeping in something in case it rains."

"*The* tent," Lee repeated, closing in on him. "As in singular?"

He didn't even spare her a look. "One tent, two sleeping bags."

She wasn't going to explode; she wasn't going to make a scene. After taking a deep breath, she spoke precisely. "I don't consider those adequate arrangements."

He didn't speak for a minute, not because he was choosing his words but because the unpacking occupied him more than the conversation. "If you want to sleep in the open, it's up to you." Hunter drew out a slim, folded piece of material that looked more like a bedsheet than a tent. "But when we decide to become lovers, the arrangements won't make any difference."

"We didn't come here to be lovers," Lee snapped back furiously.

"A reporter and an assignment," Hunter replied mildly. "Two sexless terms. They shouldn't have any problem sharing a tent."

Caught in her own logic, Lee turned and stalked away. She wouldn't give him the satisfaction of seeing her behave like a woman.

Hunter lifted his head and watched her storm off through the trees. She'd make the first move, he promised himself, suddenly angry. By God, he wouldn't touch her until she came to him.

While he set up camp, he tried to convince himself it was as easy as it sounded.

Chapter 6

Two sexless terms, Lee repeated silently as she scooped up some twigs. *Bastard,* she thought with grim satisfaction, was also a sexless term. It suited Hunter Brown to perfection. He had no business treating her like a fool just because she'd made a fool of herself already.

She wasn't going to give an inch. She'd sleep in the damn sleeping bag in the damn tent for the next thirteen nights without saying another word about it.

Thirteen, she thought, sending a malicious look over her shoulder. He'd probably planned that, too. If he thought she was going to make a scene, or curl up outside the tent to sleep in the open to spite him, he'd be disappointed. She'd be scrupulously professional, unspeakably cooperative and utterly sexless. Before it was over, he'd think he'd been sharing his tent with a robot.

But she'd know better. Lee let out one long, frustrated breath as she scouted for more sticks. She'd know there was a man beside her in the night. A powerfully sexy, impossibly attractive man who could make her blood swim with no more than a look.

It wouldn't be easy to forget she was a woman over the next two weeks, when she'd be spending every night with a man who already had her nerves jumping.

Her job wasn't to make herself forget, Lee reminded herself, but to make certain *he* forgot. A challenge. That was the best way to look at it. It was a challenge she promised herself she'd succeed at.

With her arms full of sticks and twigs, Lee lifted her chin. She felt hot, dirty and tired. It wasn't an auspicious way to begin a war. Ignoring the ache, she squared her shoulders. She might have to sacrifice a round or two, but she'd win the battle. With a dangerous light in her eyes, she headed toward camp.

She had to be grateful his back was to her when she walked into the clearing. The tent was smaller, much, much smaller, than she'd imagined. It was fashioned from tough, lightweight material that looked nearly transparent. It arched, rounded rather than pointed at the peak, and low to the ground. So low, Lee noted, that she'd have to crawl to get inside. Once in, they'd be forced to sleep nearly elbow to elbow. Then and there, she determined to sleep like a rock. Unmoving.

The size of the tent preoccupied her, so that she didn't notice what Hunter was doing until she was almost beside him. Fresh rage broke out as she dropped her load of wood on the ground. "Just what the hell do you think you're doing?"

Unperturbed by the fury in her voice, Hunter glanced up. In one hand he held a large clear-plastic bag filled with makeup, in the other a flimsy piece of peach-colored material trimmed with ivory lace. "You did know we were going camping," he said mildly, "not to the Beverly Wilshire?"

The color she considered the curse of fair skin flooded her cheeks. "You have no right to go digging around in my things." She snatched the teddy out of his hand, then balled it in her fist.

"I was unpacking." Idly, he turned the makeup bag over to study it from both sides. "I thought you knew to bring only necessities. While I'll admit you have a very subtle, experienced way with this sort of thing—" he gestured with the bag "—eye shadow and lip gloss are excess baggage around a campfire." His voice was infuriatingly friendly, his eyes were only lightly amused. "I've seen you without any of it and had no cause to complain. You certainly don't have to bother with this on my account."

"You conceited jerk." Lee snatched the bag out of his hand. "I don't care if I look like a hag on your account." Taking the knapsack, she stuffed her belongings back inside. "It's *my* baggage, and I'll carry it."

"You certainly will."

"You officious sonofa—" She broke off, barely. "Just don't tell me how to run my life."

"Now, now, name-calling's no way to promote goodwill." Rising, Hunter held out a friendly hand. "Truce?"

Lee eyed him warily. "On what terms?"

He grinned. "That's what I like about you, Lenore, no easy capitulations. A truce with as little interference as possible on both sides. An amiable business arrangement." He saw her relax slightly and couldn't resist the temptation to ruffle her feathers again. "You won't complain about my coffee, and I won't complain when you wear that little scrap of lace to bed."

She gave him a cool smile as she took his hand. "I'm sleeping in my clothes."

"Fair enough." He gave her hand a quick squeeze. "I'm not. Let's see about that coffee."

As he often did, he left her torn between frustration and amusement.

When he put his mind to it, Lee was to discover, Hunter could make things easier. Without fuss, he had the campfire burning and the coffee brewing. Its scent alone was enough to soothe her temper. The economical way he went about it made her think more kindly of him.

There was no point in being at each other's throats for the next two weeks, she decided as she found a convenient rock to sit on. Relaxing might be out of the question, she mused, watching him take clever, compact cooking utensils out of the pack, but animosity wouldn't help, not with a man like Hunter. He was playing games with her. As long as she knew that and avoided the pitfalls, she'd get what she'd come for. So far, she'd allowed him to set the rules and change them at his whim. That would have to change. Lee hooked her hands around a raised knee.

"Do you go camping to get away from the pressure?"

Hunter didn't look back at her, but checked the lantern. So, they were going to start playing word games already. "What pressure?"

Lee might have sighed if she weren't so determined to be pleasantly professional. "There must be pressures from all sides in your line of work. Demands from your publisher, disagreements with your editor, a story that just won't gel the way you want it to, deadlines."

"I don't believe in deadlines."

There was something, Lee thought, and reached for her notepad. "But doesn't every writer face deadlines from time to time? And can't they be an enormous pressure when the story isn't flowing or you're blocked?"

"Writer's block?" Hunter poured coffee into a metal cup. "There's no such thing."

She glanced over for only a second, brow raised. "Oh, come on, Hunter, some very successful writers have suffered from it, even sought professional help. There must have been a time in your career when you found yourself up against a wall."

"You push the wall out of the way."

Frowning, she accepted the cup he handed her. "How?"

"By working through it." He had a jar of powdered milk, which she refused. "If you don't believe in something, refuse to believe it exists, it doesn't, not for you."

"But you write about things that couldn't possibly exist."

"Why not?"

She stared at him, a dark, attractive man sitting on the ground drinking coffee from a metal cup. He looked so at ease with himself, so relaxed, that for a moment she found it difficult to connect him to the man who created stark terror out of words. "Because there aren't monsters under the bed or demons in the closet."

"There's demons in every closet," he disagreed mildly, "some better hidden than others."

"You're saying you believe in what you write about."

"Every writer believes in what he writes. There'd be no purpose in it otherwise."

"You think some—" She didn't want to use the word *demon* again, and her hand moved in frustration as she sought the right phrase. "Some evil force," Lee chose, "can actually manipulate people?"

"It's more accurate to say I don't believe in anything. Possibilities." Did his eyes become darker, or was it her imagination? "There's no limit to possibilities, Lenore."

His eyes were too dark to read. If he was playing with her, baiting her, she couldn't tell. Uncomfortable, she shifted the topic. "When you sit down to write a story, you craft it, spending hours, days, on the angles and the edges, the same way a carpenter builds a cabinet."

He liked her analogy. Hunter sipped at the strong black coffee, enjoying the taste, enjoying the mingled scents of burning wood, summer and Lee's quiet perfume. "Telling a story's an art, writing's a craft."

Lee felt a quick kick of excitement. That was exactly what she was after, those concise little quotes that gave an insight into his character. "Do you consider yourself an artist, then, or a craftsman?"

He drank without hurry, noting that Lee had barely touched her coffee. The eagerness was with her again, her pen poised, her eyes fixed on his. He found he wanted her more when she was like this. He wanted to see that eager look on her face for him, for the man, not the writer. He wanted to sense the ripe anticipation, lover to lover, arms reaching, mouth softening.

If he were writing the script, he'd keep these two people from fulfilling each other's needs for some time yet. It was necessary to flesh them out a bit first, but the ache told him what he needed. Carefully he arranged another piece of wood on the fire.

"An artist by birth," he said at length, "a craftsman by choice."

"I know it's a standard question," she began, with a brisk professionalism that made him smile, "but where do you get your ideas?"

"From life."

She looked over again as he lit a cigarette. "Hunter, you can't convince me that the plot for *Devil's Due* came out of the everyday."

"If you take the everyday, twist it, add a few maybes, you can come up with anything."

"So you take the ordinary, twist it and come up with the extraordinary." Understanding this a bit better, she nodded, satisfied. "How much of yourself goes into your characters?"

"As much as they need."

Again it was so simply, so easily said, she knew he meant it exactly. "Do you ever base one of your characters on someone you know?"

"From time to time." He smiled at her, a smile she neither trusted nor understood. "When I find someone intriguing enough. Do you ever get tired of writing about other people when you've got a world of characters in your own head?"

"It's my job."

"That's not an answer."

"I'm not here to answer questions."

"Why are you here?"

He was closer. Lee hadn't realized he'd moved. He was sitting just below her, obviously relaxed, slightly curious, in charge. "To do an interview with a successful, award-winning author."

"An award-winning author wouldn't make you nervous."

The pencil was growing damp in her hand. She could have cursed in frustration. "You don't."

"You lie too quickly, and not easily at all." His hands rested loosely on his knees as he watched her. The odd ring he wore glinted dully, gold and silver. "If I were to touch you, just touch you, right now, you'd tremble."

"You think too much of yourself," she told him, but rose.

"I think of you," he said, so quietly the pad slipped out of her hand, unnoticed. "You make me want, I make you nervous." He was looking into her again; she could almost feel it. "It should be an interesting combination over the next couple of weeks."

He wasn't going to intimidate her. He *wasn't* going to make her tremble. "The sooner you remember I'm going to be working for the next two weeks, the simpler things will be." Trying to sound haughty nearly worked. Lee wondered if he heard the slight catch in her voice.

"Since you're resigned to working," he said easily, "you can give me a hand starting dinner. After tonight, we'll take turns making meals."

She wasn't going to give him the satisfaction of telling him she knew nothing about cooking over a fire. He already knew. Neither would she give the satisfaction of being confused by his mercurial mood changes. Instead, Lee brushed at her bangs. "I'm going to wash up first."

Hunter watched her start off in the wrong direction, but said nothing. She'd find the shower facilities sooner or later, he figured. Things would be more interesting if neither of them gave the other an inch.

He wasn't sure, but Hunter thought he heard Lee

swear from somewhere behind him. Smiling a little, he leaned back against the rock and finished his cigarette.

Groggy, stiff and sniffing the scent of coffee in the air, Lee woke. She knew exactly where she was—as far over on her side of the tent as she could get, deep into the sleeping bag Hunter had provided for her. And alone. It took her only seconds to sense that Hunter no longer shared the tent with her. Just as it had taken her hours the night before to convince herself it didn't matter that he was only inches away.

Dinner had been surprisingly easy. Easy, Lee realized as she stared at the ceiling of the tent, because Hunter's mood had shifted again when she'd returned to help him fix it. Amiable? No, she decided, cautiously stretching her cramped muscles. *Amiable* was too free a word when applied to Hunter. *Moderately friendly* was more suitable. Cooperative he hadn't been at all. He'd spent the evening hours reading by the light of his lamp, while she'd taken out a fresh notepad and begun what would be a journal on her two weeks in Oak Creek Canyon.

She found it helpful to write down her feelings. Lee had often used her manuscript in much the same fashion. She could say what she wanted, feel what she wanted, without ever taking the risk that anyone would read her words. Perhaps it hadn't worked out precisely that way with her book, since Hunter had read more of her neat double-spaced typing under the steady lamplight, but the journal would be for no one's eyes but her own.

In any case, she thought, it was to her advantage that he'd been occupied with her manuscript. She hadn't had to talk to him as the night had grown later, the darkness deeper. While he'd still been reading, she'd been able to crawl into the tent and squeeze herself into a corner. When he'd joined her, much later, it hadn't been necessary to exchange words in the intimacy of the tent. She'd made certain he'd thought her asleep—though sleep hadn't come for hours.

In the quiet, she'd listened to him breathe beside her. Quiet, steady. That was the kind of man he was. Lee had lain still, telling herself the closeness meant nothing. But this morning, she saw that her nails, which had begun to grow again, had been gnawed down.

The first night was bound to be the hardest, she told herself and sat up, dragging a hand through her hair. She'd survived it. Her problem now was how to get by him and to the showers, where she could change out of the clothes she'd slept in and fix her hair and face. Cautiously, she crept forward to peek through the tent flap.

He knew she was awake. Hunter had sensed it almost the moment she'd opened her eyes. He'd gotten up early to start coffee, knowing that if he'd had trouble sleeping beside her, he'd never have been able to handle waking with her.

He'd seen little more than the coppery mass of hair above the sleeping bag in the dim morning light of the tent. Because he'd wanted to touch it, draw her to him, wake her, he'd given himself some distance. Today he'd walk for miles and fish for hours. Lee could stick to her role of reporter, and by answering her questions he'd learn as much about her as she believed she was learning about him. That was his plan, Hunter reminded himself, and poured a second cup of coffee. He was better off remembering it.

"Coffee's hot," Hunter commented without turning around. Though she'd taken great care to be quiet, he'd heard Lee push the tent flap aside.

Biting back an oath, Lee scooped up her pack. The man had ears like a wolf. "I want to shower first," she mumbled.

"I told you that you didn't have to fix up your face for me." He began to arrange strips of bacon in a skillet. "I like it fine the way it is."

Infuriated, Lee scrambled to her feet. "I'm not fixing anything for you. Sleeping all night in my clothes tends to make me feel dirty."

"Probably sleep better without them," Hunter agreed mildly. "Breakfast's in fifteen minutes, so I'd move along if I wanted to eat."

Clutching her bag and her dignity, Lee strode off through the trees.

He wouldn't get to her so easily if she wasn't stiff and grubby and half-starved, she thought, making her way along the path to the showers. God knows how he could be so cheerful after spending the night sleeping on the ground. Maybe Bryan had been right all along. The man was weird. Lee took her shampoo and her plastic case of French-milled soap and stepped into a shower stall.

The spot he'd chosen might be magnificent, the air might smell clean and pure, but a sleeping bag wasn't a feather bed. Lee stripped and hung her clothes over the door. She heard the water running in the stall next to hers and sighed. For the next two weeks she'd be sharing bathroom facilities. She might as well get used to it.

The water came out in a steady gush, lukewarm. Gritting her teeth, she stepped under. Today, she was going to begin to dig out a few more personal facts on Hunter Brown.

Was he married? She frowned, then deliberately relaxed her features. The question was for the article, not for herself. His marital status meant nothing to her.

He probably wasn't. She soaped her hair vigorously. What woman would put up with him? Besides, wouldn't a wife come along on camping trips even if she detested them? Would that kind of man marry anyone who didn't like precisely what he did?

What did he do for relaxation? Besides playing Daniel Boone in the woods, she added with a grim smile. Where did he live? Where had he grown up? What sort of childhood had he had?

The water streamed over her, sluicing away soap and shampoo. The curiosity she felt was purely professional. Lee found she had to remind herself of that a bit too often. She needed the whole man to do an incisive article. She needed the whole man...

Alarmed at her own thoughts, she opened her eyes wide, then swore when shampoo stung them. Damn the whole man! she thought fiercely. She'd take whatever pieces of him she could get and write an article that would pay him back, in spades, for all the trouble he'd caused her.

Clean, fragrant and shivering, she turned off the water. It wasn't until that moment that Lee remembered she hadn't brought a towel. Campground showers didn't lay in their own linen supply. Damn it, how was she supposed to remember everything?

Dripping, her chilled skin covered with gooseflesh, she stood in the middle of the stall and swore silently and pungently. For as long as she could stand it, Lee let the air dry her while she squeezed water out of her hair. Revenge, she thought, placing the blame squarely on Hunter's shoulders. Sooner or later, she'd have it.

She reached under the stall door for her pack and pulled out a fresh sweatshirt. Resigned, she dabbed at her wet face with the soft outside. Once she'd dragged it over her damp shoulders, she hunted up underwear. Though her clothes clung to her, her skin warmed. In front of the line of sinks and mirrors, she plugged in her blow-dryer and set to work on her hair.

In spite of him, Lee thought, not because of him, she spent more than her usual time perfecting her makeup. Satisfied, she repacked her portable hairdryer and left the showers, smelling lightly of jasmine.

Her scent was the first thing he sensed when she stepped back into the clearing. Hunter's stomach muscles tightened. As if he were unaffected, he finished off another cup of coffee, but he didn't taste it.

Calmer and much more at ease now, Lee stowed her pack before she walked toward the low-burning campfire. On a small shelf of rocks beside it sat the skillet with the remainder of the bacon and eggs. She didn't have to taste them to know they were cold.

"Feel better?" Hunter asked conversationally.

"I feel fine." She wouldn't say one word about the food being cold and, Lee told herself as she scooped her breakfast onto a plate, she'd eat every bite. She'd give him no more cause to smirk at her.

While she nibbled on the bacon, Lee glanced over at him. He'd obviously showered earlier. His hair glinted in the sun and he smelled cleanly of soap without the interference of cologne or aftershave. A man didn't use aftershave if he didn't bother with a razor, Lee concluded, studying the shadow of stubble over his chin. It should've made him look unkempt, but somehow he managed to look oddly dashing. She concentrated on her cold eggs.

"Sleep well?"

"I slept fine," she lied, and gratefully washed down her breakfast with strong, hot coffee. "You?"

"Very well," he lied, and lit a cigarette. She was getting on nerves he hadn't known he had.

"Have you been up long?"

Since dawn, Hunter thought. "Long enough." He glanced down at her barely scuffed hiking boots and wondered how long it would take before her feet just gave out. "I plan to do some hiking today."

She wanted to groan but put on a bright smile. "Fine, I'd like to see some of the canyon while I'm here." Preferably in a Jeep, she thought, swallowing the last crumb of bacon. If there was one cliché she could now attest to, it was that the open air increased the appetite.

It took Lee perhaps half again as long to wash up the breakfast dishes with the plastic water container as it would've taken Hunter, but she already understood the unstated rule. One cooks, the other cleans.

By the time she was finished, he was standing impatiently, binocular and canteen straps crisscrossed over his chest and a light pack in one hand. This he shoved at her. Lee resisted the urge to shove it back at him.

"I want my camera." Without giving him a chance to complain, she dug it out of her own gear and slipped the small rectangle in the back pocket of her jeans. "What's in here?" she asked, adjusting the strap of the pack over her shoulder.

"Lunch."

Lee lengthened her stride to keep up with Hunter as he headed out of the clearing. If he'd packed a lunch, she'd have to resign herself to a very long day on her feet. "How do you know where you're going and how to get back?"

For the first time since she'd returned to camp smelling like fragility and flowers, Hunter smiled. "Landmarks, the sun."

"Do you mean moss growing on one side of a tree?" She looked around, hoping to find some point of reference for herself. "I've never trusted that sort of thing."

She wouldn't know east from west, either, he mused, unless they were discussing L.A. and New York. "I've got a compass, if that makes you feel better."

It did—a little. When you hadn't the faintest idea how something worked, you had to take it on faith. Lee was far from comfortable putting her faith in Hunter.

But as they walked, she forgot to worry about losing her way. The sun was a white flash of light, and though it was still shy of 9:00 a.m., the air was warm. She liked the way the light hit the red walls of the canyon and deepened the colors. The path inclined upward, narrow, pebbled with loose stones. She heard people laugh, and the sound carried so cleanly over the air, they might have been standing beside her.

Green became sparser as they climbed. What she saw now was scrubby bushes, dusty and faded, that forced their way out of thin ribbons of dirt in the rock. Curious, she broke off a spray of leaves. Their scent was strong, tangy and fresh. Then she found she had to dash to catch up with Hunter. It had been his idea to hike, but he didn't appear to be enjoying it. More, he looked like a man who had some urgent, unpleasant appointment to keep.

It might be a good time, Lee considered, to start a casual conversation that could lead to the kind of personal information she was shooting for. As the path became steadily steeper, she decided she'd better talk while she had the breath to do it. The sweatshirt had been a mistake, too. Her back was damp again, this time from sweat.

"Have you always preferred the outdoors?"

"For hiking."

Undaunted, she scowled at his back. "I suppose you were a Boy Scout."

"No."

"Your interest in camping and hiking is fairly new, then."

"No."

She had to grit her teeth to hold back a groan. "Did you go off and pitch a tent in the woods with your father when you were a boy?"

She'd have been interested in the amused expression on his face if she could have seen it. "No."

"You lived in the city, then."

She was clever, Hunter reflected. And persistent. He shrugged. "Yes."

At last, Lee thought. "What city?"

"L.A."

She tripped over a rock and nearly stumbled headlong into his back. Hunter never slackened his pace. "L.A.?" she repeated. "You live in Los Angeles and still manage to bury yourself so that no one knows you're there?"

"I grew up in L.A.," he said mildly. "In a part of the

city you'd have little occasion for visiting. Socially, Lenore Radcliffe, formerly of Palm Springs, wouldn't even know such neighborhoods existed."

That pulled her up short. Again, she had to dash to catch him, but this time she grabbed his arm and made him stop. "How do you know I came from Palm Springs?"

He watched her with the tolerant amusement she found both infuriating and irresistible. "I did my research. You graduated from U.C.L.A. with honors, after three years in a very classy Swiss boarding school. Your engagement to Jonathan Willoby, up-and-coming plastic surgeon, was broken when you accepted a position in *Celebrity*'s Los Angeles office."

"I was never engaged to Jonathan," she began furiously, then decisively bit her tongue. "You have no business probing into my life, Hunter. I'm doing the article, not you."

"I make it a habit to find out everything I can about anyone I do business with. We do have a business arrangement, don't we, Lenore?"

He was clever with words, she thought grimly. But so was she. "Yes, and it consists of my interviewing you, not the other way around."

"On my terms," Hunter reminded her. "I don't talk to anyone unless I know who they are." He reached out, touching the ends of her hair as he'd done once before. "I think I know who you are."

"You don't," she corrected, struggling against the need to back away from a touch that was barely a touch. "And you don't have to. But the more honest and open you are with me, the more honest the article I write will be."

He uncapped the canteen. When she refused his offer with a shake of her head, Hunter drank. "I am being honest with you." He secured the cap. "If I made it easier for you, you wouldn't get a true picture of who I am." His eyes were suddenly dark, intense and piercing. Without warning, he reached out. The power in his eyes made her believe he could quite easily sweep her off the path. Yet his hand skimmed down her cheek, light as rain. "You wouldn't understand what I am," he said quietly. "Perhaps, for my own reasons, I want you to."

She'd have been less frightened if he'd shouted at her, raged at her, grabbed at her. The sound of her own heartbeat vibrated in her head. Instinctively, she stepped back, escape her first and only thought. Her foot met empty space.

In an instant, she was caught against him, pressed body to body, so that the warmth from his seeped right into hers. The fear tripled so that she arched back, raising both hands to his chest.

"Idiot," he said, with an edge to his voice that made her head snap up. "Take a look behind you before you tell me to let you go."

Automatically, she turned her head to look over her shoulder. Her stomach rose up to her throat, then plummeted. The hands that had been poised to push him away grabbed his shoulders until the fingers dug into his flesh. The view behind her was magnificent, sweeping and straight down.

"We—we walked farther up than I'd thought," she managed. And if she didn't sit down, very, very soon, she was going to disgrace herself.

"The trick is to watch where you're going." Hunter didn't move her away from the edge, but took her chin in his hand until their eyes met and held. "Always watch exactly where you're going, then you'll know how to fall."

He kissed her, just as unexpectedly as before, but not so gently. Not nearly so gently. This time, she felt the full force of the strength that had been only an undercurrent each other time his mouth had touched hers. If she'd pitched back and taken that dizzying fall, she'd have been no more helpless than she was at this moment, molded to him, supported by him, wrapped around him. The edge was close—inside her, behind her. Lee couldn't tell which would be more fatal. But she knew, helplessly, that either could break her.

He hadn't meant to touch her just then, but the demanding climb up the path hadn't deadened the need he'd woken with. He'd take this much, her taste, her softness, and make it last until she willingly turned to him. He wanted the sweetness she tried to gloss over, the fragility she tried to deny. And he wanted the strength that kept her pushing for more. Yes, he thought he knew her and was very close to understanding her. He knew he wanted her.

Slowly, very slowly, for lingering mouth-to-mouth both soothed and excited him, Hunter drew her away. Her eyes were as clouded as his thoughts, her pulse as rapid as his. He shifted her until she was close to the cliff wall and away from the drop.

"Never step back unless you've looked over your shoulder first," he said quietly. "And don't step forward until you've tested the ground."

Turning, he continued up the path, leaving her to wonder if he'd been speaking of hiking or something entirely different.

Chapter 7

Lee wrote in her journal:

On the eighth day of this odd on-again, off-again interview, I know more about Hunter and understand less. By turns, he's friendly, then distant. There's an aloof streak in him, bound so tightly around his private life that I've found no way through it. When I ask about his preference in books, he can go on indefinitely—apparently he has no real preference except for the written word itself. When I ask about his family, he just smiles and changes the subject or gives me one of those intense stares and says nothing. In either case, he keeps a cloak of mystery around his privacy.

He's possibly the most efficient man I've ever met. There's no waste of time, no extra movements and, infuriating to me, never a mistake, when it comes to starting a campfire or cooking a meal—such as they are. Yet, he's content to do absolutely nothing for hours at a time.

He's fastidious—the camp looks as if we've been here no more than a half hour rather than a week— yet he hasn't shaved in that amount of time. The beard should look scruffy, but somehow it looks so natural I find myself wondering if he didn't always have one.

Always, I've been able to find a category to slip an assignment into. An acquaintance into. Not with Hunter. In all this time, I've found no easy file for him.

Last night we had a heated discussion on Sylvia Plath, and this morning I found him paging through a comic book over coffee. When I questioned him on it, his answer was that he respected all forms of literature. I believed him. One of the problems I'm having on this assignment is that I find myself believing everything he says, no matter how contradictory the statement might be to another he makes. Can a total lack of consistency make someone consistent?

He's the most complex, frustrating, fascinating man I've ever known. I've yet to find a way of controlling the attraction he holds for me, or even the proper label for it. Is it physical? Hunter's very compelling physically. Is it intellectual? His mind has such odd twists and turns, it takes all my effort to follow them.

Either of these I believe I could handle successfully enough. Over the years, I've had to deal professionally with attractive, intelligent, charismatic men. It's a challenge, certainly, but here I have the uncomfortable feeling that I'm caught in the middle of a silent chess game and have already lost my queen.

My greatest fear at this moment is that I'm going to find myself emotionally involved.

Since the first day we walked up the canyon, he hasn't touched me. I can still remember exactly how I felt, exactly what the air smelled like at that moment. It's foolish, overly romantic and absolutely true.

Each night we sleep together in the same tent, so close I can feel his breath. Each morning I wake alone. I should be grateful that he isn't making this assignment any more difficult than it already is, and yet I find myself waiting to be held by him.

For over a week I've thought of little else but him. The more I learn, the more I want to know—for myself. Too much for myself.

Twice, I've woken in the middle of the night, aching, and nearly turned to him. Now, I wonder what would happen if I did. If I believed in the spells and forces Hunter writes of, I'd think one was on me. No one's ever made me want so much, feel so much. Fear so much. Every night, I wonder.

Sometimes Lee wrote of the scenery and her feelings about it. Sometimes, she wrote a play-by-play description of the day. But most of the time, more of the time, she wrote of Hunter. What she put down in her journal had nothing to do with her organized, precisely written notes for the article. She wouldn't permit it. What she didn't understand, and what she wouldn't write down in either space, was that she was losing sleep. And she was having fun.

Though he was cannily evasive on personal details, she was gathering information. Even now, barely halfway through the allotted time, Lee had enough for a solid, successful article—more, she knew, than she'd expected to gather. But she wanted even more, for her readers and, undeniably, for herself.

"I don't see how any self-respecting fish could be

fooled by something like this." Lee fiddled with the small rubbery fly Hunter attached to her line.

"Myopic," Hunter countered, bending to choose his own lure. "Fish are notoriously nearsighted."

"I don't believe you." Clumsily, she cast off. "But this time *I'm* going to catch one."

"You'll need to get your fly in the water first." He glanced down at the line tangled on the bank of the creek before expertly casting his own.

He wouldn't even offer to help. After a week in his company, Lee had learned not to expect it. She'd also learned that if she wanted to compete with him in this, or in a discussion of eighteenth-century English literature, she had to get into the spirit of things.

It wasn't simple and it wasn't quick, but kneeling, Lee worked on the tangles until she was back to square one. She shot a look at Hunter, who appeared much too engrossed with the surface of the creek to notice her progress. By now, Lee knew better. He saw everything that went on around him, whether he looked or not.

Standing a few feet away, Lee tried again. This time, her lure landed with a quiet plop.

Hunter saw the rare, quick grin break out, but said nothing. She was, he'd learned, a woman who generally took herself too seriously. Yet he saw the sweetness beneath, and the warmth Lee tried to be so frugal with.

She had a low, smoky laugh she didn't use often enough. It only made him want to urge it out of her.

The past week hadn't been easy for her. Hunter hadn't intended it to be. You learned more about people by observing them in difficult situations than at a catered cocktail party. He was adding to the layers of the first impression he'd had, at the airport in Flagstaff. But he had layers still to go.

She could, unlike most people he knew, be comfortable with long spells of silence. It appealed to him. The more careless he became in his attire and appearance, the more meticulous she became in hers. It amused him to see her go off every morning and return with her makeup perfected and her hair carefully groomed. Hunter made sure they'd been mussed a bit by the end of the day.

Hiking, fishing. Hunter had seen to it that her jeans and boots were thoroughly broken in. Often, in the evening, he'd caught her rubbing her tired feet. When she was back in Los Angeles, sitting in her cozy office, she wouldn't forget the two weeks she'd spent in Oak Creek Canyon.

Now, Lee stood near the edge of the creek, a fishing rod held in both hands, a look of smug concentration on her face. He liked her for it—for her innate need to compete and for the vulnerability beneath the confidence. She'd stand there, holding the rod, until he called a halt to the venture. Back in camp, he knew she'd rub her hands with cream and they would smell lightly of jasmine and stay temptingly soft.

Since it was her turn to cook, she'd do it, though she still fumbled a bit with the utensils and managed to singe almost anything she put on the fire. He liked her for that, too—for the fact that she never gave up on anything.

Her curiosity remained unflagging. She'd question him, and he'd evade or answer as he chose. Then she'd grant him silence to read, while she wrote. Comfortable. Hunter found that she was an unusually comfortable woman in the quiet light of a campfire. Whether she knew it or not, she relaxed then, writing in the journal, which intrigued him, or going over her daily notes for the article, which didn't.

He'd expected to learn about her during the two weeks together, knowing he'd have to give some information on himself in return. That, he considered, was an even enough exchange. But he hadn't expected to enjoy her companionship.

The sun was strong, the air almost still, with an early-morning taste to it. But the sky wasn't clear. Hunter wondered if she'd noticed the bank of clouds to the east and if she realized there'd be a storm by nightfall. The clouds held lightning. He simply sat cross-legged on the ground. It'd be more interesting if Lee found out for herself.

The morning passed in silence, but for the occasional voice from around them or the rustle of leaves. Twice Hunter pulled a trout out of the creek, throwing the second back because of size. He said nothing. Lee said nothing, but barely prevented herself from grinding her teeth. On every jaunt, he'd gone back to camp with fish. She'd gone back with a sore neck.

"I begin to wonder," she said, at length, "if you've put something on that lure that chases fish away."

He'd been smoking lazily and now he stirred himself to crush out the cigarette. "Want to change rods?"

She slanted him a look, taking in the slight amusement in his arresting face. When her muscles quivered, Lee stiffened them. Would she never become completely accustomed to the way her body reacted when they looked at each other? "No," she said coolly. "I'll keep this one. You're rather good at this sort of thing, for a boy who didn't go fishing."

"I've always been a quick study."

"What did your father do in L.A.?" Lee asked, knowing he would either answer in the most offhand way or evade completely.

"He sold shoes."

It took a moment, as she'd been expecting the latter. "Sold shoes?"

"That's right. In the shoe department of a moderately successful department store downtown. My mother sold stationery on the third floor." He didn't have to look at her to know she was frowning, her brows drawn together. "Surprised?"

"Yes," she admitted. "A bit. I suppose I imagined you'd been influenced by your parents to some extent and that they'd had some unusual career or interests."

Hunter cast off again with an agile flick of his wrist. "Before my father sold shoes, he sold tickets at the local theater. Before that, it was linoleum, I think." His shoulders moved slightly before he turned to her. "He was a man trapped by financial circumstances into working, when he'd been born to dream. If he'd been born into affluence, he might've been a painter or a poet. As it was, he sold things and regularly lost his job because he wasn't suited to selling anything, not even himself."

Though he spoke casually, Lee had to struggle to distance herself emotionally. "You speak as though he's not living."

"I've always believed my mother died from overwork, and my father from lack of interest in life without her."

Sympathy welled up in her throat. She couldn't swallow at all. "When did you lose them?"

"I was eighteen. They died within six months of each other."

"Too old for the state to care for you," she murmured, "too young to be alone."

Touched, Hunter studied her profile. "Don't feel sorry for me, Lenore. I managed very well."

"But you weren't a man yet." No, she mused, perhaps he had been. "You had college to face."

"I had some help, and I waited tables for a while."

Lee remembered the wallet full of credit cards she'd carried through college. Anything she'd wanted had always been at her fingertips. "It couldn't have been easy."

"It didn't have to be." He lit a cigarette, watching the clouds move slowly closer. "By the time I was finished with college, I knew I was a writer."

"What happened from the time you graduated from college to when your first book was published?"

He smiled through the smoke that drifted between them. "I lived, I wrote, I went fishing when I could."

She wasn't about to be put off so easily. Hardly realizing she did it, Lee sat down on the ground beside him. "You must've worked."

"Writing, though many disagree, is work." He had a talent for making the sharpest sarcasm sound mildly droll.

Another time, she might have smiled. "You know that's not what I mean. You had to have an income, and your first book wasn't published until nearly six years ago."

"I wasn't starving in a garret, Lenore." He ran a finger down the hand she held on the rod and felt a flash of pleasure at the quick skip of her pulse. "You'd just have been starting at *Celebrity* when *The Devil's Due* hit the stands. One might say our stars were on the rise at the same time."

"I suppose." She turned from him to look back at the surface of the creek again.

"You're happy there?"

Unconsciously, she lifted her chin. "I've worked my way up from gofer to staff reporter in five years."

"That's not an answer."

"Neither are most of yours," she mumbled.

"True enough. What're you looking for there?"

"Success," she said immediately. "Security."

"One doesn't always equal the other."

Her voice was as defiant as the look she aimed at him. "You have both."

"A writer's never secure," Hunter disagreed. "Only a foolish one expects to be. I've read all of the manuscript you brought."

Lee said nothing. She'd known he'd bring it up before the two weeks were over, but she'd hoped to put it off a bit longer. The faintest of breezes played with the ends of her hair while she sat, staring at the moving waters of the creek. Some of the pebbles looked like gems. Such were illusions.

"You know you have to finish it," he told her calmly. "You can't make me believe you're content to leave your characters in limbo, when you've drawn them so carefully. Your story's two-thirds told, Lenore."

"I don't have time," she began.

"Not good enough."

Frustrated, she turned to him again. "Easy for you

to say from your little pinnacle of fame. I have a demanding full-time job. If I give it my time and my talent, there's no place I can go but up at *Celebrity*."

"Your novel needs your time and talent."

She didn't like the way he said it—as if she had no real choice. "Hunter, I didn't come here to discuss my work, but you and yours. I'm flattered that you think my novel has some merit, but I have a job to do."

"Flattered?" he countered. The deep, black gaze pinned her again, and his hand closed over hers. "No, you're not. You wish I'd never seen your novel and you don't want to discuss it. Even if you were convinced it was worthwhile, you'd still be afraid to put it all on the line."

The truth grated on her nerves and on her temper. "My job is my first priority. Whether that suits you or not doesn't matter. It's none of your business."

"No, perhaps not," he said slowly, watching her. "You've got a fish on your line."

"I don't want you to—" Eyes narrowing, she broke off. "What?"

"There's a fish on your line," he repeated. "You'd better reel it in."

"I've got one?" Stunned, Lee felt the rod jerk in her hands. "I've got one! Oh, God." She gripped the rod in both hands again and watched the line jiggle. "I've really caught one. What do I do now?"

"Reel it in," Hunter suggested again, leaning back on the grass.

"Aren't you going to help?" Her hands felt foolishly clumsy as she started to crank the reel. Hoping leverage would give her some advantage, she scrambled to her feet. "Hunter, I don't know what I'm doing. I might lose it."

"Your fish," he pointed out. Grinning, he watched her. Would she look any more exuberant if she'd been given an interview with the president? Somehow, Hunter didn't think so, though he was sure Lee would disagree. But then, she couldn't see herself at that moment, hair mussed, cheeks glowing, eyes wide and her tongue caught firmly between her teeth. The late-morning sunlight did exquisite things to her skin, and the quick laugh she gave when she pulled the struggling fish from the water ran over the back of his neck like soft fingers.

Desire moved lazily through him as he took his gaze up the long length of leg flattered by brief shorts, then over the subtle curves accented by the shifting of muscle under her shirt as she continued to fight with the fish, to her face, still flushed with surprise.

"Hunter!" She laughed as she held the still-wriggling fish high over the grass. "I did it."

It was nearly as big as the largest one he'd caught that week. He pursed his lips as he sized it up. It was tempting to compliment her, but he decided she looked smug enough already. "Gotta get it off the hook," he reminded her, shifting only slightly on his elbows.

"Off the hook?" Lee shot him an astonished look. "I don't want to touch it."

"You have to touch it to take it off the hook."

Lee lifted a brow. "I'll just toss it back in."

With a shrug, Hunter shut his eyes and enjoyed the faint breeze. The hell she would. "Your fish, not mine."

Torn between an abhorrence of touching the still-flopping fish and pride at having caught it, Lee stared down at Hunter. He wasn't going to help; that was painfully obvious. If she threw the fish back into the water, he'd smirk at her for the rest of the evening. Intolerable. And, she reasoned logically, wouldn't she still have to touch it to get rid of it? Setting her teeth, Lee reached out a hand for the catch of the day.

It was wet, slippery and cold. She pulled her hand back. Then, out of the corner of her eye, she saw Hunter grinning up at her. Holding her breath, Lee took the trout firmly in one hand and wiggled the hook out with the other. If he hadn't been looking at her, challenging her, she never would've managed it. With the haughtiest air at her disposal, she dropped the trout into the small cooler Hunter brought along on fishing trips.

"Very good." He closed the lid on the cooler before he reeled in his line. "That looks like enough for tonight's dinner. You caught a good-sized one, Lenore."

"Thank you." The words were icily polite and self-satisfied.

"It'll nearly be enough for both of us, even after you've cleaned it."

"It's as big as…" He was already walking back toward camp, so that she had to run to catch up with him and his statement. "*I* clean it?"

"Rule is, you catch, you clean."

She planted her feet, but he wasn't paying attention. "I'm not cleaning any fish."

"Then you don't eat any fish." His words were as offhand and careless as a shrug.

Abandoning pride, Lee caught at his arm. "Hunter, you'll have to change the rule." She sighed, but convinced herself she wouldn't choke on the word. At least not very much. "Please."

He stopped, considering. "If I clean it, you've got to balance the scales—" the smile flickered over his face "—no pun intended, by doing me a favor."

"I can cook two nights in a row."

"I said a favor."

Her head turned sharply, but one look at his face had her laughing. "All right, what's the deal?"

"Why don't we leave it open-ended?" he suggested. "I don't have anything in mind at the moment."

This time, she considered. "It'll be negotiable?"

"Naturally."

"Deal." Turning her palms up, Lee wrinkled her nose. "Now I'm going to wash my hands."

She hadn't realized she could get such a kick out of catching a fish or out of cooking it herself over an open fire. There were other things Lee hadn't realized. She hadn't looked at the trim gold watch on her wrist in days. If she hadn't kept a journal, she probably wouldn't know what day it was. It was true that her muscles still revolted after a night in the tent and the shower facilities were an inconvenience at best, purgatory at worst, but despite herself she was relaxing.

For the first time in her memory, her day wasn't regimented, by herself or by anyone else. She got up when she woke, slept when she was tired and ate when she was hungry. For the moment, the word *deadline* didn't exist. That was something she hadn't allowed herself since the day she'd walked out of her parents' home in Palm Springs.

No matter how rapid Hunter could make her pulse by one of those unexpected looks, or how much desire for him simmered under the surface, she found him comfortable to be with. Because it was so unlikely, Lee didn't try to find the reasons. On this late afternoon, in the hour before dusk, she was content to sit by the fire and tend supper.

"I never knew anything could smell so good."

Hunter continued to pour a cup of coffee before he glanced over at her. "We cooked fish two days ago."

"Your fish," Lee pointed out, carefully turning the trout. "This one's mine."

He grinned, wondering if she remembered just how horrified she'd been the first time he'd suggested she pick up a rod and reel. "Beginner's luck."

Lee opened her mouth, ready with a biting retort, then saw the way he smiled at her. Not only did her retort vanish, but so did much of her defensive wall. She let out a long, quiet breath as she turned back to the skillet. The man became only more dangerous with familiarity. "If fishing depends on luck," she managed, "you've had more than your share."

"Everything depends on luck." He held out two plates. Lee slipped the sizzling trout onto them, then sat back to enjoy.

"If you believe that, what about fate? You've said more than once that we can fight against our fate, but we can't win."

He lifted a brow. That consistently sharp, consistently logical mind of hers never failed to impress him. "One works with the other." He tasted a bit of trout, noting that she'd been careful enough not to singe her own catch. "It's your fate to be here, with me. You were lucky enough to catch a fish for dinner."

"It sounds to me as though you twist things to your own point of view."

"Yes. Doesn't everyone?"

"I suppose." Lee ate, thoughtfully studying the view over his shoulder. Had anything ever tasted this wonderful? Would anything ever again? "But not everyone makes it work as well as you." Reluctantly, she accepted some of the dried fruit he offered. He seemed to have an unending supply, but Lee had yet to grow used to the taste or texture.

"If you could change one thing about your life, what would it be?"

Perhaps because he'd asked without preamble, perhaps because she was so unexpectedly relaxed, Lee answered without thinking. "I'd have more."

He didn't, as her parents had done, ask more what. Hunter only nodded. "We could say it's your fate to want it, and your luck to have it or not."

Nibbling on an apricot, she studied him. The lowering light and flickering fire cast his face in shadows. They suited him. The short, rough beard surrounded the poet's mouth, making it all the more compelling. He was a man a woman would never be able to ignore, never be able to forget. Lee wondered if he knew it. Then she nearly laughed. Of course he did. He knew entirely too much.

"What about you?" She leaned forward a bit, as she did whenever the answer was important. "What would you change?"

He smiled in the way that made her blood heat. "I'd take more," he said quietly.

She felt the shiver race up her spine, was all but certain Hunter could see it. Lee found she was compelled to remind herself of her job. "You know," she began easily enough, "you've told me quite a bit over this week, more in some ways than I'd expected, but much less in others." Steady again, she took another bite of trout. "I might understand you quite a bit better if you'd give me a run-through of a typical day."

He ate, enjoying the tender, open-air flavor. The clouds were rolling in, the breeze picking up. He wondered if she noticed. "There's no such thing as a typical day."

"You're evading again."

"Yeah."

"It's my job to pin you down."

He watched her over the rim of his coffee cup. "I like watching you do your job."

She laughed. It seemed he could always frustrate and amuse her at the same time. "Hunter, why do I have the feeling you're doing your best to make this difficult for me?"

"You're very perceptive." Setting his plate aside, he began to toy with the ends of her hair in a habit she could never take casually. "I have an image of a woman with a romantic kind of beauty and an orderly, logical mind."

"Hunter—"

"Wait, I'm just fleshing her out. She's ambitious, full of nerves, highly sensuous without being fully aware of it." He could see her eyes change, growing as dark as the sky above them. "She's caught in the middle of something she can't explain or understand. Things happen around her and she's finding it more and more difficult to distance herself from it. And there's a man, a man she desires but can't quite trust. He doesn't offer her the logical explanations she wants, but the illogic he offers seems terrifyingly close to the truth. If she puts

her trust in him, she has to turn her back on most of
what she believes is fact. If she doesn't, she'll be alone."

He was talking to her, about her, for her. Lee knew
her throat was dry and her palms were damp, but she
didn't know if it was from his words or the light touch
on the ends of her hair. "You're trying to frighten me
by weaving a plot around me."

"I'm weaving a plot around you," Hunter agreed.
"Whether I frighten you or not depends on how successful I am with that plot. Shadows and storms are
my business." As if on cue, lightning snaked out in the
sky overhead. "But all writers need a foil. Smooth, pale
skin—" He stroked the back of his hand up her cheek.
"Soft hair with touches of gold and fire. Against that I
have darkness, wind, voices that speak from shadows.
Logic against the impossible. The unspeakable against
cool, polished beauty."

She swallowed to relieve the dryness in her throat
and tried to speak casually. "I suppose I should be flattered, but I'm not sure I want to see myself molded into
a character in a horror story."

"That comes back to fate again, doesn't it?" Lightning ripped through the early dusk as their eyes met
again. "I need you, Lenore," he murmured. "For the
tale I have to tell—and more."

Nerves prickled along her skin, all the more frantically because of the relaxed hours. "It's going to rain."
But her voice wasn't calm and even. Her senses were
already swimming. When she started to rise, she found
that her hand was caught in his and that he stood with
her. The wind blew around her, stirring leaves, stirring
desire. The light dimmed to shadow. Thunder rumbled.

What she saw in his eyes chilled her, then heated her

blood so quickly she had no way to keep up with the change. The grip on her hand was light. Lee could've broken the hold if she'd had the will to do so. It was his look that drained the will from her. They stood there, hands touching, eyes locked, while the storm swirled like madness around them.

Perhaps life was made up of the choices Hunter had once spoken of. Perhaps luck swayed the balance. But at that moment, for hardly more than a heartbeat, Lee believed that fate ruled everything. She was meant to go to him, to give to him, with no more choice than one of the characters his imagination formed.

Then the sky opened. The rain poured out. The shock of the sudden drenching had Lee jolting back, breaking contact. Yet for several long seconds she stood still while water ran over her and lightning flashed in wicked bolts.

"Damn it!" But he knew she spoke to him, not the storm. "Now what am I supposed to do?"

Hunter smiled, barely resisting the urge to cup her face in his hands and kiss her until her legs gave way. "Head for drier land." He continued to smile despite the rain, the wind, the lightning.

Wet, edgy and angry, Lee crawled inside the tent. He's enjoying this, she thought, tugging on the sodden laces of her boots. There's nothing he likes better than to see me at my worst. It would probably take a week for the boots to dry out, she thought grimly as she managed to pry the first one off.

When Hunter slipped into the tent beside her, she said nothing. Concentrating on anger seemed the best solution. The pounding of the rain on the sides of the tent made the space inside seem to shrink. She'd never been more aware of him, or of herself. Water dripped uncomfortably down her neck as she leaned forward to pull off her socks.

"I don't suppose this'll last long."

Hunter pulled the sodden shirt over his head. "I wouldn't count on it stopping much before morning."

"Terrific." She shivered and wondered how the hell she was supposed to get out of the wet clothes and into dry ones.

Hunter turned the lantern he'd carried in with him down to a dim glow. "Relax and listen to it. It's different from rain in the city. There's no swish of tires on wet asphalt, no horns, no feet running on the sidewalk." He took a towel out of his pack and began to dry her hair.

"I can do it." She reached up, but his hands continued to massage.

"I like to do it. Wet fire," he murmured. "That's what your hair looks like now."

He was so close she could smell the rain on him. The heat from his body called subtly, temptingly, to hers. Was the rain suddenly louder, or were her senses more acute? For a moment, she thought she could hear each individual drop as it hit the tent. The light was dim, a smoky gray that held touches of unreality. Lee felt as though she'd been running away from this one isolated spot all her life. Or perhaps she'd been running toward it.

"You need to shave," she murmured, and found that her hand was already reaching out to touch the untrimmed growth of beard on his face. "This hides too much. You're already difficult to know."

"Am I?" He moved the towel over her hair, soothing and arousing by turns.

"You know you are." She didn't want to turn away now, from the look that could infuse such warmth through her chilled, damp skin. Lightning flashed, illuminating the tent brilliantly before plunging it back into gloom. Yet, through the gloom she could see all she needed to, perhaps more than she wanted to. "It's my job to find out more, to find out everything."

"And my right to tell you only what I want to."

"We just don't look at things the same way."

"No."

She took the towel and, half dreaming, began to dry his hair. "We have no business being together like this."

He hadn't known desire with claws. If he didn't touch her soon, he'd be ripped through. "Why?"

"We're too different. You look for the unexplainable, I look for the logical." But his mouth was so near hers, and his eyes held such power. "Hunter…" She knew what was going to happen, recognized the impossibility of it and the pain that was bound to follow. "I don't want this to happen."

He didn't touch her, though he was certain he'd soon be mad from the lack of it. "You have a choice."

"No." It was said quietly, almost on a sigh. "I don't think I do." She let the towel fall. She saw the flicker of lightning and waited, six long heartbeats, for the answering thunder. "Maybe neither one of us has a choice."

Her breath was already unsteady as she let her hands curl over his bare shoulders. There was strength there. She wanted to feel it, but had been afraid to. His eyes never left hers as she touched him. Though the force of need curled tight in his stomach, he'd let her set the pace this first time, this most important time.

Her fingers were long and smooth on his skin, cool,

not so much hesitant as cautious. They ran down his arms, moving slowly over his chest and back until desire was taut as a bow poised for firing. The sound of the rain drummed in his head. Her face was pale and elegant in the gloomy light. The tent was suddenly too big. He wanted her in a space that was too small to move in unless they moved together.

She could hardly believe she could touch him this way, freely, openly, so that his skin quivered under the trace of her fingers. All the while, he watched her with a passion so fierce it would have terrified her if she hadn't been so dazed with her own need. Carefully, afraid to make the wrong move and break the mood for both of them, she touched her mouth to his.

The rough brush of beard was a stunning contrast to the softness of his lips. He gave back to her such feelings, such warmth, with no pressure. She'd never known anyone who could give without taking. This generosity was, to her, the ultimate seduction. In that moment, any reserve she'd clung to was washed away. Her arms went around his neck, her cheek pressed to his.

"Make love to me, Hunter."

He drew her away, only far enough so that they could see each other again. Wet hair curled around her face. Her eyes were as the sky had been an hour before. Dusky and clouded. "With."

Her lips curved. Her heart opened. He poured inside. "Make love with me."

Then his hands were framing her face, and the kiss was so gentle it drugged every cell of her body. She felt him tug the wet shirt from her, and shivered once before he warmed her. His body felt so strong against hers, so solid, yet his hands played over her with the care of a jeweler polishing a rare gem. He sighed when she touched him, so she touched once again, wanting to give pleasure as it was given to her.

She'd thought the panic would return, or at least the need to rush. But they'd been given all the time in the world. The rain could fall, the thunder bellow. It didn't involve them. She tasted hunger on his lips, but he held it in check. He'd sup slowly. Pleasure bubbled up inside her and came softly through her lips.

His mouth on her breast had the need leaping up to the next plane. Yet he didn't hurry, even when she arched against him. His tongue flicked, his teeth nibbled, until he could feel the crazed desire vibrating through her. She thought only of him now, Hunter knew it even as he struggled to hold the reins of his own passion. She'd have more. She'd take all. And so, by God, would he.

When she struggled with the snap of his jeans, he let her have her way. He wanted to be flesh-to-flesh with her, body-to-body, without barriers. In his mind, he'd already had her bare, like this, a dozen times. Her hair was cool and wet, her skin smooth and fragrant. Spring flowers and summer rain. The scents raced through him as her hands became more urgent.

Her breathing was ragged as she tugged the wet denim down his legs. She recognized strength, power and control. It was only the last she needed to break so that she could have what she ached for.

Wherever she could reach, she touched, she tasted, wallowing in pleasure each time she heard his breath tremble. Her shorts were drawn slowly down her body by strong, clever hands, until she wore nothing but the lacy triangle riding low on her hips. With his lips, he journeyed down, down her body, slowly, so that the bristle of beard awakened every pore. His tongue slid under the lace, making her gasp. Then, as abruptly as the storm had broken, Lee was lost in a morass of sensation too dark, too deep, to understand.

He felt her explode, and the power sang through him. He heard her call his name, and the greed to hear it again almost overwhelmed him. Bracing himself over her, Hunter held back that final, desperate need until she opened her eyes. She'd look at him when they came together. He'd promised himself that.

Dazed, trembling, frenzied, Lee stared at him. He looked invincible. "What do you want from me?"

His mouth swooped down on hers, and for the first time the kiss was hard, urgent, almost brutal with the force of passion finally unleashed. "Everything." He plunged into her, catapulting them both closer to the crest. "Everything."

Chapter 8

Dawn was clear as glass. Lee woke to it slowly, naked, warm and, for the first time in over a week, comfortable. And for the first time in over a week, she woke not precisely sure where she was.

Her head was pillowed in the curve of Hunter's shoulder, her body turned toward his of its own volition and by the weight of the arm held firmly around her. There was a drowsy feeling that was a mix of security and excitement. In all of her memory, she couldn't recall experiencing anything quite like it.

Before she was fully awake, she smelled the lingering fragrance of rain on his skin and remembered. In remembering, she took a deep, drinking breath of the scent.

It was like a dream, like something in some subliminal fantasy, or a scene that had come straight from the imagination. She'd never offered herself to anyone so freely before, or so completely. Never. Lee knew there'd never been anyone who'd tempted her to.

She could still remember the sensation of her lips touching his, and all doubt, all fear, melting away with the gentle contact.

Should she feel so content now that the rain had stopped and dawn was breaking? Fantasies were for that private hour of the night, not for the daylight. After all, it hadn't been a dream, and there'd be no pretending it had been. Perhaps she should be appalled that she'd given him exactly what he'd demanded: everything.

She couldn't. No, it was more than that, she realized. She wouldn't. Nothing, no one, would spoil what had happened, not even she herself.

Still, it might be best if he didn't realize quite yet how completely victorious he'd been. Lee let her eyes close and wrapped the sensation of closeness around her. For the next few days, there was no desk, no type-writer, no phone ringing with more demands. There'd be no self-imposed schedule. For the next few days, she was alone with her lover. Maybe the time had come to pick those wildflowers.

She tilted her head, wanting to look at him, trying not to wake him. Over the week they'd spent in such intimate quarters, she'd never seen him sleep. Every other morning he'd been up, already making coffee. She wanted the luxury of absorbing him when he was unaware.

Lee knew that most people looked more vulnerable in sleep, more innocent, perhaps. Hunter looked just as dangerous, just as compelling, as ever. True, those dark, intense eyes were hidden, but knowing the lids could lift at any moment, and the eyes spear you with that peculiar power, didn't add innocence to his face, only more mystery.

Lee discovered she didn't want it to. She was glad he was more dangerous than the other men she'd known. In an odd way, she was glad he was more difficult. She hadn't fallen in love with the ordinary, the everyday, but with the unique.

Fallen in love. She ran the phrase around in her head, taking it apart and putting it back together again with the caution she was prone to. It triggered a trickle of unease. The phrase itself connoted bruises. Hadn't Hunter himself warned her to test the ground before she started forward? Even warned, she hadn't. Even seeing the pit, she hadn't checked her step. The tumble she'd taken had a soft fall. This time. Lee knew it was all too possible to stumble and be destroyed.

She wasn't going to think about it. Lee allowed herself the luxury of cuddling closer. She was going to find those wildflowers and enjoy each individual petal. The dream would end soon enough, and she'd be back to the reality of her life. It was, of course, what she wanted. For a while, she lay still, just listening to the silence.

The clever thing to do, she thought lazily, would be to hang their wet clothes out in the sun. Her boots certainly needed drying out, but in the meantime, she had her sneakers. She yawned, thinking she wanted a few moments to write in her journal as well. Hunter's breathing was slow and even. A smile curved her lips. She could do all that, then come back and wake him. Waking him, in whatever way she chose, was a lover's privilege.

Lover. Skimming her gaze over his face again, she wondered why she didn't feel any particular surprise at the word. Was it possible she'd recognized it from the beginning? Foolish, she told herself, and shook her head.

Slowly, she shifted away from him, then crawled to the front of the tent to peek out. Even as she reached for the flap, a hand closed around her ankle. Hunter pillowed his other hand under his head as he watched her.

"If you're going out like that, we won't keep everyone away from the campsite for long."

As she was naked, the haughty look she sent him lost something. "I was just looking out. I thought you were asleep."

He smiled, thinking she was the only woman who could make a viable stab at dignity while on her hands and knees in a tent, without a stitch on. The finger around her ankle stroked absently. "You're up early."

"I thought I'd hang these clothes out to dry."

"Very practical." Because he sensed she was feeling awkward, Hunter sat up and grabbed her arm, tugging until she tumbled back, sprawled over him. Content, he held her against him and sighed. "We'll do it later."

Unsure whether to laugh or complain, Lee blew the hair out of her eyes as she propped herself on one elbow. "I'm not tired."

"You don't have to be tired to lie down." Then he rolled on top of her. "It's called relaxing."

As the planes of his body fit against the curves of hers, Lee felt the warmth seep in. A hundred tiny pulse points began to drum. "I don't think this has a lot to do with relaxing."

"No?" He'd wanted to see her like this, in the thin light of dawn with her hair mussed from his hands, her skin flushed from sleep, her limbs heavy from a night of loving and alert for more. He ran a hand down her with a surge of possession that wasn't quite comfortable, wasn't quite expected. "Then we'll relax later, too." He saw her lips form a gentle smile just before he brushed his over them.

Hunter didn't question that he wanted her just as urgently now as he had all the days and nights before. He rarely questioned feelings, because he trusted them. Her arms went around him, her lips parted. The completeness of her giving shot a shaft of heat through him that turned to a unified warmth. Lifting his head, Hunter looked down at her.

Milkmaid skin over a duchess's cheekbones, eyes like the sky at dusk and hair like copper shot with gold. Hunter gave himself the pleasure of looking at all of her, slowly.

She was small and sleek and smooth. He ran a fingertip along the curve of her shoulder and studied the contrast of his skin against hers. Fragile, delicate—but he remembered how much strength there was inside her.

"You always look at me as if you know everything there is to know about me."

The intensity in his eyes remained, as he caught her hand in his. "Not enough. Not nearly enough." With the lightest of touches, he kissed her shoulder, her temple, then her lips.

"Hunter…" She wanted to tell him that no one had ever made her feel this way before. She wanted to tell him that no one had ever made her want so badly to believe in magic and fairy tales and the simplicity of love. But as she started to speak, courage deserted her. She was afraid to risk, afraid to fail. Instead she touched a hand to his cheek. "Kiss me again."

He understood there was something more, something he needed to know. But he understood, too, that when something fragile was handled clumsily, it broke. He did as she asked and savored the warm, dark taste of her mouth.

Soft…sweet…silky. It was how he could make her feel with only a kiss. The ground was hard and unyielding under the thin tent mattress, but it might have been a luxurious pile of feathers. It was so easy to forget where she was, when he was with her this way, to forget a world existed outside that small space two bodies required. He could make her float, and she'd never known she'd wanted to. He could make her ache, and she'd never known there could be pleasure from it. He spoke against her mouth words she didn't need to understand. She wanted and was wanted, needed and was needed. She loved…

With an inarticulate murmur of acceptance for whatever he could give, Lee drew him closer. Closer. The moment was all that mattered.

Deep, intoxicating, tender, the kiss went on and on and on.

Even an imagination as fluid as his hadn't fantasized anything so sweet, anything so soft. It was as though she melted into him, giving everything before he could ask. Once, only once, only briefly, it sped through his mind that he was as vulnerable as she. The unease came, flicking at the corner of his mind. Then her hands ran over him, stroking, and he accepted the weakness.

Only one other person had ever had the power to reach inside him and hold his heart. Now there were two. The time to deal with it was tomorrow. Today was for them alone.

Without hurry, he whispered kisses over her face. Perhaps it was an homage to beauty, perhaps it was much, much more. He didn't question his motives as he traced the slope of her cheek. There was an immediacy he'd never experienced before, but it didn't carry the urgency he'd expected. She was there for him as long as he needed. He understood that, without words.

"You smell of spring and rain," he murmured against her ear. "Why should that drive me mad?"

The words vibrated through her, as arousing as the most intimate caress. Heavy-lidded, clouded, her eyes met his. "Just show me. Show me again."

He loved her with such generosity. Each touch was a separate pleasure, each kiss a luxurious taste. Patience—there was more patience in him than in her. Her body was tossed between utter contentment and urgency, until reason was something too vague to grasp.

"Here—" He nibbled lightly at her breast, listening to and allured by her unsteady breaths. "You're small and soft. Here—" He took his hand over her hip to her thigh. "You're taut and lean. I can't seem to touch enough, taste enough." He drew the peak of her breast into his mouth, so that she arched against him, center to center.

"Hunter." His name was barely audible, but the sound of it was enough to bring him to desperation. "I need you."

God, had he wanted to hear that so badly? Struggling to understand what those three simple words had triggered, he buried his mouth against her skin. But he couldn't think, only feel. Only want. "You have me."

With his hands and lips alone, he took her spiraling over the first peak.

Her movements beneath him grew wild, her mur-

murs frenzied, but she was unaware. All Lee knew was
that they were flesh-to-flesh. This was the storm he'd
gentled the night before, the power unleashed, the demands unsoftened. The tenderness became passion so
quickly, she could only ride with it, blind to her own
power and her own demands. She was spinning too fast
in the world they'd created to know how hungrily her
mouth sought him, how sure were her own hands. She
drew from him everything he drew from her. Again and
again she took him to the edge, and again and again he
clung, wanting more. And still more.

Greed. He'd never known this degree of greed. With
the blood pounding in his head, singing in his veins, he
molded his open mouth to hers. With his hands gripping
her hips, he rolled until she lay over him. They were
still mouth-to-mouth when they joined, and her gasp
of pleasure rocketed through him.

Strength seemed to build, impossibly. She thought
she could feel each individual muscle of her body coil
and release as they moved together. Power called to
power. Lee remembered the lightning, remembered the
thunder, and lived it again. When the storm broke, she
was clasped against him, as if the heat had fused them.

Minutes, hours, days. Lee couldn't have measured
the time. Slowly, her body settled. Gradually, her heartbeat leveled. With her body pressed close to his, she
could feel each breath he took and found a foolish satisfaction that the rhythm matched her own.

"A pity we wasted a week." Finding the effort to
open his eyes too great, Hunter kept them closed as he
combed his fingers through her hair.

She smiled a little, because he couldn't see. "Wasted?"

"If we'd started out this way, I'd've slept a lot better."

"Really?" Schooling her features, Lee lifted her head. "Have you had trouble sleeping?"

His eyelids opened lazily. "I've rarely found it necessary to get up at dawn, unless it's to write."

The surge of pleasure made her voice smug. She traced a fingertip over his shoulder. "Is that so?"

"You insisted on wearing that perfume to make me crazy."

"To make you crazy?" Folding her arms on his chest, she arched a brow. "It's a very subtle scent."

"Subtle." He ran a casual hand over her bottom. "Like a hammer in the solar plexus."

The laugh nearly escaped. "You were the one who insisted we share a tent."

"Insisted?" He gave her a mildly amused glance. "I told you I had no objection if you chose to sleep outside."

"Knowing I wouldn't."

"True, but I didn't expect you to resist me for so long."

Her head came up off her folded arms. "Resist you?" she repeated. "Are you saying you plotted this out like a scene in a book?"

Grinning, he pillowed his arms behind his head. God, he couldn't remember a time he'd felt so clean, so...complete. "It worked."

"Typical," she said, wishing she were insulted and trying her best to act as though she were. "I'm surprised there was room in here for the two of us and your inflated ego."

"And your stubbornness."

She sat up at the word, both brows disappearing

under her tousled bangs. "I suppose you thought I'd just—" her hand gestured in a quick circle "—fall at your feet."

Hunter considered this a moment, while he gave himself the pleasure of memorizing every curve of her body. "It might've been nice, but I'd figured a few detours into the scenario."

"Oh, had you?" She wondered if he realized he was steadily digging himself into a hole. "I bet we can come up with a great many more." Searching in her pack, Lee found a fresh T-shirt. "Starting now."

As she started to drag the shirt over her head, Hunter grabbed the hem and yanked. Lee tumbled down on top of him again, to find her mouth captured. When he let her surface, she narrowed her eyes. "You think you're pretty clever, don't you?"

"Yeah." He caught her chin in his hand and kissed her again. "Let's have breakfast."

She swallowed a laugh, but her eyes gave her away. "Bastard."

"Okay, but I'm still hungry." He tugged her shirt down her torso before he started to dress.

Lying back, Lee strugggled into a pair of jeans. "I don't suppose, now that the point's been made, we could finish out this week at a nice resort?"

Hunter dug out a fresh pair of socks. "A resort? Don't tell me you're having problems roughing it, Lenore."

"I wouldn't say problems." She stuck a hand in one boot and found the inside damp. Resigned, she hunted for her sneakers. "But there is the matter of having fantasies about a hot tub and a soft bed." She pressed a hand to her lower back. "Wonderful fantasies."

"Camping does take a certain amount of strength and

endurance," he said easily. "I suppose if you've reached your limit and want to quit—"

"I didn't say anything about quitting," she retorted. She set her teeth, knowing whichever way she went, she lost. "We'll finish out the damn two weeks," she mumbled, and crawled out of the tent.

Lee couldn't deny that the quality of the air was exquisite and the clarity of the sky more perfect than any she'd ever seen. Nor, if he'd asked, would she have told Hunter that she wanted to be back in Los Angeles. It was a matter of basic creature comforts, she thought. Like soaking in hot, fragrant water and stretching out on a firm, linen-covered mattress. Certainly, it wasn't more than most people wanted in their day-to-day lives. But then, she reflected, Hunter Brown wasn't most people.

"Fabulous, isn't it?" His arms came around her waist, drawing her back to his chest. He wanted her to see what he saw, feel what he felt. Perhaps he wanted it too much.

"It's a beautiful spot. It hardly seems real." Then she sighed, not entirely sure why. Would Los Angeles seem more real to her when this final week was up? At the very least, she understood the tall buildings and crowded streets. Here—here she seemed so small, and that top rung of the ladder seemed so vague and unimportant.

Abruptly, she turned and clung to him. "I hate to admit it, but I'm glad you brought me." She found she wanted to continue clinging, continue holding, so that there wouldn't be a time when she had to let go. Pushing away all thoughts of tomorrow, Lee told herself to remember the wildflowers. "I'm starving," she said, able to smile when she drew away. "It's your turn to cook."

"A small blessing."

Lee gave him a quick jab before they cleaned up the dishes they'd left out in the rain.

In his quick, efficient manner, Hunter had the camp-fire burning and bacon sizzling. Lee sat back, absorbing the scents while she watched him break eggs into the pan.

"We've been through a lot of eggs," she commented idly. "How do you manage to keep them fresh out here?"

Because she was watching his hands, she missed the quick smile. "Just one of the many mysteries of life. You'd better pass me a plate."

"Yes, but— Oh, look." The movement that had caught her eye turned out to be two rabbits, curious enough to bound to the edge of the clearing and watch. The mystery of the eggs was forgotten in the simple fascination of something she'd just begun to appreciate. "Every time I see one, I want to touch."

"If you managed to get close enough to touch, they'd show you they have very sharp teeth."

Shrugging, she dropped her chin to her knees and continued to stare back at the visitors. "The bunnies I think about don't bite."

Hunter reached for a plate himself. "Bunnies, fuzzy little squirrels and cute raccoons are nice to look at but foolish to handle. I remember having a long, heated argument with Sarah on the subject a couple of years ago."

"Sarah?" Lee accepted the plate he offered, but her attention was fully on him.

Until that moment, Hunter hadn't realized how completely he'd forgotten who she was and why she was there. To have mentioned Sarah so casually showed him he needed to keep personal feelings separate from professional agreements. "Someone very special," he told her as he scooped the remaining eggs onto his plate. He remembered his daughter's comment about simmering passion and falling in love. The smile couldn't be prevented. "I imagine she'd like to meet you."

Lee felt something cold squeeze her heart and fought to ignore it. They'd said nothing about commitment, nothing about exclusivity. They were adults. She was responsible for her own emotions and their consequences. "Would she?" Taking the first bite of eggs, she tasted nothing. Her eyes were drawn to the ring on his finger. It wasn't a wedding band, but... She had to ask, she had to know before things went any further.

"The ring you wear," she began, satisfied her voice was even. "It's very unusual. I've never seen another quite like it."

"You shouldn't." He ate with the ease of a man completely content. "My sister made it."

"Sister?" If her name was Sarah...

"Bonnie raises children and makes jewelry," Hunter went on. "I'm not sure which comes first."

"Bonnie." Nodding, she forced herself to continue eating. "Is she your only sister?"

"There were just the two of us. For some odd reason, we got along very well." He remembered those early years when he was struggling to learn how to be both father and mother to Sarah. He smiled. "We still do."

"How does she feel about what you do?"

"Bonnie's a firm believer that everyone should do exactly what suits them. As long as they're married, with a half-dozen children." He grinned, recognizing the unspoken question in Lee's eyes. "In that area, I've disappointed her." He paused for a moment, the grin fading. "Do you think I could make love with you if I had a wife waiting for me at home?"

She dropped her gaze to her plate. Why could he always read her when she couldn't read him? "I still don't know very much about you."

He didn't know if he consciously made the decision at that moment or if he'd been ready to make it all along. "Ask," he said simply.

Lee looked up at him. It no longer mattered if she needed to know for herself or for her job. She just needed to know. "You've never been married?"

"No."

"Is that an outgrowth of your need for privacy?"

"No, it's an outgrowth of not finding anyone who could deal with the way I live and my obligations."

Lee mulled this over, thinking it a rather odd way to phrase it. "Your writing?"

"Yes, there's that."

She started to press further, then decided to change directions. Personal questions could be reciprocated with personal questions. "You said you hadn't always wanted to be a writer, but were born to be one. What made you realize it?"

"I don't think it was a matter of realizing, but of accepting." Understanding that she wanted something specific, he drew out a cigarette, studying the tip. He was no more certain why he was answering than Lee was why she was asking. "It must've been in my first year of college. I'd written stories ever since I could remember, but I was dead set on a career as an athlete. Then I wrote something that seemed to trigger it. It was nothing fabulous," he added thoughtfully. "A very basic plot, simple background, but the characters pulled me in. I knew them as well as I knew anyone. There was nothing else for me to do."

"It must've been difficult. Publishing isn't an easy field. Even when you break in, it isn't particularly lucrative unless you write bestsellers. With your parents gone, you had to support yourself."

"I had experience waiting tables." He smiled, a bit more easily now. "And detested it. Sometimes you have to put it all on the line, Lenore. So I did."

"How did you support yourself from the time you graduated from college until you broke through with *The Devil's Due?*"

"I wrote."

Lee shook her head, forgetting the half-full plate on her lap. "The articles and short stories couldn't have brought in very much. And that was your first book."

"No, I'd had a dozen others before it." Blowing out a stream of smoke, he reached for the coffeepot. "Want some?"

She leaned forward a bit, her brows drawing together. "Look, Hunter, I've been researching you for months. I might not have gotten much, but I know every book, every article and every short story you've written, including the majority of your college work. There's no way I'd've missed a dozen books."

"You know everything Hunter Brown's written," he corrected and poured himself coffee.

"That's precisely what I said."

"You didn't research Laura Miles."

"Who?"

He sipped, enjoying the coffee and the conversation more than he'd anticipated. "A great many writers use pseudonyms. Laura Miles was mine."

"A woman's name?" Confused on one level, reporter's instincts humming on another, she frowned at him. "You wrote a dozen books before *The Devil's Due* under a woman's name?"

"Yeah. One of the problems with writing is that the name alone can project a certain perception of the author." He offered her the last piece of bacon. "Hunter Brown wasn't right for what I was doing at the time."

Lee let out a frustrated breath. "What were you doing?"

"Writing romance novels." He flicked his cigarette into the fire.

"Writing… *You?*"

He studied her incredulous face before he leaned back. He was used to criticism of genre fiction and, more often than not, amused by it. "Do you object to the genre in general, or to my writing in it?"

"I don't—" Confused, she broke off to try to gather her thoughts. "I just can't picture you writing happy-ever-after love stories. Hunter, I just finished *Silent Scream*. I kept my bedroom door locked for a week." She dragged a hand through her hair as he quietly watched her. "Romances?"

"Most novels have some kind of relationship with them. A romance simply focuses on it, rather than using it as a subplot or a device."

"But didn't you feel you were wasting your talent?" Lee knew his skill in drawing the reader in from the first page, from the first sentence. "I understand there being a matter of putting food on the table, but—"

"No." He cut her off. "I never wrote for the money, Lenore, any more than the novel you're writing is done for financial gain. As far as wasting my talent, you shouldn't look down your nose at something you don't understand."

"I'm sorry, I don't mean to be condescending. I'm just—" Helplessly, she shrugged. "I'm just surprised. No, I'm astonished. I see those colorful little paperbacks everywhere, but—"

"You never considered reading one," he finished. "You should, they're good for you."

"I suppose, for simple entertainment."

He liked the way she said it, as though it were something to be enjoyed in secret, like a child's lollipop. "If a novel doesn't entertain, it isn't a novel and it's wasted your time. I imagine you've read *Jane Eyre, Rebecca, Gone with the Wind, Ivanhoe*."

"Yes, of course."

"Romances. A lot of the same ingredients are in those colorful little paperbacks."

He was perfectly serious. At that moment, Lee would've given up half the books in her personal library for the chance to read one Laura Miles story. "Hunter, I want to print this."

"Go ahead."

Her mouth was already open for the argument she'd expected. "Go ahead?" she repeated. "You don't care?"

"Why should I? I'm not ashamed of the work I did as Laura Miles. In fact…" He smiled, thinking back. "I'm rather pleased with most of it."

"Then why—" She shook her head as she began to absently nibble on cold bacon. "Damn it, Hunter, why haven't you ever said so before? Laura Miles is as much a deep, dark secret as everything else about you."

"I never met a reporter I chose to tell before." He rose, stretching, and enjoyed the wide blue expanse of sky. Just as he'd never met a woman he'd have chosen to live with before. Hunter was beginning to wonder if one had very much to do with the other. "Don't complicate the simple, Lenore," he told her, thinking aloud. "It usually manages to complicate itself."

Setting her plate aside, she stood in front of him. "One more question, then."

He brought his gaze back down to hers. She hadn't bothered to fuss with her hair or makeup that morning, as she had from the first morning of the trip. For a moment, he wondered if the reporter was too anxious for the story or the woman was too involved with the man. He wished he knew. "All right," he agreed. "One more question."

"Why me?"

How did he answer what he didn't know? How did he answer what he was hesitant to ask himself? Framing her face, he brought his lips to hers. Long, lingering and very, very new. "I see something in you," Hunter murmured, holding her face still so that he could study it. "I want something from you. I don't know what either one is yet, and maybe I never will. Is that answer enough?"

She put her hands on his wrists and felt his life pump through them. It was almost possible to believe hers pumped through them, too. "It has to be."

Chapter 9

Standing high on the bluff, Lee could see down the canyon, over the peaks and pinnacles, beyond the rich red buttes to the sheer-faced walls. There were pictures in them. People, creatures, stories. They pleased her all the more because she hadn't realized she could find them.

She hadn't known land could be so demanding, or so compelling. Not knowing that, how could she have known she would feel at home so far away from the world she knew or the life she'd made?

Perhaps it was the mystery, the awesomeness—the centuries of work nature had done to form beauty out of rock, the centuries it had yet to work. Weather had landscaped, carved and created without pampering. It might have been the quiet she'd learned to listen to, the quiet she'd learned to hear more than she'd ever heard sound before. Or it might have been the man she'd discovered in the canyon, who was slowly, inevitably dominating every aspect of her life in much the same way wind, water and sun dominated the shape of everything around her. He wouldn't pamper, either.

They'd been lovers only a matter of days, yet he seemed to know just where her strengths lay, and her weaknesses. She learned about him, step by gradual step, always amazed that each new discovery came so naturally, as though she'd always known. Perhaps the intensity came from the briefness. Lee could almost accept that theory, but for the timelessness of the hours they spent together.

In two days, she'd leave the canyon, and the man, and go back to being the Lee Radcliffe she'd molded herself into over the years. She'd step back into the rhythm, write her article and go on to the next stage of her career.

What choice was there? Lee asked herself as she stood with the afternoon sun beating down on her. In L.A., her life had direction, it had purpose. There, she had one goal: to succeed. That goal didn't seem so important here and now, where just being, just breathing, was enough, but this world wasn't the one she would live in day after day. Even if Hunter had asked, even if she'd wanted to, Lee couldn't go on indefinitely in this unscheduled, unplanned existence. Purpose, she wondered. What would her purpose be here? She couldn't dream by the campfire forever.

But two days. She closed her eyes, telling herself that everything she'd done and everything she'd seen would be forever implanted in her memory. Did the time left have to be so short? And the time ahead of her loomed so long.

"Here." Hunter came up alongside her, holding out a pair of binoculars. "You should always see as far as you can."

She took them, with a smile for the way he had of putting things. The canyon zoomed closer, abruptly becoming more personal. She could see the water rushing by in the creek, rushing with a sound too distant to be heard. Why had she never noticed how unique each leaf on a tree could be? She could see other campers loitering near their sites or mingling with the day tourists on paths. Lee let the binoculars drop. They brought intrusion too close.

"Will you come back next year?" She wanted to be able to picture him there, looking out over the endless space, remembering.

"If I can."

"It won't have changed," she murmured. If she came back, five, ten years from then, the creek would still snake by, the buttes would still stand. But she couldn't come back. With an effort, she shook off the mood and smiled at him. "It must be nearly lunchtime."

"It's too hot to eat up here." Hunter wiped at the sweat on his brow. "We'll go down and find some shade."

"All right." She could see the dust plume up from his boots as he walked. "Someplace near the creek." She glanced to the right. "Let's go this way, Hunter. We haven't walked down there yet."

He hesitated only a moment. "Fine." Holding her hand, he took the path she'd chosen.

The walk down was always easier than the walk up. That was another invaluable fact Lee had filed away during the last couple of weeks. And Hunter, though he held her hand, didn't guide or lead. He simply walked his own way. Just as he'd walk his own way in forty-eight hours, she mused, and stretched her stride to keep pace with him.

"Will you start on your next book as soon as you get back?"

Questions, he thought. He'd never known anyone with such an endless supply of questions. "Yes."

"Are you ever afraid you'll, well, dry up?"

"Always."

Interested, she stopped a moment. "Really?" She'd considered him a man without any fear at all. "I'd have thought that the more success you achieved, the more confident you'd become."

"Success is a deity that's never satisfied." She frowned, a bit uncomfortable with his description. "Every time I face that first blank page, I wonder how I'll ever get through a beginning, middle and end."

"How do you?"

He began to walk again, so that she had to keep up or be left behind. "I tell the story. It's as simple and as miserably complex as that."

So was he, she reflected, that simple, that complex. Lee thought over his words as she felt the temperature gradually change with the decrease in elevation.

It seemed tidier in this section of the canyon. Once she thought she heard the purr of a car's engine, a sound she hadn't heard in days. The trees grew thicker, the shade more generous. How strange, she reflected, to have those sheer, unforgiving walls at her back and a cozy little forest in front of her. More unreality? Then, glancing down, she saw a patch of small white flowers. Lee picked three, leaving the rest for someone else. She hadn't come for them, she remembered as she tucked them in her hair, but she was glad, so very glad, to have found them.

"How's this?" He turned to see her secure the last flower in her hair. The need for her, the complete her, rose inside him so swiftly it took his breath away. Lenore. He had no trouble understanding why the man in Poe's verse had mourned the loss of her to the point of madness. "You grow lovelier. Impossible." Hunter touched a fingertip to her cheek. Would he, too, grow mad from mourning the loss of her?

Her face, lifted to the sun, needed nothing more than the luminescence of her skin to make it exquisite. But how long, he wondered, how long would she be content to shun the polish? How long would it be before she craved the life she'd begun to carve out for herself?

Lee didn't smile, because his eyes prevented her. He was looking into her again, for something… Something. She wasn't certain, even if she'd known what it was, that she could give him the answer he wanted. Instead, she did what he'd once done. Placing her hands on his shoulders, she touched her mouth to his. With her eyes squeezed shut, she dropped her head onto his chest.

How could she leave? How could she not? There seemed to be no direction she could go and not lose something essential. "I don't believe in magic," she murmured, "but if I did, I'd say this was a magic place. Now, in the day, it's quiet. Sleeping, perhaps. But at night, the air would be alive with spirits."

He held her closer as he rested his neck on top of her head. Did she realize how romantic she was? he wondered. Or just how hard she fought not to be? A week ago, she might have had such a thought, but she'd never have said it aloud. A week from now… Hunter bit back a sigh. A week from now, she'd give no more thought to magic.

"I want to make love with you here," he said quietly. "With the sunlight streaming through the leaves and onto your skin. In the evening, just before the dew falls. At dawn, when the light's caught somewhere between rose and gray."

Moved, ruled by love, she smiled up at him. "And at midnight, when the moon's high and anything's possible."

"Anything's always possible." He kissed one cheek, then the other. "You only have to believe it."

She laughed, a bit shakily. "You almost make me believe it. You make my knees weak."

His grin flashed as he swept her up in his arms. "Better?"

Would she ever feel this free again? Throwing her arms around his neck, Lee kissed him with all the feeling that welled inside her. "Yes. And if you don't put me down, I'll want you to carry me back to camp."

The half smile touched his lips. "Decided you aren't hungry after all?"

"Since I doubt you've got anything in that bag but dried fruit and sunflower seeds, I don't have any illusions about lunch."

"I've still got a couple pieces of fudge."

"Let's eat."

Hunter dropped her unceremoniously on the ground. "It shows the woman's basic lust centers around food."

"Just chocolate," Lee disagreed. "You can have my share of the sunflower seeds."

"They're good for you." Digging into the pack, he pulled out some small clear plastic bags.

"I can handle the raisins," Lee said unenthusiastically. "But I can do without the seeds."

Shrugging, Hunter popped two in his mouth. "You'll be hungry before dinner."

"I've been hungry before dinner for two weeks," she tossed back, and began to root through the pack herself for the fudge. "No matter how good seeds and nuts and little dried pieces of apricot are for you, they don't take the place of red meat—" she found a small square of fudge "—or chocolate."

Hunter watched her close her eyes in pure pleasure as she chewed the candy. "Hedonist."

"Absolutely." Her eyes were laughing when she opened them. "I like silk blouses, French champagne and lobster with warm butter sauce." She sighed as she sat back, wondering if Hunter had any emotional attachment to the last piece of fudge. "I especially enjoy them after I've worked all week to justify having them."

He understood that, perhaps too well. She wasn't a woman who wanted to be taken care of, nor was he a man who believed anyone should have a free ride. But what future was there in a relationship when two people couldn't acclimate to each other's lifestyle? He'd never imposed his on anyone else, nor would be permit anyone to sway him from his own. And yet, now that he felt the clock ticking the hours away, the days away, he wondered if it would be as simple to go back, alone, as he'd once expected it to be.

"You enjoy living in the city?" he asked casually.

"Of course." It wasn't possible to tell him that she hated the thought of going back, alone, to what she'd always thought was perfect for her. "My apartment's twenty minutes from the magazine."

"Convenient." And practical, he mused. It seemed she would always choose the practical, even if she had a whim for the fanciful. He opened the canteen and drank. When he passed it to Lee, she accepted. She'd learned to make a number of adjustments.

"I suppose you work at home."

"Yes."

She touched a hand absently to one of the flowers in her hair. "That takes discipline. I think most people need the structure of an office away from their living space to accomplish anything."

"You wouldn't."

She looked over then, wishing they could talk about more personal things without bringing on that quiet sense of panic. Better that they talked of work or the weather, or of nothing at all. "No?"

"You'd drive yourself harder than any supervisor or time clock." He bit into an apple slice. "If you put your mind to it, you'd have that manuscript finished within a month."

Restlessly, she moved her shoulders. "If I worked eight hours a day, without any other obligations."

"The story's your only obligation."

She held back a sigh. She didn't want to argue or even debate, not when they had so little time left together. Yet if they didn't discuss her work, she might not be able to prevent herself from talking about her feelings. That was a circle without any meeting point.

"Hunter, as a writer, you can feel that way about a book. I suppose you have to. I have a job, a career that demands blocks of time and a great deal of my attention. I can't simply put that into hiatus while I speculate on my chances of getting a manuscript published."

"You're afraid to risk it."

It was a direct hit to her most sensitive area. Both of them knew her anger was a defense. "What if I am? I've worked hard for my position at *Celebrity*. Everything I've done there, and every benefit I've received, I've earned on my own. I've already taken enough risks."

"By not marrying Jonathan Willoby?"

The fury leaped into her eyes quickly, interesting him. So, it was still a sore point, Hunter realized. A very sore point.

"Do you find that amusing?" Lee demanded. "Does the fact that I reneged on an unspoken agreement appeal to your sense of humor?"

"Not particularly. But it intrigues me that you'd consider it possible to renege on something unspoken."

From the meticulous way she recapped the canteen, he gauged just how angry she was. Her voice was cool and detached, as he hadn't heard it for days. "My family and the Willobys have been personally and professionally involved for years. The marriage was expected of me and I knew it from the time I was sixteen."

Hunter leaned back against the trunk of a tree until he was comfortable. "And at sixteen you didn't consider that sort of expectation antiquated?"

"How could you possibly understand?" Fuming, she rose. The nerves that had been dormant for days began to jump again. Hunter could almost see them spring to life. "You said your father was a dreamer who made his living as a salesman. My father was a realist who made his living socializing and delegating. He socialized with the Willobys. He delegated me to complete the social and professional merger with them by marrying Jonathan." Even now, the tidy, unemotional plans gave her a twinge of distaste. "Jonathan was attractive, intelligent, already successful. My father never considered that I'd object."

"But you did," Hunter pointed out. "Why do you continue to insist on paying for something that was your right?"

Lee whirled to him. It was no longer possible for her to answer coolly, to rebuff with aloofness. "Do you know what it cost me not to do what was expected of me? Everything I did, all my life, was ultimately for their approval."

"Then you did something for yourself." Without hurry, he rose to face her. "Is your career for yourself, Lenore, or are you still trying to win their approval?"

He had no right to ask, no right to make her search for the answer. Pale, she turned away from him. "I don't want to discuss this with you. It's none of your concern."

"Isn't it?" Abruptly as angry as she, Hunter spun her around again. "Isn't it?" he repeated.

Her hands curled around his arms—whether in protest or for support, she wasn't certain. Now, she thought, now perhaps she'd reached that edge where she had to make a stand, no matter how unsteady the ground under her feet. "My life and the way I live it are my business, Hunter."

"Not anymore."

"You're being ridiculous." She threw back her head, the better to meet his eyes. "This argument doesn't even have a point."

Something was building inside him so quickly he didn't have a chance to fight it or reason it through. "You're wrong."

She was beginning to tremble without knowing why.

Along with the anger came the quick panic she recognized too well. "I don't know what you want."

"You." She was crushed against him before she understood her own reaction. "All of you."

His mouth closed over hers with none of the gentle patience he usually showed. Lee felt a lick of fear that was almost immediately swallowed by raging need.

He'd made her feel passion before, but not so swiftly. Desire had burst inside her before, but not so painfully. Everything was as it always was whenever he touched her, and yet everything was so different.

Was it anger she felt from him? Frustration? Passion? She only knew that the control he mastered so finely was gone. Something strained inside him, something more primitive than he'd let free before. This time, they both knew it could break loose. Her blood swam with the panicked excitement of anticipation.

Then they were on the ground, with the scent of sun-warmed leaves and cool water. She felt his beard scrape over her cheek before he buried his mouth in her throat. Whatever drove him left her no choice but to race with him to the end that waited for both of them.

He didn't question his own desperation. He couldn't. If she held off sharing certain pieces of herself with him, she still shared her body willingly. He wanted more, all, though he told himself it wasn't reasonable. Even now, as he felt her body heat and melt for him, he knew he wouldn't be satisfied. When would she give her feelings to him as freely? For the first time in his life, he wanted too much.

He struggled back to the edge of reason, resisting the wave after wave of need that raged through him. This wasn't the time, the place or the way. In his mind, he knew it, but emotion battled to betray him. Still holding her close, he buried his face in her hair and waited for the madness to pass.

Stunned, as much by his outburst of passion as by her unquestioning response, Lee lay still. Instinctively, she stroked a hand down his back to soothe. She knew him well enough to understand that his temper was rarely unguarded. Now she knew why.

Hunter lifted his head to look at her, seeing on a surge of self-disgust that her eyes were wary again. The flowers had fallen from her hair. Taking one, he pressed it into her hand. "You're much too fragile to be handled so clumsily."

His eyes were so intense, so dark, it was impossible for her to relax again. Against his back, her fingers curled and uncurled. There was a warning somewhere in her brain that he wanted more than she'd expected him to want, more than she knew how to give. Play it light, Lee ordered herself, and deliberately stilled the movement of her fingers. She smiled, though her eyes remained cautious.

"I should've waited until we were back in the tent before I made you angry."

Understanding what she was trying to do, Hunter lifted a brow. Under his voice, and hers, was a strain both of them pretended not to hear. "We can go back now. I can toss you around a bit more."

As the panic subsided, she sent him a mild glance. "I'm stronger than I look."

"Yeah?" He sent her a smile of his own. He had the long hours of night to think about what had happened and what he was going to do about it. "Show me."

More confident than she should've been, Lee pushed

against him, intent on rolling him off her. He didn't budge. The look of calm amusement on his face had her doubling her efforts. Breathless, unsuccessful, she lay back and frowned at him. "You're heavier than you look," she complained. "It must be all those sunflower seeds."

"Your muscles are full of chocolate," he corrected.

"I only had one piece," she began.

"Today. By my count, you've polished off—"

"Never mind." Her brow arched elegantly. The nerves in her stomach hadn't completely subsided. "If you want to talk about unhealthy habits, you're the one who smokes too much."

He shrugged, accepting the truth. "Everyone's entitled to one vice."

Her grin became wicked, then sultry. "Is that your only one?"

If she'd planned to make her mouth irresistible, she'd succeeded. Hunter lowered his to nibble at the sweetness. "I've never been one to consider pleasures vices."

Sighing, she linked her arms around his neck. They didn't have enough time left to waste it arguing, or even thinking. "Why don't we go back to the tent so you can show me what you mean?"

He laughed softly and shifted to kiss the curve of her shoulder. Her laugh echoed his, then Lee's smile froze when she glanced down the length of his body to what stood at their feet.

Fear ripped through her. She couldn't have screamed. Her short, unpainted nails dug into Hunter's back.

"What—" He lifted his head. Her face was ice-white and still. Though her body was rigid beneath his, there was lively fear in the hands that dug into his back. Muscles tense, he turned to look in the direction she was staring. "Damn." The word was hardly out of his mouth before a hundred pounds of fur and muscle leaped on him. This time, Lee's scream tore free.

Adrenaline born of panic gave her the strength to send the three of them rolling to the edge of the bank. As she struck out blindly, Lee heard Hunter issue a sharp command. A whimper followed it.

"Lenore." Her shoulders were gripped before she could spring to her feet. In her mind, the only thought was to find a weapon to defend them. "It's all right." Without giving her a choice, Hunter held her close. "It's all right, I promise. He won't hurt you."

"My God, Hunter, it's a wolf!" Every nightmare she'd ever read or heard about fangs and claws spun in her mind. With her arms wrapped around him to protect him, as much as for protection for herself, Lee turned her head. Silver eyes stared back at her from a silver coat.

"No." He felt the fresh fear jump through her and continued to soothe. "He's only half wolf."

"We've got to do something." Should they run? Should they sit perfectly still? "He attacked—"

"Greeted," Hunter corrected. "Trust me, Lenore. He's not vicious." Annoyed and resigned, Hunter held out a hand. "Here, Santanas."

A bit embarrassed at having lost control of himself, the dog crawled forward, head down. Speechless, Lee watched Hunter stroke the thick silver-gray fur.

"He's usually better behaved," Hunter said mildly. "But he hasn't seen me for nearly two weeks."

"Seen you?" She pressed herself closer to Hunter. "But..." Logic began to seep through her panic as she saw the dog lick Hunter's extended hand. "You called him by name," she said shakily. "What did you call him?"

Before Hunter could answer, there was a rustling in the trees behind them. Lee had nearly mustered the breath to scream again when another voice, young and high, shouted out. "Santanas! You come back here. I'm going to get in trouble."

"Damn right," Hunter mumbled under his breath.

Lee drew back far enough to look into Hunter's face. "Just what the hell's going on?"

"A reunion," he said simply.

Puzzled, with her heart still pounding in her ears, Lee watched the girl break through the trees. The dog's tail began to thump the ground.

"Santanas!" She stopped, her dark braids whipping back and forth. Smiling, she uninhibitedly showed her braces. "Whoops." The quick exclamation trailed off as Lee was treated to a long intense stare that was hauntingly familiar. The girl stuck her hands in the pockets of cutoff jeans, scuffing the ground with battered sneakers. "Well, hi." Her gaze shifted to Hunter briefly before it focused on Lee again. "I guess you wonder what I'm doing here."

"We'll get into that later," Hunter said in a tone both females recognized as basic male annoyance.

"Hunter—" Lee drew farther away, traces of anger and anxiety working their way through the confusion. She couldn't bring herself to look away from the dark, dark eyes of the girl who stared at her. "What's going on here?"

"Apparently a lesson in manners should be," he returned easily. "Lenore, the creature currently sniffing at your hand is Santanas, my dog." At the gesture of his hand, the large, lean animal sat and lifted a friendly paw. Dazed, Lee found herself taking it while she turned to watch the dog's master. She saw Hunter's gaze travel beyond her with a smile that held both irony and pride. "The girl rudely staring at you is Sarah. My daughter."

Chapter 10

Daughter... Sarah...

Lee turned her head to meet the dark, direct eyes that were a duplicate of Hunter's. Yes, they were a duplicate. It struck her like a blast of air. He had a child? This lovely, slender girl with a tender mouth and braids secured by mismatched rubber bands was Hunter's daughter? So many opposing emotions moved through her that she said nothing. Nothing at all.

"Sarah." Hunter spoke into the drumming silence. "This is Ms. Radcliffe."

"Sure, I know, the reporter. Hi."

Still sitting on the ground, with the dog now sniffing around her shoulder, Lee felt like a complete fool. "Hello." She hoped the word wasn't as ridiculously formal as it sounded to her.

"Dad said I shouldn't call you pretty because pretty

was like a bowl of fruit." Sarah didn't tilt her head as one might to study from a new angle, but Lee had the impression she was being weighed and dissected like a still life. "I like your hair," Sarah declared. "Is it a real color?"

"A definite lesson in manners," Hunter put in, more amused than annoyed. "I'm afraid Sarah's a bit of a brat."

"He always says that." Sarah moved thin, expressive shoulders. "He doesn't mean it, though."

"Until today." He ruffled the dog's fur, wondering just how he would handle the situation. Lee was still silent, and Sarah's eyes were all curiosity. "Take Santanas back to the house. I assume Bonnie's there."

"Yeah. We came back yesterday because I remembered I had a soccer game and she had an inspiration and couldn't do anything with it in Phoenix with all the kids running around like monkeys."

"I see." And though he did, perfectly, Lee was left floundering in the dark. "Go ahead, then, we'll be right along."

"Okay. Come on, Santanas." Then she shot Lee a quick grin. "He looks pretty ferocious, but he doesn't bite." As the girl darted away, Lee wondered if she'd been speaking of the dog or her father. When she was once again alone with Hunter, Lee remained still and silent.

"I'll apologize for the rudeness of my family, if you'd like."

Family. The word struck her, a dose of reality that flung her out of the dream. Rising, Lee meticulously dusted off her jeans. "There's no need." Her voice was cool, almost chill. Her muscles were wire-taut. "Since the game's over, I'd like you to drive me into Sedona so I can arrange for transportation back to L.A."

"Game?" In one long, easy motion, he came to his feet, then took her hand, stopping its nervous movement. It was a gesture that had become so much of a habit, neither of them noticed. "There's no game, Lenore."

"Oh, you played it very well." The hurt she wouldn't permit in her voice showed clearly in her eyes. Her hand remained cold and rigid in his. "So well, in fact, I completely forgot we were playing."

Patience deserted him abruptly and without warning. Anger he could handle, with more anger or with amusement. But hurt left him with no defense, no attack. "Don't be an idiot. Whatever game there was ended a few nights ago in the tent."

"Ended." Tears sprang to her eyes, stunning her. Furiously she blinked them back, filled with self-disgust, but not before he'd seen them. "No, it never ended. You're an excellent strategist, Hunter. You seemed to be so open with me that I didn't think you were holding anything back." She jerked her hand from his, longing for the luxury of dissolving into those hot, cleansing tears. "How could you?" she demanded. "How could you touch me that way and lie?"

"I never lied to you." His voice was as calm as hers, his eyes were as full of passion.

"You have a child." Something snapped inside her, so that she had to grip her hands together to prevent herself from wringing them. "You have a half-grown daughter you never mentioned to me. You told me you'd never been married."

"I haven't been," he said simply, and waited for the inevitable questions.

They leaped into her mind, but Lee found she couldn't ask them. She didn't want to know. If she was to put him out of her life immediately and completely, she couldn't ask. "You said her name once, and when I asked, you avoided answering."

"Who asked?" he countered. "You or the reporter?"

She paled, and her step away from him said more than a dozen words.

"If that was an unfair question," he said, feeling his way carefully, "I'm sorry."

Lee stifled a bitter answer. He'd just said it all. "I want to go back to Sedona. Will you drive me, or do I have to arrange for a car?"

"Stop this." He gripped her shoulders before she could back farther away. "You've been a part of my life for a few days. Sarah's been my life for ten years. I take no risks with her." She saw the fury come and go in his eyes as he fought against it. "She's off the record, do you understand? She stays off the record. I won't have her childhood disturbed by photographers dogging her at soccer games or hanging from trees at school picnics. Sarah's not an item for the glossy pages of any magazine."

"Is that what you think of me?" she whispered. "We've come no further than that?" She swallowed a mixture of pain and betrayal. "Your daughter won't be mentioned in any article I write. You have my word. Now let me go."

She wasn't speaking only of the hands that held her there, and they both knew it. He felt a bubble of panic he'd never expected, a twist of guilt that left him baffled. Frustrated, he stared down at her. He'd never realized she could be a complication. "I can't." It was said with such simplicity her skin iced. "I want you to understand, and I need time for that."

"You've had nearly two weeks to make me understand, Hunter."

"Damn it, you came here as a reporter." He paused, as if waiting for her to confirm or deny, but she said nothing. "What happened between us wasn't planned or expected by either one of us. I want you to come back with me to my home."

Somehow she met his eyes levelly. "I'm still a reporter."

"We have two days left in our agreement." His voice softened, his hands gentled. "Lenore, spend those two days with me at home, with my daughter."

"You have no problem asking for everything, do you?"

"No." She was still holding herself away from him. No matter how badly he wanted to, Hunter knew better than to try to draw her closer. Not yet. "It's important to me that you understand. Give me two days."

She wanted to say no. She wanted to believe she could deny him even that and turn away, go away, without regrets. But there'd be regrets, Lee realized, if she went back to L.A. without taking whatever was left. "I can't promise to understand, but I'll stay two more days."

Though she was reluctant, he held her hand to his lips. "Thank you. It's important to me."

"Don't thank me," she murmured. The anger had slipped away so quietly, she couldn't recall it. "Things have changed."

"Things changed days ago." Still holding her hand,

he drew her in the direction Sarah had gone. "I'll come back for the gear."

Now that the first shock had passed, the second occurred to her. "But you live here in the canyon."

"That's right."

"You mean to tell me you have a house, with hot and cold running water and a normal bed, but you chose to spend two weeks in a tent?"

"It relaxes me."

"That's just dandy," she muttered. "You've had me showering with lukewarm water and waking up with aching muscles, when you knew I'd've given a week's pay for one tub bath."

"Builds character," he claimed, more comfortable with her annoyance.

"The hell it does. You did it deliberately." She stopped, turning to him as the sun dappled light through the trees. "You did it all deliberately to see just how much I could tolerate."

"You were very impressive." He smiled infuriatingly. "I admit I never expected you to last out a week, much less two."

"You sonofa—"

"Don't get cranky now," he said easily. "You can take as many baths as you like over the next couple of days." He swung a friendly arm over her shoulder before she could prevent it. And he'd have time, he thought, to explain to her about Sarah. Time, he hoped, to make her understand. "I'll even see to it that you have that red meat you've been craving."

Fury threatened. Control strained. "Don't you dare patronize me."

"I'm not. You're not a woman a man could patronize." Though she mistrusted his answer, his voice was bland with sincerity and he wasn't smiling. "I'm enjoying you and, I suppose, the foul-up of my own plans. Believe me, I hadn't intended for you to find out I lived a couple miles from the campsite in quite this way."

"Just how did you intend for me to find out?"

"By offering you a quiet candlelight dinner on our last night. I'd hoped you'd see the—ah—humor in the situation."

"You'd've been wrong," she said precisely, then caught sight of the house cocooned in the trees.

It was smaller than she'd expected, but with the large areas of glass in the wood, it seemed to extend into the land. It made her think of dolls' houses and fairy tales, though she didn't know why. Dolls' houses were tidy and formal and laced with gingerbread. Hunter's house was made up of odd angles and unexpected peaks. A porch ran across the front, where the roof arched to a high pitch. Plants spilled over the banister—bloodred geraniums in jade-green pots. The roof sloped down again, then ran flat over a parallelogram with floor-to-ceiling windows. On the patio that jutted out from it, a white wicker chair lay overturned next to a battered soccer ball.

The trees closed in around it. Closed it in, Lee thought. Protected, sheltered, hid. It was like a house out of a play, or... Stopping, she narrowed her eyes and studied it again. "This is Jonas Thorpe's house in *Silent Scream*."

Hunter smiled, rather pleased she'd seen it so quickly. "More or less. I wanted to put him in isolation, miles away from what would normally be considered civilized, but in reality, the only safe place left."

"Is that how you look at it?" she wondered aloud. "As the only safe place left?"

"Often." Then a shriek, which after a heart-stopping moment Lee identified as laughter, ripped through the silence. It was followed by an excited bout of barking and a woman's frazzled voice. "Then there're other times," Hunter murmured as he led Lee toward the front door.

Even as he opened it, Sarah came bounding out. Unsure of her own feelings, Lee watched the girl throw her arms around her father's waist. She saw Hunter stroke a hand over the dark hair at the crown of Sarah's head.

"Oh, Dad, it's so funny! Aunt Bonnie was making a bracelet out of glazed dough and Santanas ate it—or he chewed on it until he found out it tasted awful."

"I'm sure Bonnie thinks it's a riot."

Her eyes, so like her father's, lit with a wicked amusement that would've made a veteran fifth-grade teacher nervous. "She said she had to take that sort of thing from art critics, but not from half-breed wolves. She said she'd make some tea for Lenore, but there aren't any cookies because we ate them yesterday. And she said—"

"Never mind, we'll find out for ourselves." He stepped back so that Lee could walk into the house ahead of him. She hesitated for a moment, wondering just what she was walking into, and his eyes lit with the same wicked amusement as Sarah's. They were quite a pair, Lee decided, and stepped forward.

She hadn't expected anything so, well, normal in Hunter Brown's home. The living room was airy, sunny in the afternoon light. *Cheerful.* Yes, Lee realized, that was precisely the word that came to mind. No shadowy corners or locked doors. There were wildflowers in an enameled vase and plump pillows on the sofa.

"Were you expecting witches' brooms and a satin-lined coffin?" he murmured in her ear.

Annoyed, she stepped away from him. "Of course not. I suppose I didn't expect you to have something quite so...domesticated."

He arched a brow at the word. "I am domesticated."

Lee looked at him, at the face that was half rugged, half aristocratic. On one level, perhaps, she mused. But only on one.

"I guess Aunt Bonnie's got the mess in the kitchen pretty well cleaned up." Sarah kept one arm around her father as she gave Lee another thorough going-over. "She'd like to meet you because Dad doesn't see nearly enough women and never talks to reporters. So maybe you're special because he decided to talk to you."

While she spoke, she watched Lee steadily. She was only ten, but already she'd sensed there was something between her father and this woman with the dark blue eyes and nifty hair. What she didn't know was exactly how she felt about it yet. In the manner of her father, Sarah decided to wait and see.

Equally unsure of her own feelings, Lee went with them into the kitchen. She had an impression of sunny walls, white trim and confusion.

"Hunter, if you're going to keep a wolf in the house, you should at least teach him to appreciate art. Hi, I'm Bonnie."

Lee saw a tall, thin woman with dark brown shoulder-length hair streaked liberally with blond. She wore a purple T-shirt with faded pink printing over cutoffs as ragged as her niece's. Her bare feet were tipped at the toes with hot-pink polish. Studying her thin model's face, Lee couldn't be sure if she was years older than Hunter or years younger. Automatically she held out her hand in response to Bonnie's outstretched one.

"How do you do?"

"I'd be doing a lot better if Santanas hadn't tried to make a snack of my latest creation." She held up a golden-brown half circle with ragged ends. "Just lucky for him it was a dreadful idea. Anyway, sit." She gestured to a table piled with bowls and canisters and dusted with flour. "I'm making tea."

"You didn't turn the kettle on," Sarah pointed out, and did so herself.

"Hunter, the child's always picking on details. I worry about her."

With a shrug of acceptance, he picked up what looked like a small doughnut and might, with imagination, have been an earring. "You're finding gold and silver too traditional to work with these days?"

"I thought I might start a trend." When Bonnie smiled, she became abruptly and briefly stunning. "In any case, it was a small failure. Probably cost you less than three dollars in flour. Sit," she repeated as she began to transfer the mess from the table to the counter behind her. "So, how was the camping trip?"

"Enlightening. Wouldn't you say, Lenore?"

"Educational," she corrected, but thought the last half hour had been the most educational of all.

"So, you work for *Celebrity*." Bonnie's long, twisted gold earrings swung when she walked, much like Sarah's braids. "I'm a faithful reader."

"That's because she's had a couple of embarrassingly flattering write-ups."

"Write-ups?" Lee watched Bonnie dust her flour-covered hands on her cutoffs.

Hunter smiled as he watched his sister reach for a tin of tea and send others clattering to the counter. "Professionally she's known as B. B. Smithers."

The name rang a bell. For years, B. B. Smithers had been considered the queen of avant-garde jewelry. The elite, the wealthy and the trendy flocked to her for personal designs. They paid, and paid well, for her talent, her creativity, and the tiny *B*s etched into the finished product. Lee stared at the thin, somewhat clumsy woman with something close to wonder. "I've admired your work."

"But you wouldn't wear it," Bonnie put in with a smile as she shoved tumbled boxes and tins out of her way. "No, it's the classics for you. What a fabulous face. Do you want lemon in your tea? Do we have any lemons, Hunter?"

"Probably not."

Taking this in stride, Bonnie set the teapot on the table to let the tea steep. "Tell me, Lenore, how did you talk the hermit into coming out of his cave?"

"By making him furious, I believe."

"That might work." She sat down across from Lee as Sarah walked to her father's side. Her eyes were softer than her brother's, less intense, but not, Lee thought, less perceptive. "Did the two weeks playing pioneer in the canyon give you the insight to write an article on him?"

"Yes." Lee smiled, because there was humor in Bonnie's eyes. "Plus I gained a growing affection for box springs and mattresses."

The quick, stunning smile flashed again. "My husband takes the children camping once a year. That's when I go to Elizabeth Arden's for the works. When we come home, both of us feel we've accomplished several small miracles."

"Camping's not so bad," Sarah commented in her father's defense.

"Is that so?" He patted her bottom as he drew her closer. "Why is it that you always have this all-consuming desire to visit Bonnie in Phoenix whenever I start packing gear?"

She giggled, and her arm went easily around his shoulder. "Must be coincidence," she said in a dry tone that echoed his. "Did he make you go fishing?" Sarah wanted to know. "And sit around for just *hours?*"

Lee watched Hunter's brow lift before she answered. "Actually, he did, ah, suggest fishing several days running."

"Ugh" was Sarah's only comment.

"But I caught a bigger fish than he did."

Unimpressed, Sarah shook her head. "It's awfully boring." She sent her father an apologetic glance. "I guess somebody's got to do it." Leaning her head against her father's, she smiled at Lee. "Mostly he's never boring, he just likes some weird stuff. Like fishing and beer."

"Sarah doesn't consider Hunter's shrunken-head collection at all unusual." Bonnie picked up the teapot. "Are you having some?" she asked her brother.

"I'll pass. Sarah and I'll go and break camp."

"Take your wolf with you," Bonnie told him as she poured tea into Lee's cup. "He's still on my hit list. By the way, a couple of calls from New York came in for you yesterday."

"They'll keep." As he rose, he ran a careless hand down Lee's hair, a gesture not lost on either of the other females in the room. "I'll be back shortly."

She started to offer her help, but it was so comfortable in the sunny, cluttered kitchen, and the tea smelled like heaven. "All right." She saw the proprietary hand Sarah put on her father's arm and thought it just as well to stay where she was.

Together, father and daughter walked to the back door. Hunter whistled for the dog, then they were gone.

Bonnie stirred her tea. "Sarah adores her father."

"Yes." Lee thought of the way they'd looked, side by side.

"And so do you."

Lee had started to lift her cup; now it only rattled in the saucer. "I beg your pardon?"

"You're in love with Hunter," Bonnie said mildly. "I think it's marvelous."

She could've denied it—vehemently, icily, laughingly, but hearing it said aloud seemed to put her in some kind of trance. "I don't—that is, it doesn't…" Lee stopped, realizing she was running the spoon handle through her hands. "I'm not sure how I feel."

"A definite symptom. Does being in love worry you?"

"I didn't say I was." Again, Lee stopped. Could anyone make evasions with those soft doe eyes watching? "Yes, it worries me a lot."

"Only natural. I used to fall in and out of love like some people change clothes. Then I met Fred." Bonnie laughed into her tea before she sipped. "I went around with a queasy stomach for weeks."

Lee pressed a hand to her own before she rose. Tea

wasn't going to help. She had to move. "I have no illusions about Hunter and myself," she said, more firmly than she'd expected to. "We have different priorities, different tastes." She looked through the kitchen window to the high red walls far beyond the clustering trees. "Different lives. I have to get back to L.A."

Bonnie calmly continued to drink tea. "Of course." If Lee heard the irony, she didn't respond to it. "There are people who have it fixed in their heads that in order to have a relationship, the two parties involved must be on the same wavelength. If one adores sixteenth-century French poetry and the other detests it, there's no hope." She noticed Lee's frown but continued, lightly. "Fred's an accountant who gets a primal thrill out of interest rates." She wiped absently at a smudge of flour on the table. "Statistically, I suppose we should've divorced years ago."

Lee turned back, unable to be angry, unable to smile. "You're a great deal like Hunter, aren't you?"

"I suppose. Is your mother Adreanne Radcliffe?"

Though she no longer wanted it, Lee came back to the table for her tea. "Yes."

"I met her at a party in Palm Springs two, no, must've been three years ago. Yes, three," Bonnie said decisively, "because I was still nursing Carter, my youngest, and he's currently terrorizing everyone at nursery school. Just last week he tried to cook a goldfish in a toy oven. You're not at all like your mother, are you?"

It took a moment for Lee to catch up. She set down her tea again, untasted. "Aren't I?"

"Do you think you are?" Bonnie tossed her tousled, streaked hair behind her shoulder. "I don't mean any offense, but she wouldn't know what to say to anyone not born to the blue, so to speak. I'd've considered her a very sheltered woman. She's very lovely—you certainly appear to've inherited her looks. But that seems to be all."

Lee stared down at her tea. How could she explain that, because of the strong physical resemblance between her and her mother, she'd always figured there were other resemblances. Hadn't she spent her childhood and adolescence trying to find them, and all of her adult life trying to repress them? A sheltered woman. She found it a terrifying phrase, and too close to what she herself could have become.

"My mother has standards," she answered, at length. "She never seems to have any trouble living up to them."

"Oh, well, everyone should do what they do best." Bonnie propped her elbows on the table, lacing her fingers so that the three rings on her right hand gleamed and winked. "According to Hunter, the thing you do best is write. He mentioned your novel to me."

The irritation came so quickly Lee hadn't the chance to mask it. "He's the kind of man who can't admit when he's made a mistake. I'm a reporter, not a novelist."

"I see." Still smiling blandly, Bonnie dropped her chin onto her laced fingers. "So, what are you going to report about Hunter?"

Was there a challenge under the smile? A trace of mockery? Whatever there was at the edges, Lee couldn't help but respond to it. Yes, she thought again, Bonnie Smithers was a great deal like her brother.

"That he's a man who considers writing both a sacred duty and a skilled profession. That he has a sense of humor that's often so subtle it takes you hours to catch up. That he believes in choices and luck with the same stubbornness that he believes in fate." Pausing, she lifted her cup. "He values the written word, whether it's in comic books or Chaucer, and he works desperately hard to do what he considers his job—to tell the story."

"I like you."

Cautiously, Lee smiled. "Thank you."

"I love my brother," Bonnie went on easily. "More than that, I admire him, for personal and professional reasons. You understand him. Not everyone would."

"Understand him?" Lee shook her head. "It seems to me that the more I find out about him, the less I understand. He's shown me more beauty in a pile of rocks than I'd ever have found for myself, yet he writes about horror and fears."

"And you consider that a contradiction?" Bonnie shrugged as she leaned back in her chair. "It's just that Hunter sees both sides of life very clearly. He writes about the dark side because it's the most intriguing."

"Yet he lives…" Lee gestured as she glanced around the kitchen.

"In a cozy little house nestled in the woods."

The laugh came naturally. "I wouldn't precisely call it cozy, but it's certainly not what you'd expect from the country's leading author of horror and occult fiction."

"The country's leading author of horror and occult fiction has a child to raise."

"Yes." Lee's smile faded. "Yes, Sarah. She's lovely."

"Will she be in your article?"

"No." Again, she lifted her gaze to Bonnie's. "No, Hunter made it clear he objected to that."

"She's the focal point of his life. If he seems a bit over-protective in certain ways, believe me, it's a completely unselfish act." When Lee merely nodded, Bonnie felt a stirring of sympathy. "He hasn't told you about her?"

"No, nothing."

There were times Bonnie's love and admiration for Hunter became clouded with frustration. A great many times. This woman was in love with him, was one step away from being irrevocably committed to him. Any fool could see it, Bonnie mused. Any fool except Hunter. "As I said, there are times he's overly protective. He has his reasons, Lenore."

"And will you tell me what they are?"

She was tempted. It was time Hunter opened that part of his life, and she was certain this was the woman he should open it to. "The story's Hunter's," Bonnie said at length. "You should hear it from him." She glanced around idly as she heard the Jeep pull up in the drive. "They're back."

"I guess I'm glad you brought her back," Sarah commented as they drove the last mile toward home.

"You guess?" Hunter turned his head, to see his daughter looking pensively through the windshield.

"She's beautiful, like a princess." For the first time in months, Sarah worried her braces with her tongue. "You like her a lot, I can tell."

"Yes, I like her a lot." He knew every nuance of his daughter's voice, every expression, every gesture. "That doesn't mean I like you any less."

Sarah gave him one long look. She needed no other words from him to reaffirm love. "I guess you have to like me," she decided, half teasing, "'cause we're stuck with each other. But I don't think she does."

"Why shouldn't Lenore like you?" Hunter countered, able to follow her winding statement without any trouble.

"She doesn't smile much."

Not enough, he silently agreed, but more each day. "When she relaxes, she does."

Sarah shrugged, unconvinced. "Well, she looked at me awful funny."

"Your grammar's deteriorating."

"She did."

Hunter frowned a bit as he turned into the dirt drive to their house. "It's only that she was surprised. I hadn't mentioned you to her."

Sarah stared at him a moment, then put her scuffed sneakers on the dash. "That wasn't very nice of you."

"Maybe not."

"You'd better apologize."

He sent his daughter a mild glance. "Really?"

She patted Santanas's head when he leaned over the back of her seat and dropped it on her shoulder. "Really. You always make me apologize when I'm rude."

"I didn't consider that you were any of her business." At first, Hunter amended silently. Things changed. Everything changed.

"You always make me apologize, even when I make up excuses," Sarah pointed out unmercifully. When they pulled up by the house, she grinned at him. "And even when I hate apologizing."

"Brat," he mumbled, setting the brake.

With a squeal of laughter, Sarah launched herself at him. "I'm glad you're home."

He held her close a moment, absorbing her scent— youthful sweat, grass and flowery shampoo. It seemed impossible that ten years had passed since he'd first held her. Then she'd smelled of powder and fragility and fresh linen. It seemed impossible that she was half-grown and the time had been so short.

"I love you, Sarah."

Content, she cuddled against him a moment, then, lifting her head, she grinned. "Enough to make pizza for dinner?"

He pinched her subtly pointed chin. "Maybe just enough for that."

Chapter 11

When Lee thought of family dinners, she thought of quiet meals at a glossy mahogany table laid with heavy Georgian silver, meals where conversation was subdued and polite. It had always been that way for her.

Not this dinner.

The already confused kitchen became chaotic while Sarah dashed around, half dancing, half bobbing, as she filled her father in on every detail of the past two weeks. Oblivious to the noise, Bonnie used the kitchen phone to call home and check in with her husband and children. Santanas, forgiven, lay sprawled on the floor, dozing. Hunter stood at the counter, preparing what Sarah claimed was the best pizza in the stratosphere. Somehow he managed to keep up with his daughter's disjointed conversation, answer the questions Bonnie tossed at him and cook at the same time.

Feeling like oil poured heedlessly on a rub of churning water, Lee began to clear the table. If she didn't do something, she decided, she'd end up standing in the middle of the room with her head swiveling back and forth, like a fan at a tennis match.

"I'm supposed to do that."

Awkwardly, Lee set down the teapot she'd just lifted and looked at Sarah. "Oh." *Stupid,* she berated herself. *Haven't you any conversation for a child?*

"You can help, I guess," Sarah said after a moment. "But if I don't do my chores, I don't get my allowance." Her gaze slid to her father, then back again. "There's this album I want to buy. You know, the Total Wrecks."

"I see." Lee searched her mind for even a wispy knowledge of the group but came up blank.

"They're actually not as bad as the name makes them sound," Bonnie commented on her way out to the kitchen. "Anyway, Hunter won't dock your pay if you take on an assistant, Sarah. It's considered good business sense."

Turning his head, Hunter caught his sister's quick grin before she waltzed out of the room. "I suppose Lee should earn her supper as well," he said easily. "Even if it isn't red meat."

The smile made it difficult for her to casually lift the teapot again.

"You'll like the pizza better," Sarah stated confidently. "He puts *everything* on it. Anytime I have friends over for dinner, they always want Dad's pizza." As she continued to clear the table, Lee tried to imagine Hunter competently preparing meals for several young, chattering girls. She simply couldn't. "I think he was a cook in another life."

Good Lord, Lee thought, did the child already have views on reincarnation?

"The same way you were a gladiator," Hunter said dryly.

Sarah laughed, childlike again. "Aunt Bonnie was a slave sold at an Arabian auction for thousands and thousands of drachmas."

"Bonnie has a very fluid ego."

With a clatter, Sarah set the cups in the sink. "I think Lenore must've been a princess."

With a damp cloth in her hands, Lee looked up, not certain if she should smile.

"A medieval princess," Sarah went on. "Like with King Arthur."

Hunter seemed to consider the idea a moment, while he studied his daughter and the woman under discussion. "It's a possibility. One of those delicate jeweled crowns and filmy veils would suit her."

"And dragons." Obviously enjoying the game, Sarah leaned back against the counter, the better to imagine Lee in a flowing pastel gown. "A knight would have to kill at least one full-grown male dragon before he could ask for her hand."

"True enough," Hunter murmured, thinking that dragons came in many forms.

"Dragons aren't easy to kill." Though she spoke lightly, Lee wondered why her stomach was quivering. It was entirely too easy to imagine herself in a great torchlit hall, with jewels winking from her hair and from the bodice of a rich silk gown.

"It's the best way to prove valor," Sarah told her, nibbling on a slice of green pepper she'd snitched from her father. "A princess can't marry just anyone, you know.

The king would either give her to a worthy knight, or marry her off to a neighboring prince so he could have more land with peace and prosperity."

Incredibly, Lee pictured her father, staff in hand, decreeing that she would marry Jonathan of Willoby.

"I bet you never had to wear braces."

Cast from one century to another in the blink of an eye, Lee merely stared. Sarah was frowning at her with the absorbed, absorbing concentration she could have inherited only from Hunter. It was all so foolish, Lee thought. Knights, princesses, dragons. For the first time, she was able to smile naturally at the slim, dark girl who was a part of the man she loved.

"Two years."

"You did?" Interest sprang into Sarah's solemn face. She stepped forward, obviously to get a better look at Lee's teeth. "It worked good," she decided. "Did you hate them?"

"Every minute."

Sarah giggled, so that the silver flashed. "I don't mind too much, 'cept I can't chew gum." She sent a sulky look over her shoulder in Hunter's direction. "Not even one stick."

"Neither could I." Ever, she thought, but didn't add it. Gum chewing was not permitted in the Radcliffe household.

Sarah studied her another moment, then nodded. "I guess you can help me set the table, too."

Acceptance, Lee was to discover, was just that simple.

The sun was streaming into the kitchen while they ate. It was rich and golden, without those harsh, stunning flashes of white she remembered from the cliffs of the canyon. She found it peaceful, despite all the talk and laughter and arguments swimming around her.

Her fantasies had run to eating a thick, rare steak and a crisp chef's salad in a dimly lit, quiet restaurant where the hovering waiter saw that your glass of Bordeaux was never empty. She found herself in a bright, noisy kitchen, eating pizza stringy with cheese, chunky with slices of green pepper and mushroom, spiced with pepperoni and hot sausage. And while she did, she found herself agreeing with Sarah's accolade. The best in the stratosphere.

"If only Fred could learn how to make one of these." Bonnie cut into her second slice with the same dedication she'd cut into her first. "On a good day he makes a superior egg salad, but it's not the same."

"With a family the size of yours," Hunter commented, "you'd need to set up an assembly line. Five hungry children could keep a pizzeria hopping."

"And do," Bonnie agreed. "In a bit less than seven months, it'll be six."

She grinned as Hunter's knife paused. "Another?"

"Another." Bonnie winked across the table at her niece. "I always said I'd have half a dozen kids," she said casually to Lee. "People should do what they do best."

Hunter reached over to take her hand. Lee saw the fingers interlock. "Some might call it overachievement."

"Or sibling rivalry," she tossed back. "I'll have as many kids as you do bestsellers." With a laugh, she squeezed her brother's hand. "It takes us about the same length of time to produce."

"When you bring the baby to visit, she should sleep in my room." Sarah bit off another mouthful of pizza.

"She?" Hunter ruffled her hair before he started to eat again.

"It'll be a girl." With the confidence of youth, Sarah nodded. "Aunt Bonnie already has three boys, so another girl makes it even."

"I'll see what I can do," Bonnie told her. "Anyway, I'll be heading back in the morning. Cassandra, she's my oldest," she put in for Lee's benefit, "has decided she wants a tattoo." She closed her eyes as she leaned back. "Ah, it's nice to be needed."

"A tattoo?" Sarah wrinkled her nose. "That's gross. Cassie's nuts."

"Fred and I are forced to agree."

Interested, Hunter lifted his wine. "Where does she want it?"

"On the curve of her right shoulder. She insists it'll be very tasteful."

"Dumb." Sarah handed out the decree with a shrug. "Cassie's thirteen," she added, rolling her eyes. "Boy, is she a case."

Lee choked back a laugh at both the facial and verbal expressions. "How will you handle it?"

Bonnie only smiled. "Oh, I think I'll take her to the tattoo parlor."

"But you wouldn't—" Lee broke off, seeing Bonnie's liberally streaked hair and shoulder-length earrings. Perhaps she would.

With a laugh, Bonnie patted Lee's hand. "No, I wouldn't. But it'll be a lot more effective if Cassie makes the decision herself—which she will, the minute she gets a good look at all those nasty little needles."

"Sneaky," Sarah approved with a grin.

"Clever," Bonnie corrected.

"Same thing." With her mouth half-full, she turned to Lee. "There's always a crisis at Aunt Bonnie's house," she said confidentially. "Did you have brothers and sisters?"

"No." Was that wistfulness she saw in the child's eyes? She'd often had the same wish herself. "There was only me."

"I think it's better to have them, even though it gets crowded." She slanted her father a guileless smile. "Can I have another piece?"

The rest of the evening passed, not quietly but, for all the noise, peacefully. Sarah dragged her father outside for soccer practice, which Bonnie declined, grinning. Her condition, she claimed, was too delicate. Lee, over her protests, found herself drafted. She learned, though her aim was never very accurate, to kick a ball with the side of her foot and bounce it off her head. She enjoyed it, which surprised her, and didn't feel like a fool, which surprised her more.

Dusk came quickly, then a dark that flickered with fireflies. Though her eyes were heavy, Sarah groaned about going to bed until Hunter agreed to carry her up on his back. Lee didn't have to be told it was a nightly ritual; she only had to see them together.

He'd said Sarah was his life, and though she'd only seen them together for a matter of hours, Lee believed it.

She'd never have expected the man whose books she'd read to be a devoted father, content to spend his time with a ten-year-old girl. She'd never have imagined him here, in a house so far away from the excitement of the city. Even the man she'd grown to know over the past two weeks didn't quite fit the structure of being parent, disciplinarian and mentor to a ten-year-old. Yet he was.

If she superimposed the image of Sarah's father over those of her lover and the author of *Silent Scream,* they all seemed to meld into one. The problem was dealing with it.

Righting the overturned chair on the patio, Lee sat. She could hear Sarah's sleepy laughter drift through the open window above her. Hunter's voice, low and indistinct, followed it. It was an odd way to spend her last hours with Hunter, here in his home, only a few miles from the campsite where they'd become lovers. And yes, she realized as she stared up at the stars, friends. She very much wanted to be his friend.

Now, when she wrote the article, she'd be able to do so with knowledge of both sides of him. It was what she'd come for. Lee closed her eyes because the stars were suddenly too bright. She was going back with much more and, because of it, much less.

"Tired?"

Opening her eyes, she looked up at Hunter. This was how she'd always remember him, cloaked in shadows, coming out of the darkness. "No. Is Sarah asleep?"

He nodded, coming around behind her to put his hands on her shoulders. This was where he wanted her. Here, when night was closing in. "Bonnie, too."

"You'd work now," she guessed. "When the house was quiet and the windows dark."

"Yes, most of the time. I finished my last book on a night like this." He hadn't been lonely then, but now... "Let's walk. The moon's full."

"Afraid? I'll give you a talisman." He slipped his ring off his pinky, sliding it onto her finger.

"I'm not superstitious," she said loftily, but curled her fingers into her palm to hold the ring in place.

"Of course you are." He drew her against his side as they walked. "I like the night sounds."

Lee listened to them—the faintest breeze through the trees, the murmur of water, the singsong of insects. "You've lived here a long time." As the day had passed, it had become less feasible to think of his living anywhere else.

"Yes. I moved here the year Sarah was born."

"It's a lovely spot."

He turned her into his arms. Moonlight spilled over her, silver, jewel-like in her hair, marbling her skin, darkening her eyes. "It suits you," he murmured. He ran a hand through her hair, then watched it fall back into place. "The princess and the dragon."

Her heart had already begun to flutter. Like a teenager's, Lee thought. He made her feel like a girl on her first date. "These days women have to kill their own dragons."

"These days—" his mouth brushed over hers "—there's less romance. If these were the Dark Ages, and I came upon you in a moonlit wood, I'd take you because it was my right. I'd woo you because I'd have no choice." His voice darkened like the shadows in the trees surrounding them. "Let me love you now, Lenore, as if it were the first time."

Or the last, she thought dimly as his lips urged her to soften, to yield, to demand. With his arms around her, she could let her consciousness go. Imagine and feel. Lovemaking consisted of nothing more. Even as her head tilted back in submission, her arms strengthened around him, challenging him to take whatever he wanted, to give whatever she asked.

Then his hands were on her face, gently, as gently as they'd ever been, memorizing the slope and angle of her bones, the softness of her skin. His lips followed, tasting, drinking in each separate flavor. The pleasure that could come so quickly ran liquid through her. Bonelessly, she slid with him to the ground.

He'd wanted to love her like this, in the open, with the moon silvering the trees and casting purple shadows. He'd wanted to feel her muscles coil and go fluid under the touch of his hand. What she gave to him now was something out of his own dreams and much, much more real than anything he'd ever had. Slowly, he undressed her, while his lips and the tips of his fingers both pleasured and revered her. This would be the night when he gave her all of him and when he asked for all of her.

Moonlight and shadows washed over her, making his heart pound in his ears. He heard the creek bubble nearby to mix with her quiet sighs. The woods smelled of night. And so, as she buried his face against her neck, did she.

She felt the surging excitement in him, the growing, straining need that swept her up. Willingly, she went into the whirlpool he created. There the air was soft to the touch and streaked with color. There she would stay, endlessly possessed.

His skin was warm against hers. She tasted, her head swimming from pleasure, power and newly awakened dizzying speed. Ravenous for more, she raced over him, acutely aware of every masculine tremble beneath her, every drawn breath, every murmur of her name.

Silver and shadows. Lee felt them every bit as tangibly as she saw them flickering around her. The silver streak of power. The dark shadow of desire. With them, she could take him to that trembling precipice.

When he swore, breathlessly, she laughed. Their needs were tangled together, twining tighter. She felt it. She celebrated it.

The air seemed to still, the breeze pause. The sounds that had grown to one long din around them seemed to hush. The fingers tangled in her hair tightened desperately. In the silence, their eyes met and held, moment after moment.

Her lips curved as she opened for him.

She could have slept there, effortlessly, with the bare ground beneath her, the sky overhead and his body pressed to hers. She might have slept there, endlessly, like a princess under a spell, if he hadn't drawn her up into his arms.

"You fall asleep like a child," he murmured. "You should be in bed. My bed."

Lee sighed, content to stay where she was. "Too far."

With a low laugh, he kissed the hollow between her neck and shoulder. "Should I carry you?"

"Mmm." She nestled against him. "'Kay."

"Not that I object, but you might be a bit disconcerted if Bonnie happened to walk downstairs while I was carrying you in, naked."

She opened her eyes, so that her irises were dusky blue slits under her lashes. Reality was returning. "I guess we have to get dressed."

"It might be advisable." His gaze skimmed over her, then back to her face. "Should I help you?"

She smiled. "I think that we might have the same result with you dressing me as we do with you undressing me."

"An interesting theory." Hunter reached over her for the brief strip of ivory lace.

"But this isn't the time to test it out." Lee plucked her panties out of his hand and wiggled into them. "How long have we been out here?"

"Centuries."

She shot him a look just before her head disappeared into her shirt. She wasn't completely certain he was exaggerating. "The least I deserve after these past two weeks is a real mattress."

He took her hand, pressing her palm to his lips. "You're welcome to share mine."

Lee curled her fingers around his briefly, then released them. "I don't think that's wise."

"You're worried about Sarah."

It wasn't a question. Lee took her time, making certain all the clouds of romance were out of her head before she spoke. "I don't know a great deal about children, but I imagine she's unprepared for someone sharing her father's bed."

Silence lay for a moment, like the eye of a storm. "I've never brought a woman to our home before."

The statement caused her to look at him quickly, then, just as quickly, look away. "All the more reason."

"All the more reason for many things." He dressed without speaking while Lee stared out into the trees. So beautiful, she thought. And more and more distant.

"You wanted to ask me about Sarah, but you didn't."

She moistened her lips. "It's not my business."

Her chin was captured quickly, not so gently. "Isn't it?" he demanded.

"Hunter—"

"This time you'll have the answer without asking." He dropped his hand, but his gaze never faltered. She needed nothing else to tell her the calm was over. "I met a woman, almost a dozen years ago. I was writing as Laura Miles by then, so that I could afford a few luxuries. Dinner out occasionally, the theater now and then. I was still living in L.A., alone, enjoying my work and the benefits it brought me. She was a student in her last year. Brains and ambition she had in abundance, money she didn't have at all. She was on scholarship and determined to be the hottest young attorney on the West Coast."

"Hunter, what happened between you and another woman all those years ago isn't my business."

"Not just another woman. Sarah's mother."

Lee began to pull at the tuft of grass by her side. "All right, if it's important for you to tell me, I'll listen."

"I cared about her," he continued. "She was bright, lovely and full of dreams. Neither of us had ever considered becoming too serious. She still had law school to finish, the bar to pass. I had stories to tell. But then, no matter how much we plan, fate has a way of taking over."

He drew out a cigarette, thinking back, remembering each detail. His tiny, cramped apartment with the leaky plumbing, the battered typewriter with its hiccuping carriage, the laughter from the couple next door that would often seep through the thin walls.

"She came by one afternoon. I knew something was wrong because she had afternoon classes. She was much too dedicated to skip classes. It was hot, one of those sultry, breathless days. The windows were up, and I had a little portable fan that stirred the air around without doing much to cool it. She'd come to tell me she was pregnant."

He could remember the way she'd looked if he concentrated. But he never chose to. But whether he chose to or not, he'd always be able to remember the tone of her voice when she'd told him. Despair, laced with fury and accusation.

"I said I cared about her, and that was true. I didn't love her. Still, our parents' values do trickle down. I offered to marry her." He laughed then, not humorously, but not, Lee reflected, bitterly. It was the laugh of a man who'd accepted the joke life had played on him. "She refused, almost as angry with the solution I'd offered as she was with the pregnancy. She had no intention of taking on a husband and a child when she had a career to carve out. It might be difficult to understand, but she wasn't being cold, simply practical, when she asked me to pay for the abortion."

Lee felt all of her muscles contract. "But, Sarah—"

"That's not the end of the story." Hunter blew out a stream of smoke and watched it fade into darkness. "We had a memorable fight, threats, accusations, blame-casting. At the time, I couldn't see her end of it, only the fact that she had part of me inside her that she wanted to dispose of. We parted then, both of us furious, both of us desperate enough to know we each needed time to think."

She didn't know what to say, or how to say it. "You were young," she began.

"I was twenty-four," Hunter corrected. "I'd long since

stopped being a boy. I was—we were—responsible for our own actions. I didn't sleep for two days. I thought of a dozen answers and rejected them all, over and over. Only one thing stuck with me in that whole sweaty, terrified time. I wanted the child. It's not something I can explain, because I did enjoy my life, the lack of responsibilities, the possibility of becoming really successful. I simply knew I had to have the child. I called her and asked her to come back.

"We were both calmer the second time, and both more frightened than either of us had ever been in our lives. Marriage couldn't be considered, so we set it aside. She didn't want the child, so we dealt with that. I did. That was something a bit more complex to deal with. She needed freedom from the responsibility we'd made together, and she needed money. In the end, we resolved it all."

Dry-mouthed, Lee turned to him. "You paid her."

He saw, as he'd expected to see, the horror in her eyes. When he continued, his voice was calm, but it took a great deal of effort to make it so. "I paid all the medical expenses, her living expenses up until she delivered, and I gave her ten thousand dollars for my daughter."

Stunned, heartsick, Lee stared at the ground. "How could she—"

"We each wanted something. In the only way open, we gave it to each other. I've never resented that young law student for what she did. It was her choice, and she could've taken another without consulting me."

"Yes." She tried to understand, but all Lee could see was that slim, dark little girl. "She chose, but she lost."

It meant everything just to hear her say it. "Sarah's been mine, only mine, from the first moment she breathed. The woman who carried her gave me a priceless gift. I only gave her money."

"Does Sarah know?"

"Only that her mother had choices to make."

"I see." She let out a long breath. "The reason you're so careful about keeping publicity away from her is to keep speculation away."

"One of them. The other is simply that I want her to have the uncomplicated life every child's entitled to."

"You didn't have to tell me." She reached a hand for his. "I'm glad you did. It can't have been easy for you, raising a baby by yourself."

There was nothing but understanding in her eyes now. Every taut muscle in his body relaxed as if she'd stroked them. He knew now, with utter certainty, that she was what he'd been waiting for. "No, not easy, but always a pleasure." His fingers tightened on hers. "Share it with me, Lenore."

Her thoughts froze. "I don't know what you mean."

"I want you here, with me, with Sarah. I want you here with the other children we'll have together." He looked down at the ring he'd put on her hand. When his eyes came back to hers, she felt them reach inside her. "Marry me."

Marry? She could only stare at him blankly while the panic quietly built and built. "You don't—you don't know what you're asking."

"I do," he corrected, holding her hand more firmly when she tried to draw it away. "I've asked only one other woman, and that out of obligation. I'm asking you because you're the first and only woman I've ever loved. I want to share your life. I want you to share mine."

Panic steadily turned into fear. He was asking her to

change everything she'd aimed for. To risk everything. "Our lives are too far apart," she managed. "I have to go back. I have my job."

"A job you know you weren't made for." Urgency slipped into his voice as he took her shoulders. "You know you were made to write about the images you have in your head, not about other people's social lives and tomorrow's trends."

"It's what I know!" Trembling, she jerked away from him. "It's what I've been working for."

"To prove a point. Damn it, Lenore, do something for yourself. For yourself."

"It is for myself," she said desperately. *You love him,* a voice shouted inside her. *Why are you pushing away what you need, what you want?* Lee shook her head, as if to block the voice out. Love wasn't enough, needs weren't enough. She knew that. She had to remember it. "You're asking me to give it all up, every hard inch I've climbed in five years. I have a life in L.A., I know who I am, where I'm going. I can't live here and risk—"

"Finding out who you really are?" he finished. He wouldn't allow despair. He barely controlled anger. "If it was only myself, I'd go anywhere you liked, live anywhere that suited you, even if I knew it was a mistake. But there's Sarah. I can't take her away from the only home she's ever known."

"You're asking for everything again." Her voice was hardly a whisper, but he'd never heard anything more clearly. "You're asking me to risk everything, and I can't. I won't."

He rose, so that shadows shifted around him. "I'm asking you to risk everything," he agreed. "Do you love me?" And by asking, he'd already risked it all.

Torn by emotions, pushed by fear, she stared at him. "Yes. Damn you, Hunter, leave me alone."

She streaked back toward the house until the darkness closed in between them.

Chapter 12

"If you're not going to break for lunch, at least take this." Bryan held out one of her inexhaustible supply of candy bars.

"I'll eat when I've finished the article." Lee kept her eyes on the typewriter and continued to pound at the keys, lightly, rhythmically.

"Lee, you've been back for two days and I haven't seen you so much as nibble on a Danish." And her photographer's eye had seen beneath the subtle use of cosmetics to the pale bruises under Lee's eyes. That must've been some interview, she thought, as the brisk, even clickity-click of the typewriter keys went on.

"Not hungry." No, she wasn't hungry any more than she was tired. She'd been working steadily on Hunter's article for the better part of forty-eight hours. It was going to be perfect, she promised herself. It was going to be polished like a fine piece of glass. And oh, God, when she finished it, *finished it,* she'd have purged her system of him.

She'd gripped that thought so tightly, it often skidded away.

If she'd stayed... If she went back...

The oath came quickly, under her breath, as her fingers faltered. Meticulously, Lee reversed the carriage to make the correction. She couldn't go back. Hadn't she made that clear to Hunter? She couldn't just toss everything over her shoulder and go. But the longer she stayed away, the larger the hole in her life became. In the life, Lee was ruthlessly reminded, that she'd so carefully carved out for herself.

So she'd work in a nervous kind of fury until the article was finished. Until, she told herself, it was all finished. Then it would be time to take the next step. When she tried to think of that next step, her mind went stunningly, desperately blank. Lee dropped her hands into her lap and stared at the paper in front of her.

Without a word, Bryan bumped the door with her hip so that it closed and muffled the noise. Dropping down into the chair across from Lee, she folded her hands and waited a beat. "Okay, now why don't you tell me the story that's not for publication?"

Lee wanted to be able to shrug and say she didn't have time to talk. She was under a deadline, after all. The article was under a deadline. But then, so was her life. Drawing a breath, she turned in her chair. She didn't want to see the neat, clever little words she'd typed. Not now.

"Bryan, if you'd taken a picture, one that required a great deal of your time and all of your skill to set up, then once you'd developed it, it had come out in a completely different way than you'd planned, what would you do?"

"I'd take a good hard look at the way it had come out," she said immediately. "There'd be a good possibility I should've planned it that way in the first place."

"But wouldn't you be tempted to go back to your original plans? After all, you'd worked very, very hard to set it up in a certain way, wanting certain specific results."

"Maybe, maybe not. It'd depend on just what I'd seen when I looked at the picture." Bryan sat back, crossing long, jeans-clad legs. "What's in your picture, Lee?"

"Hunter." Her troubled gaze shifted, and locked on Bryan's. "You know me."

"As well as you let anyone know you."

With a short laugh, Lee began to push at a paper clip on her desk. "Am I as difficult as all that?"

"Yeah." Bryan smiled a bit to soften the quick answer. "And, I've always thought, as interesting. Apparently, Hunter Brown thinks the same thing."

"He asked me to marry him." The words came out in a jolt that left both women staring.

"Marry?" Bryan leaned forward. "As in 'till death do us part'?"

"Yes."

"Oh." The word came out like a breath of air as Bryan leaned back again. "Fast work." Then she saw Lee's unhappy expression. Just because Bryan didn't smell orange blossoms when the word *marriage* came up was no reason to be flippant. "Well, how do you feel? About Hunter, I mean."

The paper clip twisted in Lee's fingers. "I'm in love with him."

"Really?" Then she smiled, because it sounded nice

when said so simply. "Did all this happen in the canyon?"

"Yes." Lee's fingers moved restlessly. "Maybe it started to happen before, when we were in Flagstaff. I don't know anymore."

"Why aren't you happy?" Bryan narrowed her eyes as she did when checking the light and angle. "When the man you love, really love, wants to build a life with you, you should be ecstatic."

"How do two people build a life together when they've both already built separate ones, completely different ones?" Lee demanded. "It isn't just a matter of making more room in the closet or shifting furniture around." The end of the paper clip broke off in her fingers as she rose. "Bryan, he lives in Arizona, in the canyon. I live in L.A."

Lifting booted feet, Bryan rested them on Lee's polished desk, crossing her ankles. "You're not going to tell me it's all a matter of geography."

"It just shows how impossible it all is!" Angry, Lee whirled around. "We couldn't be more different, almost opposites. I do things step-by-step, Hunter goes in leaps and bounds. Damn it, you should see his house. It's like something out of a sophisticated fairy tale. His sister's B. B. Smithers—" Before Bryan could fully register that, Lee was blurting out, "He has a daughter."

"A daughter?" Her attention fully caught, Bryan dropped her feet again. "Hunter Brown has a child?"

Lee pressed her fingers to her eyes and waited for calm. True, it wouldn't have come out if she hadn't been so agitated, and she'd never discuss such personal agitations with anyone but Bryan, but now she had to deal with it. "Yes, a ten-year-old girl. It's important that it not be publicized."

"All right."

Lee needed no promises from Bryan. Trying to calm herself, she took a quiet breath. "She's bright, lovely and quite obviously the center of his life. I saw something in him when they were together, something incredibly beautiful. It scared the hell out of me."

"Why?"

"Bryan, he's capable of so much talent, brilliance, emotion. He's put them together to make a complete success of himself, in all ways."

"That bothers you?"

"I don't know what I'm capable of. I only know I'm afraid I'd never be able to balance it all out, make it all work."

Bryan said something short, quick and rude. "You won't marry him because you don't think you can juggle? You should know yourself better."

"I thought I did." Shaking her head, she took her seat again. "It's ridiculous, in the first place," she said more briskly. "Our lives are miles apart."

Bryan glanced out the window at the tall, sleek building that was part of Lee's view of the city. "So, he can move to L.A. and close the distance."

"He won't." Swallowing, Lee looked at the pages on her desk. The article was finished, she knew it, just as she knew that if she didn't let it go, she'd polish it to death. "He belongs there. He wants to raise his daughter there. I understand that."

"So, you move to the canyon. Great scenery."

Why did it always sound so simple, so plausible, when spoken aloud? The little trickle of fear returned, and her voice firmed. "My job's here."

"I guess it comes down to priorities, doesn't it?" Bryan knew she wasn't being sympathetic, just as she

knew it wasn't sympathy that Lee needed. Because she
cared a great deal, she spoke without any compassion.
"You can keep your job and your apartment in L.A. and
be miserable. Or you can take a few chances."

Chances. Lee ran a finger down the slick surface of
her desk. But you were supposed to test the ground before you stepped forward. Even Hunter had said that.
But... She looked at the mangled paper clip in the center of her spotless blotter. How long did you test it before you took the jump?

It was barely two weeks later that Lee sat in her
apartment in the middle of the day. She was so rarely
there during the day, during the week, that she somehow expected everything to look different. Everything looked precisely the same. Even, she was forced
to admit, herself. Yet nothing was.

Quit. She tried to digest the word as she dealt with
the panic she'd held off the past few days. There was
a leafy, blooming African violet on the table in front
of her. It was well-tended, as every area of her life had
been well-tended. She'd always water it when the soil
was dry and feed it when it required nourishing. As she
stared at the plant, Lee knew she would never be capable of pulling it ruthlessly out by the roots. But wasn't
that what she'd done to herself?

Quit, she thought again, and the word reverberated
in her brain. She'd actually handed in her resignation,
served her two weeks' notice and summarily turned
her back on her steadily thriving career—ripped out
its roots.

For what? she demanded of herself as panic trickled
through. To follow some crazy dream that had planted
itself in her mind years ago. To write a book that would

probably never be published. To take a ridiculous risk
and plunge headlong into the unknown.

Because Hunter had said she was good. Because he'd
fed that dream, just as she fed the violet. More than that,
Lee thought, he'd made it impossible for her to stop
thinking about the "what ifs" in her life. And he was
one of them. The most important one of them.

Now that the step was taken and she was here, alone
in her impossibly quiet midweek, midmorning apartment, Lee wanted to run. Out there were people, noise,
distractions. Here, she'd have to face those "what-ifs."
Hunter would be the first.

He hadn't tried to stop her when she left the morning after he'd asked her to marry him. He'd said nothing when she'd made her goodbyes to Sarah. Nothing
at all. Perhaps they'd both known that he'd said all there
was to say the night before. He'd looked at her once,
and she'd nearly wavered. Then Lee had climbed into
the car with Bonnie, who'd driven her to the airport that
was one step closer to L.A.

He hadn't phoned her since she'd returned. Had she
expected him to? Lee wondered. Maybe she had, but
she'd hoped he wouldn't. She didn't know how long it
would take before she'd be able to hear his voice without going to pieces.

Glancing down, she stared at the twisted gold-and-
silver ring on her hand. Why had she kept it? It wasn't
hers. It should've been left behind. It was easy to tell
herself she'd simply forgotten to take it off in the confusion, but it wasn't the truth. She'd known the ring was
still on her finger as she packed, as she walked out of
Hunter's house, as she stepped into the car. She just
hadn't been capable of taking it off.

She needed time, and it was time, Lee realized, that

she now had. She had to prove something again, but not to her parents, not to Hunter. Now there was only herself. If she could finish the book. If she could give it her very best and really finish it…

Rising, Lee went to her desk, sat down at the typewriter and faced the fear of the blank page.

Lee had known pressure in her work on *Celebrity*. The minutes ticking away while deadlines drew closer and closer. There was the pressure of making not-so-fascinating seem fascinating, in a limited space, and of having to do it week after week. And yet, after nearly a month of being away from it, and having only herself and the story to account for, Lee had learned the full meaning of pressure. And of delight.

She hadn't believed—truly believed—that it would be possible for her to sit down, hour after hour, and finish a book she'd begun on a whim so long ago. And it was true that for the first few days she'd met with nothing but frustration and failure. There'd been a ring of terror in her head. Why had she left a job where she was respected and knowledgeable to stumble in the dark this way?

Time after time, she was tempted to push it all aside and go back, even if it would mean starting over at *Celebrity*. But each time, she could see Hunter's face—lightly mocking, challenging and somehow encouraging.

"It takes a certain amount of stamina and endurance. If you've reached your limit and want to quit…"

The answer was no, just as grimly, just as determinedly as it had been in that little tent. Perhaps she'd fail. She shut her eyes as she struggled to deal with the thought. Perhaps she'd fail miserably, but she wouldn't quit. Whatever happened, she'd made her own choice, and she'd live with it.

The longer she worked, the more of a symbol those typewritten pages became. If she could do this, and do it well, she could do anything. The rest of her life balanced on it.

By the end of the second week, Lee was so absorbed she rarely noticed the twelve-and fourteen-hour days she was putting in. She plugged in her phone machine and forgot to return the calls as often as she forgot to eat.

It was as Hunter had once said. The characters absorbed her, drove her, frustrated and delighted her. As time passed, Lee discovered she wanted to finish the story, not only for her sake but for theirs. She wanted, as she'd never wanted before, for these words to be read. The excitement of that, and the dread, kept her going.

She felt a queer little thrill when the last word was typed, a euphoria mixed with an odd depression. She'd finished. She'd poured her heart into her story. Lee wanted to celebrate. She wanted to weep. It was over. As she pressed her fingers against her tired eyes, she realized abruptly that she didn't even know what day it was.

He'd never had a book race so frantically, so quickly. Hunter could barely keep up with his own zooming thoughts. He knew why, and flowed with it because he had no choice. The main character of this story was Lenore, though her name would be changed to Jennifer. She was Lenore, physically, emotionally, from the elegantly groomed red-gold hair to the nervously bitten fingernails. It was the only way he had of keeping her.

It had cost him more than she'd ever know to let her go. When he'd watched her climb into the car, he'd told himself she wouldn't stay away. She couldn't. If he was wrong about her feelings for him, then he'd been wrong about everything in his life.

Two women had crashed into his life with importance. The first, Sarah's mother, he hadn't loved, yet she'd changed everything. After that, she'd gone away, unable to find it possible to mix her ambition with a life that included children and commitment.

Lee, he loved, and she'd changed everything again. She, too, had gone away. Would she stay away, for the same reasons? Was he fated to bind himself to women who wouldn't share the tie? He wouldn't believe it.

So he'd let her go, aches and fury under the calm. She'd be back.

But a month had passed, and she hadn't come. He wondered how long a man could live when he was starving.

Call her. Go after her. You were a fool to ever let her go. Drag her back if necessary. You need her. You need...

His thoughts ran this way like clockwork. Every day at dusk. Every day at dusk, Hunter fought the urge to follow through on them. He needed; God, he needed. But if she didn't come to him willingly, he'd never have what he needed, only the shell of it. He looked down at his naked finger. She hadn't left everything behind. It was more, much more, than a piece of metal that she'd taken with her.

He'd given her a talisman, and she'd kept it. As long as she had it, she didn't sever the bond. Hunter was a man who believed in fate, omens and magic.

"Dinner's ready." Sarah stood in the doorway, her hair pulled back in a ponytail, her narrow face streaked with a bit of flour.

He didn't want to eat. He wanted to go on writing. As long as the story moved through him, he had a part of Lenore with him. Just as, whenever he stopped, the need to have all of her tore him apart. But Sarah smiled at him.

"Nearly ready," she amended. She came into the room, barefoot. "I made this meat loaf, but it looks more like a pancake. And the biscuits." She grinned, shrugging. "They're pretty hard, but we can put some jam or something on them." Sensing his mood, she wrapped her arms around his neck, resting her cheek against his. "I like it better when you cook."

"Who turned her nose up at the broccoli last night?"

"It looks like little trees that got sick." She wrinkled her nose, but when she drew back from him, her face was serious. "You really miss her a lot, huh?"

He could've evaded with anyone else. But this was Sarah. She was ten. She knew him inside out. "Yeah, I miss her a lot."

Thinking, Sarah fiddled with the hair that fell over his forehead. "I guess maybe you wanted her to marry you."

"She turned me down."

Her brows lowered, not so much from annoyance that anyone could say no to her father, but in concentration. Donna's father hardly had any hair at all, she thought, touching Hunter's again, and Kelly's dad's stomach bounced over his belt. Shelley's mother never got jokes. She didn't know anybody who was as neat to look at or as neat to be with as her dad. Anybody would want to marry him. When she'd been little, she'd wanted to marry him herself. But of course, she knew now that was just silly stuff.

Her brows were still drawn together when she brought her gaze to his. "I guess she didn't like me."

He heard everything just as clearly as if she'd spoken

her thoughts aloud. He was greatly touched, and not a little impressed. "Couldn't stand you."

Her eyes widened, then brightened with laughter. "Because I'm such a brat."

"Right. I can barely stand you myself."

"Well." Sarah huffed a moment. "She didn't look stupid, but I guess she is if she wouldn't marry you." She cuddled against him, and knowing it was to comfort, Hunter warmed with love. "I liked her," Sarah murmured. "She was nice, kinda quiet, but really nice when she smiled. I guess you love her."

"Yes, I do." He didn't offer her any words of reassurance—it's different from the way I love you, you'll always be my little girl. Hunter simply held her, and it was enough. "She loves me, too, but she has to make her own life."

Sarah didn't understand that, and personally thought it was foolish, but decided not to say so. "I guess I wouldn't mind if she decided to marry you after all. It might be nice to have somebody who'd be like a mother."

He lifted a brow. She never asked about her own mother, knowing with a child's intuition, he supposed, that there was nothing to ask about. "Aren't I?"

"You're pretty good," she told him graciously. "But you don't know a whole lot about lady stuff." Sarah sniffed the air, then grinned. "Meat loaf's done."

"Overdone, from the smell of it."

"Picky, picky." She jumped off his lap before he could retaliate. "I hear a car coming. You can ask them to dinner so we can get rid of all the biscuits."

He didn't want company, Hunter thought as he watched his daughter dash out of the room. An evening with Sarah was enough, then he'd go back to work. After switching off his machine, he rose to go to the door. It was probably one of her friends, who'd talked her parents into dropping by on their way home from town. He'd brush them off, as politely as he could manage, then see if anything could be done about Sarah's meat loaf.

When he opened the door, she was standing there, her hair caught in the light of a late summer's evening. He was, quite literally, knocked breathless.

"Hello, Hunter." How calm a voice could sound, Lee thought, even when a heart's hammering against ribs. "I'd've called, but your number's unlisted." When he said nothing, Lee felt her heart move from her ribs to her throat. Somehow, she managed to speak over it. "May I come in?"

Silently, he stepped back. Perhaps he was dreaming, like the character in "The Raven." All he needed was a bust of Pallas and a dying fire.

She'd used up nearly all of her courage just coming back. If he didn't speak soon, they'd end up simply staring at each other. Like a nervous speaker about to lecture on a subject she hadn't researched, Lee cleared her throat. "Hunter..."

"Hey, I think we'd better just give the biscuits to Santanas because—" Sarah stopped her headlong flight into the room. "Well, gee."

"Sarah, hello." Lee was able to smile now. The child looked so comically surprised, not cool and distant like her father.

"Hi." Sarah glanced uncertainly from one adult to the other. She supposed they were going to make a mess of things. Aunt Bonnie said that people who loved each other usually made a mess of things, for at least a little while. "Dinner's ready. I made meat loaf. It's probably not too bad."

Understanding the invitation, Lee grasped at it. At

least it would give her more time before Hunter tossed her out again. "It smells wonderful."

"Okay, come on." Imperiously, Sarah held out her hand, waiting until Lee took it. "It doesn't look very good," she went on, as she led Lee into the kitchen. "But I did everything I was supposed to."

Lee looked at the flattened meat loaf and smiled. "Better than I could do."

"Really?" Sarah digested this with a nod. "Well, Dad and I take turns." And if they got married, Sarah figured, she'd only have to cook every third day. "You'd better set another place," she said lightly to her father. "The biscuits didn't work, but we've got potatoes."

The three of them sat down, very much as if it were the natural thing to do. Sarah served, carrying on a babbling conversation that alleviated the need for either adult to speak to the other. They each answered her, smiled, ate, while their thoughts were in a frenzy.

He doesn't want me anymore.

Why did she come?

He hasn't even spoken to me.

What does she want? She looks lovely. So lovely.

What can I do? He looks wonderful. So wonderful.

Sarah lifted the casserole containing the rest of the meat loaf. "I'll give this to Santanas." Like most children, she detested leftovers—unless it was spaghetti. "Dad has to do the dishes," she explained to Lee. "You can help him if you like." After she'd dumped Santanas's dinner in his bowl, she danced out of the room. "See you later."

Then they were alone, and Lee found she was gripping her hands together so tightly they were numb. Deliberately, she unlaced her fingers. He saw the ring, still on her finger, and felt something twist, loosen, then tighten again in his chest.

"You're angry," she said in that same calm, even voice. "I'm sorry, I shouldn't have come this way."

Hunter rose and began to stack dishes. "No, I'm not angry." Anger was possibly the only emotion he hadn't experienced in the last hour. "Why did you?"

"I…" Lee looked down helplessly at her hands. She should help him with the dishes, keep busy, stay natural. She didn't think her legs would hold her just yet. "I finished the book," she blurted out.

He stopped and turned. For the first time since she'd opened the door, she saw that hint of a smile around his mouth. "Congratulations."

"I wanted you to read it. I know I could've mailed it—I sent a copy on to your editor—but…" She lifted her eyes to his again. "I didn't want to mail it. I wanted to give it to you. Needed to."

Hunter put the dishes in the sink and came back to the table, but he didn't sit. He had to stand. If this was what she'd come for, all she'd come for, he wasn't certain he could face it. "You know I want to read it. I expect you to autograph the first copy for me."

She managed a smile. "I'm not as optimistic as that, but you were right. I had to finish it. I wanted to thank you for showing me." Her lips remained curved, but the smile left her eyes. "I quit my job."

He hadn't moved, but it seemed that he suddenly became very still. "Why?"

"I had to try to finish the book. For me." If only he'd touch her, just her hand, she wouldn't feel so cold. "I knew if I could do that, I could do anything. I needed to prove that to myself before I…" Lee trailed off, not able to say it all. "I've been reading your work, your earlier work as Laura Miles."

If he could just touch her... But once he did, he'd never let her go again. "Did you enjoy it?"

"Yes." There was enough lingering surprise in her voice to make him smile. "I'd never have believed there could be a similarity of styles between a romance novel and a horror story, but there was. Atmosphere, tension, emotion." Taking a deep breath, she stood so that she could face him. It was perhaps the most difficult step she'd taken so far. "You understand how a woman feels. It shows in your work."

"*Writer*'s a word without gender."

"Still, it's a rare gift, I think, for a man to be able to understand and appreciate the kinds of emotions and insecurities that go on inside a woman." Her eyes met his again, and this time held. "I'm hoping you can do the same with me."

He was looking into her again. She could feel it.

"It's more difficult when your own emotions are involved."

She gripped her fingers together, tightly. "Are they?"

He didn't touch her, not yet, but she thought she could almost feel his hand against her cheek. "Do you need me to tell you I love you?"

"Yes, I—"

"You've finished your book, quit your job. You've taken a lot of risks, Lenore." He waited. "But you've yet to put it all on the line."

Her breath trembled out. No, he'd never make things easy for her. There'd always be demands, expectations. He'd never pamper. "You terrified me when you asked me to marry you. I thought about it a great deal, like the small child thinks about a dark closet. I don't know what's in there—it might be dream or nightmare. You understand that."

"Yes." Though it hadn't been a question. "I understand that."

She breathed a bit easier. "I used what I had in L.A. as an excuse because it was logical, but it wasn't the real reason. I was just afraid to walk into that closet."

"And are you still?"

"A little." It took more effort than she'd imagined to relax her fingers. She wondered if he knew it was the final step. She held out her hand. "But I want to try. I want to go there with you."

His fingers laced with hers, and she felt the nerves melt away. Of course he knew. "It won't be dream or nightmare, Lenore. Every minute of it will be real."

She laughed then, because his hand was in hers. "Now you're really trying to scare me." Stepping closer, she kissed him softly, until desire built to a quiet roar. It was so easy, like sliding into a warm, clear stream. "You won't scare me off," she whispered.

The arms around her were tight, but she barely noticed. "No, I won't scare you off." He breathed in the scent of her hair, wallowed in the texture of it. She'd come to him. Completely. "I won't let you go, either. I've waited too long for you to come back."

"You knew I would," she murmured.

"I had to, I'd've gone mad otherwise."

She closed her eyes, content, but with a thrill of excitement underneath. "Hunter, if Sarah doesn't, that is, if she isn't able to adjust…"

"Worried already." He drew her back. "Sarah gave me a pep talk just this evening. You do, I assume, know quite a bit about lady stuff?"

"Lady stuff?"

He drew her back just a bit farther, to look her up and down. "Every inch the lady. You'll do, Lenore, for me, and for Sarah."

"Okay." She let out a long breath, because as usual, she believed him. "I'd like to be with you when you tell her."

"Lenore." Framing her face, he kissed both cheeks, gently, with a hint of a laugh beneath. "She already knows."

A brow lifted. "Her father's daughter."

"Exactly." He grabbed her, swinging her around once in a moment of pure, irrepressible joy. "The lady's going to find it interesting living in a house with real and imaginary monsters."

"The lady can handle that," she tossed back. "And anything else you dream up."

"Is that so?" He shot her a wicked look—amusement, desire, knowledge—as he released her. "Then let's get these dishes done and I'll see what I can do."

* * * * *